A CAYO HUESO MYSTERY
# DEAD AND BREAKFAST

A CAYO HUESO MYSTERY

# DEAD AND BREAKFAST

## KIMBERLY G. GIARRATANO

FOR MY KIDS

# CHAPTER ONE

Liam Breyer stood at the pool's edge and wiped his sweaty brow with the ratty hem of his blue T-shirt. The Florida sun was potent, even for early October, and the heat made his head throb. Liam dipped the skimmer into the murky water and scooped out a soggy palm frond. He swung the net over to the top of the white fence and tapped it on the splintering wood. The giant leaf disappeared into the neighbor's yard. Somewhere a chicken clucked. He sighed, brought the skimmer back to the surface of the water, and did it again. This was what he had become. A pool boy for a decrepit old hotel.

Palm fronds and dead flies littered the pool's surface. Not to mention beetles that floated belly up like blackened candles. It would take a while to clean out the gunk, and he hadn't even gotten to vacuuming the pool floor yet. Then he would have to shock the water with chlorine. He carefully leaned over and peered into the cloudy water. Green algae clung to the bottom of the stepladder. He nodded. Yup, a ton of chlorine.

Not that any of this mattered. The rusty patio furniture sat untouched, and a film of dirt and grime had settled on its surface. He even left his cell phone on the table, afraid it would fall out of his pocket and into the gross water, and he'd have to dive in to retrieve it.

Despite the heat, there wasn't one tourist by the pool. Liam hadn't seen a guest all morning, although he swore he could hear a baby crying, or maybe that was just his hangover making him hallucinate. Nope, the Cayo Hueso Dead and Breakfast didn't have many guests, or at least none that Liam had seen, and no one that seemed in the mood to swim. Who'd want to relax here?

Liam flicked a mosquito from his bicep. His grandfather used to talk about this place like it was a palace. Back in its heyday, whatever that meant. What difference did it make to him? He was paid no matter what, albeit it poorly and not very often. Evelyn Abernathy made it clear that she was doing Liam a favor by employing him, although, as he peered around at the empty beer bottles peeking out from behind neglected shrubs and large cracks in the patio concrete, he knew that wasn't the case at all. Granted, this was the only job he could get. In Key West, where college grads competed for jobs waiting tables, Liam Breyer was lucky to be working at all.

Evelyn had pursed her lips when Liam told her he only recently acquired his GED. All she had said to him was, "The hotel needs to be in tip-top shape for Fantasy Fest. You'll have to do."

Gee, thanks, lady.

Liam hung up the skimmer along two hooks on the white fence. Flecks of white paint rained down on his knuckles. He opened the patio shed, the door squeaking on rusty hinges, and stepped inside. The air outside was humid and sticky, but inside the shed, a surge of cool air swirled around Liam. He was suddenly overtaken by a strong earthy smell. He grabbed the pool vacuum and hose, and hightailed it out of there.

Liam had heard the rumors about the Cayo Hueso. Haunted, they said. Half of Key West was supposedly haunted. Hell, even the ladies' room at the goddamn Hard Rock Cafe on Duval Street was haunted. What made this place so unique? Of course, Liam didn't believe in ghosts. He'd never seen one, and the kooks who claimed they had were just that—kooks. People would believe almost anything if they wanted to, but he had to admit, this place made his skin itchy.

Liam slipped his hand into his pocket and fingered the diamond ring he'd slid in there for safekeeping. Pops told him he could take anything he wanted from the little wooden box. "It's all your abuela's costume jewelry, I imagine," Pops had said. "I'm not one to hold on to the past." Liam didn't think this ring classified as *costume jewelry*, but what did he know. Liam would pawn it and pay back Pops for the scooter.

Liam crouched by the filter and connected the vacuum hose. He stood up and submerged the vacuum into the pool as bubbles flittered to the top. Liam grumbled under his breath. He was finally old enough to be his own man, only to return home to Key West bankrupt. Liam planned to make something of his life. The vacuum sucked up a dead beetle. This was not it.

As he pushed the vacuum along the cement floor, something metallic caught his eye. Liam squinted into the water. Whatever it was glinted. A necklace maybe. His pulse quickened. Maybe he'd come into more money than he thought.

Liam rose and retrieved the skimmer from the fence. The skimmer pole wouldn't be long enough to reach the pool's eight-foot depth while he stood, so he crouched by the water's edge. He plunged the net into the water and scooted the metal object along the cement floor. His heart sank. It was a necklace, but there wasn't a diamond or even gold. This was silver and rectangular, like one of Pops's old dog tags from the navy, similar to the one Liam wore around his neck.

He tried to scoop up the dog tag, but he kept pushing it away from the net. Someone must've lost it swimming. Liam cringed. Who would swim in this pool? The algae alone made him nauseous.

Something else beneath the water's surface caught Liam's eye. He leaned farther over the pool and waited for the ripples in the water to steady. When they did, the face of a young woman stared back at him. He whipped his head around, but no one stood behind him. When he turned back to the water, the woman's mouth had twisted up in amusement. She climbed out of the water and clawed his face.

Liam screamed as the woman dragged him below the water's surface.

Autumn Abernathy was Windexing the mirror when the music box slid across the nightstand, pushed by an invisible hand.

Autumn shook her head, as if exasperated by a petulant child. "No, Katie."

The olive wood music box suddenly popped open, and the tinkling of a sweet lullaby filled the room. Autumn sighed and ran the dust rag over the dresser and along the mirror's ornate wooden frame. She didn't pay much attention to her own reflection, which looked unfamiliar if she wanted to be honest with herself. After six months in Florida, her normal pale skin was tanned and freckled. A bit of sunburn streaked her nose and cheeks. Her dark hair had frizzed from the humidity, and a lovely line of sweat ran down her cleavage. Autumn felt perpetually uncomfortable in her skin. That's what happened when you took a Jersey girl and plunked her into hotter-than-Hades Key West.

Sometimes, Autumn imagined waking up from a dream and finding herself back in New Jersey. Her parents were still together. Her father hadn't cheated and gotten remarried. Oh, and he and Jennifer didn't have a baby on the way. Gross. And Autumn would be hanging out with her best friend and going to the movies just like they used to. Instead, Autumn spent most Friday nights watching old films with her mom and Aunt Glenda.

Autumn glanced past her disheveled appearance and focused on the music box. Katie was up to something, she just wasn't sure what. The music box snapped closed.

Autumn whipped around, her ponytail smacking her cheek. She rubbed her arm across her sweaty forehead, leaving a smudge of dust on her skin. "Seriously, Katie. Don't mess with Aunt Glenda's music box. It was a gift from Uncle Duncan." Darn, she shouldn't have mentioned that. Katie loved to screw with Aunt Glenda. After all, it was Katie's ghostly presence that drew in the guests who worshipped the occult.

Autumn waited a beat. "Fine. Don't talk to me." She went to the closet and rustled out a set of threadbare cream bed sheets. "Why don't you haunt Mrs. Paulson in the January Room? She's been bitching all week that she hasn't seen a ghost. *And she paid to see a ghost.*" She mimicked Mrs. Paulson's heavy Southern accent.

Autumn yanked the floral coverlet off the four-poster bed. Changing the bed linens of total strangers used to skeeve her out, but she had gotten accustomed to it. The Florida heat, however, she would never appreciate. In New Jersey right now, she'd be unpacking her sweaters and heading to Starbucks for warm pumpkin spice lattes. In Key West, the only thing she ever ordered were iced coffees, extra ice.

"Mrs. Paulson," Katie said, materializing, "is a fat old cow and I have no intention of entertaining her. I don't care what she paid for. It's not like Aunt Glenda pays *me*." Katie glided over to the window, the sunlight filtering through her semi-translucent form. A sly smile crept along her pale pink lips. "Now, that boy outside over there, he's someone I'd like to know better. He's groovy, don't you think?"

Autumn slid a case onto a pillow. "His name is Liam, and don't mess with him." Autumn purposefully evaded her last question. He *was* handsome if you liked boys with dark hair and tanned skin. She didn't know if she did. In New Jersey, she'd only dated Ryan Jacobs, and he was blond. And kinda pasty.

Katie pouted. "Why not? You don't think he'd find me pretty?"

Tall with long straight blonde hair parted in the middle, Katie wore bell-bottoms and a tight striped sweater that showed off her large breasts. She wasn't just pretty, she was a knockout. A dead knockout.

Autumn sighed. "You're pretty."

Katie examined Autumn's green tank top and cotton shorts. "You could be pretty too, if you did something with your hair."

Autumn combed her fingers through her brown ponytail. "It's too hot to do something with it."

Katie shook her head. "You have no imagination." She peeked out the window. "Do you think I should say hello?"

"Absolutely not. You'll freak him out. Besides, he won't be here long. Mom hired him to help get the Cayo ready for Fantasy Fest. After November first, she plans to let him go." Autumn wondered if Liam knew of her mom's intentions. "So, don't get attached. Why don't you bother Mrs. Paulson before she complains to my mom for the billionth time?"

"Humph. Is that all you think I'm good for?" Katie nudged the music box closer to the edge of the dresser.

Autumn's hand shot out. "Aunt Glenda will be crushed if you break it."

Katie smiled mischievously. "Duncan died forever ago. She needs to let go and stop living in the past." Autumn watched as the box teetered on the edge.

"Katie," Autumn warned, but before she could leap over the bed to save it, Katie had knocked the music box off the nightstand, smashing it to pieces. Then she disappeared.

Autumn cursed and gathered up the wooden fragments. She'd have to tell Aunt Glenda what Katie had done, but not within earshot of her mother, Evelyn. Her mom bristled anytime Glenda or Autumn spoke of ghosts.

Autumn's phone buzzed in her pocket. She set the broken wooden pieces on the dresser and checked the screen. Her breath caught. Her father! Last night, she had sent him a pathetic email begging him to let her come back home. Despite the fact that her father had cheated with a woman barely out of college, Autumn felt like she was the one being punished for his infidelity. After all, she wasn't allowed to stay in her childhood home.

Her dad texted a response:

I know I said we could reexamine you moving in with us, but it's not a good idea right now. Jennifer is struggling a bit with the pregnancy. Besides, she is thinking of starting her own online business, making kids' clothes, and we can't guarantee we can convert the attic back into your bedroom. Your mother also wouldn't approve. I miss you tons, sweetheart, and we'll definitely talk about setting up a visit soon. Once the price of airfare comes down.

Enjoy the Florida weather. It's getting cold here. Sweater weather. Brrr.

Autumn's stomach rolled.

Autumn saw there was another text from Natasha and she brightened. Tasha was her Hail Mary. If anyone could come through for her, it was her best friend.

What up, Chiquita? My parents said ixnay on moving in with us for senior year. Can't you move back in with your dad?

Autumn slumped onto the bed. Okay, so begging for a place to stay in New Jersey wasn't working. She was all out of options until she went to college in the Northeast next fall. Autumn would have to suck it up until then.

She finished cleaning the room, retrieved the smashed music box, and closed the door. The March room would stay vacant for at least another two weeks, until the partygoers arrived for Fantasy Fest.

Autumn bustled down the stairs and into the hotel lobby. Aunt Glenda stood at the reception desk, holding a blue feather duster. She brushed a small elephant figurine, her fingers adorned with gold rings.

Timothy watched Aunt Glenda from his perch

behind the desk. He smoothed down his lavender tie, a bold fashion choice for a teenager, but Timothy never acted like any teen Autumn knew.

He put his hand on the figurine and picked it up in one swift motion. "Miss Glenda, why don't you let me do that?"

"I'm just trying to be useful." Glenda pouted. "Between you, Evelyn, and Autumn, I feel like I have nothing to do anymore."

Autumn approached her aunt and presented the broken pieces of the music box. "I'm terribly sorry. Katie's in a mood."

Aunt Glenda's eyes misted. "Is that Duncan's music box?"

"Yeah," said Autumn.

Glenda clutched the pieces to her chest. "I'd be more upset at her, but I feel for the poor dear. I think it's all that sexual frustration."

Timothy nearly choked on his gum.

Glenda clucked her tongue. "Well, she was only sixteen when she overdosed. Supposedly as boy crazy as they come."

Evelyn Abernathy poked her head out of the back office and whispered, "Is Mrs. Paulson gone?"

Timothy waved her out. "At least for the day. She signed up for a booze cruise."

"Lovely," Evelyn said dryly. She brushed her auburn hair off her forehead. Unlike the guest rooms, the lobby lacked air-conditioning and offered no relief from the relentless humidity. Only a weak breeze flowed through the sliders' screen door. "Autumn, is the March room finished?"

"Yes, Mom. All done." Often, Autumn felt like her mother's employee, rather than her daughter.

"All right, honey. Why don't you go upstairs and do your homework?"

But before Autumn could reply, a scream sliced through the lobby, followed by the sound of a body thrashing in the pool.

# CHAPTER TWO

Liam struggled against the weight gripping his ankle. He felt fingers curl around his skin and drag him down, but there was no one else in the water with him. He clawed at the surface as he struggled for breath.

Suddenly, the weight disappeared and Liam swam up. He broke through the surface and gulped in air. His eyes flew open and locked on to the face of a girl with light skin and dark hair. He cried out and submerged back into the enveloping water. Liam popped up again and flung the pool water from his hair.

The girl, who Liam now recognized as Evelyn's daughter, extended her hand to him. "You okay?"

Liam swam to the pool's edge and hoisted himself out without taking her hand. Greenish water ran down his clothes in rivulets. His body trembled. The old lady, Glenda, hurried over to him with a towel and draped it over his shoulders. Evelyn was there too, her face a mask of suspicion. And Timothy, his hand covering his wide mouth, was desperately trying not to laugh, and failing.

Liam's cheeks burned. Only the girl, what was her name? Summer? No, Autumn. She didn't look so much concerned as curious.

"Were you attacked by an animal?" Autumn tilted her chin at Liam's face.

Liam touched his cheek and winced. His fingertips grazed a scratch. To tell them what really happened would require a lengthy explanation and a psych evaluation. "Yeah. A cat, I think."

"You think?" Evelyn's brows rose.

"I mean, it was a cat."

"Autumn, dear," Glenda said. "There's a first-aid kit in the shed. Grab it and see to William's cheek, won't you?"

Evelyn sighed loudly, as if this whole scene was a nuisance to her. She waved Glenda inside. Liam heard her whisper to Autumn as she passed, something about rabies. He wanted to hide under the stained rug in the lobby. Timothy stayed and stared at him, smiling like an idiot.

Liam flopped down onto a nearby patio chair, his thigh bumping up against a rusty screw that scratched his skin. He was a mess. His sneakers were soaked, never mind his T-shirt and shorts. Good thing he left his cell phone on the table.

Liam stripped off his shirt and threw it to the concrete below. It made a loud smacking sound, the way wet cotton did when it connected with cement. Autumn returned and froze, her eyes locked on Liam's bare chest. Liam watched her cheeks color before setting the first-aid kit on the table. She opened it up and drew out peroxide and gauze. She stood directly in front of him, but averted her gaze from Liam's torso, and tilted up his chin. In doing so, Liam was able to appreciate Autumn's warm brown eyes and long lashes.

"Hold still." She dabbed the peroxide on his cheek, and he winced. "So, a cat, huh?"

Liam didn't meet her gaze. "That's what I said."

Autumn squirted ointment onto a cotton ball and pressed it onto his cheek. "Was this cat also pretty? About five-foot-six? See-through? Perpetually stuck in the 70s?"

"Girl." Timothy's voice dragged out the letter *r*. "You think Katie did that?"

Autumn appraised Liam, her hand hovering over his cheek. "I know it wasn't a cat."

Liam pushed Autumn's hand away from his face. He held her hand for a moment before saying, "I don't know what you're playing at here, but you're freaking me out."

Autumn straightened. "You know the Cayo is haunted, don't you?"

He stared at the cracked concrete. "Everyone says that."

"Well then, why don't you admit that it was Katie who hurt you and not some cat?" she asked.

Liam squinted at her. Was this girl for real? Did she really believe this crap? "I don't believe in ghosts if that's what you're asking. I'm not a freak."

Autumn blanched. She turned away and closed the first-aid kit. "Course not. I was kidding anyway." Her voice trailed off. "I'll just go put this back." She opened the shed door and slipped inside.

"Damn, boy," Timothy said. "Way to make a girl feel special."

"I don't believe in ghosts," Liam said again, this time more forcefully.

"No one said you had to," Timothy said. "But we both know it wasn't a cat that hurt you. So, if pretty Miss Katie attacked you, then let us know. She can be downright aggressive when she wants to be."

Liam leaned back against the chair's worn plastic. He knew that whatever it was that scratched him was not a ghost. That was total bullshit. But, it was also not a cat. He traced his fingers back over his face and counted five long scratches. He must've hurt himself in his panic. He was tired and had drank too much punch at the beach party. Plus, he had arrived home only days ago. He hadn't adjusted to the time difference and all that traveling on the bus. He felt slightly relieved. He was exhausted and hung-over. *Of course, I thought I saw a woman in the water. I'm not crazy. Just still drunk.*

Timothy sighed loudly and started back toward the lobby. Liam cleared his throat and Timothy paused. "This Katie," Liam said. "I'm just curious. What does she look like?"

Timothy's eyes widened ever so slightly. "Katie's a blonde. Unmistakably blonde."

*So, then not the girl from the pool.*

Liam gave a slight nod. Timothy didn't say anything after that. He waited for Autumn to join him and together they went inside the Cayo, leaving Liam alone to puzzle out his thoughts.

Autumn entered the lobby and slumped into a wicker chair near the window. She shouldn't have been so bothered by Liam's *freak* comment. After all, what did the opinion of a high-school dropout mean to her? And yet, it stung. So what if she bought into the notion of ghosts? They spoke to her! Well, Katie did at least. If the Cayo had other ghosts, they sort of kept to themselves.

Autumn wasn't exactly sure why she could see spirits, although she suspected it was an inherited trait. Evelyn used to talk about her weird grandmother who would have conversations with the air. Aunt Glenda claimed to see spirits too, but she was only Autumn's great aunt through marriage.

Timothy compared ghosts to radio waves and people to radios. Each ghost had its own frequency and some people could tune into that ghost's frequency, like adjusting the dial on an old radio. But most people were broken radios. No matter how much they tried to clear the static, they would not get reception. Autumn, on the other hand, was a universal receiver. There wasn't a ghost around that she couldn't spot. Or at least, that was how it seemed.

In her old home in New Jersey, Autumn was sensitive to the odd noises in the house. When she was little, she'd often see a young girl in braids and a white smock dress playing outside. A little girl who had lived in the house over a century ago. Autumn knew spirits existed, but her mother didn't believe. In New Jersey, the strange noises in the house were made by the wind. Or a squirrel in the attic. The little girl in braids was just a dream. Her mother never took her seriously. Evelyn was a broken radio. She never saw spirits.

Timothy went to lobby desk and retrieved a sketchbook and a set of colored pencils from a black attaché case. Even in the heat, Timothy appeared polished. His charcoal vest was perfectly tailored to his thin frame and his tie lay flat, only a small silver pin to adorn it. His dress shirt held no hint of perspiration, nor was there a line of moisture along his brow. His black hair shone of pomade, not sweat. Must be that young Bahamian blood. Autumn plucked her damp tank top from her sweaty chest.

Timothy's head bent over his paper, his pencil scratching furiously. Autumn stood, went over to the desk, and rang the brass bell to be annoying. Timothy didn't even glance up.

"Whatcha doin'?" she asked.

He swiped the bell before Autumn could ring it again. "Sweet child, leave me alone. I'm drawing some ideas for the D and B website."

Autumn rolled her eyes. She hated it when he called her "sweet child." Timothy was nineteen, only two years older than her. "My mom wants you to redesign the website?"

"Uh-huh," he said. "She's paying me to revamp it. It's called rebranding." He smiled and held up his sketch. "This should be a nice addition to my portfolio."

It was a new logo. A picture of a pristine Key West Victorian with white paint and teal shutters. In reality, those teal shutters would be hanging on for dear life by a lone rusty screw and that white paint would be peeling off in ribbons. More interesting, though, was what was written inside the logo. *Cayo Hueso Bed and Breakfast*. Not Dead and Breakfast as Aunt Glenda had named it.

"She wants to change the name? Aunt Glenda can't be too happy about that. It's a haunted hotel. Not some cottage retreat in Vermont."

Timothy shook his head. "I just do what I'm told."

"Well, someone should tell my mom the ghosts aren't going anywhere just because she wants them to," said Autumn.

"Go tell her yourself. She's in her office." He nodded toward the back room.

Autumn thought about doing that, but decided against it. What did she care if her mother wanted to reinvent this place? Autumn wasn't planning on staying here long enough to see that plan through. Or at least, that's what she told herself.

Thumps came down the stairs and the large silhouette of Mrs. Paulson emerged in a tight, floral dress. Apparently, Mrs. Paulson hadn't left for her booze cruise yet.

"You there." The woman pointed at Autumn. "That darn ghost will not make herself known to me, but she sure as hell has no problem playing jokes. She stole my brooch and set it on the chair with the pin sticking up." She rubbed her buttocks and Autumn bit her lip to stop from laughing.

"I'm sorry, Mrs. Paulson." Autumn couldn't help but stare at Mrs. Paulson's sausage toes, her nails painted bright orange. "Katie can be very, uh, temperamental."

Mrs. Paulson puffed out her chest. "I don't care. I paid to be haunted, not annoyed. And there's something going on with my water. One minute it's cold, the next minute, it's boiling like a Georgia summer."

Autumn's mother popped her head out of her office and approached the reception desk. Timothy slunk down on his stool.

"Mrs. Abernathy, I expect better accommodations or I'll be posting a negative review on Vacation Raters." Before she could wait for a response, Mrs. Paulson adjusted her straw hat on her bloated head and stormed out the front door.

"Another satisfied customer," Autumn said.

Evelyn Abernathy glared at her daughter. "You think this is funny? It's women like that who can destroy our business. Another negative review and this place will go bankrupt."

"What are you worried about?" Autumn asked. "We have a full house for Fantasy Fest." The Cayo Hueso had twelve guest rooms, each named after a month. And last time Autumn checked, all the rooms had a booking for Fantasy Fest, Key West's ten-day bacchanalian party. Granted, it would be a few weeks before they'd be occupied, but it was something.

Evelyn sighed. "If we make it to Fantasy Fest. Anyway, ten days a year is not enough to keep us afloat. This place needs to be booked all the time." She softened her eyes. "And please stop encouraging your Aunt Glenda."

Autumn balked. "What do you mean?"

"I mean, telling her the things *Katie* did." Evelyn used air quotes when she said Katie's name. "I overheard you before. Your aunt believes so strongly in these spirits, she won't consider turning this into a proper guesthouse. She's afraid she'll upset the ghosts, not to mention Uncle Duncan. The poor man's been dead ten years, let him rest in peace." She pinched the bridge of her nose. "No more of this haunted nonsense. It brings in the nuts." She tilted her chin at the door Mrs. Paulson had sauntered out moments earlier. "It's you who broke the music box while you were dusting, just admit it."

Autumn wondered if her own mother thought she, too, was a nut like Mrs. Paulson and Aunt Glenda. She now knew Liam thought so. "I didn't break the music box."

Evelyn gave another exasperated sigh. "If we don't get decent paying customers in through that door all year round, then we'll all be out of a job." She frowned at Timothy and then to Autumn. "And a place to live."

Autumn brightened. "Then it's back to Jersey?"

Her mother shook her head. "Nope. El Paso."

"With Grandma?" Autumn groaned, her smile gone. "You're joking."

Evelyn lightly patted Autumn's cheek. "Like most things in this place, I'm dead serious. Now why don't you go upstairs and study? You have school tomorrow."

"I know." The heat of frustration crawled up Autumn's body like mercury in a thermometer. Why did her mom always have to treat her like a child?

Autumn started to head upstairs to her bedroom, but instead, she smacked right into Liam's wet torso.

# CHAPTER THREE

Liam didn't see Autumn, or he would've prepared for the impact. She slammed into his chest, and he instinctively embraced her, wrapping his arms around her while still holding on to his wet T-shirt.

"Oof." Autumn pulled away. Liam glanced at her flushed cheeks, and he wondered if he looked as embarrassed as she did.

Even after Liam had spent several minutes putting back the pool supplies, his shorts were still soaked. They dripped water on Autumn's shoes. Liam glanced down at the puddle on the old wood floor. "Sorry about that."

"No, I'm sorry. I should be more careful where I walk."

Well, he couldn't argue with that. There was an awkward silence before Evelyn cleared her throat.

Liam suddenly felt the need to cover himself up. "Can I borrow a dry shirt?" He wasn't sure who would offer to help. Timothy was so lean, Liam imagined ripping one of his shirts Incredible Hulk-style.

Luckily, Aunt Glenda barreled around the corner. A navy polo shirt with thin white stripes on the collar and sleeves lay draped over her arm. She held the shirt out to Liam. "It belonged to Duncan. You kids would call it vintage now."

Liam hesitated to accept the shirt. Pops told him how the old lady felt about her dead husband. He would've preferred a simple, white cotton T-shirt so he could slink back to work with dignity or out the front door never to return. He couldn't believe he had fallen into the pool. *It's crazy to think I was dragged in. Ghosts don't exist and they definitely don't drown people. Right?* His head pounded as if a coal miner had taken a pickax to his skull.

Liam turned his body away from the prying eyes and slipped the polo shirt, which smelled faintly of mothballs and mildew, over his head. He smoothed the shirt's hem over his hips and then looked up to see Timothy, Autumn, Evelyn, and Glenda all watching him curiously. His skin crawled under their gaze. *I bet they're thinking I'm just another Breyer loser.* Liam wondered if this job was worth the awkwardness.

Glenda gently placed her hand on Liam's shoulder. "You probably should just go home."

Liam wasn't prepared to be fired. But part of him knew to expect it.

"Don't worry," Glenda said kindly. "I'll still pay you for a full day. You come back tomorrow when you've had a good rest."

"Oh, okay," Liam said, surprised. So he wasn't being fired. He still felt reluctant. He wasn't sure he was comfortable taking the old lady's money without finishing the work. "I'll make up the hours tomorrow."

Glenda smiled broadly and clapped. "Wonderful. I must say, in that shirt, you look just like—" but before she could finish, there was a strange rattle and a loud crack.

"Watch out!" Autumn cried, just before she rammed Liam into the reception desk. His back stung from the force. A brass chandelier crashed down onto the floor, right where he had stood.

"Jesus!" cried Evelyn as she stared up at the ceiling. She whirled to Liam. "Are you all right?"

For a moment, her concern touched Liam until he realized she was probably only worried about a lawsuit. He nodded.

"How the hell did that happen?" Evelyn asked, breathless.

Everyone followed Evelyn's gaze, except for Liam. He'd had enough of this place. He didn't care what strings or favors Pops had called in; he wasn't coming back here. Not ever.

Evelyn stared at the broken chandelier, which sat on the floor in a heap of brass. She clucked her tongue. "How much do you think that's going to cost to replace?"

Glenda clutched her chest. "That chandelier's been in the house for decades." She frowned at Liam, grabbed a paper bag from the reception desk, and shoved it into his hands. "Here. Take some of Cora's cookies for your grandfather. They're key lime. Her specialty." Glenda's voice trembled as she pushed him toward the door.

"Okay." Liam tried to catch his breath. He wanted to tell the old lady that he'd return the shirt, but he knew that wasn't likely to happen.

Glenda waved him out the door. Liam didn't need to be told a second time. On his way out, Evelyn hissed, "That boy is bad luck. We should hire someone else."

"Pish, Evie. His grandfather and my Duncan were close friends," said Glenda. "Besides, the poor boy was attacked." He didn't wait to hear the rest.

Liam strode over to his scooter, a beat-up 1984 Honda Elite with scratched gold paint and a torn leather seat that he had bought cheap. He kicked a palm leaf out from under the bike and unbuckled the helmet from the handlebars. He took the paper bag and his cell phone and tossed them in the small trunk space on the back of the bike. He was just about to snap on his helmet when Autumn came barreling out of the Cayo.

"Wait!" she cried.

Liam sat up straighter. What did she want now? Couldn't he just get out of here? The humiliation seemed never ending.

Autumn halted at the bike and pushed a strand of hair from her face. She handed him a bunch of crumpled bills.

"What's this?"

"It's your day's pay. Aunt Glenda thinks you won't return. She wanted you to have what she promised."

Autumn's face soured, and Liam couldn't help but think she looked pretty.

Liam wasn't used to such generosity. He was more accustomed to glares and suspicious glances. He peeked back and saw Evelyn watching from the window. Yeah, like that.

Liam returned the money to Autumn's palm. "Tell her she can pay me weekly like we agreed."

Autumn appeared thoughtful for a moment. "So you'll be back?"

Liam buckled the helmet's strap under his chin. "Yeah."

"Okay, I'll let Aunt Glenda know." She hesitated before turning to leave.

Liam gently caught her wrist. "I'm sorry I implied you were a freak. I didn't mean for it to sound that way."

"Sure you did." Her smile drooped. "It's not the first time a guy has called me that. It doesn't bother me."

"It should," Liam said. "It was rude, and I apologize. Also, thank you for pushing me out of the way of that falling light fixture."

"Chandelier," she corrected.

"Whatever. I could've been hurt. We both could've." The words hung in the air.

Autumn nodded and gave a slight wave before heading back inside the Cayo Hueso. Liam watched her go and caught another glimpse of Evelyn's disapproving face.

Liam was sick of those looks. He didn't want to be some divorcee's minimum-wage lackey. He wanted to work for himself. He wanted to create something of value so that if his father or his deadbeat mother ever came back to Key West, they'd regret running out on him. Unfortunately for Liam, he just didn't know how.

Autumn entered the Cayo's foyer with its ornate moulding and antique rug. She stared up the long carpeted staircase and blew the bangs off her forehead. The last thing she wanted to do was homework, but if she was ever going to get into a decent college back north, she needed to keep her grades up. She rested her hand on the bannister when Evelyn, who was fussing with brochures on the hallway table, cleared her throat.

"I need to talk to you about something." Her mother motioned toward her office. "Can you come into the back?"

Dreading a talk with her mother, Autumn stalled before following on Evelyn's heels like a Cocker spaniel.

Her mother's office was nothing more than a glorified storage closet, although it did have a small circular window that let in natural light, but little air circulation. Evelyn had claimed the office the minute they had unpacked from their move, grumbling something about never having a proper place to work at the Abernathy's hardware store. Autumn scanned the pile of folders stacked on the desk and the packages of toilet paper shoved into the corner. Autumn didn't think this was a proper place to do anything, let alone manage a hotel.

Evelyn sat in her black office chair and pointed to a folding chair next to the desk. Autumn hated when Evelyn did this stuff—called her into the office like an employee instead of just talking to her like a mom.

Autumn plopped into the chair and carefully tucked her knees under the desk. "What's up?"

Evelyn jiggled the mouse before turning the computer monitor toward her daughter. It was the email Autumn had sent her father a few days ago. Autumn's stomach soured. She wasn't sure what upset her more—that her father had betrayed her by forwarding the email to her mother, or that Evelyn had seen how far Autumn was willing to go to move back home.

Evelyn's eyes darkened a little. "I know you're not happy about being in Florida, but you can't keep asking your dad to move back in with him." Evelyn swallowed. "He has a new life now, and we're not a part of it."

"That's only true for you," Autumn said. Evelyn blanched, and Autumn regretted her words. "I mean, he's still my father. And I'm still his daughter, even if he is remarried."

"To a child," Evelyn snapped. "Ugh, Jennifer is only a few years older than you." She dropped her voice. "Do you hate it here that much that you'd want to return to the man who destroyed our family? Do you hate me that much?"

Autumn cringed inwardly. Why did her mother always have to make everything about her? "I don't hate you, Mom." Autumn picked up a brass apple, a paperweight, and cupped the fruit in her hand. The apple-picking season was coming to an end in New Jersey. She and her parents used to go to Meadow Farms every September and pluck juicy red apples from the trees. "I miss home. I miss cool temperatures and dried leaves and bonfires."

Evelyn reached over and patted Autumn's hand. "I miss that stuff too. Fall was my favorite time of year. I mean, I named you after the season, for goodness sake. But Key West has its own benefits. Like turquoise water and palm trees. Besides, we have an opportunity to make a new life here. To start fresh and leave the past behind."

Autumn didn't want to leave the past behind. She liked the past. In the past, her parents were happily married. "Key West is nice. For now."

Evelyn knitted her brows. "What do you mean for now?"

"Well, I'm not living here forever. I'm applying to college in New Jersey."

Evelyn slumped back into her chair. "There's something I need to tell you."

Suddenly, Evelyn's words felt heavier than that stupid brass paperweight. "What?"

"There isn't money to send you to college in the northeast."

Autumn gripped the edge of the desk. "What do you mean no money? I have a college fund. Don't I?"

Evelyn shook her head, but didn't glance up. "You had a college fund. You have to understand. The hardware store was hemorrhaging money and the divorce left me and your father broke."

Autumn felt tears threatening to come. "What did you do with my college fund?"

"Your aunt needed some cash to keep this place running and so I used it as an investment."

"You spent my college fund on this dump!" Autumn leaped up, and her eyes fell on the paperweight. She suddenly felt the urge to hurl the brass apple at that tiny glass window.

"Autumn!" Evelyn rose. "I get that you're upset, but don't you see? This place could be our future."

"You mean your future! My future is gone because there's no money for college."

"You can go to community college. We'll figure something out." She reached for Autumn's hand again, but Autumn snatched it away.

"I'm going to college next year in New Jersey, whether Dad wants me home or not. I'll find a way." Autumn stormed away from her mother's cramped office and thundered up the stairs to her bedroom.

# CHAPTER FOUR

Autumn and her mother shared a set of rooms and an adjoining bathroom on the Cayo's third floor, which was technically the finished half of the attic; the other half was for storage. Here, the rooflines pitched, forcing Autumn to duck her head as she entered her bedroom. She made a beeline for the ancient air-conditioning unit in the window and flicked on the switch. It sputtered to life and then roared.

She longed for the kind of crisp fall afternoon where a fleece pullover provided enough warmth so that cool air on her cheeks didn't make her shiver. She missed orange pumpkins and bursts of red leaves. She couldn't appreciate the Florida heat, especially because it seemed so relentless.

When Autumn felt better, well physically better, she pushed herself off the air conditioner. The anger simmered underneath her skin. Her mother blew her college fund on this crappy hotel. Autumn loved her Aunt Glenda, and she didn't want to see the Cayo fail, but not at the expense of her college education. What had her mother been thinking?

Taking a deep breath, Autumn grabbed her laptop off the squat pine nightstand. She sat on her bed, put a pillow on her thighs, and rested the computer on top of it like a makeshift desk. Everything in Autumn's bedroom was makeshift. From the mismatched pine furniture to the squeaky brass bed to the lavender and blue walls that were the result of Uncle Duncan running out of paint. Her mother's bedroom was just on the other side of the bathroom they shared. Way too close for Autumn's comfort.

After six months of living there, she still hadn't put up any posters or personal items other than a couple of framed photographs on the dresser. In the photo of Autumn and her father last October at the Apple Festival, her father's arm was draped around her as she held a bushel full of Jonagolds. The other photo showed her and Natasha, arms linked at the Homecoming game sophomore year. They had known each other since first grade. Although, aside from a few text messages, Instagram comments, and that email she sent earlier, Tasha rarely contacted Autumn anymore.

Autumn opened up the laptop and connected to the Cayo Hueso's spotty Wi-Fi. In addition to some trigonometry homework and an English paper, Autumn had to write her college admissions essays, although now she questioned the point of it all. She needed a sack of money to land in her lap.

Autumn had emailed the chair of the journalism department at Candlewick College, a small liberal arts school in New Jersey, for guidance. Autumn worried her lack of journalism experience would prevent her from being accepted into the program, which, according to the college website, limited the class size.

Autumn logged into her email account and exhaled when she saw the woman had responded.

Dear Ms. Abernathy,

I'm so delighted that you are interested in our award-winning journalism department, and I look forward to reviewing your application this winter. In response to your question regarding scholarship opportunities, we do have one special award—the Thomas Henderson Investigative Journalism Scholarship Award. Students must prove exceptional journalism skills in reporting and leadership either through a professional newspaper internship or via the high school editorial staff. Some of our previous winners have even conducted true crime research using police records. The scholarship application is due the same time as your college admissions packet. All materials can be found on the website.

Best of luck,

Bridget P. Crimson

Autumn's gut twisted. Aside from some research papers in history, Autumn had no real journalism or leadership experience. Her portfolio held a few measly clippings about student government meetings and prom committee finance issues. And she left New Jersey just when the news editor position opened up at her high school paper. Autumn was as qualified for the scholarship as her Aunt Glenda. Getting out of Florida seemed hopeless.

If Evelyn hadn't yanked Autumn away from home, she'd be the editor of her high school paper by now.

"What's so great about New Jersey anyway?" said a voice beside her.

Autumn jumped, nearly knocking the computer to the floor. Katie's hands were on her hips. Clearly, she had been reading over Autumn's shoulder. Autumn snapped the laptop closed. "God, you scared me. Why aren't you using those creepy powers on Mrs. Paulson?"

"That bloated peacock can't see me. I've tried. So what's so great about New Jersey?"

"It's home."

Katie swept her arms around Autumn's bedroom as if she was showcasing it for *The Price Is Right*. "Isn't this home now?"

Autumn shook her head. "Not to me it isn't."

Katie glided over to the photo of Autumn and Natasha on the dresser. "I was originally from New York. Came to Key West for Christmas break to hang out with my cousin Duncan."

Autumn raised a brow.

"I'm from his mother's side of the family," Katie pointed out. "You and I are not related. Had I just stayed home, I'd probably still be alive. Instead I overdosed on Quaaludes. Although, if I were alive, I'd be old. Probably in my fifties or something." She grinned as if the memory had been pleasant and not grisly. "And I'd never get to see Liam without a shirt on. He is totally far out."

Autumn rose from the bed. Whenever Katie was in the room, she felt like she had to stay on guard. "I told you not to mess with him. You could've seriously hurt him."

Katie flipped her long hair. "I didn't."

Autumn narrowed her eyes. "Come on, don't lie to me. I saw the scratches on his face. The guy was completely freaked out."

Again, there was that pout. "I didn't do anything to him, let alone touch him. I'm not sure I can, although that does sound like fun. I'd love to put my hands on his—"

"If you didn't scratch him, how did he get those marks on his cheek?" She wondered if for a moment Liam was telling the truth about the cat.

Katie waved her hand, dismissing Autumn's question. "There's another ghost here."

"You mean the young mother with the baby?" Autumn thought she knew all about the spirits at Cayo Hueso, even if she hadn't seen them all. Some ghosts were just more elusive than others. Aunt Glenda was never sure who the young mother was, but Autumn often heard the wailing of the infant. She shuddered just thinking about them.

Katie shook her head. "No. A different spirit. A darker one."

"Who? I've never seen another ghost." Aunt Glenda claimed Uncle Duncan haunted the Cayo too, but Autumn doubted it. She'd like to think her uncle would visit her—he used to entertain her with magic tricks when he was alive.

Autumn breathed out a puff of air that lifted her chestnut bangs off her forehead. "Why haven't I seen that ghost?"

"Murdered spirits aren't very outgoing."

Autumn's eyes widened. "This ghost was murdered?"

"So it seems."

"Hm." Autumn didn't say it aloud, but she wondered why a spirit, who had been murdered, would be visible to Liam. Who was he to her? Autumn slid the ponytail holder out of her hair. "I don't get it. I've never heard anything about a murder at the Cayo. Aunt Glenda would've said something."

"Would she?" asked Katie, as if that were explanation enough.

"Huh." Autumn stared at her lavender walls and tapped her bottom lip with her finger. "I'm going to the pool."

"What for?"

Autumn glanced at her closed laptop.

*Some of our previous winners have even conducted true crime research using police records.*

A smile spread across her face. Perhaps, getting that scholarship was not hopeless after all.

"I don't know yet," said Autumn. "I'm going to investigate."

Liam leaned against the railing at Mallory Square and squinted at the warm, turquoise water. It was the kind of day when the sun ducked in and out of the clouds as if playing hide and seek with a child. One moment, the sky was bright and as clear as the Caribbean Sea. The next, clouds darkened and threatened thunderstorms. Currently, the water sparkled like a diamond.

Liam glanced at the cruise port and watched tourists scamper down the pier. A palm tree billowed in the gentle breeze. This was home for him. Following his dad to the desolate oil fields in North Dakota had been a mistake, even if it was to make quick money. Truth was, Liam had missed Key West.

Someone clapped Liam on the shoulder.

"Dude, I'm so glad you're back in town," Randall said, smiling.

Randall's light brown hair hung longer than it used to. Duct tape patched up not just the holes in the pockets of his ratty board shorts but also the splintered edges of his skateboard.

Liam gave Randall's shoulder a playful punch. "What can I say? My blood runs warm."

"I didn't see you last night at the party."

Liam pinched the bridge of his nose, hoping to subdue the pounding in his skull. "I was there. What was in that punch?"

Randall laughed. "Dude, you should know better than to sample the local brew. It's always spiked. You're still dry?"

Too many Breyer men relied on alcohol to manage. Liam was not going to be one of them. "Yup."

Randall peered at Liam through dark eyes. "What's with the shirt? You look like you should be auditioning for *Mad Men*."

"Very funny. I kinda fell into a pool." Randall raised his brows. Liam waved him off and glanced out at the water. "So, what's up?"

Randall leaned against the railing and faced the square. His eyes scanned the small crowds, resting every now and then on the figure of a beautiful girl. "You know my cousin Keith with the boat?"

Liam nodded. He remembered Keith as a kid—a pudgy mess with curly blonde hair and dirt smudges on his face. Randall said he'd become a fisherman but was getting sick of being on the water.

"Yeah."

"Well, he has a lead on a fleet of scooters we can buy at a steep discount to fix up to sell."

Liam scratched his cheek. He wasn't a decent scooter mechanic like Randall. He wondered why his old friend was even mentioning it.

"What kind and how many?"

"A few Kymcos, some Havanas, but mostly Mios. About fifteen bikes."

"That's quite the assortment. Where'd he'd find them? An auction?"

"Yeah," Randall answered quickly. "Anyway, to get all fifteen will cost eight grand."

Liam whistled. "That's a lot of money."

"Not for fifteen bikes. They're cast-offs, but with our skills, we can make them look brand new again.

We buy them cheap, fix them up, and sell them at a profit. Keith did the math, and we could walk away a few grand richer. Each."

"You keep saying 'we.' I know nothing about scooters." Liam scanned the square. He watched a street performer, a brown-haired girl who reminded him of Autumn, spin five hula-hoops at once. The swirling hoops hypnotized him.

"Once you sell the bikes, then what?" asked Liam.

Randall squinted into the sunlight. "What do you mean?"

"I mean, then what? You fix scooters. You sell them. What's next? Is that what you want to do your whole life? Buy scooters on the cheap and sell them on Craigslist?" Liam stepped aside so a man on a unicycle could ride past. Liam knew he was being unfair to Randall. The kid was raised by his alcoholic grandfather in an RV park on Stock Island. Randall didn't have dreams. He just needed to find a way to eat.

"I don't know, dude. I know I can fix scooters. Except . . ."

*Ah. Here's the real reason Randall met me out here today.* "You don't have eight grand." Although, Randall didn't know this yet, but neither did Liam.

"Well, we don't need the whole eight from you. Keith will put in half and you'll put in half. I'll do the grunt work and then you, with your Don Draper good looks, will help sell the bikes to hot, young girls for a nice profit margin."

"There's a big flaw in this plan," said Liam. "I don't have four grand. I barely have four dollars."

Randall groaned. "I thought you were making Rockefeller up north. What happened?"

"It's a long story." Even though Randall would understand Liam's plight the most, Liam wasn't in the mood to rehash what had happened in North Dakota. The whole story just made Liam feel worse about himself, if that was even possible. "I don't want to get into it. All I can tell you is I don't have the money. And my part-time job pays almost less than nothing. Besides, I don't want to invest in repairing scooters. If I'm going to put my money toward something, I want it to last. I want to create something."

"What? Like your own business?"

Liam's gaze darted around the square to a middle-aged man with a yellow trucker hat that read Canton Corp in big, black letters. A young woman with long, blonde braids giggled with her friends as they listened to one of Mick Canton's tour operators give a spiel about snorkeling. A scooter with neon green paint and the name Canton Sunshine Tours on the side was parked along the shops. The name Canton was everywhere in Key West because Mick Canton practically owned the whole island. What would that be like—to be so rich and powerful that your name was on everything?

"Yeah. Like my own business." Liam didn't know how to repair scooters, but he knew how to ride them. He knew all the nooks and crevices of the island. He was a Conch, a Key West native. He could show tourists parts of this island they'd never see in a Canton brochure. "Why don't we run our own scooter tour company?"

Randall scoffed. "We missed the boat on that by thirty years. Canton figured out a way to bundle all his tour operations. You rent a scooter, book a snorkeling trip, and jump on Blazevig's haunted city tour all for a low, low price. We can't compete with that."

Liam pursed his lips, impressed with Randall's common sense. "You're right. But we know the Keys. We could lead guided scooter tours, take the tourists to the best spots on the island. Off the beaten path, ya know?" Liam's pulse quickened as he imagined the possibilities.

"Dude, that sounds like a ton of responsibility."

Liam rolled his eyes. "Come on. Don't you want to put your name on something? If we open up our own business, it's ours, and no one can take it away from us." Liam pointed toward a squat, bald man struggling to raise the blue umbrella on his hot dog cart. "Even that guy is his own boss."

Randall inhaled the aroma of dirty water hot dogs and licked his lips. "I don't want to get on Canton's radar."

"We won't. He owns all of Key West. Why would he spend any time worrying about us? We're nothing to him."

Randall gently nudged Liam in the ribs. "We could even bundle packages with my cousin's boat. We could do charters."

Liam grinned. "Now, you're thinking. Canton can't own everything. He can't own us."

Randall waved his hand in a high arch. "We could call the place 'Keys to Your Heart Scooters and Tours.'"

A girl on a Canton Corp bicycle rode past them. "Your cousin is a Bell too, right?"

Randall nodded.

"Then, let's call it Breyer and Bell Scooter Tours." Liam liked how that sounded. Also, every time Mick Canton drove past their shop, he'd see the Breyer name. Liam grinned and squeezed Randall's shoulder.

"But you can't even come up with the four grand needed to secure the bikes," Randall said, squashing Liam's excitement. "How are we going to fund a business?"

Liam raked his hands through his hair, damp with sweat. "I'm doing odd jobs at the Cayo Hueso. Of course, I'm only making enough to fill my ride with gas at this point."

Randall laughed. "Get out of here. I didn't even know the Cayo was still open. Dude, see any ghosts?"

Without meaning to, Liam touched the scratch on his cheek. "You don't believe in that crap, do you?"

Randall appeared thoughtful for a moment. "Not sure, man. This whole island is filled with haunted places. How many people have claimed to see ghosts? Everyone can't be crazy, ya know?"

Liam had never thought about it like that before.

"Does Old Glenda Reynolds still run the place?" Randall asked.

"She's there, but her niece Evelyn has taken over. Got her daughter, Autumn, working there too. They're from New Jersey."

"Is this Autumn hot?" asked Randall.

Liam recalled Autumn's light touch as she pressed the ointment into his skin. He was a stranger to her, and she hadn't hesitated to patch him up. He smiled at the memory.

"Say no more," Randall said.

"Nah, it's just. Yeah, she's pretty, but she's different too. Not like . . ."

"Not like Victoria and those rich bitches she hangs out with," Randall finished.

"Autumn's nice. Her mother, on the other hand, rides my ass like I'm free labor. The money's crap too, but it's work."

Randall clapped Liam on the back. "Don't fret, my man. We'll get Breyer and Bell Tours up and running and you can say adios to the spooky Cayo." Randall tapped his chin. "Do you have any money to give my cousin so he knows you're serious? Perhaps, Keith can float the rest of the cash if you invest some of your own dough."

Liam watched a sailboat glide across the water with a man on board scrambling to hoist the sails. Liam patted his shorts pocket. "Well, I have a ring to pawn."

"Hope this ring has a giant diamond. Can I see it?"

Liam slipped his hand into his pocket to take out the ring when his stomach dropped to his knees. "Oh, crap."

"What?"

"The ring. My grandmother's ring."

Randall's mouth gaped open. "You were going to pawn your grandmother's ring. That's cold."

"Pops said I could. It was in a box of stuff she never wanted." Liam paced. "He thought I could get a grand for it at least." He dropped his shoulders and hung his head. "I know where the ring is."

"Where?"

Liam shuddered when he thought about the dark-haired woman. The one he hoped he had hallucinated. "The bottom of the Cayo's swimming pool."

# CHAPTER FIVE

Autumn stood at the edge of the pool and squinted into its cloudy depths. She wasn't sure what she was seeking—the face of the murdered ghost she supposed, but unlike Katie, this ghost was elusive. And unpredictable. After all, until today, Autumn had never even heard of this spirit.

Autumn examined the water and pursed her lips. This seemed like a stupid plan. Even if she discovered more about the murdered girl, there would be no way to prove what had happened to her. She couldn't exactly record the testimony of a ghost.

Then Autumn spotted something shiny glinting at the bottom of the pool. She grabbed the pool skimmer from the fence and submerged the net until she was gliding it along the floor. It took her a few tries before she was able to cradle the tiny object in the net. She swung the skimmer toward her and plucked the object from the skimmer. Her breath caught.

It was a ring.

And not just a cheap ring either, but a gold one with a square-cut diamond, larger than the one on Evelyn's now-defunct wedding band. How had this beautiful ring ended up in the pool? Between the algae on the liner and the dead beetles, no one had stepped a toe in the pool.

Except for Liam.

Of course, Liam! He fell in. But still, what was he doing with a women's engagement ring? Was it a present for a girlfriend? She brushed aside a stab of jealousy. She didn't know Liam well, and she refused to crush on a boy she'd just met. All he had going for him right now was his looks, and Autumn knew that a relationship based on a superficial attraction wouldn't last. Just ask Evelyn. Autumn's parents had been voted most beautiful couple in high school. Now they were the most bitter.

Autumn held up the wet ring, mesmerized as the diamond sparkled in the sunlight. She suddenly understood why the entire English department crowded around Ms. Waldron's ring finger after she got engaged.

What would this ring look like on her? Autumn glanced back at the Cayo to make sure no one was coming outside before slipping the ring on to her finger.

"Check that out," she said aloud. "It fits." Autumn stretched out her hand to admire the sparkle.

Suddenly, she felt overcome with a sense of dizziness. She stumbled away from the edge of the pool, grabbed the side of the old patio table, and steadied herself. Black spots floated in front of her until they darkened her vision completely. Her heart pumped so loudly she thought she could hear it. Sweat bloomed under her arms. Intense pressure climbed her torso as though invisible arms were squeezing her in a bear hug. Her nerve endings tingled. A bright light flashed.

The pain in her chest subsided, but everything still seemed fuzzy, as if she was viewing the world underwater. She blinked several times to clear her vision. Autumn crumpled against the table until she felt well enough to stand up.

She had read magazine articles of young girls suddenly stricken by incurable diseases. Could that be what was happening to her?

She hugged herself and then wiggled her fingers, trying to regain sensation. She caught sight of slender fingers on a tanned, dark-skinned right hand. This did not look like her hand. Autumn ran her fingers down her body, sliding them over silky white fabric with pearly buttons. She was wearing a blouse? Autumn peered over the side of the pool into crystal clear water and caught a glimpse of her reflection. It wasn't her face that appeared.

Autumn's eyes darted around the patio. The Cayo's white peeling paint appeared fresh and unmarked. The pool's typical green tint shimmered clear and blue. The once-rusted patio table looked smooth and clean. The round-faced clock that hung next to the doors ticked away. Eight o'clock. That couldn't be right. It was still afternoon.

This was the Cayo's patio and yet it wasn't. This was the Cayo of years ago. The one Autumn had seen in Aunt Glenda's old photos. Had she hit her head?

Autumn heard the melodic sound of a girl's laughter. A slender girl, standing near the gate that led to the street. She had short dark hair that flipped up at her shoulders and wore a white blouse with an embroidered crest and a red plaid skirt that stopped at her knees. Autumn glanced down at her matching attire. The red knee socks itched. She lifted a strand of her hair and brought it in front of her face. It was dark, like a walnut, and matched the other girl's.

The girl appeared by Autumn's side, linked her arm, and rested her head against Autumn's shoulder.

"There you are, Inez. The boys want to go out on Ralphie's boat. Do you want to come?"

*Ralphie? That name sounds familiar.*

"No, I don't," came a strange voice. It sounded harsh, with just a lilt of an accent. Autumn didn't mean to be angry, but she couldn't help how she sounded. She couldn't control the words coming out of her mouth.

The other girl pursed her lips and motioned toward a young man with brown wavy hair, dressed in a dark blue sailor uniform with white stripes on the sleeves. He was muscular and tan, but is back was turned toward them, and Autumn couldn't see his face. "Don't be angry, Inez. I saw him first." She smiled, more gently this time. "Que guapo, no?"

*I'm in Inez's body. Inez who?*

"Don't rub it in, Mariana. Fue mío primero," her voice said. *Dammit, I wish I had taken Advanced Spanish.* "Which sailor?"

A tall, broad shouldered man with blond hair and a wide grin, also dressed in a Navy uniform, gave the girls a slight wave. There was something familiar about him, but Autumn couldn't place his face.

"He's just as handsome," Mariana admitted. "And he seems to like you." But something inside Autumn suggested she desired the other sailor—the one whose face she couldn't see. She suddenly felt a stab of jealousy.

Mariana brightened. "He asked to be introduced." She brushed past Autumn and went over to the tall sailor with the easy smile. Mariana whispered in his ear and the sailor's brows rose in amusement. Autumn glanced away. She, nor Inez, seemed interested in this sailor. Autumn wanted to explore the Cayo and seek out Uncle Duncan, who must've been a young man, but she couldn't force her body to move. *I must be inside a memory. What year is this?*

Autumn caught a glimpse of Inez in the reflection of the French doors. Unlike Mariana, Inez had heavy bangs that sat on her forehead and thick dark eyebrows. She was a beauty like Mariana, but Inez's countenance appeared sharper than Mariana's. If Mariana was all soft, curvy lines, Inez was hard angles and edges.

Autumn directed her attention toward the young sailor, whose face she still couldn't see. She wanted to tap him on the shoulder, force him to look at her, and demand he pay attention to her. That definitely wasn't something Autumn would do.

Mariana waved Inez over. "Come on. Don't be such a square." The tall sailor laughed, and heat spread through Autumn's body. She bunched up her fists. The other sailor finally turned around. His sloped nose. Those Caribbean blue eyes. That dark, wavy hair. He winked at Autumn—no, Inez—and said, "It'll be fun."

If Autumn had any control over this body, she would have gasped. He looked just like—

"Hey all!" a voice rang out.

Autumn turned to see her Uncle Duncan, now young with his tousled brown hair and sparkling hazel eyes, approach the group. A lanky, skinny fella, who reminded Autumn of one of those complete skeletons from biology class, was in tow. He hid shyly behind Autumn's uncle.

Duncan approached Inez and grinned before he clapped the bony sailor on the back. "Ralphie and I are ready to go. The boat's waiting. You coming, Inez?"

*So, that's Ralphie. How do I know him?*

Just then, the tall, blond sailor joined Autumn. "Of course she's coming. We're all going."

"What's your name, sailor?" Autumn felt herself smile, but the feelings inside were all jumbled up. She wasn't happy.

The blond sailor held out his hand. "I'm Mick. Mick Canton."

Suddenly, Autumn's vision blurred, and the pressure in her chest waxed and waned. She struggled to breathe. Her eyes twitched, and she shut them tight. When she opened them again, she was back in her familiar, drab surroundings.

She collapsed into the patio chair and let out a deep breath. Her whole body shook. "Whoa."

That had never happened to her before, but then again, she'd never put on a dead girl's ring before. Autumn wished she hadn't been pulled so quickly from the vision. She enjoyed seeing Uncle Duncan. He had died when Autumn was a small child, but she remembered him as a joyous, carefree man with a mischievous streak.

Perhaps Inez wanted help puzzling out her memories. And so far, Autumn thought she had unearthed at least one clue. She knew why Inez had targeted Liam.

Liam's grandfather lived in New Town, a section of Key West north of George Street. While Old Town was lined with charming and historic Victorians and roosters parading up and down the sidewalks, New Town's small, one-story Floridian ranches lacked the ornate decorations and soft pastels of Old Town. Pops's white one-story had faded blue trim and a single carport.

Pops could sell his home tomorrow and make a fortune—if he wanted to. But as Pops said, "Where am I going to retire? I already live in Florida."

Liam pulled his scooter up the driveway and killed the engine. He took off his helmet and wiped the sweat from his brow with his forearm. He grabbed Cora's cookies and his wet shirt from the small cargo hold. The brown paper bag was soggy, and he imagined the cookies were too.

Liam opened the screen door and called out, "Pops, you here?"

"Yeah, sport." His grandpa coughed. "In the kitchen."

Liam found Leo Breyer at a small, round table reading the newspaper. Bifocals perched on the tip of his nose. A salami sandwich lay half-eaten on a chipped ceramic plate. And rather than use a napkin, Pops wiped his hands on his wrinkled khaki shorts. "You're home late. How was your first day at the Cayo?"

Liam opened up the fridge and found a can of soda. He popped it open. "Humiliating."

Pops raised an eyebrow. "Where'd you get that shirt?"

Liam sipped the soda, the cold liquid burned his throat. "Glenda Reynolds gave it to me because I fell into the pool. Go ahead and laugh."

Pops shook out the crease in the newspaper before turning the page. "Wasn't going to."

"Seriously, Pops. The people at that place are nuts. They believe in ghosts."

"You needed a job. I got you a job." Pops adjusted his glasses. "Besides, there are worse things to believe in."

Liam chugged the soda and burped. He crushed the can and tossed it into the recycling container by the back door. "I don't really want to go back there, but . . ."

"But, what?" Pops asked.

Liam pressed his face against the door's dirty windowpane and stared at the round, white rocks that covered the yard where grass might normally grow. "I need the money. I'm going into business with Randall."

"That dummy?"

Liam dropped into the chair next to his grandfather. "He's not a dummy. Well, he knows scooters, at least. Anyway, think about it. There's enough tourists and business in Key West to go around and it's time we get a piece of the pie."

Pops covered his face with the newspaper. "I was wrong. *You're* the dummy."

Liam pulled the newspaper away from Pops. "This is a chance for the Breyers to rise to the top in Key West. You see how people treat you at the VFW, like you're not good enough, and me—"

Pops's blue eyes appeared dull. "People don't treat you badly because of who I am. They treat you badly because of who you are."

Liam balked. Well, that stung.

Pops put down the newspaper and peered at Liam. "I think you should forget this scooter business. You can't compete with a big shot like Mick Canton. Why don't you apply to college?"

Liam hated how his grandfather had such little faith in him. "Cuz, Pops, I need money. College costs a whole lot of money." He stared out the back door and thought about Evelyn bossing him around. "No, I want to work for myself."

"Okay, sport. Just don't be surprised if this all blows up in your face." He nodded at Liam's borrowed polo shirt. "You gonna go back to the Cayo? You'll make me look bad if you don't."

Liam didn't think the Breyer family could look worse, but he didn't want to disappoint the old man. "Yeah, I'll go back." He remembered Cora's cookies and tossed the brown paper bag onto the table. "For you."

Pops peered inside the bag and smiled. "Job perk for your old grandpa." He reached inside and then frowned. "They're all wet." Pops shrugged and popped a piece of cookie in his mouth. "Still good. Did you get a few bucks for the ring at Louie's?"

Liam's mouth went dry. "I'm gonna do it tomorrow." He felt bad for lying, but Pops already lacked confidence in Liam. Confessing he lost his abuela's ring wouldn't help his cause. Liam wanted to go back to the Cayo and search for the ring, but was too embarrassed to face Autumn or her mother. He'd have to return later when no one was there.

"You look pale," said Pops. "You all right?"

"Uh, yeah. I'm just gonna hit the hay. I'm spent."

"Hung-over, you mean," Pops mumbled.

"Unlike you, I didn't mean to drink so much."

"Thanks for the judgment." Pops rolled his eyes. "You're eighteen years old and you went to a party. I didn't expect less." He nodded toward a piece of scrap paper tacked up on the fridge by a broken magnet. "Your father called. He's doing better. Wants you to give him a call soon."

Liam took down the piece of paper with an un-familiar area code scribbled on it. "Sure, Pops. Will

do." He headed toward his bedroom and crumpled the scrap of paper inside his palm. When he
passed the bathroom, he dropped it inside the toilet
and flushed.

## CHAPTER SIX

Shortly before bedtime, Autumn was on her knees rummaging through an old steamer trunk in the attic when Timothy appeared.

"Girl," he said, his voice hinting at annoyance. "Your mother heard noises up here and sent me to check it out. Do you think I like running up and down the stairs?" He fanned himself in the doorway. "What are you doing up here? It's hotter than hell."

Autumn wiped a line of sweat from her forehead with the back of her hand. "Just give me a sec." She removed an old black-and-white photo from a box in the trunk and sat back. "Well, freak me." In the photo stood a group of four young sailors, their arms around one another's shoulders.

Timothy rolled his eyes. "What are you playing at?"

Autumn crouched, careful of the steep slant in the ceiling. She waved the old photo at Timothy, who plucked the picture from Autumn's fingers before turning it over. "Duncan, Ralphie, Mick, and Leo, 1966." He furrowed his brows. "What made you go looking for this? Besides pretty boy looking exactly like his grandfather."

Autumn peered at the picture. "Is that who it is?"

"Who else would look just like him? Anyway, how do you think he got the job? Boy didn't even get his high school diploma, and your mama agrees to hire him."

"You don't have a college degree," Autumn pointed out.

"I'm working toward it." Timothy sounded huffy. "Anyway, what made you think to look for this?"

Autumn pointed to the top of a dusty box where she had set the ring. Her voice teetered on giddiness. "I channeled her." Her chest swelled with pride. At the Cayo, lots of people saw ghosts, but no one had ever channeled a spirit before. This was big.

"You what?" Timothy's voice rose an octave.

"I got inside her memories. The ghost's name is Inez. I don't have a last name, but she knew Duncan and Leo and Mick."

Timothy picked up the ring and examined it. "This must've been hers. But how did you get it?"

"It was at the bottom of the pool. I bet it slid out of Liam's pocket when he fell in."

"You mean was pulled in, don't you?" Timothy carefully set the ring back on the box. "So your pretty boy and this ghost are connected somehow."

"That's the thing. I think it's Liam's grandfather with the connection to the ghost. The resemblance is uncanny. Besides, too many coincidences can't be coincidence. And he's not *my* pretty boy."

"Sure he isn't." Timothy fanned himself with the photo. "Go see your mama. We'll figure this ghost thing out another time."

Autumn grinned.

"What are you so happy about?" Timothy asked. "This doesn't have anything to do with you."

"It doesn't yet." Autumn snatched back the picture. "But it gives me a chance to investigate—just what I need to earn that journalism scholarship."

"Girl, you're going to insert yourself into a mystery you have no business being in. And besides, the minute you mention the word *ghost*, you can kiss that scholarship opportunity goodbye. You better give pretty boy back his ring. Something tells me he needs the ring more than you do."

"I'll give him the ring when he asks for it."

Timothy clucked his tongue. "Give Liam back his ring. And don't channel ghost girl." He pointed at her. "Evelyn said to tell you it's time for bed. I'm heading home." And with that, he strode away.

Autumn's face soured. *It's not even ten yet.* Autumn waited until she could no longer hear Timothy's steps. She picked up the ring and slipped it on to her finger and waited for the black dots to appear. This time she was ready.

Liam woke sometime after midnight covered in sweat. He had dreamed that the brunette from the pool clawed out his eyes before her face morphed into Autumn. Despite the malfunctioning air-conditioner in his room, Liam couldn't rid his body of the goosebumps that had erupted along his arms and neck. He rose from the bed and threw on a pair of black mesh shorts and an old white undershirt before finding the keys to his scooter. He slipped out his bedroom window, so as not to wake his grandfather, and quietly rolled his scooter to the end of the block. Then he started the engine and drove back to the Cayo.

At this time of night, Key West was quiet, but not eerily so. The only sounds were the buzz from his scooter and the laughter of a few tourists staying at a nearby hotel.

Liam drove along Fogarty and then traveled to Eisenhower. He parked a few houses down from the Cayo, just in case Evelyn or Autumn were still awake. He didn't want to explain his presence at this time of night.

Liam unlatched the old white gate and slipped into the Cayo's darkened patio. He sidled around the edge of the pool, careful to avoid the inky black water. He swallowed a lump in his throat. *Find the ring and get out of here.*

Liam glanced up at the Cayo's darkened attic windows. He sucked in his breath, turned on the small flashlight on his cell phone, and aimed the beam toward the water's surface. He felt like an idiot having driven here in the middle of the night. He shouldn't have lost the damn ring in the first place.

The light only skimmed the top, and he couldn't see the pool's floor. Liam decided to check the pool filter. It was possible the drain sucked the ring into it.

Liam's heart raced as he walked around the lima-bean-shaped pool. He squatted, quietly lifted the plastic lid off the filter, and aimed the flashlight into the hole. Nothing glinted. He removed the strainer and rummaged around. Liam grimaced and shuddered as his hand grazed thick dead beetles and slimy leaves. Unfortunately, he came up empty.

"Looking for this?" A husky voice breathed into his ear.

Liam nearly toppled into the water, his heart hammering in his chest. He rose from his crouch to face Autumn, dressed in plaid boxer shorts and a thin blue tank top. His gaze trailed her body and then landed on her hand, outstretched in front of her, the diamond ring catching the moonlight.

Liam let out a breath. "Thank you. I thought it was lost forever." He reached out to take the ring off Autumn's finger, but she snatched her hand back.

Autumn waved her pointer finger at him. "No, no, sailor. This isn't yours. You don't get to take it."

*Sailor?* "Autumn, are you okay?"

Autumn stepped forward so that mere inches separated them. She smelled like jasmine, and her T-shirt was so painfully thin. Liam tried to look everywhere but directly at her. His thoughts were jumbled, and it took him a moment to find the words. "Can I have my ring back? It was my abuela's."

Autumn tapped her finger against Liam's lips.

"Shhhh." Liam stared into Autumn's dilated pupils. She laughed or cackled—Liam couldn't decide which.

"I could've been yours, Lion," she cooed.

"Give me the ring, Autumn," Liam said firmly.

"No." Autumn drew her face in close and brushed her lips against Liam's mouth.

Liam's body tingled as if an electric current had passed through Autumn's lips and into his mouth. But this moment seemed wrong. Felt off. He cried out when Autumn bit his lower lip. He pulled away and ran his tongue over his mouth, tasting blood. He pushed Autumn off him.

"What's wrong with you?" He wiped at his mouth with the back of his hand. A streak of red, like the smear of paint, bloomed on his skin.

Autumn cackled again and wiggled her fingers in some kind of seductive wave before slipping through the sliding glass doors.

She never did give him back the ring.

What the hell just happened? Liam rushed out of the patio and ran to his scooter parked down the block. His breath came out in huffs. He straddled the bike and was about to flee until he remembered that Autumn called him Lion.

That was Pops's nickname in the navy.

The next morning, Autumn adjusted the strap on her messenger bag and climbed the steps to the Keys of Excellence Charter School. Her eyelids felt as though small weights were pulling them down. She'd had a restless night's sleep, possibly dreaming about Liam, but she really couldn't remember now.

Someone yelled out, "Hey, Joisy girl!"

Autumn squeezed her eyes shut and pretended not to hear. She stepped toward the entrance and a lithe blonde girl blocked her way. "Going somewhere?"

Even without looking up, Autumn knew it was Victoria Canton who stood there with her hands on her perfect waist. There were girls like Victoria back home in Jersey. Rich. Entitled. Nasty. But Autumn never had confrontations with them. And in the unlikely event she had gotten cornered by one of the bitchy girls, Natasha had been there to back her up. God, what she wouldn't have done to have someone on her side now.

"Just to class, Victoria." Autumn didn't bother hiding her exasperation. "Same as everyone else." Victoria remained in her path. Autumn saw from the corner of her eye a group of Victoria's friends off to the side. They stood at attention like soldiers waiting to be called into battle. "You need anything from me or can I get to class?"

Victoria glanced at her friends and then back at Autumn. "Yeah, I need the notes for American Lit. I heard McNulty is giving a pop quiz later this afternoon."

Autumn lifted the flap of her messenger bag and thumbed through her folder. She found the stapled group of notes, four pages on Hemingway, and handed them over to Victoria. To be honest, Autumn felt sorry for Victoria since no amount of money seemed to help her do well in school.

"Thanks," Victoria said, without a hint of gratitude in her voice. "How you can study with all those ghosts thrashing about is beyond me." She leaned in and said in a loud whisper, "Do they talk to you?" The soldier clique snickered in the background.

Autumn sidled past Victoria. "Actually, yes. Hemingway was 'thrashing' about in one of the guest rooms, and he had plenty to say about himself." She tapped the side of her head with her finger. "I'm going to ace this pop quiz. Hemingway said so." Autumn grinned, surprised by the sudden surge of bravery in confronting her bully.

Victoria growled. Her two leggy friends headed over, until Victoria held up her hand to stop them. Her attention fixated on the street where a tanned guy was pulling up alongside the curb in his beat-up scooter. Autumn watched Victoria bound down the cement steps, crying, "Liam!"

Autumn couldn't help but roll her eyes. "Figures," she mumbled. Of course, Liam of all people would know Victoria Canton.

Liam pressed the kickstand to the asphalt with the toe of his sneaker and dismounted the bike. He removed his helmet and set it in on top of the seat. Victoria went to wrap her arms around Liam's neck, but he grabbed her wrists and gently pushed her back. Victoria pouted like a three-year-old.

"I didn't come to see you." Liam tilted his chin at Autumn by way of greeting.

He must have come to ask her about the diamond ring. Autumn sighed. Timothy was right. He must need it for something. But, of all places, why had he felt compelled to talk to her here? Autumn wondered if she could slip away undetected. She needed more time with the ring if she was going to discover what happened to the ghost. She retreated toward the steps, but Liam called out, "Autumn!"

She slumped her shoulders and scuttled down the steps. *Just get this over with.* But the moment she came face-to-face with him, she felt this desire to both kiss him and scratch his eyes out at the same time. *What is going on with me?*

"Your lip is all puffy," Autumn said.

Liam arched his brows so high Autumn thought they'd fly off his forehead. "Uh, yeah. That's what happens when someone bites your lip."

Autumn glanced from Victoria to Liam and grimaced.

Liam's eyes widened. "Uh, no."

Autumn shrugged. "What you do in your own time is your business."

Liam crossed his arms and stared intently at her. She fidgeted under his gaze.

"You mean, you don't remember?" he asked.

"Remember what?"

Liam's eyes darted to Victoria, who stood there with her hands on her hips. "I think we should talk about this later."

Victoria's lip curled up. "How do you even know each other?"

This time, Liam answered. "I work for her great aunt."

"At the haunted hotel?" Victoria's eyebrows shot up into perfectly manicured arches.

"A job's a job. We can't all be born rich."

Victoria frowned, but then she purred, "I didn't break up with you because you didn't have money."

Now, it was Autumn's turn to be incredulous. "You guys used to date?"

Victoria smiled and moistened her lips. "We did more than date." She laughed and linked her arm through Liam's elbow.

Autumn's stomach soured. "I'll see you back at the Cayo." She ran up the stairs, hoping to reach homeroom before the second bell. Autumn thought she heard her name again, but this time, when she ducked her head down and pretended not to hear, no one got in her way.

When Autumn returned to New Jersey, Victoria Canton and her god-awful friends would be a distant memory.

# CHAPTER SEVEN

Liam watched Autumn enter the school building. He shouldn't have come here. He should have gone straight to the Cayo. He could have spoken to Autumn later. But his shift would end before she got home from school, and he really needed that ring back. Plus, he didn't think Evelyn would like it if he hung around after he was off the clock.

Well, the ring was safe at least. But Liam's skin crawled just the same. Did Autumn really not remember kissing him last night? Or was she playing him?

One problem at a time.

Liam pinched the bridge of his nose and said to Victoria, "Why did you have to say that?"

She tucked a strand of blonde hair behind her ear. "Say what?"

"'We did more than just date,'" he mimicked. "You know that isn't true."

She scoffed. "You can't possibly care what she thinks. She's related to a crazy woman. Plus, she's from New Jersey."

"You really haven't changed one bit, have you?"

Victoria skimmed her finger down Liam's shoulder and drew circles along his forearm. She knew how to touch him, how to get his pulse to quicken. She also knew how to use him for a good time, before throwing him away. Liam brushed her hand off his arm. "Quit it, Vicky. I'm not interested."

Liam noticed that Victoria kept glancing back at her group of friends, who were staring at them as if hypnotized. "You're such a hypocrite. What do you care what *they* think? They told you to dump me because I was a loser."

Victoria whipped her head back and faced him. "No one tells me what to do. Besides, I never said you were a loser."

Liam straddled the scooter and buckled his helmet on his head. "No, you just treated me like one. I have to go to work. I only came here to ask Autumn something, and you scared her off."

"Sure you didn't," Victoria said, laughing. "You know I go here."

"Whatever, Vic." Liam inserted the key into the ignition.

Victoria touched Liam's hand. "I heard you need some start-up capital for a business venture. Maybe, I can help you with that."

Liam cursed under his breath. "Randall."

"Stop by my house sometime. And we can discuss how I can finance your operation." She hurried up the steps to join her group of friends. Liam watched as the girls bowed their heads and laughed.

"Breyer!" A deep voice barked his name.

Liam startled as a black SUV rolled up alongside him, sandwiching him between the street and the sidewalk. Mick Canton sat in the passenger seat, his arm draped over the open window, his Rolex glinting in the sunlight. He cracked his neck muscles before adjusting his sunglasses atop his full, albeit graying, hair. Mick's driver, a burly man with a flattop, rested thick fingers on the steering wheel.

Liam had learned early that the best way to handle Mick was to pretend like the man didn't intimidate him. Key word: *pretend*. Mick thrived on weakness, and he could smell it like a shark smelled chum in the water.

Liam feigned a smile. "Can I help you, Mr. Canton?"

Mick flicked a mosquito off his forearm. "Doubtful. I thought you were making your money in the Dakotas, drilling for oil." The way Mick said it made it seem like Liam had gone off to earn money on Mars.

Liam felt a burgeoning headache. "Didn't work out."

"Course not," said Mick, his wide mouth turning up at the corners.

Liam cringed. "Okay, well if that's all—"

"Not quite young man. Now that you're back, I want to make it clear that you should stay away from my granddaughter."

Liam watched a beetle scuttle along the sidewalk. "I promise you that Victoria and I have no plans to get back together. That ship has sailed."

Mick sucked on his teeth. "No hard feelings, son. I just don't want her getting hurt."

"She broke up with me," Liam said.

Mick smirked. "That's not what I meant. "You see, a girl like Victoria, with money and influence, is an easy target for boys like yourself."

Liam balled his fists. He stepped toward the SUV and Burly Flattop opened his car door. Mick put his hands out to stop him. "Not necessary, Finn. Young Liam wasn't making any threatening movements. Were you?"

Liam didn't respond.

Mick chuckled and motioned for Finn to start the car. "I hope *not* to see you around, Breyer." Then the SUV sped off, kicking up bits of gravel on its way out.

With shaky hands, Liam turned on the scooter. He was late for his shift at the Cayo. After his confrontation with Mick, taking orders from Evelyn would be a treat.

Autumn always cut through City Cemetery on her way home from school. The Cayo was directly on the other side of the cemetery, off Pine Street. When she and Evelyn first moved there in the spring, Autumn used to spend hours reading the creepy epitaphs, sometimes gliding her fingers along the ancient skulls embedded in the headstones. Eventually, she realized that despite the cemetery being a huge tourist destination, some people in Key West still had beloved family members buried there. Like Mr. Blazevig, who, on most days, tended to the graves of his dead wife and son. Today was no different.

"Hi, Mr. Blazevig," Autumn said cheerfully.

The man was crouched on all fours, leaning toward a squat headstone and holding a garden trowel. He was digging out weeds that had crept up over the stone. Unlike the larger, grandiose grave markers in City Cemetery, the Blazevigs' stones were modest and close to the ground.

Autumn never asked Mr. Blazevig directly, but Aunt Glenda said his son died in Afghanistan, and Mrs. Blazevig succumbed to pneumonia a few years ago.

Mr. Blazevig stood up and wiped his hands on his dingy white shirt. He leaned over the black iron fence that separated his family plots from the walkway where Autumn stood. "Why, hello, dear. How was school?"

Mr. Blazevig was tall and scrawny with sunburned skin. He had wispy, white hair and a jovial laugh. Aunt Glenda referred to him as a kind soul, but there was something about Mr. Blazevig that seemed tormented.

Autumn shrugged.

"That good, huh?"

"Just some mean girls at school." No matter how good the rest of her day went, Victoria Canton always managed to seep under Autumn's skin.

Mr. Blazevig's narrowed his dark eyes. "Never had patience for bullies. They'll get their comeuppance, don't you worry."

Perhaps. Victoria's life seemed next to perfect. Autumn couldn't imagine the popular and rich mean queen would ever have to worry about paying for her dream college.

"Anyway." Autumn tried to muster a smile. "My mom needs me at the D&B."

Mr. Blazevig wiped sweat from his brow. "Your mom is trying her hardest to get that place back on its feet. She's smart, if you ask me. Say, you don't think she could spare you a few nights a week?"

Autumn adjusted the strap on her messenger bag that was cutting into her shoulder. "What do you mean?"

Mr. Blazevig scratched his cheek. "Well, I could use another tour guide to take over some shifts. Um . . ." His cheeks reddened. "The doctor thinks I shouldn't work so much."

Mr. Blazevig ran a moderately busy ghost tour company where he escorted visitors around Old Town, showing them Key West's most haunted attractions and telling stories of tragic demise. He did at least two tours a night, every night. And then he was back at the cemetery the next day, tending to the graves.

"Can I think about it?" Truth was, Autumn's mother kept her pretty busy at the Cayo Hueso. If she wasn't cleaning rooms, she was organizing Glenda's old files, helping Cora prepare dinner, or sweeping the front porch. Plus, she hesitated to take on extra work, especially since she needed time to complete her scholarship application.

"Of course, dear." He smiled at her, although the corner of his eyes drooped. He returned to pruning the growth surrounding the headstones.

Autumn fingered the diamond ring in her skirt pocket. She yearned to slide it back on her finger and channel Inez again, but she needed to stall. Autumn glanced at the time on her cell phone. Liam was hopefully finishing up his shift and getting ready to leave the Cayo. If Liam confronted her about the ring, Autumn knew she couldn't lie to him. Although, her gut told her Liam already knew she had it.

Autumn directed her thoughts to the old photo she'd found in the attic. The one with her uncle and his Navy pals. If she were going to properly investigate Inez's death, she'd need to gather more information. And Mr. Blazevig, who was somewhat of an expert in all things paranormal, would be a good start.

"Mr. Blazevig?"

His head was still bent over his work. "Yes?"

"Do you know a ghost story about a woman named Inez? She died at the Cayo Hueso sometime in the mid-1960s?"

The old man tensed his shoulders for a moment. "Uh, can't say that I have, Autumn."

Autumn dug around in her bag. "I have one more question. I found an old photo at the Cayo of Uncle Duncan and some navy buddies. I was wondering if you could identify them for me."

Autumn already knew everyone in the photo, but she was fishing for something. She handed the photo to the old man.

Mr. Blazevig straightened and brushed the dirt from his threadbare pants. He removed reading glasses from his shirt pocket before holding the photo at arm's length.

"I recognize Uncle Duncan, of course." Autumn pointed to a tall, skinny gentleman. "Is that you?"

Mr. Blazevig laughed. "Sure is. I was always a bean pole." He tapped his crooked finger on the largest man. "That strapping Nordic gentleman is Mick Canton. Scandinavian on his mom's side. And that man is Leo Breyer. We were all stationed together at the naval base here. We did our tours overseas, but somehow we all managed to come back to the island."

Autumn nodded. "You guys were close, weren't you?"

Mr. Blazevig handed Autumn back the photo. "We were very good friends for a long time. I was so sad when Duncan died. He and I were particularly close. Like the brother I never had."

Autumn had wondered if her uncle was the glue that held them together and if his death made them drift apart. Because as far as she knew, Mr. Blazevig, Leo, and Mick never saw one another anymore. But then she discovered that there had been a girl they knew—a girl who had died and was now haunting the Cayo. Maybe their suspicions of one another damaged their friendship.

"Thanks, Mr. Blazevig." Autumn slipped the photo back into her bag. "I'll let you know about the job."

"Please do." He crouched back down on his knees and plunged the shovel into the dirt to remove a clump of weeds. "It's not too often I find a person I can trust."

"How do you know you can trust me?"

"Because you're Duncan's niece."

Autumn waved goodbye. She slowly made her way along the path and thought about trust. A sweet, old man like Mr. Blazevig wouldn't lie to her about knowing Inez, but maybe he would circumvent the truth. He said he'd never heard of a ghost story about Inez, but that didn't mean he hadn't met her in real life. Because he had.

*"There you are, Inez," the girl said. "The boys want to go out on Ralphie's boat."*

Mr. Blazevig was the tall, skinny sailor from Inez's memory—Ralphie.

Liam entered the pool shed and left the door wide open, bringing in the natural sunlight and heat. This made him feel better, less claustrophobic. He rummaged through some old buckets, moldy pool noodles, and a broken fishing rod, hoping to unearth a shovel. His shift ended twenty minutes ago, but a stray cat dropped a dead bird at the foot of the steps leading out to the courtyard, and Evelyn had asked Liam to take care of it. Liam doubted he was receiving overtime pay for this.

"Get a shovel from the pool shed," Evelyn had instructed. "Bury it in the back, behind the Marlberry. No one goes there."

There was something about the way Evelyn ordered him around that felt familiar. Sometimes, it reminded him of the principal at his last high school. The one who told him that his presence would not be missed. After that, he dropped out and got his GED. Other times, Evelyn barked at him like his former babysitter after he dumped Legos all over Pops's kitchen floor. There was just something about the woman and that something hated Liam. He must have reminded her of someone too.

Liam squinted at a dusty corner of the shed. "Aha." The sound of his own voice calmed his nerves. This whole place made him doubt his sanity.

Just as Liam reached for the shovel, he felt a shove from behind. He tumbled over a galvanized bucket and landed awkwardly on the wood floor. A rusty nail, with its sharp tip pointed upward, was centimeters from his face. Liam attempted to push himself up, but found his feet tangled in old rope.

"Jesus." He kicked the rope off his sneakers, hoping to free himself from the net of junk. Just as he pulled himself up, the edge of the shovel grazed his eyebrow. As if some unknown force had picked up the heavy tool and swung at him with all the intention of decapitating him. The shovel clanged loudly to the floor. Liam's heart raced and his breath caught before he clamored out of the shed.

# CHAPTER EIGHT

A little while later, Autumn was sneaking through the lobby—desperate to avoid Liam, whose scooter still sat outside—when her mother beckoned her from the office. Autumn leaned against the doorframe. "What's up?"

Evelyn dropped a pen onto the ledger and faced her daughter. "Tell me about your day."

Autumn blinked. It had been a long time since her mother inquired about her school day. Finally, she shrugged. "Haters gonna hate."

Evelyn tilted her head. "Victoria again?"

Autumn nodded. For a second, she was tempted to squeeze into the chair next to Evelyn's desk and disclose all that she had learned about Inez in the past two days, but she thought better of it. Bringing up ghosts would only make Evelyn bristle.

"Victoria's certainly not the nicest girl on the island," her mom said.

"Did you know Liam used to date her?" Autumn regretted the words the moment she uttered them. She knew her mom already disliked Liam. Her comment could only solidify that opinion, which she didn't think was fair.

"Well," her mom said, clucking her tongue. "I'm not surprised. Certainly shows Liam's true colors." Evelyn glanced at the glow of the computer monitor. "I hope you'll be the bigger person and be nice to Victoria even though she may not deserve it. Her grandpa owns most of Key West. And he's taken a particular interest in the Cayo. I'm considering asking him to be an investor."

Autumn scrunched her face. She thought it funny that Liam should be harshly judged for dating Victoria, but not Autumn for being a phony and sucking up to her.

Evelyn pressed her fingers into her eyes before sipping her coffee. "I better get back to work. These accounts are a mess."

Autumn took that as her cue to leave. As she turned to go, her mother asked, "Can you find Mrs. Paulson extra towels?"

Autumn sighed. Her investigation into Inez would have to wait.

After nearly tripping over the old shovel, Timothy stumbled onto the patio with a sour expression. "I swear, your shenanigans are going to get me killed. Or worse, you're gonna make me tear my dress shirt."

Liam sat on the patio chair, feet away from him, dabbing at a cut above his eye with the hem of his T-shirt.

"Should I get the first-aid kit? Again?" Before Liam could protest, Timothy called out, "Mama!"

Cora Newbold popped her head out the door, took one look at Liam, and emerged a moment later with a large, white handbag. She unzipped her bag and removed a clear pouch that held Band-Aids, gauze, and ointment.

Cora was heavy-set and wearing a turquoise blouse and matching head wrap. She and Timothy shared the same dark eyes and wide nose, but Timothy's chin ended in a point. Cora's round face was maternal and soft, although she was no nonsense as she rummaged through the medical supplies. She gingerly lifted a dark curl away from Liam's cut. He wondered if this was what it was like to be cared for by a mother.

"How did this happen?" Cora's accent was thick with the islands.

Liam inhaled her spicy, citrus perfume. "I tripped over a shovel. There's so much crap in the shed."

Cora narrowed her eyes at the blood on his forehead. "Is that so?"

"Yes," said Liam in a tight voice.

Cora gave him a halfhearted nod, but Liam could tell that she didn't believe him. "It seems that the ghost has it out for you."

He sighed. This again. Sure, he thought he saw a girl in the pool, but ghosts just don't go around drowning people. Stuff like that doesn't happen. "I don't believe in ghosts."

Cora dabbed at Liam's cut with a piece of gauze. A line of red blood bloomed on the white cotton. He winced as she applied pressure. "That's the thing about ghosts. You don't have to believe in them, but they believe in you."

She placed Liam's hand onto the gauze and ordered him to hold still while she rummaged through the first-aid kit for ointment.

"What does that even mean?" he asked. "They believe in you?"

Cora twisted the cap off the bacitracin and squeezed the cloudy gel onto a bandage, which she stuck to Liam's forehead. "My ancestors believe that spirits seek out the living when they need assistance."

"If this spirit needs my help, then why does she keep trying to kill me?" Liam scoffed.

"Ah-ha!" Timothy cried out. "So you do admit that ghost girl took a swing at you with a shovel? Did she also bust your lip?"

"I'm not admitting anything," said Liam. "It's crazy to think that ghosts are real. Or that they can lift heavy shovels."

"Hush," said Cora with a wave. "There *are* presences in this house. And this one, in particular, is trying to communicate with you."

"Why?" Liam asked.

Timothy examined his well-manicured nails as if they were more interesting than this conversation. "You might want to talk to Miss Autumn. She has some theories."

Liam rose and touched the now-bandaged cut on his head. "That's ridiculous."

Cora closed the first-aid kit. "My son is right. Autumn seems very connected to the spirit world. Unlike any young person I've ever met. She's a conduit for the dead."

Someone cleared their throat and they all froze. No one had heard Evelyn's footsteps as she entered the patio. "Liam, did you take care of the bird?"

"Not yet, Mrs. Abernathy. I got clocked by a ghost." Liam glanced at Timothy and Cora, waiting for a laugh, but their eyes widened and they both gave imperceptible nods. Okay, so don't talk about ghosts in front of the boss lady.

Evelyn's eyes flitted around the pool area. "Please take care of it before you go home." She said to Cora, "Mrs. Paulson requested grouper for dinner. Is that doable?"

"Sorry, not today, Mrs. Abernathy. There was no one to go to the wharf." Cora slid the first-aid kit into her bag and headed inside with Evelyn, who muttered something about "guests expecting fresh seafood."

Timothy lingered outside with Liam. "Talk to Autumn. By the way, she has your ring."

"I know."

"You know?"

"Yeah, she flashed it at me before she did this." Liam pointed to his swollen lip.

"She hit you?"

"No, she bit me."

"Miss Autumn bit your lip?" Timothy sounded incredulous. "When?"

"Last night. After midnight."

Timothy put his hands on his hips. "You came back here at night to search for the ring?"

"Crazy, right?"

Timothy's pupils grew. "On second thought, *I'm* going to talk to Autumn. You go bury that bird and then go home. Your ring is safe for now."

"What do you mean 'for now'?"

But Timothy had already slipped through the sliding glass doors. Liam remained outside alone, with a cut on his forehead, about to say a eulogy for a bird.

After returning from the January room where she left Mrs. Paulson a fresh stack of towels, Autumn hurried to her bathroom. She turned on the hot tap and waited for the shower to steam up. That was the thing about truly old houses—the water pressure sucked, and it took an eternity for the water to be anything but arctic cold.

Autumn faced the bathroom mirror and slid the ponytail holder out of her hair. The brunette strands were stringy, damp from sweat. Mascara caked under her lashes, leaving flecks of black in the creases below her eyes. She saw herself as Liam must have seen her yesterday. A mess.

Autumn thought back to Inez. The way she carried herself. Tall. Elegant. Important. Being inside Inez's memories gave Autumn an understanding of what it was like to be a woman people noticed. And yet, despite Inez's self-confidence and beauty, she longed for something too. Not a something, Autumn realized, a someone. Someone she couldn't have.

Steam billowed around Autumn. The ring glinted next to the soap on the sink, taunting her. Calling her. Timothy would rat her out to Liam any moment, so it was now or never.

Autumn slipped the ring on her finger and steadied herself against the edge of the pedestal. She waited for the slight wave of dizziness.

This time when Inez climbed inside Autumn's body, the ghost didn't transport Autumn back in time. She hovered inside her and whispered, "What do you want to know?"

Autumn glanced at her reflection. An amber ring circled her normally brown irises. "Who are you?" Autumn felt an invisible hand guide her as she traced a letter into the steamy condensation: a lowercase *t*.

Okay, that's a start. No true last name, but it shouldn't be too hard to get information on a girl named Inez T., who died in the 1960s.

Autumn grew bolder. "Who killed you?"

Again, her hand lifted, as if guided by another force, and she wrote L-E-O on the glass.

Autumn gasped. "Are you sure?" She stared at her reflection, but Inez didn't answer.

"Take me back," Autumn demanded, "into your memories. Take me back to the day you died."

Autumn's vision clouded and then cleared. Leo Breyer loomed in front of her, his face an angry mask. Autumn's gaze darted around, but they weren't in the patio. They stood in corridor with doors on both sides. A school? The only illumination came from the gymnasium. Leo continued to yell at her.

A shadow lurked behind him, but Autumn couldn't make out the form. Man or woman, she wasn't sure.

Spittle came out with Leo's words, and his skin grew reddened, as if he was on fire.

"I can't take you anymore," he screamed at her.

Autumn shrank back and laughed.

Leo's eyes widened. He raised his hands as if to strike, and then blackness.

Autumn felt lighter. The spirit had lifted and was gone. Her vision cleared and she was back in her bathroom.

"Dammit!" Autumn cried.

She heard a pounding on the door. Her mother. "Are you almost done in there?"

"Just a minute," she called back.

Autumn stepped into the hot shower and let the water wash away her sweat and grime. The ghost told her what she wanted to know, but she couldn't shake her uneasiness. Inez didn't seem exactly trustworthy. Autumn needed proof. Proof that Leo was in fact Inez's killer, or proof that he wasn't. Either way, she needed Liam's help.

Liam cradled the dead bird in the shovel and carried it to the far corner of the yard where the Cayo's back fence butted up against the neighbor's property. A large banyan tree pushed against the fence, and its roots protruded from the earth. The trunk reminded Liam of a sea monster rising from the ocean, unfurling its tentacles. The tree must've been a hundred years old, at least.

The Marlberry grew underneath the Banyan tree, the shade providing just the right amount of darkness for the shrub's bright green leaves and pink flowers. It was a pretty, albeit neglected garden. Just the right place to bury a dead animal. No one came back there.

Liam spotted a gap in the tree roots and considered it a fitting place to bury the bird. He dug a small hole in between the roots and scooped out the dirt, forming a pile of earth. He wouldn't need to dig deep—the bird was barely the size of his palm.

Using the tip of the shovel, he nudged the bird into the tiny hole and then went to pile on the dirt. But something stopped him. Liam crouched and examined the dirt mound. He poked at it with his finger and uncovered a round brass pin, roughly the size of a quarter. Liam brushed off the loose dirt and held it up, hoping to read the inscription in the fading afternoon light. He could barely make out the name. St. Veronica's School for Girls.

The pin seemed familiar, but Liam couldn't remember why. He slipped it into his pocket, and covered the dead bird with dirt.

After he and Randall got their business off the ground, Liam swore he would not think about dead things, animals or people, for a long, long time.

Shortly before dinner, Autumn sat on her bed, a history textbook lay in her lap. Timothy knocked on Autumn's bedroom door.

"What's up?" she asked Timothy, who was dressed in a gray suit vest with a light blue shirt underneath. No bowtie. "Gotta date?"

"I have study group tonight."

"Cyrus?" Autumn wagged her brows.

A smile crept up on Timothy's face. "Maybe. Not that it's any of your business." Timothy leaned against the doorframe and softened his stance. "Listen, I know you think I'm all beauty and no brains—"

Autumn laughed.

Timothy narrowed his eyes. "But I'm telling you something important. You cannot keep channeling that ghost. She'll kill you."

Autumn rose and went over to the sputtering air-conditioning unit. She smacked the metal box until it roared back to life. "You're being dramatic. The ghost only wants my help."

"Something tells me she doesn't."

"What's that supposed to mean?"

Timothy scratched his cheek. "This spirit seems pretty bitchy. And not bitchy like Katie either, but more mean-spirited." He laughed. "No pun intended."

Autumn whipped around. "She deserves justice, doesn't she?"

"Who are you kidding?" Timothy couldn't keep the annoyance out of his voice. "That's not what you're doing. You're exploiting her to get a college scholarship."

"I'm not! She's confused and unstable, and she's likely to hurt Liam. Not me."

"Channeling a ghost is risky. You do it too often, she'll take over your soul. You won't be Autumn Abernathy anymore. You'll be Inez in Autumn's body."

"I've only channeled her twice. First, when I put on the ring and had no idea that would happen. And second, a little while ago in the bathroom."

Timothy held up three fingers. "Three times. You've channeled her three times."

"Huh?"

Timothy leaned against the mismatched painted walls as if he was straddling the border of two countries, and crossed his arms over his chest. "You channeled her in your sleep last night. And you bit Liam's lip in the process."

Autumn felt her stomach flip flop. "That couldn't have happened. I don't remember seeing him." Although, she recalled a dream about lions.

"Were you wearing the ring in your sleep?"

Autumn had placed the ring next to her on the bedside table. She shook her head.

"Crap. Things are progressing faster than I thought. That's what happens when you let a ghost into your body. She thinks it's her new home and she'll evict you right quick." Timothy pushed off the wall and smoothed down his vest. "The boy knows you have his property anyway. He's expecting it back."

Autumn sighed heavily. "I didn't even learn much. All I got was her last initial and she called out Leo Breyer as her killer."

Timothy held up his hand. "Hold up. She named Liam's grandpa as the murderer?"

"Yup."

"Sounds like your work is done, then. Ghost girl solved her own crime. Now you just need to communicate that to her, and she'll leave Liam alone. Case closed."

"How can I do that if I don't channel her?"

"Ask Miss Katie to relay the message." Timothy pointed a thin finger at Autumn. "Don't talk to her yourself. Got it? This ghost was dormant a long time, and one look at Liam Breyer and she's awake. She wants something, and it isn't help. I'd insist you give me the ring for safekeeping, but I don't want to be responsible for that boy's haunted jewelry. Lord knows I don't need to channel a dead girl."

Autumn crossed the room and made a big show of locking the ring in a black box on top of her dresser. "You happy?"

Timothy relaxed his shoulders. "Yes. I'll see you tomorrow." He shut the door.

Autumn flopped back onto her bed. She hated how Timothy always acted like he was so smart, although Autumn had to admit he was right most of the time. Except for this. Autumn didn't think Inez's murder was a closed case. In fact, she thought Inez's murder investigation was just beginning.

Autumn slid her cell phone off the top of the bedside table. She withdrew the piece of paper with Liam's cell phone number that she copied from her mother's files and texted him a message.

Meet me in the Cayo patio tomorrow before school so I can return the ring.

She hit send. She bit her lip and wrote him another message.

And FYI the ghost's name is Inez T. Ring any bells?

Liam never replied.

# CHAPTER NINE

That same evening, Liam huddled at his grandfather's kitchen table and picked at the spaghetti.

"What's the matter? You don't like it? Sylvia from down the block made the sauce." Pops grunted. "I think she has a thing for me."

Liam laughed, but it sounded hollow. "It's fine. Good, actually. I guess I'm not that hungry."

His grandpa sipped his beer and wiped his mouth. "Something bothering you, kid? Like that cut on your forehead?"

Liam tapped his fork lightly against the ceramic bowl. "I have a lot on my mind. And the cut is fine. It doesn't hurt too bad."

Leo leaned back and opened up his arms. "Come on, sport. Talk to your old Pops."

Liam heaved a big sigh. "Do you believe in ghosts?"

"Ghosts? I thought this was going to be a frank discussion about the meaning of life. Or about girls."

"It's about that too. But, seriously, do you believe in ghosts?"

Leo threw down his napkin. "I knew I shouldn't have asked Glenda to hire you. That place has got you spooked." He stood and lumbered to the fridge. "Did you hear some weird noises?" He rummaged around the side door for parmesan cheese and plunked it on the table. He sat back down and readjusted the napkin. "Or see a woman in a white sheet?" Leo smirked.

Clearly, his grandfather was making fun of him. Leo had a way of talking to him like he cared and couldn't give two shits all in the same breath. He did it to Liam's father too. But for some reason, Liam decided to be honest with his Pops, if only to say it aloud and move on. Weird stuff happened at the Cayo and Liam couldn't keep tricking himself into normality anymore.

"Yeah. I did see a woman. A young woman with dark brown hair."

Leo scoffed. "Sure it wasn't Glenda's pretty niece?"

"No. She had a dark mole right below her eye." Liam touched his cheek to show the spot.

Pops stopped smirking, and his face paled. "Is that all?"

Liam moved a piece of spaghetti around his plate and recalled Autumn's text message, the one he hadn't answered. "Autumn claims the ghost's name is Inez. Go ahead and laugh if you want, but it's just too weird. Not sure why she came after me, but—" Liam didn't have a chance to finish. His grandfather sprung from his chair and vomited Sylvia's spaghetti dinner into the kitchen sink.

Liam jumped up. "You okay? You need me to call the doctor?"

Leo ran the faucet, gargled water, and spit into the sink. He wiped his mouth with a hand towel. "I'm fine. It just went down the wrong pipe." Pops returned to the table and slunk into his chair. He pushed away his dinner.

Liam shifted uncomfortably in his seat. Something sharp was digging into his pocket. He removed the pin he had found by the tree at the Cayo and laid it on the table.

Pops glanced down at the pin, and he sucked in a breath. He picked up the pin and ran his thumb across the engraving. "I haven't seen this thing in years."

"Wait, you recognize this?"

"Well, yeah. Didn't you find this in your abuela's jewelry box? It's her class pin."

Liam leaned back in his chair and crossed his arms. "No. I found it buried at the base of a tree in the Cayo's backyard."

"Well, that's a coincidence."

Liam arched his brow. "There seems to be a lot of coincidences at the Cayo." He got up from the table and gently squeezed his grandpa's shoulder. "And that can't be a coincidence."

The following morning, Autumn stood close to the pool's edge and stared into the green water as if in a trance. She jumped at a light touch. She would've toppled into the water if it wasn't for the strong grip of a hand.

"Whoa." Liam pulled her upright. "Close one."

Autumn caught her breath, her cheeks flushed, embarrassed that she had almost gone headfirst into the greenish water. "Yeah, thanks." Liam loosened his grip on her silky, floral blouse. The one that was so practically see-through she had to wear a camisole underneath. She wasn't sure what possessed her to dress-up, but Autumn felt a peculiar need to show Liam she wasn't always a sweaty, gross mess. To prove that she fit in Key West just as much as the pretty girls in her high school.

Autumn took a step back from the pool and from Liam. She inched her fingers into her shorts pocket and slid out the gold ring. She watched Liam's face visibly relax before he opened up his palm. Autumn placed the ring inside Liam's palm and closed his hand over it. "I'd take really good care of this." Autumn regretted having to give up the ring. She'd gotten a glimpse into the life of her mystery ghost, and she wanted to know more. But Timothy's warnings, plus the fact that she supposedly kissed Liam and didn't remember, made the decision for her.

Liam looked into Autumn's brown eyes. "Thanks. I was worried this was gone forever."

Autumn stared at Liam's bruised lip and averted her gaze. She could feel the heat climbing her neck. "I shouldn't have held on to it for so long."

As if checking for damages, Liam examined the ring in the morning light. Like Autumn could ruin a diamond. "I'd give you a hard time about it, but I'm just relieved to have it back. You didn't find any dog tags in the pool too, did ya?"

"Dog tags?"

Liam pushed his shirt collar aside to uncover a metallic rectangle attached to a silver chain. "Like this?"

Autumn shook her head.

"Weird." Liam dropped his necklace under his shirt.

"Right." Autumn needed more information about the ring, such as how Liam came to possess it. "The setting looks quite old, like the ring might be antique."

Liam's eyes brightened. "Hmmm. I wonder if Louie will give me more money for it then."

"You're gonna sell it to Pawn Louie? Why would you do that?" Everyone in town knew about Pawn Louie. Evelyn had even dropped off a few of the Cayo's antiques, including some of Aunt Glenda's forgotten record albums, hoping they'd bring in extra cash.

Liam tensed his shoulders. "It's none of your business why." He glanced at the sliding glass doors. "I better get inside. Your mom has a list of repair jobs for me." He started toward the door, and Autumn cleared her throat.

"You shouldn't sell the ring." She searched for a reason. "It looks sentimental."

Liam rolled his eyes as if he had no time for explanations. "My abuela never even wore it. I doubt it's worth anything."

"Then don't sell it. Hold on to it for a little while longer. Just until I can figure things out."

"Figure what out?" Liam asked impatiently.

"That ring is connected to the ghost."

"That's impossible. It belonged to my grandmother."

"Was her name Inez?" Autumn whispered.

"No," Liam said. "Mariana."

Autumn gasped. "Mariana was your grandmother? So, she and Leo got married?" A weird surge of jealousy burned Autumn's ribs. Her hand flew to her chest to quell the acid.

Liam blanched. "What's going on with you? First, you bite my lip. Then the weird text. Are you playing me?"

"No," she said, insulted. "I don't remember kissing you."

"You bit me," he clarified. "Not kissed. There's no mistaking the difference."

Autumn cringed. "Here's the thing. I have some insight. About the ring. And the rightful owner."

Liam pointed at himself. "I'm the rightful owner."

"No, you're not."

"Oh, really?"

"This ring belonged to a woman named Inez." She gestured at Liam's cheek. "The ghost who scratched your face. I wouldn't have been able to channel her otherwise."

Liam pulled away and laughed uneasily.

"You don't believe me, I get it. But when I put the ring on, I can channel her—see inside her past. It's the reason I don't remember talking to you that night. She gets into my head just as much as I can see into hers. And I become her."

Liam twisted his body toward the Cayo. "I really have to get to work, and you have school."

"I'll prove it to you." Autumn plucked the ring from Liam's finger, and before he could stop her, she was already losing focus.

Suddenly, Autumn was inside Inez's body again. This time she was at the beach, her dark tanned legs stretched out in front of her, her toes digging into the sand. A muscled arm embraced her and she felt lips graze her collarbone. She glanced up at Mick. Inez ran her fingers through his sandy blond hair and laughed. But the emotion felt hollow, as if Inez wasn't joyful in the moment. Autumn watched Leo Breyer bob in the ocean waves, his arms protectively encircling Mariana. And then Autumn screamed—a sound so primordial, she awoke on the cement patio floor, to where Timothy was yanking the ring off her finger. He placed it in Liam's palm.

Anger bubbled inside her. "Why'd you do that?"

"I told you it's not safe."

Liam hovered over her, speechless. Autumn wondered if he thought they were performing for him. There was no way he believed her.

"I saw something," she said, her voice hoarse.

Liam furrowed his brow, but despite all that skepticism, she could tell he was curious. "What?"

"I became her again. Inez. Except this time I was on the beach, and I was laughing, yet angry. I wasn't alone either. Mick was with me. He had his arm wrapped around my shoulder and he kissed me right here." She touched her bare skin below the collar of her shirt.

Liam's eyebrows shot up. "Mick Canton? That's gross. You have major issues."

"We weren't the only people on the beach either. Mariana was there. And . . ."

Autumn glanced at Timothy for a second, and he nodded in assurance. "Tell him."

"Leo," she said.

"Leo? As in my Pops?"

"Yes." Autumn's voice was barely a whisper.

Liam's face reddened, and he clenched his fists at his sides. "This crap isn't funny. You're telling me a murdered ghost knew my grandpa?"

"Not just knew your grandfather, but I think she was in love with him." Inez never showed Autumn that part, but Autumn could sense it. "Maybe she's confused. Spirits can get like that. It's just—"

"Just what?"

"You have her ring," she said.

"No, I have my abuela's ring, and her name was Mariana. Mariana Cruces."

"Cruces? I saw that word in my Spanish textbooks. It means—"

"Crosses." He rubbed his face.

*Crosses! It wasn't a 'T' Inez had shown me in the bathroom mirror. It was a cross.* Autumn's excitement grew. "Mariana was Inez's sister."

"My abuela didn't have a sister. She was an only child." His eyes flitted back and forth like he was trying to work out his family tree in his head. But rather than concede Autumn might be on to something, Liam backed away from her, his hands out as if trying to placate an unstable person. "I need a break from this." He turned on his heels and headed back to the Cayo.

Autumn smacked her forehead. She'd put on the ring to show off a little, thinking Liam would believe her once he saw what happened. But he just thought she was teasing him. Or worse, that she was insane.

Timothy clucked his tongue. "Girl, I told you not to channel her again."

"Because you said it was dangerous," she argued.

Timothy drew a circle in the air around Autumn's hurt face and then glanced at the patio door where Liam had just entered. "Well, wasn't it?"

# CHAPTER TEN

Later, during his afternoon break, Liam ran out of the Cayo Hueso and down the street, leaving his scooter, which was wet from an afternoon rain shower, parked outside the hotel. He needed to get out of the hotel to breathe. He felt bad for dismissing Autumn that morning, but there was something not right with her. She didn't strike him as the type of girl to play cruel jokes, but neither had Victoria, and look how that ended up.

Maybe Liam could buy into the notion of ghosts haunting the Cayo, but the fact that Autumn could channel a dead girl—that seemed too insane, even for Key West.

Liam stopped running. He would have to apologize to Autumn. Again. Despite the crazy crap surrounding him since he started at the Cayo Hueso, she was the only one who made him feel visible. He laughed. Funny, how it took a girl who thought she saw ghosts to make him feel noticed.

Liam rounded the corner and headed into Louie's Pawn Shop. Louie Casanova had been in business since before Liam was born. Pops used to say that Louie was shadier than the base of a willow tree. Unfortunately for Liam, there wasn't a more honest racket in town. If he wanted quick cash, he'd need to go to Louie's.

When Liam opened the pawnshop's front door, a cold blast of air assaulted him. Louie had the air conditioning turned all the way up. Liam had never been a fan of artificially cold air. He'd just as well take the humidity if it meant warm, salty breezes from open windows.

Shuddering, Liam approached the glass counter on the far side of the shop. He nervously tapped his fingers along the display case as he examined rows of wedding bands, antique pocket watches, and silver coins—all someone's treasures at one point. Liam wasn't sure why he was so anxious. He'd pawned stuff before to make money. Old cufflinks of Pops he never wore. Some subwoofers his father had stored in the crawl space. Nothing potentially worth as much as Abuela's ring, though.

Liam glanced into the back office where Louie hunched at the desk, cradling a telephone against his ear and waving his arms in big exaggerated motions. Louie looked like a cross between a turtle and a rat. Louie caught Liam's eyes and held up a thick pointer finger, letting Liam know he'd be with him in a minute. That minute felt interminable. Liam wanted to sell the ring and get out of there. But as he turned the smooth gold around his pinkie finger, he couldn't help but think about Autumn's performance this morning as she splayed out on the patio floor, her eyelids fluttering as if in a dream state. Was she really expecting him to believe that this ring somehow transported her into the body of a ghost?

He shook his head, if only to answer himself. Nah. He was no fool. To believe Autumn channeled a spirit meant Liam was no different than the kooks in this town trying to sell the tourists on haunted tours. Like Pops's old navy buddy, Ralph Blazevig.

"Come on, come on," Liam said under his breath, his patience waning.

The brass bell on the front door chimed, and Liam craned his neck to see Mick Canton saunter up to the counter in pressed chinos and a designer golf shirt. Mick eyed Liam and sneered. Mick used to treat Liam with indifference when he was dating Victoria. But now, he was outright hostile.

Within moments, Louie was off the phone and scurrying to the front of the store, bypassing Liam and extending his meaty hand to Mick. "Good to see you. What brings you by?"

Mick's presence took up so much of the space alongside the counter that Liam felt forced to move down. Liam studied the men's bracelets in the case below and feigned interest as he listened to Mick and Louie's conversation.

"Some merchandise was stolen from one of my warehouses," Mick said in a low voice. "You wouldn't happen to know anything about that?"

Liam watched from the corner of his eye as Louie backed away from the counter and held up his hands. "Now, you know I would never accept stolen goods." Louie didn't hear Liam scoff, or if he did, he pretended not to. "Especially anything that might have your stamp on it."

Mick grinned and Louie appeared to relax. "I'm not accusing you of fencing my property. But I know you hear things in this town." Mick dropped his Cheshire-cat smile.

Liam wondered what exactly had been taken. It didn't have to be big money for Mick to come down to this dump. Mick didn't let the smallest pawn get one over on him, even if it amounted to nothing.

Louie shook his head. "Sorry, Mick. My intell isn't what it used to be, but I can make some inquiries."

Mick leaned over the counter and patted Louie's shoulder. "That's a start." Mick twisted his thick neck and narrowed his eyes at Liam. "That's twice this week I've seen you. Let's not make this a habit."

Blood bubbled underneath Liam's skin as if he was an active volcano. He slapped the ring on the counter, and it clanged against the glass. "Louie, are we going to do business or what?"

Louie gave Mick an apologetic glance, but Mick waved him away, as if to say, *take care of the boy.* Louie grabbed his jeweler's magnifying glass from underneath the counter, but before he could examine the ring, Mick snatched it off the counter. His voice sounded tight, almost hoarse. "Where'd you get this?"

"I didn't steal it if that's what you're implying. It was in a box of my grandmother's stuff."

"Doubtful," Mick mumbled, but Liam heard him as clearly as if the man had screamed it in Mallory Square. Mick's typical ruddy features drained of their color.

"You look a little pale there, Mick. Feeling all right?" Liam said.

"Don't you worry about me." Mick's lip curled into a sneer. "I'm always okay."

"Whatever." Liam gestured to Louie. "I'm on a break from work. I don't have much time."

"Where ya working, kid?" Mick asked.

"At the Cayo Hueso."

"Is that where you found this?"

Liam gave Mick an icy glare. "I told you, it was my grandmother's." He turned to Louie. "Can you tell me what it's worth or not?"

Mick rubbed his big thumb along the diamond solitaire and laid the ring on the counter. "First rule of negotiating is never ask your opponent what something is worth. You tell 'em what it's worth. What's this ring worth to you?"

Louie went to pick up the ring, his curiosity piqued, but Mick laid his hand on top and held the ring prisoner to the glass.

"What's it worth to you?" Mick repeated.

Liam stuttered. "I, I." In his head, he could hear Randall hiss, "Four grand." But Liam's tongue felt heavy in his mouth. This was a windfall for him, and he couldn't even speak. He squeaked out his price.

Mick's eyebrow shot up. "It didn't cost four grand when it was new, I bet you that much. Besides, what does a kid like you need with that much money?"

Liam squirmed under Mick's gaze. *Don't tell him.* Liam rapped the counter with his knuckles. "Know what? I'll come back later."

Mick held up his hand. "I'm done here." He glanced once more at the ring before pointing at Louie. "Don't forget to keep your ears open about my merchandise." Mick watched as Louie's Adam's apple bobbed. He grunted in satisfaction and left, the bell on the door signaling his exit.

As soon as Mick's hulking figure had disappeared from sight, Liam and Louie both exhaled sighs of reliefs. For different reasons, of course.

Louie slid a jeweler's monocle over his eyes and peered at the ring. "Okay, Mr. Impatient. Let's see what we've got here."

Autumn found Aunt Glenda sitting at her vanity table, dabbing a drop of perfume on the base of her neck. For a brief moment, Autumn could see her aunt the way Uncle Duncan probably had—as a young, vivacious redhead.

Autumn gently rapped on the doorframe. "Uncle Duncan must have been the envy of all his friends."

Aunt Glenda smiled in the mirror, although the smile didn't seem to reach her eyes. "Oh, I don't know about that. I'd like to think your uncle and I were like two puzzle pieces and only we fit together.

His friends used to tease him about me—they said I was spacey and silly. One of his friends actually told him I was only good for one thing." She arched her brow.

Autumn balked. "That's awful. I hope Uncle Duncan punched him out."

"I'd say he did." Glenda chuckled. "Gave ol' Mick a shiner right before he went home to his parents."

Autumn bounced down on the bed. She wanted to tread lightly here, but she was curious. "Mick as in Mick Canton? Is that when Uncle Duncan and Mick stopped being friends?"

Aunt Glenda slowly lowered the hairbrush. She looked thoughtful as if she was selectively choosing her words. "No. Not then. Anyway, I told Duncan not to worry about it."

"So they stopped being friends after the navy?"

Glenda squirmed in her chair. "Yes, after. Although it wasn't so much that they stopped being friends, it was that life happened. I mean, you get serious with a girl and then get married. When Ralphie met Lena, we hardly saw him anymore. And then Mick started making money, and he became a bit ruthless in that sense." She leaned over and gently patted Autumn's knee. "So . . . how's school going? Are you making friends?"

Ugh. Aunt Glenda was crafty. Just when Autumn thought she could make some headway, the old woman directed the conversation to school. Autumn sighed. "Not really."

Aunt Glenda joined her on the bed and smoothed out a wrinkle in the burgundy bedspread. "It's because you're different. I know your mom thinks ghosts are just make-believe, but she hasn't had to deal with the spirit world her whole life." She gently bumped Autumn's shoulder. "You'll adjust."

"Liam thinks I'm crazy." To Autumn's surprise, her voice shook.

"You like William, don't you?" Aunt Glenda sounded soft and maternal and nothing like Evelyn.

Autumn picked at a loose thread on the comforter. "I don't really get him. He insists he doesn't believe in ghosts, but he's been attacked twice already."

Glenda circled her arm around her shoulder. "I'd say that Liam and his grandfather have some trust issues. Leo loved Mariana with a fierce passion, but their marriage was riddled with problems. And Liam's mother abandoned him when he was a toddler. The Breyer men have been hurt plenty for one lifetime. Try to be kind to Liam—he could probably use a friend as much as you."

Autumn stood and leaned against the tall, mahogany post. "I am being kind to him. I keep warning him about Inez, but he won't listen."

Glenda's eyes grew round. "Who?"

"Inez Cruces. She's the one who is trying to kill Liam."

Glenda leaped up and grabbed Autumn's shoulders. "How do you know that's her name? Did she tell you?"

"Not really," Autumn said slowly. "I mean, she did, but not at first. I sort of channeled her."

Glenda gasped. "Do you know how dangerous that is?"

Autumn broke away from her aunt's hold. "I do now. Timothy gave me an ear-full. Anyway, have you ever heard of her? Inez? I think she died in 1966."

Glenda bristled. "She was Mariana's sister."

"I know," said Autumn, anxious for new details.

"Well, you should also know that she wasn't a nice person. Not just in death, but in life. She nearly separated Liam's grandparents," Glenda whispered and her gaze flitted around the room. Did her aunt fear Inez? "I can't believe she haunts this place. That can only mean—"

"She died here," Autumn finished. "You didn't know?"

Glenda paled. "She'd gone missing the night of the spring dance. She had a fight with her sister over Leo and stormed out of the gymnasium at St. Veronica's. No one saw her again."

"When was that?"

Her aunt clasped her hand. "Promise me you won't take this further. Ignore her, and she'll go away."

"I don't think she will," Autumn growled, tightening her grip on her aunt's hand.

"You're hurting me, dear," Aunt Glenda squeaked.

Autumn snatched back her hand. "I'm so sorry." A darkness rolled over her, reminding Autumn of storm clouds over the Atlantic. Timothy was right—Inez had taken residency inside her body.

Autumn's head swam with questions, but before she could interrogate her aunt further, Evelyn appeared at the door, looking put out.

"There you are, Autumn. Cora needs help preparing dinner. Also, sometime tomorrow, I'd like you to tidy up the April room. We have a new guest checking in on Friday." Evelyn's voice sounded light. Interesting how only talk of new business could make Evelyn happy.

Glenda pressed her hands into Autumn's back and steered her toward the hallway. "She'll be right there." Then Aunt Glenda closed her door on both Autumn and her mother.

Evelyn put her hands on her hips. "Well, that was rude. I wonder what's the matter with Glenda."

Autumn glanced at her aunt's now-closed door. Mr. Blazevig, Aunt Glenda, and, most likely, Leo Breyer were all keeping secrets. But was it because they feared Inez or were afraid of what Autumn would discover about Inez's murder? Either way, Inez's spirit wasn't leaving anytime soon.

# CHAPTER ELEVEN

On Thursday afternoon, Autumn held a photo in front of Liam's face.

He glanced at her. "What's this?"

"You tell me." Her face reflected a mixture of impatience and mistrust. Liam wasn't sure what to make of her.

He had been sitting at the Cayo's round kitchen table, eating a sandwich from a deli around the corner. It was his afternoon break, although he didn't miss seeing Evelyn's pinched face as she kept popping in with the excuse she was adjusting the dinner menu when really she was only checking her watch. He wiped his hands on his cargo shorts and took the photo from Autumn's hands. Their fingers grazed and he felt a slight jolt.

Liam stared at the photo of the four sailors. It was exactly the same picture Mick Canton had in his home office. He remembered seeing it when he and Victoria dated. "Where did you get this?"

"I found it in the attic." She pointed to the curly haired sailor on the far right. "That's Uncle Duncan. He and my grandpa were brothers. My grandpa said

I have his dark hair." She smiled at Liam like she was proud of the connection. Liam loved his grandfather, but he was certain he never smiled with pride at the mention of genetic similarities between him and Pops.

"I've seen this photo before," he said. "So?"

She gestured to the photo again. This time her finger zeroed in on Leo Breyer. "So, you look just like your grandfather."

He nodded. "I know."

Autumn shook her head in disbelief. "I mean *just* like him. You're clones."

Liam scoffed. Leo Breyer was a crotchety old man full of cryptic pieces of caution that did him no good. When Liam decided to drop out of high school so he could work with his dad in the northern oil fields, Leo didn't do anything to stop him. He only said, "See you in the summer, kiddo." When Liam asked Pops about his mother, Leo kept his mouth shut. "Not my place to say." Sure, young Leo Breyer and Liam might have looked identical, but the similarities stopped at the physical. Liam was going to make something of his life regardless of the deadbeats who gave him his start in this world. "Again, so?"

"Flip it over," said Autumn, annoyed.

Liam sighed and turned over the photo. There was something written on the back. *Buddies for life.* Had his grandpa and his friends ever imagined one day they'd barely speak to one another?

Autumn sat down at the table and ran her fingers over the scratches in the wood. "Liam," her voice was soft, gentle as if she was his preschool teacher telling him his mother had not yet arrived to pick him up from school, "Inez keeps attacking you. *You.* Why would she do that?"

Liam swallowed a bite of food. A hunk of salami scraped his throat. "I don't know."

"Don't you think it's odd that she would come after you? You weren't alive when she was alive. But—"

"But what?"

"But someone who resembled you was around in 1966."

Liam hated all this cryptic talk. "You're saying my grandfather killed this girl." The words sounded as ridiculous aloud as they did in his head. Pops wasn't the aggressive type. He was the passive-aggressive type. The avoiding type. "That's not possible."

"I don't know your grandfather," she said.

"That's right. You don't."

"But, he definitely knew her."

Liam dropped his salami on rye on top of the wax paper it came wrapped in. He wasn't hungry anymore. He realized that Autumn truly believed in the spirit world. But he was remembering Pops's reaction the other night at dinner when he mentioned Inez's name. That kind of visceral response couldn't be faked. "You said yourself that she's a confused spirit. She probably doesn't know who killed her. Or what happened."

Autumn blew a strand of dark hair from her face. It would've been a cute gesture had they not been talking about his elderly grandfather killing a girl when he was a teenager.

"Ask your grandfather about it," she said quietly.

"Autumn, I'm not—"

"She named him."

Liam sputtered, "Wha-what do you mean she named him?"

"The ghost, Inez, she named Leo Breyer as her killer." Autumn uttered the words slowly and deliberately as if afraid Liam wouldn't comprehend what she was saying. Truthfully, he couldn't.

"That's impossible. Not to mention ridiculous."

Pops might've known the dead girl, but he definitely didn't kill her. Liam stood and threw his napkin on top of his sandwich. "Seriously. I'm done with this."

"But—"

"No! I don't want to hear it anymore. My grandfather would never hurt someone. Let it go." Autumn slumped her shoulders, but Liam wasn't done. "Why are you doing this? Do you get off on calling people murderers?"

"No! I need to make sense of this. You don't understand what it's like to be haunted all the time."

Liam thought about his mother. How her clothes still sat in boxes in the spare bedroom closet. How if he tried, he might be able to smell her perfume. He was haunted—just not by ghosts.

"I could've proved all this to you if you'd just held on to the ring," she said.

Liam scooped up the remains of his sandwich. His break was officially over, and he was grateful. His head throbbed with nonsense about ghosts and money. Randall had been bugging him for his share of the cash. Four grand, but Louie's best offer was 2,000 dollars.

Liam sighed. "Well, I didn't. So try acting like a normal girl or something." He didn't mean to sound so cruel, but he couldn't take back the words now. Why was he such a dick all the time? "I'm sorr—" But his apology came too late. Autumn had left the kitchen, the old door swinging.

Shortly before dinner, when Cora and Evelyn were busy in the kitchen composing the menu for the week, Autumn sneaked back into the attic. Her mother would be suspicious if she caught Autumn up there, or she'd accuse her of hiding to avoid work, especially since Autumn hadn't gotten around to tidying up the April room for the new guest.

Autumn pulled her damp T-shirt away from her sweaty skin. If it was eighty-five degrees outside, then it had to be 105 degrees in the attic. Air circulation didn't exist up here.

Liam might have sold the ring, but Autumn vowed to figure out what had happened to Inez. Autumn decided she wouldn't let Liam's words bother her anymore. Because once Autumn solved Inez's death, then she knew the journalism committee would award her the scholarship money. After all, what other candidate would have solved a murder? And then Autumn would be back in New Jersey next September sipping warm lattes and sunbathing on the green lawns before class. Very collegiate.

Autumn shuffled around, hoping to find what she needed and make a quick escape. After all, she had uncovered one photo. There might be photographic evidence proving Inez existed.

Katie materialized, her ghostly form slowly coming into focus. "What are you doing?" Her voice sounded like a mixture of boredom and interest.

Autumn nearly tripped over an old box of Uncle Duncan's magic tricks. "Trying to find something that proves Inez was here in the late sixties. I can't rely on a ghost's testimony to write my scholarship essay, so I'm hoping to uncover more photos. Maybe one with Inez actually in it."

Katie didn't seem too impressed, but she glided around the attic, tilting her head into crevices and narrowing her eyes at boxes. Autumn didn't think Katie had x-ray vision, but ever since Inez was able to touch Liam in the pool, she had to admit she didn't know as much about ghosts as she thought.

Autumn opened up trunks, but she couldn't bring herself to touch the old hat boxes, moldy and soft from years in the Key West humidity.

"What about this?" Katie nodded toward a gray metal box on the floor by the window. "It's a little rusty, but it seems to require a key. You know what they say, 'if it's important, lock it—'"

"Up." Autumn went over the gray box and picked it up. It wasn't large or heavy for that matter. A small metal box one might use to protect cash at a garage sale. Or a firebox. "Do you see a key?" she asked Katie.

Katie looked around. "That might be a lost cause. Usually if something is locked the key is also hidden, don't ya think?"

"You know, I had a diary when I was a kid. It had a key too. Except I was known for losing things, so I put the key somewhere I could find it easily. Somewhere in plain sight." Autumn scanned the attic, which was encased in red light from the setting sun. A crimson beam of sunlight climbed the walls and shone on a collection of antique porcelain dolls. The kinds of dolls popular in scary movies and stories. Except one of the dolls was male. A sailor. On a hunch, she went over to the doll, its white sailor jacket cloaked in dust, and plucked it from the shelf. Autumn shook the dust off the doll and coughed.

"He has a little pocket on his sailor uniform," Katie noted.

"So he does." Autumn slipped her fingers inside and removed a tiny key.

"Jackpot," Katie said.

"Great minds think alike." Autumn inserted the key into the lock and opened the box.

"Are there gold doubloons inside?" Katie joked.

Autumn brought the box closer to the window. She stood it on top of an old trunk and rummaged through. There were a few trinkets inside. Some medals from the navy, a gold anchor pendant, a small studio headshot of a baby boy. Autumn didn't bother removing any of the items since they didn't seem to link to Inez.

Autumn found a few more photos of Uncle Duncan and Ralph, dressed in their Navy uniforms and standing with their arms around each other. Uncle Duncan had a wide, easy grin, as if he'd never been happier than that moment. There was a photo of Mr. Blazevig wearing a goofy smile and holding a wooden cane in the manner of Gene Kelly from *Singing In the Rain*. That was one of Aunt Glenda's favorite movies.

Autumn found another photo of Leo and Mick with beer bottles in their hands, mischief plastered on their faces. No pictures of Inez, though. Autumn shrugged and pocketed the photos anyway. She thought her mother would want to frame a few and hang them up in the reception area. Show the guests what the Cayo used to look like in its heyday.

Autumn lifted her hair off the nape of her neck and fanned her skin. "Rats. I better get downstairs before my mother notices. Or Aunt Glenda." Autumn made her way toward the door.

Katie glided behind and giggled. "I haven't seen one of these in decades."

Autumn paused and glanced behind her. Katie pointed a slim, translucent finger toward an opened hatbox—the one Autumn had bypassed when she first entered the attic. Except, before the box had been closed, and now it was opened. Inside lay a stack of warped comic books, their paper edges curled with humidity and time. The one on top had a faded illustration of a sailor in sailor whites with two curvaceous women flanking him. One was a brunette, and the other was blonde.

Katie laughed, almost to herself. "I read that one. I had sneaked into Duncan's room looking for his stash of pot when I found his comic book collection. I devoured the whole collection in an afternoon."

Autumn felt herself growing impatient, but it wasn't often Katie experienced nostalgia. "It was that good a story? What was it about? A love triangle?"

"Oddly," said Katie, staring up at Autumn with her big, blue eyes. "It was." And then she vanished.

# CHAPTER TWELVE

Liam sat at the kitchen table deep in thought. If Autumn was to be believed—and at this point, he wasn't sure how trustworthy she was—then that diamond ring, and his grandparents, were connections to a ghost. A ghost who was related to his abuela, who might have been in love with his grandfather, and who fingered Pops as her killer. It was all too weird to believe. Then why did Liam feel so uneasy?

Between the photo and the ring, Liam wondered if he and Autumn could have a conversation that didn't revolve around death. In hindsight, maybe Liam should've held on to the ring just a little longer. But Louie seemed interested in cutting him a fair deal, and Mick's interest in the whole thing made Liam's skin crawl.

It was best he sold it. Perhaps now, everyone— Randall, Autumn, even the bitchy ghost—would leave him alone.

Liam didn't hear his grandpa enter the kitchen until the old man slammed the fridge door, startling him. Pops cracked back the tab on a can of beer and chugged a long sip. He nodded at his grandson. "Got a lot on your mind?"

Liam pursed his lips. "Something has been bothering me about that diamond ring."

Pops belched. "All the more reason to sell it."

That was a strange answer. Didn't he want to know what was bugging Liam about the ring? Unless Pops already knew. "Are you sure it was Abuela's ring?"

Pops scoffed. "Of course I'm sure. It wasn't your mother's if that's what you're worried about. That woman left you nothing."

"That's not what I meant. It just didn't look like something Abuela would wear, that's all."

Pops placed his beer on the Formica table before sitting down across from Liam. He took a sip. "How would you know? You were only ten when she died." Pops stared past Liam and into the backyard, his eyes glazing over. What was his grandfather thinking? "Besides, who else's ring would it be?"

Liam decided to take a chance. "Inez."

"Don't know who you mean." Pops got up and patted Liam's shoulder. "I'm tired, kiddo. Had a tough day at bocce. I'm going to take a nap."

Liam rose to meet Pops's eyes. "You know exactly who I mean. She had dark hair and a mole. Olive skin. She was a knock-out."

"You're describing your grandmother." Pops smiled.

"No, this woman was not Abuela. She was Abuela's sister and tough as nails with a jealous streak."

Pops swallowed as if he was ingesting a marble. "Who told you this? Glenda?"

Liam couldn't very well mention Autumn's role in all this, or that a ghost accused him of murder. Pops would want to know how a seventeen-year-old Jersey girl was able to unearth demons from his past. "I ran into Mick Canton at the pawn shop. He spotted the ring and then said the weirdest thing."

Pops ran his hand along his gray scruff. "Yeah? What's that?"

"'It didn't cost four grand when it was new, I bet you that much.' What do you think he meant by that?"

"You'd have to ask Canton."

Liam pounded his fist on the table, which surprised his aging grandfather—the man who had raised him, who had taken him to Little League games and attended parent-teacher conferences. The man who, up until lately, he had trusted implicitly. "You know I can't ask Canton. So, I'm asking you because you know the answer."

Pops leaned back against the fridge and crossed his arms. The anchor tattoo stretched over his wrinkled skin. "Mick Canton knows how much the ring initially cost because he gave it to Inez."

Liam fell into the chair. "They were engaged?"

"Yup."

"Then how did Abuela get the ring?"

"Your grandmother said Inez and Mick had a fight. One of many. Inez threw the ring at Mick and Mariana picked it up, afraid it would get lost."

"What was the fight about?" asked Liam.

Pops pushed himself off the fridge and held up his hands in mock surrender. "I don't know. Ask Mick Canton."

"Here ya go, Mr. . . ." Autumn trailed off as she opened the door to the April room on Friday afternoon, wishing that she had prepared it better. An hour ago, she had set out to dust the antique furniture and vacuum the oriental rugs, but all she managed to do was wipe down the mirrors before nausea overcame her. Perhaps the room's faint scent of salt and fish was to blame. The guest had arrived early anyway.

"Fletcher," the man replied. "Kevin Fletcher."

"Mr. Fletcher," she said, stifling a burp. *What is wrong with me?* "I hope you enjoy your stay at the Cayo Hueso." She waved her arms around, showcasing the soft, mint green paint. "This is the April room."

Mr. Fletcher wagged his bushy eyebrows. "The April room?"

"All the rooms are named after a month. My uncle's idea. There are twelve rooms."

"Huge place. Not all occupied?"

"No." Autumn walked over to the bathroom and flicked on the lights. "Here's your personal guest bath. There's a hair dryer in the top drawer of the vanity." She glanced at the man's thinning gray hair. "Uh, or not. Cora makes breakfast at seven a.m., but will only keep the eggs hot until eight thirty. No later. After that, she says they taste like rubber. There's a pad and paper on top of the nightstand and the Bible in the top drawer."

Mr. Fletcher grunted and pointed to his chest. "Atheist."

Autumn pointed at herself. "Jewish on my paternal grandma's side."

Mr. Fletcher laughed.

Autumn clapped her hands. "Anything else you need?"

"Yeah, can you suggest some things to do?"

Was he for real? He was in Key West—a tourist mecca. There were a million things to do. "Most of our guests enjoy the Haunted Key West Tour run by Mr. Blazevig. He takes you on a walking tour of Old Town and shows you all the haunted spots. Of course, you're already staying in one."

"I'm not really the believing type," he said. "I think it's all a load of nonsense. No offense."

*Sure, no one's a believer until they confront a ghost.* "Why are you staying here? The only reason people come to the Cayo is to be haunted. We're famous for our ghosts."

"I came to Key West to relax and work, and this place has the cheapest rate in all of Old Town." Mr. Fletcher examined the room and shrugged. "Also, the only vacancy on such short notice."

"If you don't mind my asking, what kind of work do you do?"

"I used to be a lawyer. But now I report on crime."

"Like murders? Stuff like that?" Her mind spun. She wondered if he'd be willing to take a look at her scholarship application. Maybe even give her some revision notes. Or better yet, write her a letter of recommendation.

She decided not to ask him just yet as she had no evidence, nor theories, on Inez's murder.

"Yup. Stuff like that," he said. "Not the stuff of sweet dreams."

"Well then, sounds to me like you deal with ghosts all the time."

He set his suitcase on the bed. "Clever girl. You might be right about that."

Autumn stared at the floral bedspread with the pink hibiscus pattern. Suddenly, she saw a flash of tangled arms and legs.

Another flash. Inez kissing Mick.

The bile climbed Autumn's throat.

Another flash.

*I love you, Inez.*

*Te amo, Mick.*

Autumn leaned against the desk, her weight jostling the keys and Mr. Fletcher's computer.

He dipped his head. "Are you okay? Do you want me to get your mom?"

Autumn squeezed her eyes closed and then opened them. The room appeared brighter, although her mind felt impaired and dull. "I'm okay. Just the heat getting to me."

"Ah. A northerner. Am I right? You'll get used to it."

Autumn pressed her palm to her temple. "I don't think I'll ever get used to this place." And she meant it.

"Autumn!" Evelyn called from downstairs.

"Gotta go." Autumn deposited the room key on top of the small, pine desk next to the man's laptop.

"See you at dinner." Before Autumn closed the door, she noticed a handprint on the bureau mirror, one she had sworn she wiped away only an hour ago.

Liam parked his gold scooter in the street outside Autumn's school and waited for her, paying no attention to the students scurrying around him.

When Autumn emerged into the sunlight, he waved. She rolled her eyes and hustled down the steps, walking quickly past him. But Liam was faster. He gently touched her arm.

"Hey, slow down."

"Why?" she asked, without looking at him. "I'd think you'd rather talk to someone *normal*. I'm sure Victoria is around here somewhere. Besides, my mom needs me at the Cayo." She glanced down at his tanned fingers, still curled around her arm.

"Okay, I deserve that." Liam lowered his voice. "I was hoping we could talk about things. Supernatural things. And your mom isn't expecting you home."

She peered at him through thick lashes. "What do you mean?"

"I suggested I pick up the day's catch at the pier since Mrs. Paulson wanted a seafood dinner and your mother seems anxious to impress the new guest. But then Evelyn insisted you come with me. I don't think she trusts me." His voice softened and he realized how he must had sounded—hurt. He secretly hoped Autumn would feel bad for him. In suggesting he get the fish, he was trying to get into Evelyn's good graces. Although he didn't anticipate working at the Cayo too much longer, he still didn't want her treating him like he was a thief counting the silver. He wasn't prepared for Evelyn to insist Autumn come too. That was an added bonus.

Liam heard one of Victoria's minions call out, "What's the ghost freak doing with Liam?" Autumn winced. He pretended not to hear the comment.

"I don't know," Autumn said, her voice trailing.

Liam sensed she wouldn't want to climb on the back of his scooter until he apologized. "I'm sorry about what I said last week. But you need to see it from my perspective. I prefer to think the Cayo brings out the worst in my imagination, and then you come along and tell me the ghosts are . . ."

"Real?"

"Possible," he clarified. "Nothing about any of this seems real. Not coming home to Key West. Not my job at the Cayo Hueso. Not you." He stared at her and watched as her cheeks colored. "Besides, I know my grandfather didn't hurt that ghost girl. But, maybe I know who could have."

Autumn adjusted the strap on her bag and arched her brow. Liam handed her a purple helmet, which he had taken from the small cargo space on the back of the seat. "Come on. We can talk."

Autumn still hesitated. Somewhere behind her, Victoria's shrill voice cried out, "What's *she* doing with him?" Victoria hurried down the steps. Autumn glanced quickly at Liam before grabbing the helmet, slapping it on her head, and jumping on the back of the bike.

"Let's get out of here," she said and they sped off toward the wharf.

Autumn wrapped her arms around Liam's waist. His pulse immediately quickened. Victoria never wanted to ride on his scooter, and when she did, it was mostly after he cajoled her. No one owned cars in Key West. At least no one he knew. Most friends had bicycles or scooters. Some just walked. Only problem was, you couldn't get off the island without a car. Scooters were not meant for Highway 1.

Liam parked next to a food truck that served breakfast until ten. The lot was empty except for rogue roosters, who pecked at the sand and sparse blades of grass. Autumn dismounted and adjusted her floral dress. Liam tried and failed not to stare at her tanned legs.

The boats would be arriving soon. Liam tilted his chin toward the water. "Fish is coming off the *Benny Blue Eyes*."

"Huh?"

"It's the name of the fishing boat." Liam inhaled the salty air and wrinkled his nose at the overpowering stench of fish. It reminded him of the patio area at the Cayo and that made his skin itch. Liam swiped the surface of his phone to reveal the time. "The boat should be here soon." He led Autumn to an empty part of the pier, and they sat down.

Autumn dangled her legs over the edge of the dock and swung them to and fro like a small child. She squinted into the bright rays of the setting sun. Liam joined her, his legs bent and his hands splayed behind him. At first, they were both quiet, just watching the fishing boats coming and going. Liam remembered when Pops would bring him out on the water. Except now, instead of being mesmerized by dolphins, Liam was hypnotized by Autumn's shapely legs.

He leaned into Autumn. "Pops used to take me on his little catamaran when I was a kid. I'd dream of catching a shark."

Autumn raised her brow into a high arc.

Liam shrugged. "I was six. What did I know? I wanted to put it in a fish tank at home. Pops said I could if I caught one. Of course, I never did."

"Your Pops had a good sense of humor."

"Oh yeah, he's a real comedian."

Autumn shifted her weight a bit. Liam's skin prickled at seeing how close she was to him.

"It's nice your grandpa was around," she said. "My mom's mother lives in El Paso. My dad's parents died when I was little."

"Pops wasn't just around. He basically raised me. My mom split when I was three, and then my dad took jobs wherever he could find them. Eventually, he left the Keys to drive tractor-trailers. I think my dad left because my mom did. It sort of messed him up. I know it messed me up." Liam shut his mouth. He was revealing too much. But talking to Autumn felt natural. With Victoria, Liam downplayed his humble upbringing, but Autumn didn't come from money. Her life seemed as screwed up and weird as his.

Autumn picked at some loose threads on her skirt. "My parents got divorced last year. My dad cheated on my mom with the woman who managed the accessories shop down the street from my parents' hardware store."

Liam raised his eyebrow. "Accessories?"

"You know, hair bows, necklaces—that sort of thing. Anyway, my parents' store was tanking because of the big chain places around the corner. Right before the divorce, they closed shop. Jennifer moved into our old house and out of desperation, we moved in with Aunt Glenda. My mom used to do bookkeeping for the hardware store, so she's working on making the Cayo profitable. I think it makes her feel important." Autumn adjusted her sunglasses on her face. "Anyway, my dad kept saying that the divorce wasn't my fault. That I shouldn't blame myself. It had nothing to do with me." She scoffed. "The thing is, it had everything to do with me. It affected me more than them. They separated from each other, which is what they wanted. It wasn't what I wanted at all."

"Better than fighting," he said.

"There was no fighting in my house," Autumn said, her voice eerily quiet. "There was only silence. That was worse."

Liam put his arms around her shoulders and gave her a squeeze. It was meant as a friendly, comforting gesture, but the contact electrified his body. He quickly let her go and an awkward silence enveloped them both.

Autumn inched away from Liam. His cheeks grew hot with embarrassment.

Liam cleared his throat. "Pops has always been a quiet guy. Whenever I screwed up, and it was often, he would never yell or scream. He'd just give me one of those side-glances, and I could tell he was disappointed. That's how he and I are different. Pops is not a risk-taker. He's a big believer in minding your own business. Accepting the status quo. So you see? There's no way my grandfather could've killed a girl. It's just not in him."

"Especially since he raised you. He must be a decent person." She gave him a small smile.

"But she named him," said Liam.

Autumn nodded. "She wrote his name in my foggy bathroom mirror."

Autumn didn't strike Liam as a liar and she didn't seem crazy. Perhaps, there were things in this world that Liam would never understand. Could never understand. But, he'd have to accept them anyway. But, why would a ghost lie about who killed her? Because she *had* to be lying. Pops wasn't a murderer. Liam shuddered. "Creepy."

"Inez also flashed me back to a memory where your grandpa was yelling at her. He was so angry."

"Inez seemed to make a lot of people angry with her."

"What do you mean?"

Liam sat up straighter and peered out at the ocean. He listened to the melodic lapping of the waves against the dock. The Breyers were a lot of things—deadbeats, dropouts, drifters. They were flawed men, but they weren't killers. Liam confided in Autumn what Pops had said yesterday. That Inez and Mick had been engaged and that they had fought so fiercely, Inez threw her engagement ring in Mick's face. "I know Mick Canton doesn't take kindly to humiliation."

Autumn pushed her sunglasses to the top of her head and faced Liam. "Enough to kill?"

# CHAPTER THIRTEEN

Autumn wasn't quick to buy into his suspect. Sure, Inez and Mick were a couple, but why would he kill her and why wouldn't Inez name him? As a ghost, would she still protect him? "I suppose we could look into that, but Mick really loved Inez." She remembered being in the April room and seeing those flashes of them together. Heat rose to her cheeks. "I know he can be ruthless in business, but murder? I don't know."

Liam shrugged. "I wouldn't put it past him."

Autumn tapped her lips with her finger. "Mr. Blazevig was awfully cagey when I brought up Inez's name, and even Aunt Glenda didn't like Inez."

"You just named two of the nicest old people I've ever met. No way they did it."

"Who knows what they were like all those years ago."

"People don't change who they fundamentally are."

"Maybe." Autumn watched the fishermen dock the boat and unload the fish from various vessels. Sometimes, she felt like she was in a movie. Here it was, late afternoon, and she was swinging her legs over crystal clear ocean water. Back in New Jersey, she'd most likely be watching television while she did her trigonometry homework. Autumn had always accepted her routines. Key West stomped on that monotony.

Autumn brought her knees up to her chest, careful not to flash boaters her underwear. "Why do you trust me all of a sudden?"

"It's not that I didn't trust you before. But she's tried to kill me twice now. At some point, I need to think of self-preservation." Liam faced her and cocked his head to the side. "But I need you to be honest with me. What's in this for you?"

Autumn squinted at him before sliding her sunglasses down over her eyes. "I want to study journalism and I'm using Inez's disappearance for a scholarship application."

"Uh-huh," he said, even as a smile tugged at the corners of his mouth. "You're that desperate to freeze your butt up north?"

Even as Autumn bathed in the sunlight and welcomed the soft, ocean air, she still grinned when she thought of crisp, fall breezes. "I'm a Jersey girl. It's in my DNA."

"Well, I'm a Conch." He pronounced the word with a hard K sound at the end.

"A what?"

"Most people come to the Keys on vacation and leave. Then, there are those who've lived here their whole lives. Natives. They're called Conchs."

"Oh," she said. "Well, I'm definitely not a Conch."

"Well, you could've been dragged somewhere worse." Autumn detected a bit of defensiveness in his voice. "I don't get it. What's so great about New Jersey?"

Autumn wiped away a line of sweat from above her lip. *Attractive.* "What's so great about here?"

Liam pointed at the dying sun. The rays fanned out in golden arcs. "You can't tell me you have this in Jersey?"

She shrugged. "We have the shore. But more importantly, we have seasons. My family loved fall. My parents named me Autumn for God's sake. Right now, if I were home, I'd be taking my sweaters out of storage. My mom would be prepping the house for Halloween and my birthday. We'd head out to the orchards and pick apples. Then we'd hit the pumpkin patch and I'd spend at least thirty minutes scouring the ground for the most symmetrical pumpkin I could find. Not too big. Not small. And totally round. My dad would carry it around for me and seatbelt it in next to me. He did that last year, and I was turning seventeen. Then we'd finish the day with apple cider donuts. My dad would build a fire and my mom would serve up hot apple pie and ice cream. She'd only close the windows if it got too cold to sleep." She closed her eyes and breathed deep, trying to envision the autumn colors of red and gold. Instead, she smelled rotting fish and salt.

Liam sat upright. "It doesn't sound like you want to go back to New Jersey."

Autumn wondered if Liam was deaf. Did he not hear what she had said? "It doesn't?"

"Nah. It sounds to me like you want to go back in time." He laughed, but Autumn failed to see the humor. "You want to go back to when your parents were happily married and everything was warm and cozy."

"What's so wrong with that?" she asked softly.

"There's nothing wrong with it, but it's pointless. You can't make that happen. Moving back to Jersey isn't going to give you what you want."

Autumn watched the undulating ocean waves. She knew Liam was right. She couldn't get her family back, but Jersey was familiar. She understood how the Northeast worked. The changes in weather invigorated not just her, but everyone around her. In the Keys, the stagnant and oppressive temperatures unnerved Autumn and made her skin itch. Time stood still here and she couldn't adjust. She was neither tourist nor a Conch. Autumn didn't belong anywhere.

"Do you know what Cayo Hueso means?" Liam asked.

Autumn shook her head.

"It's the original Spanish name for Key West. It means Bone Key. When the Europeans landed here, the island was covered in bones. Used to be a graveyard for the natives."

"Really?" she asked.

"See? You find that interesting. For a girl who embraces the dead, you're more at home in Key West than any other city in the country."

"I don't know about that." Autumn spied a line forming near the boat. She stood up and smoothed down her dress. "Fish is up."

Liam nodded and rose to his feet.

Autumn wondered if Liam could see the disappointment wash over her face. She wasn't in a rush to go home and have her mother order her about like a scullery maid. There was something Autumn didn't quite understand. "You pawned the ring. Why not just leave the Cayo and you'll never have to worry about Inez?"

"The ring only brought in a little money. I need more cash." Liam pointed to a short guy in cargo shorts and a stained white T-shirt. "You see that guy over there?"

The boy reminded Autumn of the slackers who sneaked cigarettes outside the high school gym. "Yeah."

"That's my buddy, Randall. He may not look like much, but he's loyal, and he's a good mechanic. He and I are going into business together. Randall and I come from . . . well, let's just say our last names are not the most popular around here. But he and I are going to make something of ourselves." Liam's eyes gleamed. "I'm gonna grab the fish and we'll head back."

She said, "Sure," and watched Liam make his way over to his friend. She hung back but could still hear their conversation.

Randall clapped Liam on the shoulder. "Good to see you, bro."

"You too. We came for the grouper," Liam said.

Randall pointed to a squat guy in a red, smeared apron. "Keith'll hook you up." Randall tilted his head and glanced beyond Liam. "Who's the cutie?" Autumn blushed.

Liam spun around. Autumn pretended to be fascinated by the tops of her sandals. She leaned against the railing and let the breeze play with the hem of her dress. "That's Autumn, my boss's daughter."

Randall laughed. "That's a thing with you isn't it, dude? You're always liking the boss's daughter. Victoria?"

Autumn bristled. Victoria didn't have any redeeming qualities, so what attracted Liam to her? Other than her obvious good looks. Autumn hoped Liam wasn't that shallow.

"I never worked for her grandfather," Liam said.

"Everyone in this town works for Mick Canton," Randall quipped. "Oh, speaking of working. You got the money?"

Liam handed Randall a padded envelope. "There's two grand there. Be careful with it."

"I will, don't you worry." Randall bumped Liam's fist with his own. "We are in business. Keith is going to put up six. But I'm gonna need more than this. This isn't going to cut it."

Randall glanced past Liam and grinned at Autumn. She glared back.

"I'm working on it. But I can't make Evelyn pay me more. Anyway, we have to sit down and figure out where we're going to set up shop. I'd feel better once we have real concrete plans."

"Good news is we have a spot already." Randall handed Liam a heavy, wrapped package. "My granddad's been sitting on a piece of land by the salt ponds. It's not ideal, but it's ours."

"You're kidding me?" Liam's eyes grew wide. He slapped Randall on the back. "That's awesome!"

"Even more awesome is that Granddad promised me that land one day." Then he grumbled, "Least he could do. The drunk. Anyway, this plan of yours might work after all."

Liam brightened. Autumn hoped for Liam's sake this worked out. She didn't know him well, but she knew him well enough to know he needed some good luck in his life. Also, her mother wasn't going to keep him employed too much longer.

Randall tapped his shorts pocket where he now hid 2,000 dollars. "Gotta split. Catch ya mañana?" He walked backward and pointed at Liam. "Oh, Victoria is having a party. You gotta come, dude. Should be epic."

"No way, man. I'm not crazy enough to get back into that mess," Liam said.

"Bring the cutie," Randall called back as he disappeared into the throng of people crowding the dock.

Liam joined Autumn. His cheeks held a pinkish cast and Autumn wondered if he was blushing. "Ready to go?"

She nodded, and they made their way back to Liam's parked scooter. He placed the packaged fish in the trunk and handed her the bike helmet. Once again, Autumn couldn't help but think that if she were back home, she wouldn't be doing this. If anything, she'd be holed up in her room, listening to music and working on a chemistry lab. Not purchasing fish that had been caught in a net barely an hour ago and escorting it on the back of a scooter driven by a very cute Liam Breyer.

*People in the Keys definitely don't live for the weekend like they do up north.*

Autumn wrapped her arms around Liam's waist as he sped off for home. Suddenly, the palm fronds seemed greener. The roosters, with their bright red crests, paraded up and down the sidewalks as if signaling to Autumn to take notice. She watched a six-toed tabby clean its paws as it balanced on a white picket fence. The singing and laughter emanating from a group of tourists rose above the scooter's buzzing so that Autumn felt like she was surrounded by an orchestra of joy. Autumn thought maybe Key West was finally seeping into her bones, or perhaps it was really Liam.

Liam parked the scooter alongside the curb outside the Cayo Hueso. Autumn hopped off the back.

She collected the fish from the trunk. "Thanks. I had a nice time."

"Me too."

Autumn hesitated, not quite ready to go inside. "Although, I'm sorry you pawned the ring. I hope your business takes off."

Liam bit his swollen lip and winced. Autumn still couldn't believe she had done that. Well, Inez had done that.

"I don't want to be the reason you don't get that scholarship. I just needed the money, ya know?"

"Oh, I know," she said. "Money would make both of our lives so much better."

He laughed. "If it makes you feel any better, I had my regrets about selling it."

"Really?"

"I even went back to Louie's the next day to see if I could buy it back."

"What happened?"

Liam turned on the scooter. "I was too late. Someone had already bought it. See you tomorrow." Liam waved as he sped home on his bike.

The next afternoon, Liam stood along the Cayo Hueso's pool, skimming the dead bugs and leaves off the water's surface. Except, rather than looking down, he stared across at the battered old fence that separated the Dead and Breakfast's backyard from the neighbor's. The fence was in desperate need of a paint job, one Liam would surely be asked to do soon. Across the way, Liam could hear some chickens clucking and the neighbor yelling at her husband.

He kept skimming the same spot over and over again. He made 2,000 dollars selling the ring, but he had to come up with another two grand to ensure his stake in the business. A business he envisioned. Otherwise, Randall's cousin would have to bring someone else into the fold. And knowing Keith Bell, that someone would be shady and hard to manage.

Victoria's offer of financing his business flashed in his brain, but he quickly cast it aside. Money from her had strings attached, and he knew that he did not want to be her puppet.

Liam felt the familiar buzzing in his pocket. He lifted the phone from his cargo shorts and frowned at it, recognizing the number. He decided, against his better judgment, to answer.

"Victoria, how the hell did you get this phone number?"

"Randall gave it to me," she said, clearly not taking the hint.

Liam rolled his eyes and cursed Randall in his head. Victoria used to never give Randall the time of day, now they were chatting behind his back. "I'm at the Cayo. What do you want?" In the background, Liam could hear her friends giggling.

"I want to invite you to my party," she said. "This Friday night."

"I have to work."

"Oh, come on, Liam. You probably get off around seven or eight?"

"Around then."

"The party won't start until later," she said, her voice pleading. "You can even bring a friend."

"A friend, huh?"

Liam could practically envision her smiling, thinking she had him. "Totally. The more the merrier. Pilar is single now. She broke up with Tyler a week ago. Maybe you can set her up." Victoria must have thought he'd bring one of his high school buddies to the party.

"Good to know." He spotted Evelyn giving him the evil eye from the lobby window. "I gotta go. Boss lady doesn't like me talking on my cell phone."

"Okay." Victoria quickly added, "It's at my house on Sunset Key. You remember where it is."

"I remember," he said dryly. "I really gotta go."

"Okay, come after your shift is over and don't forget to bring your friend." Then she hung up.

Liam pressed the end call button and slid the phone back into his pocket. He pushed the skimmer into the water and scooped out some leaves. He knocked the net against the fence and went back to retrieve more leaves. That's when he saw Inez's face sneering at him. He cried out and stumbled backward, right into Autumn.

She caught him and spun him around. "Whoa, Liam. You okay?"

Liam shook his head, as if waking himself up from a dream, or in this case, a nightmare. "I'm fine." He took a long pause before asking, "Hey, do you want to go to a party?"

# CHAPTER FOURTEEN

Autumn leaned against the railing of the ferry and stared at the warm water, lit up by a stream of white moonlight. Liam was right about one thing. She didn't have this in Jersey. The ferry moved quicker now, traveling from the cruise port to the pier at Sunset Key.

"I can't believe I agreed to this," she said.

Autumn's mother had not been pleased her daughter was going out. "What about movie night?" she had asked.

"It's Friday," Autumn replied, as if she always went out on Friday evenings, rather than watching old black-and-white movies on Turner Classics with her mom and aunt.

"Evelyn, let the dear girl go on a date," Aunt Glenda had said.

"It's not a date," Evelyn and Autumn said together. Autumn gave her mom a questioning look. What was it about Liam she didn't like?

"I mean," Autumn had said. "He didn't make it sound like a date."

Glenda smiled and tapped Autumn's bare shoulder. "Right dear. That's why you're wearing such a pretty dress. Because it's not a date?"

You know, for a kooky old woman, she sure was shrewd.

In the end, Evelyn allowed her daughter to go out. Although, she instituted a brand new curfew. Midnight. And the strict instructions that Autumn was not to touch one ounce of alcohol.

Liam glanced over at Autumn's sour face. "Come on, it will be fun?"

"Did you just make that a question?" she asked.

"No?"

Autumn laughed. "Victoria is going to hate this." Her eyes widened with a thought. "Is that why you brought me? Because you knew it would her piss off?"

Liam glanced down at the churning water and grinned sheepishly. "No. Maybe."

Autumn nudged him with her shoulder. But then her voice took on a more serious tone. "Do you want her back?"

Liam jerked his head up. "No."

"She is beautiful," Autumn said, as if that detail alone justified his feelings.

"She is beautiful," he repeated. "And she knows it. Victoria comes from a very wealthy family. A family used to getting what they want all the time. People like the Cantons make it hard to say no."

Autumn nodded along as if she understood, but her dealings with the wealthy Cantons were only through

Victoria, who mostly needed Autumn's English notes to pass her exams. Autumn knew Victoria struggled with her studies and wondered what kind of ridiculous expectations were placed on the girl. For a moment, she felt a twinge of sympathy, but as the ferry docked at Sunset Key and the mansions came into focus, Autumn found it easy to brush aside any sorry feelings.

Liam clasped Autumn's hand to help her off the boat. "Ready?"

"No," she said, brushing her dress down. But she was smiling.

Autumn stood outside Victoria Canton's Sunset Key home and stared with her mouth agape. To say it was a large house would be an understatement. It wasn't so much that the house was tall, as most homes in Florida weren't known for height, but that it was expansive. Liam watched Autumn twist her neck to see from one end of the house to another. Unlike Key West, Sunset Key had new and rich construction. Here, homes sat on larger pieces of land with Olympic-size pools and water slides. The Canton home was bathed in a warm orange glow from the lights embedded in the well-manicured landscaping.

Autumn's voice came out high-pitched. "This is where Victoria lives?"

"Yup," Liam said. "This is Canton wealth right here."

"She could buy and sell me without thinking." Autumn inhaled a deep breath. "I shouldn't have agreed to let you bring me here. She's going to know why you did it, and she's going to make me pay for it."

Liam chuckled. "Just be Jersey strong." Then without thinking about, he found Autumn's hand and intertwined his fingers. His pulse quickened when she didn't pull away. "Come on."

The two approached the ornate teak front door. A young girl in a bikini top and denim skirt flanked one of the columns like a soldier on guard. Probably one of Vicky's freshman minions. She clutched a glass fishbowl. But instead of fish, cash swam inside.

The girl smacked her gum. "Twenty dollars. Each." She gave Autumn a pointed look.

Autumn blanched. "You're charging us to go to the party?"

Liam slipped his hand inside his back pocket and removed his wallet. He slipped two twenty-dollar bills from his wallet and folded them inside the bowl. "It's for a good cause." The freshman nodded and the two went inside.

Autumn said nothing, and Liam hoped he hadn't embarrassed her. He leaned into her and whispered, "Victoria's sister is probably running for Conch Queen for Fantasy Fest. She's raising money for AIDS research. She's been fundraising all year."

Autumn nodded and relaxed her shoulders. Although she couldn't tear her eyes away from the interior decor of the house. Liam could only imagine what she was thinking.

For Liam, the house hadn't changed much. Sure the entranceway had a new piece of modern art, probably some priceless collectible worth more than Pops made in his entire life. When they entered the grand foyer, Liam wasn't surprised to see a woman in a black vest bearing a tray of tiny quiches.

"What is this place?" Autumn whispered. "It's like we stumbled into a ritzy Bar Mitzvah."

Liam inhaled a quiche. "Victoria's parties start out this way. Catered food. Soda. Open pool. But then when her parents and grandfather head out on their boat for the night, things become less innocent." Autumn examined Liam's face, and he quickly added, "Or so I've heard."

"Right," she said.

Just then, Liam heard someone call his name. Victoria came bounding down the stairs in a strapless yellow dress that barely covered her butt, a colorful green drink in hand. She skidded to a halt when she saw Autumn, the green liquid swirling and threatening to slosh out of the martini glass.

Liam grinned. "You said to bring a friend."

Victoria didn't so much as flinch. "I did. Hi, Autumn. Didn't think you were allowed out before sundown."

Autumn didn't miss a beat. "I live with ghosts, not vampires."

Victoria sidled up to Liam. "Food is in the kitchen. Booze is in the pool house." She whispered seductively, "Please take advantage of my hospitality." She removed a maraschino cherry out of her drink and popped it into her mouth. She placed the stem into Liam's palm. Heat rose to his cheeks as she sauntered away. Victoria's mission to make Autumn uncomfortable made Liam feel equally itchy. Why in the world did he think it was a good idea to come here? Part of him thought that if Victoria saw him with Autumn, she'd back off. Now, he realized that seeing Autumn only strengthened her resolve. Vicky did like a challenge.

Liam led Autumn to the kitchen. At one point, Liam thought he recognized the song playing on the stereo until he realized a boy band was performing live outside by the pool. He rubbed his hands together. "One thing about Victoria's parties is the food is outstanding." He bit a grilled shrimp. He smiled as he chewed and picked another shrimp off the platter and put it in Autumn's mouth. Her eyes closed for a second. Warmth radiated from his chest.

"You're right." Autumn grabbed another shrimp. "These are delicious." She laughed for a second. "Parties back home were nothing more than some bowls of pretzels and a keg in the backyard."

"How high class." Victoria popped her blonde head in between Autumn and Liam. She linked her arm through Liam's. "Grandfather wants to see you. I told him all about your business model and he wants to hear about it."

Liam's eyes widened. "Who told you about our business model?" His eyes closed. "Randall. I'm gonna kill him when I see him." He sighed. "Vicky, your grandfather isn't going to be happy when he hears I'm trying to start up a small tour company."

"Don't be stupid. You think he cares about a little competition?" She pointed to a close door at the end of a hallway. "He's in his study, waiting for you." She smiled at Autumn. "Did Liam tell you that our grandfathers were navy buddies?"

Autumn nodded, but said nothing. Liam imagined Autumn thinking of all the things she'd like to tell Victoria about her grandpa and a young Cuban girl he knew once.

"They were great friends back in the day," said Victoria, her voice sickly saccharine. "I'll keep Autumn busy while you and Grandfather have a chat."

Liam reminded himself to tear into Randall the next time he saw him. That kid could not keep his big mouth shut. Liam didn't want Mick Canton's help. He just wanted to make something of himself without anyone interfering. But it was too late. Vicky was pushing him toward the study door. All he could hear was squealing as the boy band finished another song.

Liam's apologetic face was no consolation for leaving Autumn alone with Victoria Canton and her bitchy friends.

Jenna Anderson and Pilar Rubio suddenly flanked Victoria's side, their Amazonian statuettes casting shadows against Autumn's slight frame. Their stares could cut glass. Autumn held out her hands in mock surrender. "Look, Victoria. I didn't come here to start a war. Liam and I aren't a *thing*, okay?"

Victoria laughed. "I don't think of you as a threat, silly."

Autumn wanted to drop her guard, but something told her not to. She suddenly felt like she couldn't breathe. "Um, where's the ladies' room?"

"The ladies' room?" Victoria asked. "This isn't the Olive Garden. The guest bathroom is down the hall." She pointed her perfectly polished pink nail toward a narrow hallway with several doors on either side.

Autumn mumbled a thanks before practically running in that direction. She opened the bathroom door and went inside to hide. For a guest bathroom it was pretty spacious. A large Jacuzzi tub sat under a wide picture window. Blue green glass tiled the shower. Two square sinks rested atop the marble vanity. Autumn nodded to herself in approval. She could hide out here all night if she had to. She didn't have to actually use the bathroom, but she figured if she stayed put, Victoria and her friends would get bored and forget about her.

Sure enough, when she poked her head out the door a few minutes later, the girls were gone. Autumn exhaled. She started heading toward the kitchen where she last saw Liam, but an open door, directly across the hall, caught her attention. She spotted a glimpse of lavender.

Autumn's attic bedroom in New Jersey had light lavender walls. She wondered if her stepmother, Jennifer, had repainted them when she converted Autumn's bedroom into a craft space. Curious,

Autumn walked across the hall and gently pushed open the door, revealing a beautiful room with white wainscoting and a four-poster bed in deep mahogany. A soft purple shade covered the walls and satin drapes adorned the windows, which were really French doors. Someone had clustered pillows on a large ottoman covered in purple paisley fabric. So many pillows. A black plush letter V leaned against the headboard. Autumn's breath caught. This was Victoria's room. Autumn knew she should have gotten out of there as fast as she could, but she couldn't help but admire the luxuriousness. She'd never seen anything like it. If rooms at the Cayo Hueso looked half as beautiful as this, Evelyn wouldn't have to grovel to the Mrs. Paulsons of the world for a decent review on Vacation Raters.

Tall bookshelves lined one wall and held decorative items like glass vases and crystal animals. Autumn tilted her head to the side and read the titles of a stack of books. *Passing the SATs. Physics for Dummies. Realizing Your Potential. Overcoming Dyslexia. How to Survive College with a Learning Disability.* Wow. Victoria wasn't lazy about her studies. She was struggling and too embarrassed to ask for help.

"See something interesting?" came a voice from behind.

Autumn whipped around. Victoria glared at her. The Amazonian agents stood next to her like pillars.

Autumn's stomach dropped. She hadn't meant to snoop. "I'm sorry. I saw the lavender walls and the door was open and your room is just so pretty. I didn't mean to pry."

Victoria's eyes widened and then narrowed. "You know what Autumn, you haven't seen the backyard yet, have you?"

"Huh?" Autumn's gut churned.

"The backyard," said Victoria. "Everyone is outside dancing and hanging out with the boys." She went over to Autumn and pushed her toward Jenna and Pilar, who each took Autumn's arms, practically dragging her away.

"Listen, girls," Autumn said as they escorted her down the hallway. "Let's not do anything crazy."

"We're just showing you the patio," Pilar said in her usual bored tone.

Autumn began to sweat as the girls forcefully walked her through the house. *Maybe they just want me outside with the rest of the party. I can understand that.* They pulled her through the French doors that led from the large living room to the pool area. Kids from the charter school—a few girls from American Lit, the Italian foreign exchange student from her calculus class—stopped to stare at her. And Autumn had to admit, she was starstruck by the band. Natasha would never believe that she got to see a live performance from the boys of—but Autumn didn't have a moment to finish that thought.

Victoria suddenly flanked her, gripped Autumn tightly by the shoulder, and gave her a hard push backward into the pool.

# CHAPTER FIFTEEN

Liam could smell the cigar smoke before he set foot inside the room.

"Come in, boy," Mick called out to him. "Don't be lurking in the shadows. It's rude."

Liam straightened. "Yes, sir."

Mick Canton laid his cigar on the edge of a crystal ashtray. When he stood up from his desk, Liam realized just how imposing a figure Mick was. He had a Papa Hemingway way about him. Broad and tall and dressed in a Havana-style white button down shirt. Mick had to be at least six foot three, if not taller. Liam thought he saw an old anchor tattoo on his right forearm. Just like Pops. Always a sailor.

Mick clapped him on the back. "I meant to ask you at Louie's, how's your grandpa doing these days?"

Liam was surprised by this question and Mick's friendly demeanor. In all that time he had dated Vicky, Mick never seemed interested in what Pops was up to. "He's fine. Retired now."

When Liam had been dating Victoria, Pops hinted that men like Mick Canton were powerful and rich for a reason and didn't want their pristine granddaughters messing around with poor Conch boys.

Mick came around his desk and pointed Liam to a brown leather chair. Liam sat. Was this the same man who accosted him on the street only a week ago?

"So." Mick picked up his cigar and took a few puffs. "Did Louie give you a fair price for the ring?"

"Very fair," Liam lied.

Mick blew smoke in Liam's direction. "Good. I guess you'll be using the money for your start-up."

Liam shifted nervously in the chair. Stupid Randall. There was no way Mick would let a couple of punk high school dropouts infringe on his business.

"Relax," said Mick, reading Liam's thoughts. "There's plenty of tourist dollars to go around."

Liam tried to shake off the tension in his shoulders.

"Besides," Mick said, "I've been in the business long enough to know that customers are willing to pay for quality, not some hokey rip-off." He chuckled to himself. "That's why they come to my tours and only my tours."

Liam didn't respond. He didn't see the point. Mick would never admit that someone else could create something of value, especially if it competed against Canton Corp.

"Come." Mick gestured for Liam to stand up. "Let me show you something."

Mick draped his beefy arm around Liam's shoulders, forcing Liam to slouch under the weight. He steered him along to the stone fireplace, an odd thing for a

Floridian home. Above the mantel hung a swordfish, and below a photo of Mick next to the giant fish. Mick scanned the mantel, which also held trophies and many other family photos. His finger landed on a small black-and-white picture in a sterling silver frame, which had tarnished over time. He plucked the frame from the mantel and presented it to Liam.

Liam studied the photograph. A group of four men, not much older than Liam, all dressed in dark blue Navy uniforms. Two female figures stood to the side of the photo, their faces cut off. Liam recognized the tallest man as Mick. Liam smiled when he saw Pops. It was the same smile.

"You look just like your old man," Mick said softly.

Liam ran his finger over the photo. In the background, Liam noticed the familiar house. "Was this taken at the Cayo?"

"Yes. We used to have the best parties there. Doesn't your grandfather have photos from then?"

The only photos of Pops that Liam had seen were one on his wedding day when he was in his mid-twenties and one of him holding Ray, Liam's father. Mostly, Liam only knew the Pops that was wrinkled and hunched over. Who smoked cigars when he thought no one would be home for a while. Who still believed Ray was a good man even though he never raised his own son, choosing to find work in every state but Florida.

Liam smiled, mostly to himself. Four friends, sailors about to conquer the world. What could be better? A sense of adventure. Driving out to his dad's job, Liam had seen a lot of America, but only the crappy parts. Liam pointed to a shapely leg in a plaid skirt. "Who's this?"

"Probably one of the girls from St. Veronica's," Mick said gruffly. His eyes drifted past Liam.

Liam wanted to utter Inez's name and gauge Mick's reaction, but he couldn't be so cruel. If what Autumn had seen was real, then he had loved Inez only to have his heart broken.

Mick set the picture back on the mantel. "The Cayo Hueso seems to be in dire straits."

Liam shrugged. "It's seen better days, that's for sure."

"Well, when I heard Glenda's niece came all the way down from New Jersey to keep that place afloat, I figured things couldn't be good. Shame. Duncan was a good friend, but Glenda became unhinged after he died. Kept going on and on about ghosts and the spirit world. Duncan would be ashamed if he knew how quickly she ran his hotel into the ground. House has been in the family for generations."

Liam felt uneasy under the weight of Mick's shoulder.

"She's probably getting desperate to sell the old place," Mick said.

Liam wasn't thinking about the Cayo Hueso anymore. He was studying another old photo of Mick, his arm draped around a lithe blonde bride. For some reason, he thought about his parents and wished he had seen their wedding photo. Liam mumbled, "Uh huh." This seemed to please Mick, who slapped him heartily on the shoulder.

Liam disengaged himself from Mick's grasp. Apparently, when he was on the old man's turf, Mick become tamer and friendlier. Liam decided to hedge his bets. "So, there are no hard feelings about my scooter business?"

Mick stubbed his cigar out in the ashtray. "Of course not. I'm not worried about the likes of you. Most businesses fail. Yours won't be any different."

"Hush," came a soft voice. "That's no way to speak to one of Victoria's friends."

Victoria's grandmother, Bernadette Canton, leaned against the doorframe. She was tall, slim, with her blonde hair pinned elegantly off her neck. Her smile took up most of her face. There was something about her that reminded Liam of Victoria. Unlike Mick, Bernadette had always been nice to Liam. Or at least, *nicer*.

Mrs. Canton limped into Mick's study, her walk affected by polio when she was a kid, and rested her slender hands on her husband's shoulders. "There's more than enough business in Key West to go around. You can't control everything." She massaged Mick's shoulders. "Victoria is asking that the adults leave the house now. I think she's feeling embarrassed by her old grandparents."

Mick grunted. "I'll have the captain bring around the boat."

Liam wondered what Autumn would think about this conversation. Boats. Captains. It would probably solidify all her negative opinions about living in the Keys. Better she not hear it then.

Autumn! Shoot! He left her all alone. He inched toward the door, trying to politely make his exit, when he heard a scream.

Autumn thought a million things as she was falling backward into the pool. Her home in New Jersey for one. The dark bannister that she used to slide down when she was a kid. The neighbor's tabby cat, who used to catch and kill yellow finches and leave them at their back door. Her mother hated that. But her last thought when she was falling was her large four-poster bed. The one she could fall into and hide under mounds of soft blankets whenever the world had let her down. That was what she wished for as the warm water enveloped her.

Autumn stayed underwater until she was desperate to breathe before erupting to the surface and a bombardment of laughter. She emerged from the pool. The hem of her dress clung awkwardly to her thighs, the way wet clothes did against skin.

Autumn's chin trembled, a sure sign she was about to cry. But when she saw Victoria's smug face greet her, Autumn bit her lip and lifted her head. No way was she going to let this spoiled, rich bitch get the best of her.

Autumn flung her long hair over shoulder, droplets of water scattering everywhere. Victoria held her hands up to protect herself from the spray. "Thanks for inviting me," Autumn said through gritted teeth. "Awesome party."

She steeled herself against the stares and walked back into the house. Liam met her in the kitchen.

"Oh, crap," he said. "You're all wet."

"I am." Her voice wobbled. "I was pushed into the pool. Can we go now?"

Liam pulled off his button down shirt, leaving a thin T-shirt underneath, and draped it over Autumn's shoulders.

Autumn relaxed, but only for a moment. "Grab more of those shrimp and let's get the hell out of here."

Liam bit his lip to suppress his laughter. "Whatever you say." He swiped a cocktail napkin, palmed several grilled shrimp, and followed Autumn out the ornate front door.

Autumn slipped off her sandals and carried them in her hands. All she could think about was getting back home to New Jersey. Liam could make her see how wonderful island living could be, but girls like Victoria made Autumn realize that no matter how warm and tropical Key West was, it could never be home. All vacations came to an end.

Liam turned off the scooter and dismounted first before he helped Autumn off the bike. They hadn't said much on the ferry. Okay, they said nothing to each other on the ferry. Liam could only imagine how much anger Autumn must've felt toward him. After all, it was his moronic idea to drag her to the party of a jealous ex-girlfriend. Liam hadn't been thinking too smart lately. He'd been too distracted. Autumn had a lot to do with that.

Autumn's clothing had dried some in the warmth of the night. Her dark hair, still damp, cascaded down her back. She looked beautiful, and he wanted to tell her that but feared the backlash.

"Listen," he said, his voice soft and hushed. "I'm so sorry about what happened. I know Victoria can be a bitch, but I had no idea she'd do something like shove you into the pool."

She held up her hand. "You don't have to apologize."

"I feel like I do."

She shook her head, her hair undulating like waves breaking on the shore. "It's my fault. I shouldn't have been there."

Liam reached for her hand. Her skin felt warm and soft. "You should be wherever you want." He wanted to say, "Even if that means New Jersey and not here in Key West with me." But he didn't. Again, she just shook her head.

"That's not what I meant." She seemed to be lost in thought, and Liam didn't want to intrude.

Instead, he nodded. "Okay, let me just walk you to the door." But Autumn had already bolted ahead. She had taken only a few steps on the path, before Liam whispered, "I keep messing up."

Autumn paused, her back still to him, her shoulders drooped. She spun on her heels and charged toward him. Liam didn't budge. Autumn stopped inches in front of his face. Her eyes searched his and she seemed like she wanted to say something, but instead she just pressed her lips to his. At first, he was stunned, but he instantly wrapped his arms around her waist and drew in her body. His skin heated up as if he'd been lying in the sun. He'd never felt so alive. Until the porch light went on and Evelyn poked her head outside.

"Autumn, is that you?"

And they broke apart.

# CHAPTER SIXTEEN

Autumn winced at the sound of her mother's voice. She didn't know why she kissed Liam. One moment she was so angry at her stupidity for going into Victoria's room—school would be a nightmare on Monday, that was for sure—and the next moment, she felt this tug inside her body, pushing her toward him. Even though she had been kind of irritated with Liam for inviting her to that party, she still wanted to be near him, and she wanted to keep on kissing him—if it wasn't for her mother.

She parted from Liam and walked backward toward the Cayo Hueso, giving him a small wave. He smiled and it warmed her over, making her sweat just a bit despite her damp clothes.

Evelyn greeted her when she came inside, a hot steaming mug of coffee in her hands. "You're home earlier than I expected." Her brows knitted at Autumn's appearance. "You look disheveled."

Autumn didn't say anything. She didn't want to get into the details about how the bitchy girls at school were out to get her. And after that kiss with Liam, it didn't seem important anymore. "How come you're not in bed?"

Her mom sipped from her coffee mug. "Can't sleep. Worried about the bills."

Autumn nodded. She knew the Cayo wasn't doing well, but she'd assumed her mom was a worrywart. Aunt Glenda made it seem like there was enough money in savings to keep the place afloat for a while. Maybe that wasn't true. "Is there something I can do to help?"

Evelyn pursed her lips, and the gesture made Autumn's stomach clench. Autumn was trying to be nice, but Evelyn's expression hinted at an unpleasant response. "Actually, there is. I'm going to need you to take a pay cut."

Autumn stepped back. A pay cut? How was she supposed to save money for school? She was already scrounging her earnings away. "How much of a pay cut?"

Her mother shifted her weight. "I was thinking we suspend your salary until we can bring in more business."

Autumn balked. She wasn't expecting that. "How am I supposed to save for college? Candlewick is my cheapest option, and it's still like twenty-five grand a year."

"It's not your cheapest option." Evelyn patted her daughter's shoulder. "You could always do a year of community college in Florida."

Autumn squirmed away from her mother's touch and backed up against the dark wood paneling in the foyer. "I want to go back home."

Evelyn sighed. "Please, Autumn, be reasonable. If I can't ask you to do this, then I'll have to fire Liam, and we need him here during the day to do the heavy lifting while you're at school. If it makes you feel better, I'm not making any money either."

"No, it doesn't make me feel better."

"We need to change our expectations." Her mother frowned, although her attention seemed focused on a crack in the wall and not Autumn's feelings.

"We?" Autumn's voice hit a shrill note. "This is my future we're talking about. What about Dad?"

Evelyn's eyes hardened. "He'll pay some, but don't expect more from him. You shouldn't rely on your father to keep his word."

"What kind of parent blows their child's college fund on an investment and then makes her work for free? Like a slave? Doesn't that sound ridiculous to you?"

"Would you rather I fire Liam? You two are getting cozy. Do you want to be the reason he loses his job now?" Evelyn put her mug down on the vestibule table. "Look. I'm sorry to do this to you. It's possible we can make this place great again. Profitable. But we're hemorrhaging money, and I need you to help me. I want you to go to college. I want you to be a success. But please, just be a little more understanding. Okay?"

Autumn pushed past her mother. "I'm going to bed."

Evelyn always said she wanted what was best for Autumn, but most days, her mother only wanted what was best for Evelyn.

The first thing Autumn did after flopping on her bed was retrieve her cell phone. She sent out a text to the number on Mr. Blazevig's ghost tour brochure.

It's Autumn Abernathy. If that job is still available, I'd like to start work right away.

Mr. Blazevig replied with a smiley emoticon, pretty tech savvy for a seventy-year-old man. Unfortunately for Autumn, she didn't have much to smile about.

Liam walked alongside Autumn. Unlike most evenings when the air was so thick with humidity Liam swore he could carve out a chunk with a knife, tonight held a tinge of crispness. He watched Autumn inhale deeply. She was practically skipping down the sidewalk, which was weird because when he saw her earlier, she had held up her hand and said, "Fair warning. I'm in a mood." But now Autumn grinned as if all her troubles had hitched a ride on the cool breeze that meandered through the streets.

"I feel like I can breathe," she said. "I bet I could wear a light cardigan." She laughed. Liam liked the sound.

"Are you cold?" He wasn't sure why he asked. He wasn't wearing anything heavier than his T-shirt and couldn't offer her a hoodie like a real gentleman.

Autumn glanced at him, her eyes twinkling. "Are you kidding? This feels amazing. The weight of all that humidity is gone. You know, you didn't have to walk me to Duval." Autumn was on her way to meet Ralpah Blazevig, dodging tourists and roosters on their way to Duval.

"We should've taken the scooter," said Liam.

"Are you kidding? On a night like this? I'd rather walk." Autumn hopped over a crack in the sidewalk. "Sorry about snapping at you before. I'm mad at my mom."

Liam wasn't sure whether he was relieved or upset that they hadn't discussed the kiss. Last night, for the first time in a long while, he slept without dreaming and woke up anxious to see Autumn. But right now, she seemed more excited about the drop in temperature than about him.

They turned the corner in silence, and Liam gently touched her elbow, easing them to a stop. "Did I get you in trouble? Did your mom get upset about the—" He couldn't bring himself to say *kiss*. He saw a deep blush creep up Autumn's neck.

"No. She didn't—I don't even think she saw. It's about money."

"Oh."

"She isn't going to pay me anymore for working at the Cayo."

"This is my fault," Liam said. "I should quit so your mom has more funds."

Autumn squeezed Liam's hand, and it took all his resolve not to lean into her for another kiss. "The truth is, she needs you at the Cayo more than she needs me. I'll earn more money working for Mr. Blazevig than I will at the Cayo, anyway. I'm pissed at her because she makes decisions without consulting me. I don't blame you at all."

Liam exhaled. "I thought maybe you were mad at me because of all the crap with Victoria and me kissing you—"

"I kissed you."

A smile crept up on his face. "Well, that is true."

Autumn pressed against the thick trunk of a palm tree with her hands behind her back. "A month ago, the craziest thing happening at the Cayo was a guest checking in. I couldn't get away fast enough."

"And now?" he asked.

She grazed the tip of her black hi-top sneaker along a crack in the cement. "And now, I don't know. I'm not gonna lie. I'd do anything to go back to Jersey. Go to my high school's crappy football game. They always lose. Hang out with Natasha at the bonfire." Her voice got soft. "But then, I'd probably want . . ." She didn't finish her thought. Instead she said, "Do you think you'd ever leave the Keys?"

The presence of tourists thickened the closer they got to Duval Street. Fantasy Fest was still a week away, but the city was getting crowded. Liam listened to the cacophony of scooters and electric cars buzzing through the streets. Close by, he heard laughter and music. There was a party just about everywhere in Key West.

Liam shook his head. "I did leave Key West, and that didn't turn out so well. Also Pops is getting older now, and I need to stick around for his sake."

Autumn watched the tourists. Liam thought he could see the gears inside her head churning.

"Can I ask you a personal question?" she said. "You can totally say no."

Liam couldn't imagine saying *no* to Autumn ever. "Shoot."

"How come you need money if you were working in North Dakota for a whole year? I thought guys were making small fortunes up there."

Liam blinked at her. He opened his mouth to speak, but snapped it closed. Why was this so hard to share? He had confided so much to her already. But Liam worried about what Autumn would think of him if she knew he had to pay for his father to go to rehab.

"I shouldn't have asked. It's not my business." Autumn checked the time on her phone. "I better get going, anyway. You don't have to walk me the rest of the way." She smiled sincerely, although that did little to alleviate the anxiety in Liam's stomach. Just when he thought he was getting close to Autumn, he pushed her away.

Liam wanted to escort her to Duval Street. *Hell, I'd walk her to New Jersey if it meant I could hang out with her more.* But he respected her desire to be alone. "Sure. I have some things to do anyway."

Autumn kissed Liam on the cheek before she turned and headed toward the meeting spot for Mr. Blazevig's haunted tours. Liam couldn't help but notice that her chin was tilted down and her eyes watched the sidewalk instead of the life going on around her.

He ran his hands through his hair and exhaled. Liam wanted to warn himself away from Autumn, but he knew that was pointless. He was in danger of falling for Autumn, even as she admitted how badly she wanted to leave the Keys.

# CHAPTER SEVENTEEN

Autumn spotted Mr. Blazevig standing near the large Banyan tree at the base of the old Porter Mansion on Duval Street. He stood hunched over a small table set up on the sidewalk and fussed with brochures. He smiled and made grand gestures with his hands as he chatted with tourists. He appeared slightly younger than the sad man she often saw in the City Cemetery, the widower tending to the graves of the two people he loved most.

Autumn dodged a couple in white shorts and Panama hats and crossed Duval. This section of Old Town reminded her of a carnival. Bodies pressed in on all sides. Laughter and music filled the empty spaces and light flooded the street. The scent of grilled burgers wafted among the breeze, tempting hungry tourists. Everyone was happy to be in Key West. Admittedly, even Autumn. Her time with Liam made her longing for New Jersey weaken ever so slightly.

Evelyn, on the other hand, didn't seem too thrilled with Autumn's decision to work for Mr. Blazevig. "Midnight tours?" she had said, her brow furrowing.

"Only on the weekends," Autumn explained.

"Is that safe?"

Autumn shrugged off her mother's worries. She wanted to say, "You should've thought of that before you fired me." But instead she said, "I'll be fine."

When Autumn and her mother moved here, Evelyn made a point of taking Autumn to the Hemingway House and the Butterfly Conservatory and Fort Zachary. All the places Evelyn deemed "safe" and "respectable." Autumn thought it was pretty ridiculous of Evelyn to bring her down here only to show her the touristy stuff. If Key West was going to be her home, then she needed to understand it—even the seedy parts.

"There you are, dear." Mr. Blazevig pulled Autumn out of her daze. His hands trembled slightly as he aligned the brochures on the table. "We'll get started in about ten minutes, but first I want to tell you how to register customers, take reservations, and get credit card info for billing."

"Uh, okay." Autumn thought she was just giving the tour. She assumed Mr. Blazevig would handle the money and the people. She was only supposed to show up and talk.

Autumn did her best to take mental notes as Mr. Blazevig explained his detailed, if antiquated, system for booking customer reservations and collecting deposits. "I conduct tours every night at seven and nine o'clock, except for the weekends when I do special midnight tours," he said.

"Every night?" she asked, surprised at how this seventy-year-old man had the energy to walk the streets of Key West, practically giving a performance. It had to be exhausting.

He nodded. "I was thinking of cutting out the midnight tours, but they're popular." He related a few other details that Autumn tried hard to remember, but her head spun.

"Do you typically do all this . . . by yourself?"

The old man thumbed through a three-ring binder. "Who else would do this, dear?"

"You never had part-time help?"

"My wife's nephew worked for me a few years back, but then he moved away. There are not many people I can trust." He gave a weak smile.

Sadness bloomed in Autumn. Mr. Blazevig was a lonely old man. "Show me how to do the credit card slips again." Mr. Blazevig gave her a wink and then spent the next few minutes explaining how he kept his books. Autumn found it interesting and even suggested a phone app to help manage the accounts. She wondered why her mother never bothered to do the same thing with the Cayo. Autumn could be more assistance than just cleaning toilets.

After a few moments, Mr. Blazevig glanced up and noticed a small group had gathered in front of the mansion. Autumn watched as he tied a red bandana around his neck and topped his head with an old straw hat. If she squinted, Mr. Blazevig looked like Hemingway in his glory days. She watched the man transform. As if possessed, Mr. Blazevig became someone else—an actor.

"Welcome to the Haunted Ghost Walk of Key West," he told his audience. For a moment, the sounds of Duval Street hushed. Autumn focused on Mr. Blazevig's voice. "Tonight, you will hear unbelievable tales of ghosts and legends. Did you all know Key West is one of the ten most haunted cities in America?"

The crowd murmured and some shook their heads.

Mr. Blazevig tipped his hat. "Well, when a city is founded on the skeletons of those who lived here before, it creates a powerful energy that does not leave. Cayo Hueso means Bone Key." Autumn wished Liam had stuck around for this. But their conversation had gotten awkward, and Autumn couldn't blame him for distancing himself.

As Mr. Blazevig spoke about the history of Key West, she tried to pay close attention to the details, especially if she would have to recite it next week. He led them across the street and told the audience to take plenty of photos. They were to look for orbs, little balls of light that appear for no reason in their photos. "They say it's evidence of ghosts."

Autumn watched the group. Everyone was smiling and listening to Mr. Blazevig's melodic voice. She had to hand it to the man, he could entertain a crowd. Not to mention weave a good story. If she were going to be a writer, she'd need to do these same things, except in print.

Mr. Blazevig pointed to the second floor window at the Hard Rock Cafe. "You ladies be cautious, you hear? There's a ghost by the name of Robert, who haunts the women's bathroom." Autumn laughed with everyone else and examined the old Victorian house. Her eye caught on the silhouette of a familiar-looking guy. He slouched against the street lamp as he typed into his phone. She searched her memory until she could come up with the name—Randall. She turned her attention back to Mr. Blazevig, who was now leading them down the street on the way to a haunted graveyard.

At one point, the group stood outside an abandoned storefront with large windows taped up with butcher paper. Mr. Blazevig recalled a sad story about children dying in a fire and Autumn shuddered.

Mr. Blazevig asked the tour group to place their hands against the glass. "Some people say they can feel the heat from the flames." Some of the tourists shook their heads. An older woman crossed herself and spat on the sidewalk. When Mr. Blazevig waved his hands to lead the group toward City Cemetery gates, Autumn saw Randall lurking in the distance, attempting to hide behind another building and doing a terrible job of it. He had his phone out again and was snapping photos.

Autumn considered cornering him, until Mr. Blazevig called her over. "Come, dear, we're heading to City Cemetery." Autumn hesitated, but in the end, she followed.

City Cemetery didn't typically make Autumn's skin crawl. During the day, the white headstones shone in the sunlight like marbled artifacts of another era. But at night . . . well, that was something else. Even being with a crowd of people, Autumn still felt the little hairs on her arm rise.

In fact, no one in the group made a sound, except for Mr. Blazevig. He lowered his voice as he waved his hands over the locked wrought iron gates. "City Cemetery is famous for its nefarious habitants and peculiar epitaphs."

Autumn listened to the old man tell a story about a woman poisoned by her husband's mistress. As the tour group proceeded, Autumn hung back. She pressed her cheek against a cool gravestone and listened. Footsteps. The sound of shuffling feet. And tapping. Her stomach dropped. Especially when she lost sight of the tour group.

Her heartbeat quickened until she heard the beeping. *Wait a minute.* She moved alongside the fence before clamping her hand down on Randall's shoulder. His scream could be heard in Miami.

"Gotcha," she said.

Randall slammed against the metal fence and clutched his chest. "You scared the crap out of me!"

His cell phone dropped to the ground. Autumn bent down to retrieve it, but something on the screen caught her eye—a photo of the tour. She wiped away dust that covered the screen. She held the phone in front of his face. "You're spying on us!"

Randall shrugged her off. "Just getting a few ideas."

"You're stealing Blazevig's tour. You'll steal his clients too."

Randall held out his hands in mock surrender. "Everyone does it. There are a ton of these tour group operations. You think anyone has something original to say?"

Autumn shook her head. "Mr. Blazevig runs a unique business. Does Liam know you're doing this?"

Randall smiled then. "Liam's my boy. He'll be cool with it."

Autumn hoped he was wrong.

"Besides, Blazevig doesn't have many more years doing this stuff. He'll need to leave it to the young guys."

"Yeah. Go tell that to Mick Canton." Autumn pushed off him and handed him back his phone. "Go home, Randall. You'll never hold a candle to men like Mr. Blazevig."

Randall smoothed down his T-shirt. "Whatever, Jersey girl. I can see why Victoria doesn't like you."

Autumn shrugged. "And you can see why I don't care."

"Later," Randall called to her as he headed along the side street.

Autumn ran to catch up to Mr. Blazevig, who smiled and joked, "Ghost slow you down?"

Autumn watched Randall slink out of sight. "More like a ghoul."

Liam woke the following morning to find a text message waiting for him from Autumn. He rubbed the sleep from his eyes before scanning the screen.

*Your friend Randall is a spy. Followed me on my ghost tour and took notes.*

Liam breathed out a heavy sigh and leaned against his headboard. He'd have to talk to Randall. It was one thing to try and take a cut of Mick Canton's lucrative business, but he didn't want to steal clients from old Mr. Blazevig. The man was harmless, not to mention, an old army buddy of Pops. Also, a ghost tour on scooters seemed kind of stupid. *What is Randall doing?*

His phone vibrated with another text message from Autumn.

*Mom wants to know if you can come in early. She has an errand for you. Sorry.*

"Sure, why not?" Liam said to no one in particular. If anything, he'd get paid a little more, and he could see Autumn again. It didn't sound so bad. That is until he arrived at the Cayo Hueso.

Evelyn barely let him say hello to Autumn, before she shoved a long piece of paper into his hands. Liam cocked his head to the side and peered around Evelyn's pinched face, hoping to catch a glimpse of Autumn. He could see she was wearing a yellow tank top and white shorts. Her ponytail swung as she swept the patio. She looked beautiful.

Evelyn cleared her throat and nodded at the slip of paper. "It's a list of provisions for Fantasy Fest. We're booked for the entire ten days, so I'm going to need you to go out and pick up everything that I've written on that list."

Liam glanced at the paper and perked up. This could take a while. A few hours alone with Autumn was something he'd arrange for free. Evelyn was paying him to hang out with her daughter.

Evelyn dangled a set of keys from her fingers. "You and Timothy can take my car. It has adequate trunk space."

"Hold up," said Liam. "You want me to go with Timothy?"

Timothy ducked his head out of Evelyn's office and pursed his lips. "It's no picnic for me either, sugar."

"No offense," said Liam. "It's just, are you sure you can spare him? I just thought I could go with Autumn." Liam knew what Evelyn's reaction would be the minute the words left his mouth.

She narrowed her eyes. "Autumn will help me here. You go with Timothy."

Liam took the car keys and blew out a breath. Timothy came around the reception desk. He smoothed his white button shirt and adjusted his bowtie in the mirror. "Come on, lover boy. Let's get this over with."

Liam and Timothy emerged into the daylight and approached a blue Prius with Jersey plates parked along the curb. Liam held out the keys. "You want to drive?"

Timothy vigorously shook his head. "I don't drive."

Liam's eyes widened. "What about a scooter?"

"Never learned."

How do you get around?"

"I ride my bike," he said simply.

Liam went around to the driver's side and opened the door. He didn't understand how Timothy, who always looked so polished and put together without an ounce of sweat staining his impeccable wardrobe, rode his bicycle in the wretched humidity.

Timothy climbed into the passenger's side and buckled his seatbelt. "I know what you're thinking, and, baby, all I can tell you is it's my Bahamian blood. I adapt well to heat."

Liam started the engine. "So, basically, you don't sweat like the rest of us because of your Bahamian blood?"

"That's right."

Liam put the car in drive. "I guess you could say it's because you were born that way."

Timothy rolled his eyes at the Lady Gaga reference. "Ha ha, lover boy. Now drive to the market. We've got plenty to do."

Liam stood on the back of the shopping cart and coasted down the aisle like he used to do when he was a kid. He skidded to a stop in the produce department where Timothy had spent nearly a quarter of an hour inspecting bananas.

"Seriously, dude," Liam said. "Pick out yellow ones."

"Again, your wit is to be admired," Timothy said. "My mother wants these bananas for muffins but they need to be overripe."

Liam picked up a bunch of bananas developing a brown tinge on the skin. He thrust them at Timothy. "Get these."

"Too ripe. By the time the guests arrive, these won't be fit for a dog." He made a big point of glancing at Liam as he said this.

Liam exhaled. "This is taking forever."

Timothy clucked his tongue. "Be thankful you're out of the Cayo for an afternoon, and you don't have Evelyn breathing down your neck."

It never occurred to Liam that Timothy would find Evelyn overbearing. He thought she just had it out for him. "Does she bug you too?"

Timothy plucked a bunch of bananas that were neither green nor beginning to brown, and put them in the cart. "She's been on my case all week to get that website done. But she wants to be made aware of every change I make. I can't be micromanaged like that." He glanced at Liam. "Of course, in your case, she's just being a mama grizzly with you."

Liam picked up three apples from a nearby table and juggled them. "What does that mean?"

"It means Evelyn sees how you ogle Autumn. She's protecting her baby."

Liam caught the apples in rapid succession. "I don't ogle Autumn. I just like her is all."

"A lot."

"Yeah, a lot. So?" Liam put the apples back down on the table.

"So, lover boy, Ms. Evelyn just got out of a long marriage to a man who cheated on her. My guess is she hates all men, myself excluded, right now. Besides, isn't Miss Autumn going to college in New Jersey next year?"

"Well, you never know. She might stick around."

Timothy made a check mark on the shopping list and then gave Liam a pointed look. "Please. The girl may sweat you a little, but don't be thinking she's going to give up her dream of returning home for your bony ass."

Liam clutched his chest and feigned hurt. "Thanks."

"Just sayin'." Timothy nodded toward the meat department. "Come on. We've got a ton more to buy and my mama ain't getting any younger."

Liam followed Timothy with the cart. But his childlike antics had dissipated, and he couldn't get Timothy's words out of his head.

*Don't be thinking she's going to give up her dream of returning home for you.*

That was just Liam's luck with women, wasn't it? He was never good enough for them to stick around.

# CHAPTER EIGHTEEN

Autumn sat at her desk in her bedroom and tapped the pen against the notebook. It was hard to focus on her AP History homework when she wanted to focus on Liam instead. Autumn had to admit that there was no Liam Breyer in New Jersey. She would definitely miss not seeing him every day when she started college next fall.

Lunch had been stressful, if uneventful. Cora served up the fish Bahamian style. Mrs. Paulson complained as much as she always did. The knife was dirty. Her water had specks floating in it. The dinner was served too late. But she couldn't complain about the delicious food.

Mr. Fletcher, on other hand, voiced nothing but compliments. Autumn could tell the man hadn't been taken care of in a long time. She wondered when he had last eaten a vegetable. Autumn's mother visibly relaxed in front of Mr. Fletcher and tensed up whenever Mrs. Paulson so much as cleared her throat. It was enough to drive anyone over the edge. But then Autumn thought back to her afternoon at the pier with Liam, and a sly smile crept up on her face.

Autumn shook her head in an attempt to focus on her schoolwork. Goosebumps erupted on her arm.

"Ugh, homework," Katie said, appearing from nowhere. "That's one thing I don't miss about being alive. But seeing that dreamy look on your face tells me you weren't thinking about homework just then." Katie wagged her brows. "You want to make out with Liam, don't you?"

"Seriously?" asked Autumn.

Katie's lips curved into a pout. "What? You're not going to confide in me? Don't you think he's groovy?"

Suddenly, Autumn's cell phone buzzed. She swiped it off the desk, assuming it was Natasha giving her a play-by-play of Homecoming events. Her friend had been texting more often ever since Autumn sent an email about Liam.

Whatcha up to? Liam texted.

Autumn smiled, a rosy glow erupting on her cheeks. She wrote back, Homework. You?

Definitely not homework. Going to see Randall tomorrow.

Give him hell for me.

You know I will.

Katie read over Autumn's shoulder and squealed, "You're flirting! Reminds me of letters passed around at school. Do people do that anymore?"

Autumn nodded as she typed. "Some do."

There was a moment before Liam responded. Night,

Autumn. She wrote back good night, before setting down the phone.

"He's totally into you," said Katie. "I bet he's a good kisser."

Autumn felt the heat rise to her cheeks.

Katie squealed. "Ooh! I knew it. You kissed him. Tell me everything."

"No way."

"Who am I going to blab to?"

"Fair enough." She turned to Katie. "Well—" But then the phone buzzed again. Autumn picked it up and laughed.

"What's so funny?" Katie asked.

Autumn held up the cell phone's screen so Katie could read the message.

Send my love to the pretty blonde ghost.

Katie grinned and glowed brighter than she had in days. "Autumn, don't mess this up."

But before Autumn could ask her what she meant by that, Katie had disappeared.

The following morning, Liam rapped gently on the aluminum front door to Randall's granddad's trailer, which occupied a postage-size lot off Laurel Avenue on Stock Island, just a short scooter drive from Pops's place.

Liam hadn't been there in years, not since Mr. Bell had called Pops an uppity cheat. Pops said it had something to do with a bad round of bocce ball at the VFW. Liam hoped Randall's grandfather was over it now because he really needed to talk business with his friend.

Liam waited on the small porch. The weathered gray boards wobbled under his feet. He didn't hear any noise, so he leaned over the porch to peer in the dingy window. A blue recycling bin sat underneath. He rapped on the door again and called out, "Randall!"

A moment later, Randall opened the screen door in his ratty cargo shorts and no shirt. He yawned and adjusted his baseball cap, which he wore backward. Randall clapped Liam on the shoulder, but waited until the jet noise above subsided before saying, "Sorry, dude. I was napping."

"You texted me last night," Liam pointed out. "Said to see you first thing this morning."

Randall led Liam to a set of beach chairs leaned against the lattice that covered the trailer's undercarriage. The faded awning provided some relief from the sun.

Liam wiped sand off the seat before sitting down. He rested his sneakers on the rough patch of grass and adjusted his sunglasses. Liam forgot how much he used to enjoy coming here, more so when Randall's grandfather was nowhere to be seen. Despite the noise pollution from the airport, Stock Island held a certain industrial charm. For Liam, it was like going back in time.

Randall folded his hands behind his head and sighed. "This, right here, is the life." He knocked the lid off a cooler and reached inside for a beer. "You want one?"

"Nah, dude." Liam checked the time on his phone. "It's not even nine." He looked around for the old Pontiac. "Where's your grandfather?"

Randall shrugged. "Don't know. Don't care. I haven't seen him since yesterday."

"Aren't you worried?"

"Nope." Randall opened the tab on the can, took a swig, and belched.

"Okay." Liam would be freaking out if Pops didn't come home. Although, his first instinct would be to ring the neighbor's door. "Anyway, was Keith able to get the bikes?"

Randall nodded. "He's storing them in his garage in the backyard."

"All fifteen?" Liam vaguely remembered Keith's house. The garage was nothing more than a glorified shed.

"Yeah. We moved them there late last night. Had to borrow a truck and everything. Hence, why I was still sleeping when you knocked."

"Okay," said Liam, but his insides churned a bit with anxiety. What kind of business partner would Randall be? Would he sleep in on weekends, leaving Liam to do all the management? "You're not gonna be like this when we start our business, are you?"

Randall cocked a brow. "Like what?"

Liam waved his arms around the trailer site. "Slackerish."

Randall pushed away the comment with his hand. "I'm the one who was up at midnight, hauling scooters. What were you doing? Hanging out with your girlfriend?"

Liam held up his pointer finger. "First, I wasn't hanging out with Autumn, and you know that because you were spying on her! And second, she's not my girlfriend."

"Whatever," said Randall, downing another sip.

"And what were you doing spying on Autumn to begin with? We're not doing haunted ghost tours."

Randall belched. "I know that."

"Then?"

"Autumn made an assumption, and I let her think we were ripping off old Blazevig."

Liam shifted in his chair. "Then why were you following her?"

Randall put his beer down and flattened a few random blades of grass. "I was asked to."

Liam rose and rummaged for a can of soda from the cooler. "Did Vicky tell you to spy on her? I really didn't imagine her to be the jealous type. Anyway, tell Vic she can worry about herself. I know what I'm getting into."

"Do you?"

Liam pulled back the tab and took a sip. The sweet, ice-cold liquid that traveled down his throat felt like relief. "Anyway, let's talk business and not my love life."

"Fair enough." Randall crushed his beer can and tossed it toward the recycling bin. He missed by inches, but stayed seated.

"What do we need to do to your granddad's lot to make it usable?"

"Well, there's a small structure on the land. We could use that as sort of a kiosk. We need permits and a lawn mower."

"Okay," said Liam. "The lawnmower isn't an issue. I'm sure I can borrow one from the Cayo. But permits . . . how much do you think that will cost?"

Randall shrugged. "I figured since I did the heavy lifting, you could check into getting the permits."

"Sure," said Liam. He could make a trip to town hall. Hopefully, permits weren't expensive. "Once that's done. We can set up. Get the bikes repaired and on the premises. I guess our last issue is advertising. We need to tell tourists we're here. The salt ponds are not exactly on the tourists' radar."

"I'll make print T-shirts with a logo." Randall grinned.

"Do we have a logo?"

"Uh, no."

Liam sighed. "I'll ask Timothy at the Cayo to design something. He's savvy with that stuff."

"Sounds like you're really fitting in over there," Randall muttered.

Liam finished the soda and tossed the can into the recycling container. Slam dunk. "I don't know if I'm fitting in. It's a family run business. I'm not exactly family. But everyone is nice enough." Except for Evelyn.

Randall dug his heels into the dirt and leaned back in his chair. "Vicky's right. You will get hurt."

"Stop telling Vicky stuff. I had to have a talk with Mick about our start-up."

Randall bolted upright. "He knows?"

Liam did a double take at Randall. "You think when you confide in Victoria, she keeps her mouth closed? You should know better than that."

Randall scraped his nail against a piece of hard plastic that jutted from the armrest. "And he didn't seem pissed?"

"Not that I could tell. But you know Mick Canton. He's just biding his time until he—"

The boys turned their heads toward the sound of a car's engine approaching. Randall groaned and grumbled, "Granddad's home."

Liam watched as Fred Bell parked his midnight blue Pontiac in front of the trailer, narrowly missing the trailer's rickety porch. He struggled to climb out of the drivers' seat. "What are you two losers doing?"

"Nothing, Granddad."

The old man stumbled around his car. His brown slacks were stained and shredded at the hem. His shoelaces were untied. A red scratch cut across his bulbous nose and his glasses hung crooked on his face.

"Where've you been anyway?" Randall asked, getting to his feet and helping his grandfather up the little porch.

"I was at the Green Parrot, and then I hung out with old Ralphie for a little while. I fell asleep in my car."

"Ralph Blazevig?" Liam asked.

Fred's eyes searched Liam's face as if trying to place him. "Yeah. We go way back." He chuckled and then hiccupped. "I used to hit on his sister."

A noise of disgust escaped Liam's mouth.

"Just like your Pops," Fred sneered. "Too good for everyone else."

Liam retreated a step. "I'm gonna take off."

Randall nodded as he held his grandfather's elbow. "See you later, dude."

Liam put on his helmet and started the scooter's engine. He watched Fred Bell stumble into his rundown trailer. Pops had always been a drinker, but he'd never been as bad as Randall's grandfather. Liam made a mental note to replace Pops's beers with a six-pack of cola.

Autumn felt uneasy during dinner, which probably explained her upset stomach. She'd picked at her fish fillet, only taking a few bites, and pushed the rest of her meal around the edges of her plate. A childish tactic and an unnecessary one. Evelyn was so distracted with the budget reports that she didn't even flinch when Autumn announced she had homework and asked to be excused. Her mother shoved a piece of bread in her mouth and waved Autumn away without so much as a glance in her daughter's direction.

Autumn needed fresh air, so she wandered into the patio area. Even though she hadn't moved around much, sweat pooled under her arms and at her temples. She peeled her blouse from her skin, but it was no use. Autumn pressed the back of her clammy hand to her forehead. *Am I coming down with something?* Maybe, but these symptoms seemed different. She had no sniffles, no congestion. Not even a sore throat. Her stomach rolled, and only a handful of crackers could alleviate the nausea. Perhaps Autumn's queasiness could be attributed to the stress of living in a haunted hotel.

"Inez?" Autumn asked the still night air. "Are you here?" She was greeted with silence.

Autumn walked around the patio, stepping over cracks in the concrete that had been hastily repaired by Uncle Duncan years ago. Autumn examined a rust stain on the concrete, probably made from a pool of water that had sat on the patio too long. The rust reminded Autumn of blood, and she wondered how Inez had died. So far, all she knew was that the woman was murdered, but how?

Autumn glanced back at the Cayo, making sure her mother wasn't lurking in the window. Evelyn never liked it when Autumn spoke to spirits. Although Evelyn was convinced Autumn had only been talking to herself. The Cayo was quiet.

"Was this how you died?" Autumn pointed to the pool. "Were you drowned?"

Autumn heard a cackling laugh.

Without the ring, she had no way to pull Inez to her. No way to access the ghost's mind. She'd hoped speaking to her aloud would provoke the spirit, but Inez couldn't be controlled that way. Autumn considered a different tactic.

"You drowned, didn't you? Maybe, no one killed you. Maybe you just drank too much and slipped on the wet patio. It's not the first time that has happened. Some silly high school girl has one too many whiskey sours or whatever you guys drank back then. She isn't paying attention and she falls, knocks her head on the edge of the pool, and tumbles into the water. And there's no one to save her."

Autumn jerked back as if two hands have shoved her hard. Inez was present and probably pissed. *Good. If I can't use the ring to call her, maybe I can use reverse psychology.*

"Admit it, Inez. You killed yourself by being stupid—" A punch smashed into her chest and Autumn cried out. The swirling blackness quickly followed.

Autumn sucked in a breath. She exhaled as someone clasped her hand and swayed with her. Her heels clacked on the Cayo's pristine cement patio. A recognizable the song, The Supremes' "My World is Empty Without You" emanated from the record player which was set up on a bridge table near the French doors. She felt a hot breath in her ear.

Mick held Inez close as they danced. He wore the dark blue uniform with white stripes on the sleeves. Just like the night they met in Autumn's first vision. The diamond glinted on Inez's finger. "My grandmother's ring looks beautiful on you," said Mick.

Inez admired the glitz. "It does, doesn't it?"

Mick twirled Inez around, and she bumped into a soft body behind her.

Glenda's faced pinched with annoyance and her eyes searched frantically. "Has anyone seen Duncan?"

Inez moved her hips and spun around the redhead. "He's probably hiding from you."

"Inez," Mick warned.

"What? She's a ditz. No wonder Duncan's a queer." Inez laughed.

*Did queer then mean the same thing it means now?*

Inez yelped as Glenda yanked Inez's hair. "Get off me, puta."

Glenda ran her fingers across Inez's face, drawing blood. Inez screamed and charged Autumn's aunt. Autumn wished she could stop her, but Mick had pulled her back and hissed in her ear, "Let it go or she could hurt the both of you."

*The both of you?*

Duncan came bounding near the pool with Ralph on his heels. "What's going on here? We heard a scream."

Glenda wiped furiously at her eyes.

Mick answered, "Nothing. The girls wigged out a little over the music. Wasn't anything."

Duncan tilted up Glenda's chin and whispered, "Is that right?"

Inez taunted, "Tell him. Go on."

Glenda glared at Inez before she nodded. "I wanted to hear The Rolling Stones, that's all. Inez disagreed. Things got heated. It's nothing."

Duncan shot Mick a pointed look as Mick shrugged his broad shoulders. Duncan led Glenda away from the patio and inside the Cayo, leaving Mick alone with Inez.

"Why do you have to say those things?" Mick asked.

"What? I'm saving the chica from her misery," said Inez with an air of indifference. "She shouldn't be with someone who can't really love her."

*Inez should take her own advice.*

Autumn felt that queasiness hit her insides again. She pushed Mick away and retched into a nearby shrub.

"I heard it doesn't last long," Mick said from behind. "Maybe a few weeks."

Autumn hurled again. Her mind spun. The sudden nausea. Mick's protectiveness. Autumn remembered seeing Jennifer retch into a trashcan during a video call with Autumn's dad.

"Don't worry, pumpkin," her father had told Autumn. "Jennifer's okay. It will only last a few weeks."

When Autumn stood up, she was back in the present day. Inez having left her body, but having told Autumn something very important.

Inez was pregnant.

# CHAPTER NINETEEN

Tuesday morning Liam gently rapped on the wood moulding outside reception. Evelyn sat at a small table in the lobby, eating a bagel while pouring over some books. Autumn was there as well. The minute he saw her, his chest swelled. He watched as her cheeks reddened too.

Autumn had texted him last night to tell him about Inez and the baby. He hoped they'd have time to discuss it before school, but glancing at Evelyn's hunched shoulders, it didn't seem likely.

"Morning, Mrs. Abernathy. Where would you like me to start today?"

Evelyn didn't even lift her gaze from the ledger. She held out her hand with a piece of notebook paper dangling from her fingertips. "I have a list here for you. There's a leak in the August bathroom. Mr. Fletcher mentioned hearing a constant dripping last night across the hall, and he was none too pleased about it."

"I didn't hear him complain," Autumn said. "And I saw him this morning at breakfast."

Her mother looked up from the ledger as if seeing everyone in the room for the first time. "That's because he is too much of a gentleman to say anything. But it would've annoyed anyone trying to sleep, I can tell you that. It's our job to see that guests' needs are met even before they know what those needs are."

Liam knitted his brows in confusion. It sounded to him like Evelyn was spewing something she must've read in a book. *How to Run a Hotel for Dummies.* And she thought they were all dummies. "Okay," he said. "I'll go upstairs and take care of it. Do you know where the leak is coming from?"

"I believe the bathtub." She dropped her gaze back to the ledger in front of her. "I imagine the faucet needs tightening." She nodded toward the chair next to her. On it was a red metal toolbox, circa last century. Liam grabbed it and took that as his cue to get to work. Autumn opened her mouth like she wanted to utter an apology for her mother's coldness, but she could only shrug.

Liam climbed the stairs, the metal tools rattling inside the box like bones in a coffin. The humidity was worse upstairs. He wiped a bit of sweat from his upper lip and scanned the worn wooden signs on the door. The September room was on his right. He squinted at the wood on the door and ran his finger over the faded A. August. He inhaled deeply and opened the door.

The first thing that hit him was the wet air. Evelyn had said that the last guest to stay there was a high-maintenance middle-aged woman from Texas in town for a singles event.

He listened carefully for the dripping. Drip . . . drip. The droplets fell softly, as if from a short distance. He opened up the bathroom door and spotted a curling iron still plugged into the socket near the base of the tub. Did no one notice this when the previous guest had left?

The old claw foot tub nearly overflowed with water. Not only had the faucet been leaking, but the tub drain had been clogged too. Liam put down the toolbox on the tile floor and peeked inside the tub. The droplets made little rings that dissipated as they rippled through the water.

Liam stifled a gag. Whatever was clogging that tub had to be gross. If it was a hairball, he knew it would be seconds before he could reach the toilet in time to barf up breakfast. Liam could handle blood, but hairballs he could not. He leaned over and braced one arm against the far end of the tub. He squeezed his eyes shut, thrust his hand into the water, and stuck his fingers into the drain. Streams of water flowed freely from the tub, drenching his shoes.

*I'm not being paid enough money to do this.* Liam grazed something soft, not rough like hair, but silky like a piece of cloth. He pushed his fingers farther into the drain in an effort to grab it. It was no use. He yanked his hand out and opened up the toolbox, searching for a pair of pliers.

He exhaled when he found them. The old toolkit was good for something. He leaned over the tub and put the pliers into the drain, trying to pinch the cloth between the pliers' teeth.

Liam smelled something burning. A curling iron, smoking from the heat, floated in the air, inching toward him. A vein in his neck pulsed rapidly as if it was about to explode. Liam froze, his eyes glued to the sizzling iron. He swallowed hard, glancing at the door, readying his escape. But then he was shoved into the bath. Water overflowed. An invisible hand pressed down on his head. The curling iron, still plugged into the socket, lingered over the tub. If it fell in, he was toast. Electrocuted. Liam struggled to grab the edge of the porcelain tub. His face broke the surface of the water and he screamed. "Help!"

Autumn charged toward him. She smacked the curling iron away, and cried out. The wretched thing clanged to the tile floor. Autumn shook out her hand and hissed.

"Dammit, Inez." Autumn cradled her injured hand for a moment before reaching in and helping Liam out of the water. "She nearly killed you. Again. We have to get rid of her."

A cry of frustration cut the air, followed by a baby's wail. Liam shuddered.

"I'm serious, Liam." Autumn helped him climb out of the tub. He slipped on the tile floor, but she caught him and they embraced awkwardly. "This is the third time. She's tried to drown you, take off your head, and now electrocute you. When are you going to get it? This is serious."

"Your mother is going to think I'm crazy. This is the second time I've fallen into water while working."

"Forget my mom." Autumn tilted Liam's chin and forced him look at her. "What are we going to do about this?"

"Did you see her?" he asked.

Autumn dropped her hand. "Sorta, kinda. I saw a female form. She had dark hair, but unlike Katie, her features were blurry. Like bad television reception."

"Speak of the devil." Katie appeared and glided over to Liam, who didn't seem to register her apparition.

"He can't see you," Autumn said. "You're gonna have to adjust your reception."

Katie squeezed her eyes tightly together. Autumn watched her silhouette brighten. "How about now?"

Liam gasped and fell against the pedestal sink.

"It worked," Autumn said dryly.

Liam's face paled. "I can't believe what I'm seeing."

Katie pouted. "I'm not a what. I'm a who. God, it's like you've never seen a woman before."

Liam sat on the edge of the tub, which had now drained, with his mouth agape. He stared at Katie as if she was a piece of art he was trying to decipher.

Autumn snapped her fingers in Liam's face. "Focus."

"I can't." He pointed at Katie's apparition. "I'm seeing a ghost. A real ghost."

Katie put her hands on her hips. "Well, thank you

for noticing." She jutted out her chin. "I was just like you once. A living person. Try to pretend I'm still that girl. I'm just a little see-through now."

Liam's voice trembled. "Okay. I'll try."

The piece of cloth that had been the source of the clog lay on the floor like a giant spitball. "What is that?" Autumn asked.

Autumn gently laid a hand on Liam's shoulder and tried to steady him as he bent to pick up the rag. "It looks like some kind of handkerchief."

He opened up the soggy ball. There was the letter B embroidered on it in blue thread. It also had an old brown stain.

*Blood*? "Is that yours?" Autumn asked Liam.

"Do I look like the kind of guy who carries around old handkerchiefs?" He raised his brow.

"No," Autumn and Katie said at the same time.

"It probably belonged to the former guest, Mrs. Benson," Autumn said. "I mean, that makes the most sense."

Katie flickered slightly. "It sounds like Inez is trying to tell you something. And that B," she pointed at Liam, "is a clue."

"She thinks Leo Breyer killed her," Autumn said. "B for Breyer."

"Pops is a lot of things, but he's no murderer. He's harmless."

Autumn remembered Leo's scowl in her vision. He didn't look harmless then. But she wouldn't mention that now.

"If she thinks I'm my grandfather, then doesn't it make sense that she would be confused as to who killed her?" Liam asked.

Katie thought about that for a moment before saying, "Yes. She's either missing her own memories or she's linking separate events from her past. Either way, you don't have the full picture."

Autumn said, "When I get inside her head. I'm at the mercy of what she shows me. I can't make her see the truth."

"Sounds to me like she's trying to make *you* see the truth," said Katie.

"Yeah, well, I know Liam didn't kill her. Do you think if we called her to a séance, she'd understand that Liam isn't Leo?"

Katie scoffed. "You've got to be kidding. I'd never come just because some fools called me to a table draped with a maroon cloth."

"Well, would Inez?" Autumn asked.

Katie shrugged and flitted around the bathroom. "She might. She likes messing with you guys."

Liam tilted up his head at Autumn. "How do we go about contacting her?"

"Don't ask her," Katie said. "Just because she can see ghosts doesn't mean she can control them. Two very different things. What you need is a medium."

"A medium?" Liam asked. "Where do we find one of those?"

Katie smiled and waved her arms in a dramatic fashion. "Luckily for you, right under your nose."

"Timothy," Autumn whispered.

"Yes," said Katie. "That beautiful Bahamian downstairs, who unfortunately wouldn't be into me, is your medium. You want to talk to Inez. Talk to Timothy."

Timothy stood at the reception desk, doodling on a thin pad of blue paper that had *Cayo Hueso* scrawled across the top.

"What are you jackals looking at?" Timothy said without glancing up from the pad.

"A medium," Autumn and Liam said together.

Timothy dropped his pen. "Aw, hell no. Who told you I was a medium?"

"Katie," Autumn said.

Timothy rolled his eyes. "I told you to contact ghost girl through Katie, not *through* me."

"I need you to do it. Remember? 'It's too dangerous for you, Autumn,'" She mocked Timothy's know-it-all voice.

"Well, I thought ghost girl was visiting you in your sleep."

"I can't wait to do things on her schedule because she keeps trying to kill Liam. We have to put an end to this."

Liam grabbed a white towel off the reception desk and wrapped it around his torso, hoping to dry his sopping wet clothes. Evelyn left stacks of towels around the Cayo, as if she expected guests to use the pool. Liam seemed to be the only one who actually used them. "I pawned the ring," Liam said. "And she tried to kill me. Again."

"I've also had phantom morning sickness for the past week," said Autumn, rubbing her stomach. "We need someone who knows what they're doing."

"That's clearly not you two." Timothy straightened his turquoise bowtie. "Unfortunately, the problem remains. You're still going to need something belonging to the spirit to force her to come to the table."

That stopped Autumn's momentum, and Liam could see the disappointment in her face. It did sound like an impossible task. Find something belonging to a strange ghost from fifty years ago.

Liam wanted to kiss her disappointment away. "Don't worry. Maybe there's a way around it."

"Uh-uh," Timothy said. "No loopholes when it comes to the dead. Also, I'm not contacting any spirit until Evelyn and Miss Glenda are gone from here."

"We're screwed," said Liam.

"Not necessarily." Timothy jutted his thumb toward the wall calendar. "The ladies are going to Miami tomorrow. They have a meeting with a bank, hoping to get a small business loan."

"How long will they be gone?" Liam asked.

"Overnight," he replied. "You have one evening to do this thing. Better find something of the dead girl's quickly."

Liam looked at Autumn's expression. It was a mix of emotions he couldn't quite figure out. Determination, maybe and . . . hope. It was at that moment that Liam had never felt more attracted to the Jersey girl.

"What?" she asked.

Liam just smiled, mostly to himself. "Nothin'."

That night, Liam laid in bed in his boxer shorts and a holey Radiohead T-shirt that resembled Swiss cheese. It was after eleven and sleep would not overtake him.

His cell phone buzzed, and Liam grabbed it off the nightstand. It was a text from Autumn.

I've searched the attic and turned up nothing.

No object. No séance. No control.

Frustrated, Liam threw his phone into the top drawer of his nightstand and heard a rattle. Liam fumbled around and pricked his finger on a sharp object. He sucked the blood droplet off his finger and picked up the St. Veronica's pin he found in the Cayo's backyard.

Leo said his grandmother had a pin too. Liam quietly opened his bedroom door and padded down the hall to Pops's room. He listened to his grandpa's rhythmic breathing. The old man was sound asleep.

Liam crept into the bedroom and slid his abuela's jewelry box off the dresser and then snuck back out. He tiptoed to his bedroom and shut the door.

Liam clicked on his lamp, sat cross-legged on his bed, and opened the carved wooden box. He dug through gold earrings, Abuela's wedding band, a cross, and lastly a round pin with the St. Veronica's insignia. Liam held up both pins to the light. They were identical. Except, the clean pin was his grandmother's. The other one still had dirt caked in the crevices.

Liam brushed off some flecks of dirt. *So whose pin is this?*

He texted Autumn. I think I may have found something. He snapped a photo of the pin and hit send.

Liam put his phone and the pin on the nightstand and laid down for sleep with a burgeoning smile. He liked being the hero.

# CHAPTER TWENTY

The next evening, Liam poked his head into the lobby. Mr. Fletcher stood at the reception desk, talking to Autumn, who was pointing at places on a map of Key West.

"Are they gone?" Liam asked, before fully stepping inside.

Mr. Fletcher raised a brow, and shook his head. "You kids." He folded the map and slipped it into the pocket of his dinner jacket, the kind with suede patches on the elbows. Liam's father used to have a jacket like that. He wondered for a moment if Mr. Fletcher had children and then shook the image from his head.

"Enjoy your dinner," Autumn called to Mr. Fletcher as he left the lobby. The man nodded once before closing the door.

Timothy came around with candles. "Fletcher gone?"

Autumn nodded. "And Mrs. Paulson checked out this morning."

"Good riddance," he said. "We'll go out by the pool since that's where things, uh . . . began. Also, it seems to be a place of energy."

Autumn pulled open the patio door and ushered the boys outside like a doorman. "Right this way."

The anxiety that had settled in Liam's stomach now radiated throughout his whole body. He shook his fingers, hoping to rid himself of the nervous energy. This nightmare couldn't end fast enough.

Timothy pointed to a spot near the pool. Autumn spread out a flannel plaid blanket, the kind you might bring on a fall hayride or Christmas carriage ride. The three of them sat down, and for a moment, Liam enjoyed the blanket's softness on his skin, until he reminded himself of what they were there to do.

Timothy set the candles around the blanket, careful not to get them too close to the flannel. "No need to be set on fire," he joked, although his voice sounded strained.

Liam dug around his pockets for a lighter. It had been a few years since Pops gave up cigarettes, but Liam kept the lighter. He never knew when he might need it. Like now. Liam clicked the lighter, the small flame sprung to life, and lit the candles. On a stifling Key West night, there was little risk of a breeze blowing out the flames.

Once that was done, Timothy nodded as if to signal to everyone to buckle down. It was time to get serious. He sat cross-legged on the blanket and intertwined his fingers, which he positioned in his lap. Liam wasn't sure what he was expecting. Yoga maybe. Liam decided to do the same and mimicked Timothy's posture. Autumn sat on her knees. She looked at Liam briefly, but then turned her gaze on Timothy.

Timothy closed his eyes and exhaled deeply. "I'm finding my center." So, it was like yoga. Timothy held out his hand.

Liam fished into the back pocket of his shorts and thrust the St. Veronica's pin into it.

Again, Timothy took several deep breaths and called for Inez in a low voice.

The candlelight flickered. The cacophony of insects died down to a barely audible hum.

"Inez," Timothy said. "If you're here, please make your presence known. We would like to speak with you."

Timothy's voice grew deep and authoritative. Clearly, this séance was something he had done before. When and how often was he called upon to communicate with the dead?

"Inez," Timothy said sharply. "Can you communicate with us?"

Liam heard a crackling sound. A pale silhouette emerged over the pool, startling him. Goosebumps erupted along his flesh, and he shuddered in the hot, humid air.

"She's not coming," Katie said.

Timothy opened his eyes. He slumped a bit at the sight of the blonde ghost.

Autumn deflated. "What's going on?"

The skin around Katie's eyes appeared dark and hollow. Usually, Katie's colors were vibrant if only slightly transparent. But now her complexion seemed sallow and pale. "She's angry."

"Why won't she talk to us?" Timothy grasped the pin. "She has to—we have a connection."

Katie shook her head at the oval pin. "That's not hers. It can't be, or she'd be forced to come to the circle."

Autumn scrunched her nose. "Crap. She's screwing with us. She knows what she's doing."

"Don't be so sure," Katie said. "She's unstable and confused."

"I don't think she is. She knows what she wants."

Liam swallowed hard. "I'm afraid to ask what."

Autumn hugged her arms around herself. "Revenge."

"Lovely," Liam said, standing up. He dusted off his shorts. His grandparents managed to piss off Inez, and now she wanted to seek revenge against him. It would be just like the adults in his life to do something stupid that he had to fix.

Timothy crawled to the candles and blew them out one by one. He went to collect them, but the glass was too hot to touch. "I hate to be involved in this more than I have to be, but we need to stop her. She tried to kill lover boy three times, and she's doing something weird to Miss Katie."

Katie nodded in agreement. "Her energy is dark and zapping mine."

"And how do we stop her?" Liam asked, the anger seeping into his voice. He didn't mean to come across as anxious, but deep down, Liam was freaked. He couldn't quit and leave Autumn and her mom in the lurch. No one he knew would agree to work here. Plus, he felt uneasy about leaving Autumn alone in this place with the ghost. How could he assure himself she was safe if he couldn't see her every day?

"We keep trying," Autumn said, her voice firm. "We need to know more about what happened the night she disappeared. To do that, we need to start asking questions. I'll talk to Aunt Glenda again and Mr. Blazevig."

"I'll keep poking around the attic," Katie offered. Liam thought it was a nice gesture, considering Katie didn't have to help. But being dead had to be boring, and perhaps this was the most entertainment Katie had seen in years.

"I'll see what I can dig up in my mom's old books," Timothy said.

"And I'll . . ." Liam's voice trailed. He wanted to say, harass my Pops, but he still wasn't sure he could do it. Instead, he made a suggestion even less appealing. "Call my dad. He might know some things."

That seemed to satisfy Autumn and actually made Liam feel better. That is, until the candles exploded.

Glass shards exploded like shrapnel. Autumn ducked and covered her head with her hands. Luckily for all of them, the glass fragments sprayed the concrete patio, missing their legs.

"What the hell was that?" Liam cried out.

Timothy smoothed down his hair. "I guess miss ghost thang is not pleased."

Autumn surveyed the damage. "Next time we do this, she'll play nice. She won't have a choice."

Timothy let out a long sigh. It sounded to Autumn like he had been holding his breath for quite a while. "Maybe there shouldn't be a next time."

"What do you mean there shouldn't be a next time?" Autumn asked as she headed over to the toolshed. She needed a broom to sweep up the mess. "We all agreed to get to the bottom of this. Don't you want to know what happened to her?"

Liam pushed a giant glass shard with his sneaker and chimed in. "Not if it means pissing her off and getting hurt."

Autumn reached into the shed. The floodlights illuminated the cluttered mess inside. She grabbed the broom and closed the door. "She's already pissed off. But if we don't . . . what's the expression?" Autumn snapped her fingers.

"Kick her to the curb?" Timothy finished.

"Okay. If we don't kick her to the curb, she's likely to kill Liam and take down the Cayo with her."

"Maybe, I should just quit," Liam said, his voice barely a whisper.

"What? No." Autumn knew her mother was going to fire Liam after Fantasy Fest, but she wasn't willing to let go of him so soon. Besides, she had plans to convince her mother to let Liam work for the Cayo permanently. Autumn swept up the shards, until Timothy held out his hand. He nodded at the old clock on the patio wall. It was nearly seven. "I'll do that. Don't you have a ghost tour to lead?"

Mr. Blazevig. Shit. Autumn blew the bangs off her forehead. "This isn't over!" The last part she yelled into the evening air, hoping Inez would hear her warning. Then she turned to Liam. "Don't make any rash decisions just yet."

Liam kissed Autumn's forehead. "You neither. I'll walk you to Duval."

Autumn smiled and led the way out through the gate and into the street.

Early Friday morning, Evelyn barged into Autumn's room and shook her awake. Autumn draped her arm across her face and groaned. "Mom, it's barely light out."

Evelyn bounced on her daughter's bed. "I know, but we're expecting a full house today." Autumn slid her arm off her face and caught her mother's giddy look. Her eyes twinkled. "To think, this place up and running at full capacity. If we can just make the Cayo Hueso the best hotel they've ever been to, then I bet they'll tell their friends. It will certainly dilute those bad Vacation Rater reviews. And should help us secure a new business loan."

The sunlight streamed in through the gauzy curtains. Autumn sat up and yawned. "This is going to be a great ten days. You'll see."

Her mother patted her daughter's leg. "If things go well and the Cayo turns a profit, we can talk about college in the northeast."

Autumn didn't know what to say. Somehow, her mother insisting she go to college in Florida solved a problem she didn't want to face. Did she want to stay here for Liam or not? One thing was for sure, she was curious about Fantasy Fest.

Evelyn bounded to her feet. "Get showered and dressed. I need you to run down to the florist for a fresh bouquet for the lobby. And please sweep the patio. I swear those palm trees drop those massive leaves to annoy me." And just like that, the mother-daughter bonding moment was over as Evelyn submitted a list of chores for Autumn to do before breakfast.

Once Evelyn left, Katie appeared in Autumn's room. Autumn gave her a friendly smile. "Well at least she's happy." Autumn cocked her head to the side and examined the ghost's eyes. They weren't blue anymore. Instead, her irises were black orbs.

"You okay?" she asked Katie.

Katie blinked slowly. "Inez is sucking up my energy. Like a vacuum."

"Are you sure?"

"Yes." Katie could barely glide over. "Bad hotel reviews are the least of your mom's worries."

Autumn approached Katie, who hovered cautiously near the window. Katie put her hands up and squinted at the bright sunlight. "What do you mean?"

"Inez has plans," Katie said. "Big plans."

But before Autumn could ask what Katie meant, she disappeared. Autumn felt a rush of cold air caress her skin, and she shivered. Autumn whirled around in a circle. "Katie?" But she'd barely had time to ponder the situation when Evelyn called her down to work.

Ten minutes later, Autumn descended the stairs, her hair still damp from her speedy shower. Her mother greeted her with a paper list.

"What would I have done had you had school today?" Evelyn asked, shaking her head.

Autumn shrugged. For some reason, the charter school let everyone have the week of Fantasy Fest off, even though most, if not all the events were for the eighteen and over crowd, which was something Evelyn reminded Autumn of frequently.

"Remember," said Evelyn. "Check-in is typically at three, but I've agreed to let guests arrive early so that they may uh . . . partake in the festivities." She handed Autumn a dust rag. "Please dust the rooms, except for Mr. Fletcher's. Do his room after he leaves for the day."

"What's this?" came a male voice. Evelyn spun around and smiled. If Autumn didn't know better, she'd think her mom was blushing. Mr. Fletcher had appeared from the small dining room, carrying a newspaper under the crook of his arm and sipping a cup of Cora's freshly brewed coffee in an *I Heart NJ* mug.

"I was just telling Autumn to clean the April room after you left for the day." Evelyn smoothed down her hair.

"Oh, no need." Mr. Fletcher tucked the paper under his arm. "I wouldn't want her to miss out on the Goombay Festival."

The Bahama Village Goombay Festival was the kick-off event for Fantasy Fest located in the Bahama Village, off Duval and Petronia. From what the girls at school said, it was a fun street fair, and there wouldn't be much nudity. It was the nighttime festivities and barely clad revelers that would make Autumn blush.

Evelyn dismissed this with a wave of her hand. "Autumn's not going to that."

"What's this I hear about the Goombay Festival?" Aunt Glenda entered the lobby wearing a gauzy, coral dress and grasping a blue feather duster. "Evelyn dear, I do hope you won't work Autumn to the bone. She should go."

Evelyn's mouth hung open and she sputtered, "Ab-absolutely not. Fantasy Fest is ten days of . . . of . . ."

Autumn put her hands on her hips. "Ten days of what?"

"Debauchery," she said finally.

Mr. Fletcher held back a laugh, although unsuccessfully.

"Nonsense," Glenda said. "The Goombay Festival is the tamest of all the events during Fantasy Fest. At worst, all Autumn will see is a half-naked man."

Mr. Fletcher nearly choked on his sip of coffee.

Evelyn's voice grew shrill. "There will be thousands of people there. It isn't safe."

"Mom!" Autumn said, mortified.

"You can't keep her cooped up in the Cayo all ten days," Glenda said. "Let her go with Liam after everyone's settled."

Evelyn's eyebrows shot up. "I don't think that's a good idea."

"How about this?" said Mr. Fletcher. "I'll accompany Autumn and Liam to the festival later if that's all right with Evelyn."

"That would be nice. Thank you." Evelyn grinned at Mr. Fletcher. But then they heard the sound of glass shattering in the kitchen. "I better go see what that is." She darted away from the lobby.

Autumn accepted Mr. Fletcher's now-empty coffee mug. "You don't have to babysit me."

He set the newspaper inside a brown leather attaché case. The kind Autumn's father had once upon a time. "If anything you'll be babysitting me. I have no idea where this Goombay Festival even is. I figured I should see something of Fantasy Fest before I get too submerged in my research."

"What are you working on?" Autumn asked.

Mr. Fletcher shrugged. "I'll let you know when I dig up something interesting. Right now, it's just a lead. What time do you want to leave?"

"Liam is done with his shift around four o'clock. I'll ask him to come."

Mr. Fletcher nodded and tipped his hat, an old-fashioned gesture Autumn found charming. She now understood why her mother blushed.

# CHAPTER TWENTY-ONE

Liam walked alongside Autumn, his hands deep inside his pockets, and stared at the sidewalk. Mr. Fletcher flanked his other side, whistling with a file of papers tucked under his arm. It would've been such a casual walk had it all not felt like an awkward, chaperoned date.

Liam had not planned on going to the Goombay Festival after his shift. He'd attended so many times before, having come here when he was ten years old, dressed up as a zombie pirate, chasing the other boys from his school in and out of the tourists' legs.

A man wearing a pink rubber octopus on his head accidentally brushed up against Liam as they entered Bahama Village. He apologized and tipped his drink in Liam's direction.

Autumn rubbed her arms. "I feel so out of place." She wasn't wearing a costume, just a blue tank top and jean shorts.

Liam chuckled. "Truer words have never been spoken, Jersey girl."

Autumn didn't laugh, and Liam worried he had

offended her. "If I had known we'd be here, I would've dug around for a get-up. Usually Fantasy Fest is exhausting, so I don't go out until midweek."

"No big deal," Autumn said.

They passed red and white tents serving up tart lemonade. Liam inhaled the aromas of jerk chicken, fried fish, and conch fritters. His stomach grumbled, but he didn't have much cash. Liam moved aside for a member of the Junkanoo band, clad in bright blue and orange, wearing a tuba around his neck and torso. The music had always been Liam's favorite part of Goombay. At any given moment, he could hear calypso, reggae, and even 90s alternative in various parts of the festival.

A woman in a string bikini and blue body paint smiled as she sidled past Mr. Fletcher. He cleared his throat. "A tame event, huh?"

"This is nothing," Liam said. "Wait until later in the week where practically everyone is naked. Anyway, you come to Goombay for the music and the food. There's nothing like it anywhere else in the world."

"That may be, but this is where I leave you," Mr. Fletcher announced.

"Fantasy Fest not your scene?" Liam asked.

The man shook his head. "I'm forty-five years old, and I've just bumped shoulders with a thousand people in only sixty seconds. I'm going to find a quiet place to do research."

"Good luck," said Liam.

Mr. Fletcher gave him a pained nod and hunched his shoulders against the thick crowds.

"I don't really understand what he's doing in Key West during Fantasy Fest if he doesn't want to be in Key West during Fantasy Fest," Liam said.

Autumn stared after the man. "He said something about his editor forcing him here. I guess he should've researched Key West a little better before booking his trip in October."

"Well said." Liam thought about the conversation he and Pops had last night.

"Tell me the truth, kiddo," Pops had said in between sips of beer. "Do you like Glenda's niece?"

Liam didn't answer him right away. Instead, and without meaning to, he grinned like an idiot.

Pops scoffed. "That goofy smile tells me everything."

Liam poured a glass of orange juice and grabbed a box of chocolate puffs from atop the refrigerator. He plunked it down on the kitchen table and rooted inside for a handful of cereal. Before popping some in his mouth he said, "Yeah, but what does it matter? She's going back to New Jersey for college. Plus her mother hates me."

Pops dismissed this comment with a wave and a big belch. "Eh. All mothers hate their daughters' boyfriends. It's a rule. Your abuela didn't like your mother very much when she first met her."

Liam crunched on his cereal, but it tasted like dust. Pops rarely spoke about his mother or grandmother.

"She said your mother acted like a hussy who would break your father's heart. Man, was she right. Abuela was being protective. Just like Autumn's mother."

Liam swallowed his breakfast and washed it down with a sip of juice. "Yeah, well, Autumn isn't my girlfriend."

"How do you know? Did you ask her?"

Liam dropped a handful of puffs in a bowl. "Guys don't just ask girls to be their girlfriends." Liam thought about how he and Victoria started dating. They had one English class together before Victoria invited him to a party at her mansion. He drank a little, and then before he knew it, they were making out in the pool. Monday morning before the first bell, Victoria had linked her arm through Liam's and introduced him to her clique as her boyfriend. There had never been any discussion. He probably would've never agreed to the relationship. But that was how he became Victoria Canton's property. Thinking about it, he would've liked to have been asked.

As he strolled around the Goombay Festival with Autumn at his side, Liam really appreciated how slow and organic their whatever-it-was-called relationship was evolving. It felt natural. And that's how Liam liked things to be.

The Junkanoo gathered in formation as they prepared to parade down the street. A band member slid his trombone while another pounded furiously on his drums. Liam tapped his foot to the music. "You're not in a rush to go home, are you?" he asked Autumn.

Autumn turned to him and gave him a wicked grin. "Not at all. What did you have in mind?"

Liam scratched his head in such a way that Autumn suspected that he had no idea where to go next. "Do you want to hear music at the main stage on Emma Street?" He practically yelled to be heard above the din.

"You want to just walk to the water?" Autumn's voice rose to match his. She winced, wondering if it was a lame suggestion. She wanted to experience Fantasy Fest, not bow out like Mr. Fletcher, but she didn't want to compete with loud music for Liam's attention.

Fortunately, Liam smiled and they walked to the Southernmost Point. Tourists jammed around the large black, red, and yellow buoy and snapped photos.

"So what do you think of Fantasy Fest so far?" Liam asked.

Autumn shrugged. "Not quite as raunchy as I had thought."

He grinned. "You ain't seen nothing yet."

Autumn blushed and looked around. A tall blonde, dressed in a mermaid costume with a tiara, entered the cafe on the other side of the street. Autumn tilted her chin up at the cafe nearby and saw a banner that read, "Raise money for AIDS research."

"Where's happening here?"

Liam leaned in to Autumn. "It's the coronation of the king and queen of Fantasy Fest. Every year they raise money for AIDS research."

A muscular man in nothing but a white speedo smiled at Autumn before grazing past her and heading into the cafe. "Let's go in."

Liam spread his arms wide. "After you."

Autumn's eyes widened. The "cafe" was a cafe in name only. It was a gorgeous open-air restaurant that sat right on the beach. It was also packed.

"You want something to drink?" Liam asked.

"Just a soda," Autumn said.

"You got it. Wait here."

Autumn decided to push through the throng of people and head toward the back of the cafe and watch the waves break on the sand. She remembered summer vacations at Long Beach Island down the Jersey Shore, before her parents' business hit hard times. Her folks would rent a beach house for a week, and she and her father would boogie board on the surf. Her mom would pack half a dozen books to read in her beach chair. They'd spend hours in the water and then at night they'd grab a table at the nearest seafood restaurant. It was her favorite part of summer. And as she stared at the warm Florida waters lapping at the sand, she wondered why she hadn't appreciated this more until now.

A shrill voice rang out. "Oh my God, what are you doing here? I didn't think you ever left the haunted hotel." A laugh followed.

Autumn whipped her heard around. Victoria stood with her hands on her hips. Her ocean blue strapless dress barely covered her boobs.

Autumn's insides churned. Just as she was enjoying the ocean, the sight of Victoria ruined it.

"Jeez, Victoria. It's a free country." Autumn felt childish using that old comeback, but it did seem fitting in this case. "Do I go around asking why you're wherever you are?"

Victoria played with a diamond necklace that draped her swanlike neck. "That's the difference between us. I belong here and you don't."

Although Autumn wouldn't utter it aloud, this time, she felt Victoria was right.

Just when Autumn considered shoving Victoria into the ocean, Liam showed up holding two sweaty glasses filled with a bubbling soft drink. Autumn snatched the glass out of his hand and chugged the sweet liquid. It felt cool going down, but the carbonation burned her throat. She put the glass down on a bar ledge and wiped her mouth with the back of her hand. Classy, but she didn't care.

Victoria stood gaping at Liam. "You came here together?" Her voice hit a high-note that sounded like nails on a chalkboard. Even Liam flinched.

"Vicky? Why are you here?"

Victoria's eyes flamed. "It's my sister's coronation. She's the Queen of Fantasy Fest. She raised the most money for AIDS research."

"Good for her." He caught Autumn's eye. "Well, we're gonna go."

Victoria blocked Liam's exit. "At my party, I thought you guys came as friends. But are you guys, like, *together*?"

Autumn didn't know how to respond. She wasn't

sure what she and Liam were. They were friends, that she was positive about, but they also kissed. Autumn's last relationship had progressed similarly. They were friends first and they went to the movies a bunch of times with a group. But while she assumed they were dating, the boy didn't. Which she found out when their junior prom was announced and he had asked another girl.

"Uh," was all Autumn could muster.

Liam stared at Autumn, and for a moment, Autumn felt like everything had quieted down. He said in a low voice, "What do you think? Would you like to be my girlfriend?"

Heat rushed to Autumn's cheeks. She didn't even steal a glance at Victoria to see how she was taking it. Autumn beamed. "I'd love to." Liam held out his hand and she clasped his fingers. Together they sidled past Victoria and into the Key West evening.

Liam didn't want to say goodnight to Autumn, but he also couldn't wait to go home and tell Pops that she agreed to be his girlfriend.

Evening rolled upon them. The sun had set below the horizon without Liam even noticing. At some point, and with his last five dollars, Liam stopped to buy Autumn ice cream, and they meandered slowly toward the Cayo. The streets were no less crowded, but the tourists were heading toward Duval while he and Autumn walked away from it.

Autumn seemed entranced with her soft-serve cone. As he watched her tongue dance around the chocolate and scoop the sprinkles into her mouth, he found himself desperate to kiss her. But then she stopped and got a faraway look in her eyes.

"You didn't ask me to be your girlfriend to make Victoria jealous, did you?"

"No." He leaned against a white picket fence that bordered the front of a light pink Victorian. "Do you know why I asked you to be my girlfriend?"

"Cuz you like me?" Autumn teased.

"Yes." He laughed. "And because once upon a time, Victoria announced to everyone that I was her boyfriend. Like she owned me or bought me at some department store. She never asked me to be her boyfriend."

"So you asked me to be polite?"

"I asked you because I like you. A lot. Asking in front of Victoria was just extra fun." He grinned broadly

Autumn licked her ice cream. "She makes school a living hell for me."

"Don't let her. No one should have that much power over you." Even as the words left his mouth, he knew he was a hypocrite. He let people have power over him. Victoria, for starters. His dad. Pops, sometimes. Hell, even Mick Canton.

"Did you ever talk to your Dad about Inez?" Autumn asked, as if she was reading his mind.

Liam sighed. "Talking to my dad is . . . difficult. He's in rehab." They stopped in front of the Cayo. All the guests must had gone out for the night, except for Mr. Fletcher, whose room was illuminated from the street. "That's what I didn't want to tell you before. My dad is a drunk. He crashed a truck into a tree and almost killed himself. I had to check him into rehab, or he'd be in jail right now."

Autumn squeezed his hand. "I'm sorry about your dad, but I'm glad you told me."

"I'm glad I told you too. I'll try calling him. He might know something about Inez."

She offered him a reassuring smile. "We'll get down to the bottom of this."

Liam smiled too. "I like how you say 'we.'"

"Well, I don't want Inez hurting my man, now do I?" Her grin broadened.

Liam laughed and then came in close. "I'd like to kiss you now."

Autumn giggled. "Are you asking to be polite?"

"I'm not asking." Liam's heart pounded as he tipped his head down and kissed Autumn on the mouth. She leaned against him and he slipped his hands into her hair. Unfortunately, the moment was disrupted by a blood-curling scream.

"Crap." Autumn pulled away from Liam. "Did that come from the Cayo?"

Liam put a protective arm around Autumn, which warmed her despite the chilling scream. "I think it did."

"Inez!" Autumn cried and she sprinted down the path and into the Cayo, Liam right on her heels.

Autumn flung open the door and hurried into the lobby. Glenda rested against the reception desk, fanning herself with a brochure for a booze cruise.

Timothy stood beside her, urging her to take a sip of water.

"What the hell is going on?" Autumn's panic rose despite Timothy's obviously bemused expression.

"A chicken exploded," he said matter-of-factly.

Autumn blinked in rapid succession, trying to register his words. "I'm sorry, what did you say?"

Timothy put his hands on his hips. "I said, a chicken exploded."

"Like in the oven?"

Timothy pointed to the patio. Autumn and Liam both turned their gaze outside. But Autumn didn't need clarification when she spotted a red, bloody glob on the patio door glass.

She swallowed hard. "I better go outside."

"I'm coming with you," Liam said.

Autumn opened the sliding door, careful not to further disturb the bloody mass on the glass. She got a whiff of an odor, which she could only assume was raw chicken meat, and decided to breathe through her mouth.

Evelyn was sitting in one of the plastic patio chairs, her face drained of color. Red splotches covered her white Capri pants, like a Jackson Pollack painting. Mr. Fletcher rested his hand on her shoulder, but he removed it once he saw Autumn. Cora, in her blue floral dress with black braids coiled up on her head like a turban, hovered near her mother. It was odd for Autumn to see Cora outside of the kitchen. Even more odd that she was waving a small purple stone all over the patio.

"Mom, are you okay?"

Evelyn's voice came out in a hoarse whisper. "I only came outside to shoo away the chicken. It got into the yard through the hole in the fence, and I didn't want it getting into the pool. I was afraid of something happening to it. I took the broom from the shed and tried to coax it back over." Her voice was on the edge of a sob, and Autumn bent down to squeeze her mom's shoulders. "The poor thing exploded. I don't know how that happened."

Mr. Fletcher cleared his throat. "I've never heard of anything like this."

"It's that evil spirit." Cora brandished her amulet over the concrete.

Evelyn put her face in her hands. "We're ruined. When the guests come back, they're going to see this and flee. I tried calling the police, but they're too busy with Fantasy Fest to investigate a report about an exploding chicken." She began to laugh hysterically.

"Mom, go inside and get cleaned up." Autumn surveyed the patio. "Liam and I will hose everything down. The guests are all gone. They're here to party and drink. I doubt they'll realize what happened. We'll get bleach and no one will know."

"I'll help," said Mr. Fletcher.

Evelyn stood on shaky legs. "Oh no. We can't have you do that. You're a guest."

"It's the least I can do for all the hospitality you've shown me. Go to your room and rest. You've been traumatized."

Evelyn, her face still pale, sputtered.

"I insist," Mr. Fletcher said.

Autumn escorted her mother to the lobby. Aunt Glenda and Timothy left, presumably to the kitchen for tea to calm Glenda's nerves. "I'm going to get plastic bags and gloves and bleach. You go to bed."

Evelyn nodded. "Thank you, Autumn. You're a good girl. I'm sorry I gave you such a hard time about Goombay."

"That's okay," Autumn said.

"But, just to be safe, I'd really like it if you stayed here for the remainder of Fantasy Fest. Just until things get back to normal. Such a freak accident."

But Autumn knew it had not been an accident. It had been Inez. The appearance of Katie in the lobby confirmed it.

"She's evil." Katie's eyes were dark hollows. "Tonight a chicken. Tomorrow, a person."

Autumn gave Katie a not-now nod even as goosebumps erupted along her flesh. "Sure, Mom," Autumn said. "I'll be here for you."

Evelyn smiled weakly and retreated upstairs to her room. But Autumn knew the safest place in Key West was anywhere but the Cayo Hueso Dead and Breakfast.

# CHAPTER TWENTY-TWO

The following morning, Liam rested against his scooter in the parking lot of the Cuban Coffee Queen while he sipped his latte. He and Autumn had been up late scrubbing chicken guts off the patio. It had been a gory, gross mess, and Liam was pretty certain he wouldn't be eating poultry for a long time.

Liam caught a few hours of sleep only to be woken up by the buzzing of his cell phone—a text from Randall asking him to meet him on the corner of Thompson and South Street. He got up, showered, and threw on cargo shorts and a blue shirt, a gift from Victoria, who said the blue brought out the turquoise in his eyes, and stopped for coffee.

He sipped his coffee, which only heightened his nervousness. Usually, the warm liquid, even on a hot morning, relaxed him—but not today. He finished the beverage and tossed the empty cup into the trash. Then he hopped on his scooter and sped down Margaret Street, dodging lively tourists, to meet Randall at his cousin's house.

Liam pulled up in front of a one-story white bungalow with green trim and dismounted from his bike. He carried his helmet under his arm. He'd never been to Keith's house before and proceeded with caution until Randall appeared from around the corner and waved Liam around back.

Liam followed Randall into a small rocky area.

"I figured you'd be up when I buzzed," Randall said, his voice almost a slur.

"I wasn't up. Have you been drinking?" Liam's face colored when he realized how judgmental he sounded. "Forget I asked."

"Nah, it's cool." Randall removed a key from the pocket of his ratty board shorts. "I was partying on Keith's boat last night. I guess I still haven't sobered up."

Liam scanned the yard. Both he and Randall stood in front of a white outbuilding, only slightly smaller than Randall's trailer. The outbuilding was painted white, to match the house Liam presumed, but the wooden slats were unevenly spaced. Only one window, no bigger than a placemat, had Plexiglas and shimmered in the morning light. Next to the building, Liam spied a broken kitchen chair, a wire trellis, and random cardboard boxes. "So, this is Keith's house?"

"Yup. He owns it, free and clear," said Randall.

Liam never understood why men like Keith and Randall's granddad would hold on to valuable Key West property rather than sell it, especially since they all needed the money. Then again, Key West was home, and if you could live here, why wouldn't you?

Randall opened the shed's rickety door. He glanced around the yard and then beckoned for Liam to follow him.

Liam swallowed a lump in his throat. After the incident at the Cayo, Liam was wary of sheds in general, but he pushed aside his fear and followed Randall inside.

Liam immediately tried to cut through the humidity with his hand. "Dude, you should take off that Plexiglas."

"No way, man," said Randall. "I don't want to risk anyone snooping and stealing these bad boys."

Liam scanned the row of scooters. Somehow, Randall and Keith managed to stuff fifteen bikes inside the narrow space. "So, this is our fleet?"

"This is our fleet," Randall said proudly.

Liam crouched to inspect one of the bikes. He ran his finger over scratches in the paint and checked out another bike. More scratches. Each bike had a one-inch square space where the paint was faded. As if some plate had been removed.

"Don't worry. Keith has a buddy who works at a body shop. He's going to sand down the dents and repaint the bikes all the same color. This way, they look like they belong to our shop."

Liam wanted to ask more about how the bikes got the scratches, but Randall pulled color swatches from his pocket.

"These were the two I liked best."

Liam frowned. This was supposed to be a partnership, but he was being presented with only two color options. One blue and one orange. Liam's annoyance crept in.

"I'm partial to Midnight Blue myself." Randall tapped the little card stock. "But I'll defer to you, dude."

Liam read the name on the orange swatch and made a decision. "I like Autumn Afternoon best."

Randall playfully elbowed Liam in the arm. "I figured you would." Randall took the color swatches back and slid them in his pocket. He ushered Liam out of the sweltering hot box and closed the door, making sure to secure the lock with a key.

"Listen, I'm going to need five hundred dollars from you for the paint job," Randall said.

Liam balked. "I don't have five hundred of anything. I gave you all my money."

Randall sighed. "Dude, this whole business idea was yours, and you have no cash to bankroll it? Keith's already put up double his share."

"Sorry, *dude*. I'm trying as best I can. I sold a piece of my grandmother's jewelry to get this started. I can see about picking up a second job."

Randall rested his hand on Liam's shoulder, but Liam shook him off.

"Don't be like that. We're buds. Amigos."

"I'll figure it out." Liam made his way toward the street where his scooter was parked.

"Please do, bro," Randall called out. "I'd hate to see you pushed out."

That same morning, Autumn rolled over in bed and smiled. At one point, she'd had a delicious dream that she could not remember, but she thought Liam was in it. She wiped sweat from her chest and noticed the familiar hum of the air conditioner was silent.

Katie popped in, interrupting Autumn's good mood. Autumn squinted at the ghost, who was hardly visible in the bright sunlight streaming through the windows.

"I can barely see you," Autumn said.

"I barely feel like I'm here," Katie whispered.

"What time is it?"

"Not even eight. Your mother is already downstairs, waiting for you."

"Of course she is. God, it's Saturday. And I spent all of last night hosing chicken guts off the concrete. You'd think I could get some rest." Autumn stretched and went over to the air conditioner. She smacked it several times. "Stupid machine. Today of all days." Autumn felt clammy and damp in her pajamas. "I'm going to shower. Then I'll report for duty." She gave Katie a mock salute, but Katie said nothing. *Poor girl. She used to think that was funny.* Before she could chastise the ghost for her loss of humor, Katie had disappeared.

Autumn entered the bathroom. The cool tiles soothed her bare feet. She twisted the showerhead. Usually, it took a few minutes for the old pipes to deliver hot water to the attic space. Autumn put her hand under the water to gauge the temperature. She yelped. The water was scalding. Autumn fussed with the faucet, trying to lower the temperature. But even on the coldest setting, the water did not cool. Steam filled the bathroom and fogged up the mirrors.

Autumn wrapped her hand in the plastic shower curtain to turn off the scalding water. When she turned around, there were words written in the steamy mirror. *Come and get me.*

Autumn steeled her eyes. "I will. Don't you worry."

Autumn hustled downstairs in a pair of terry cloth shorts and a peach tank top. Her mother would not approve, but without a shower, she didn't see the need to put on anything nice. She halted when she saw a middle-aged and slightly overweight couple, coated head to toe in blue body paint and not much else. Correction, they had strategically placed leaves covering their private parts. *There goes my appetite.*

Evelyn faced the couple, her features a mask of control. "I'm terribly sorry. I'll get on the phone to the plumber as soon as we're done."

The man shook his head. "I think I could settle for cold water, but that water temperature is likely to scald someone. They'll have a good mind to sue."

"What room are you in Mr. . . . ?" Evelyn asked.

"Mr. Emerson. And it's the July room. I have to wash off this blue paint. It's getting itchy." He scratched his butt cheek.

"Of course." Evelyn whispered to Autumn, "Please notify the guests that we are fixing this right away."

Autumn wanted to protest, but one look from her mother, and she was running back upstairs. She knocked on the door to the February room. A man in a goatee opened it. He scratched his hairy chest and smiled at Autumn a bit too friendly. "Aren't you a nice wake-up call?"

Autumn stepped back. "I'm sorry to disturb you, but we're having problems with the water. My mom has called the plumber."

The man grinned. Autumn suspected he was still drunk. She peeked around him and saw a naked woman in his bed. Autumn wasn't positive, but she thought the woman was wearing fish scales. "No worries. Wake me before dark." He closed the door in Autumn's face.

Autumn woke up most of the guests. And most of them appeared to be intoxicated.

Last, she knocked on Mr. Fletcher's door. As expected, he was dressed, but he still hadn't shaved. "Everything okay?"

After seeing practically a dozen naked bodies, Autumn felt relieved the man was in clothes. "There's a problem with the water. It's boiling. Mom's on the phone with the plumber, but I just came to warn you."

"I showered just a minute ago."

"You did? And your skin isn't peeling off?"

He chuckled. "No. My water wasn't hot. It was cold. And pretty refreshing."

"Well that's odd. Everyone else has scalding water."

Mr. Fletcher shrugged. "Maybe the plumber will be able to figure it out."

"Maybe." But Autumn wasn't convinced.

After an emergency weekend visit, which cost Evelyn $125 an hour, hour-and-a-half minimum, the plumber concluded someone turned the hot water heater up as high as it could go. As for Mr. Fletcher's cold water, the plumber just scratched his head and said he couldn't understand how that happened.

Liam parked his scooter outside the Cayo. But before he could take off his helmet, Autumn came running out to greet him.

He smiled, but his smile dropped once he saw Autumn's exhausted expression and limp hair.

"What's the matter? Everything okay?"

Autumn exhaled. "Mom said to tell you not to come in today. She had to pay a plumber and she can't afford to pay you too. I meant to text you, but I was running around."

Liam slouched a bit. "Okay." It wasn't what he wanted to hear. "What about later this week?"

Autumn nodded. "She said Tuesday."

Tuesday was several days away. It sucked not to see Autumn for that long. "I wanted to talk to you about your birthday?"

"What about it?"

"I'd like to take you out," he said. "To celebrate."

"It's a week away. Hopefully, things will calm down by then." Autumn bit her lip and looked back at the Cayo. "I gotta go around the corner to the hardware store and pick up putty. The plumber ran out."

"I'll get it for you," he said, hoping to prolong their time together.

"It's fine. I'll do it. If you do it, then my mom will feel like you're working, and she'll consider you on the clock. And . . ."

"I get it. No worries." His face softened. "We'll talk later."

Autumn nodded, and Liam watched her run around the corner. He waited a few moments before he turned the key in the ignition and sped toward Duval.

With an unexpected day off and his stomach growling, Liam drove to Caroline Street for mahi tacos from the food truck. While waiting in line behind a woman wearing robot body paint, Liam heard a familiar voice call his name. How was it possible in a sea of thousands of costumed tourists, she always managed to find him?

Liam slowly turned around and let out an annoyed breath. "Victoria."

She flicked a strand of blonde hair over her shoulder and smoothed down her red sequined bikini top. She wore a less revealing skirt with it. "I always thought you avoided Fantasy Fest, but I've seen you twice now."

"I was hungry," said Liam as if that were reason enough. "And I thought you'd be on Sunset Key avoiding the crowds like you do every year."

"Grandma organized a diamond necklace raffle for charity at the Southernmost Beach Cafe later in the week. She's meeting her auxiliary ladies to finalize details."

"That's cool she volunteers for stuff like that." Liam meant what he said. He'd always liked Victoria's grandmother.

Victoria shrugged. "She's nice like that."

"You could be nice like that."

Vicky adjusted the sunglasses on her head. "You mean I could be nice to Autumn?"

"For starters."

Victoria laughed. "I'm not going to invest the time in being Autumn's friend and neither should you."

Liam moved up in line. All he wanted was to get his tacos and find a quiet place to eat. But Victoria didn't seem to get the hint.

"Seriously, Liam. Autumn does nothing but talk about New Jersey. You should hear her in class. Whenever college plans come up, it's about Rutgers. Or Seton Hall. Or Montclair. She has no plans to stick around the Keys after graduation. Which means she has no plans to stick around you."

"Harsh, Vicky."

"It's the truth. I should know. I had to listen to that from you."

He raised his brows.

"Oh, don't you remember? For months, you talked of nothing but meeting your dad in North Dakota. What? Thinking my feelings wouldn't be hurt? I wasn't special enough for you to stick around. What makes you so sure you're special enough for miss east coast to give up her plans for you?"

Liam never thought about how he hurt Vicky's feelings when he took off. She was always surrounded by friends, not to mention enormous wealth. Up until now, he wasn't even sure she had feelings. Like she was a vampire with no heart.

"Whatever, Vic. You're just saying this shit because you don't want to see me happy."

Victoria's chin wobbled slightly and for the briefest of moments, Liam worried she was on the verge of tears. Instead, she cleared her throat and said, "You're wrong. I don't want to see you *unhappy*. Because when someone you love leaves you, it sucks." She put on her sunglasses.

Bernadette Canton emerged from the cafe, dressed in a linen suit, and clasped her granddaughter's hand. "There you are! I approved the table settings and the necklace is stunning."

"Nice to see you again, Mrs. Canton," Liam said politely.

Bernadette smiled, pulling the skin taut across her face. "Likewise, William." Bernadette, like Glenda, always used his full name.

Victoria reached out to Liam and touched his arm. "The charter school is having a winter formal in a few weeks. Are you going to go?"

Liam knitted his brows.

"Oh, you didn't know? Autumn didn't ask you?" A smile played on her lips.

"To be honest, I haven't thought that far ahead," said Liam.

"Well, you have to come. Everyone loves a dance."

Bernadette shifted her weight off her bad leg. "Not everyone, Victoria." She nodded toward the street.

"Come, dear. Finn is waiting for us around the corner. I still have a few more errands to run."

Victoria nodded and pivoted on her heels. "Enjoy your tacos."

Liam watched her go with a heaviness in his chest. Perhaps with everything going on with the Cayo, Autumn forgot to mention the school dance. *Maybe she doesn't want to go. Or maybe she doesn't want to go with me.*

Liam approached the food truck and placed his order.

"Were those the Cantons?" said the guy behind the window as he handed Liam a cardboard bowl and several napkins.

"Yup," said Liam, his voice practically a sigh.

The guy whistled. "Those are some powerful people. Untouchable."

Liam glanced behind him, still expecting to see Victoria and Bernadette Canton waltzing like royalty among their Key West subjects, but they were long gone. *Untouchable? Were they really? Was anyone?*

# CHAPTER TWENTY-THREE

That night, Autumn flopped on the bed and buried her sweaty face in the floral bedspread.

"Tough day?" Katie asked, her voice raspy.

Autumn rolled over on to her side to look at the ghost. "Well, after the whole boiling lava water fiasco this morning, Mom discovered that the fridge had been unplugged. The cheese, milk, and who knows what else went rancid. I had to drive to the supermarket to restock only to come home and find Mom scrubbing the floor. Apparently a guest had puked. That last one I'm pretty sure had nothing to do with Inez."

"But the other things?" Katie asked.

"Definitely her."

"How's your mom doing?"

Autumn raised her brow. It was unusual for Katie to show compassion for Evelyn, or Glenda, for that matter. Evelyn pretended ghosts didn't exist, which insulted Katie. Glenda knew about Katie, but used her like a sideshow in a carnival, which also insulted Katie.

"She's at the end of her rope. We finally have a packed house, and everything is going wrong."

Katie floated over to Autumn, her form fading fast in the dark room. "I need you to hurry up and banish Inez. She's getting more and more out of control. I'm afraid."

Autumn sat up in her bed and hugged her knees. The last thing she would want would be for Inez to stay here, causing havoc, and for Katie to disappear. Where would Katie even go?

"You don't want to know," Katie said, reading her mind. "Inez can push me into a dark place. It's not like seeing the light. It's the opposite. I don't want to get sucked in there."

The pit in Autumn's stomach grew. She was supposed to be solving Inez's murder and pursuing the scholarship, but she'd been having too much fun with Liam, not to mention helping her mother run the Cayo, to make a dent in the investigative work. Autumn's scholarship deadline wasn't until December. But Katie's deadline just got moved up.

The problem was, something inside Autumn kept her from moving ahead. If a bit of Inez was still inside Autumn, then why wouldn't Inez want Autumn to uncover her killer? Didn't she want justice?

Autumn needed to focus. "How do we banish Inez?"

"You need to remove her hold on the physical world."

"By uncovering her killer?"

"As a start. I don't know. Maybe."

Autumn got up from the bed and paced the room. She went over to the air conditioner unit and turned it on. It blared to life, blowing cold air. Finally, she could think. Except her head felt crowded, like there was too much information crammed in there. Or too many people. She turned to Katie, her eyes narrowing. "And if I don't solve her murder?"

"If you don't, this won't end well."

"For who?" asked Autumn in a slight Cuban accent.

Katie's lip trembled and she retreated. "Autumn, come back."

Autumn shook her head, trying to clear out the junk clouding her thoughts. "I'm sorry, Katie. Where was I?"

But Katie had already disappeared.

That following Tuesday, Liam and Autumn hopped off Liam's bike as they arrived at the salt ponds to deliver cash to Randall. Liam should have never said anything, but when he mentioned to Autumn that he needed 500 dollars to cover more business expenses, Autumn didn't hesitate to open up her sock drawer and hand him a wad of bills.

"I can't take this," he had told her. "You need it more than I do."

Autumn pressed the money into his hand. "You'll pay me back. I know you will."

"Of course I'll pay you back. As soon as the scooter shop is up and running, I'll reimburse you nine hundred dollars."

Autumn laughed. "I think that's high interest."

They had approached the plot of land where Liam and Randall planned to set up shop only to find a bulldozer ramming into the shack. The little building crumbled. The wood splintered into toothpicks.

Liam's stomach dropped to his knees. He ran over to the construction worker, waving his hands above his head.

"Liam, wait!" Autumn called to him.

But Liam was an unstoppable force. This was Randall's property, and there was no way Randall would bulldoze the shack. They couldn't afford to construct something better.

"Stop!" Liam called out. The bulldozer reversed on its caterpillar tracks. The worker, having spotted Liam, lowered the bucket. He shut down the machine.

"What's the matter, kid?"

"What are you doing? You're destroying the property."

"I'm supposed to, kid. The owner wants it cleaned up."

"Randall Bell?" Liam asked.

"No, Canton Corp. They own this now." He put on his headphones and turned on the machine. It roared to life. Liam jumped back just in time.

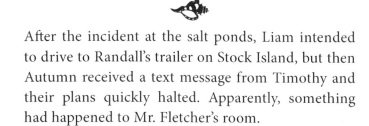

After the incident at the salt ponds, Liam intended to drive to Randall's trailer on Stock Island, but then Autumn received a text message from Timothy and their plans quickly halted. Apparently, something had happened to Mr. Fletcher's room.

"Can you drive me back?" Autumn asked.

Liam exhaled and mumbled, "I'm gonna throttle Randall when I see him."

Autumn kissed Liam's cheek. "Let's get back to the Cayo and deal with one problem at a time." Lately, there seemed to be a whole lot of problems.

Autumn walked inside the Cayo's lobby with Liam close behind her. She felt his light fingertips on the hem of her shirt, and it gave her chills.

Mr. Fletcher stood at the reception desk, waving frantically and talking in a hushed whisper.

"Is everything okay?" she asked.

Mr. Fletcher gave an imperceptible nod. "I don't want to alarm your mother, but someone was in my room."

"Someone who?" Autumn's voice rose an octave. Mr. Fletcher motioned for her to lower her voice and peered into the back office.

"Like a guest?" she whispered.

Mr. Fletcher bit his lip. "Maybe. But I had locked the room. I made sure of it."

Autumn clutched her chest, a gesture that was a little more dramatic than she intended. "You don't think it was a Cayo employee, do you?"

"Well, not an employee exactly," he said, rather vaguely. He motioned through the empty space around him.

Timothy's eyebrows shot up. "Mr. Fletcher, are you a believer?"

The man tapped his stubbly chin. "I think you all better come to my room. Just don't tell your mother." Autumn nodded quietly and put a finger to her lips.

Mr. Fletcher hurried upstairs and Autumn, Liam, and Timothy followed.

Mr. Fletcher put his hand on the doorknob and turned it slowly. When he opened the door, Autumn stifled a gasp. His stuff had been thrown all over the place. The dresser drawers were open, clothes scattered like a bomb had gone off. The papers on his desk were tossed about the room as if a gale force wind had swirled them around in a funnel cloud. Even the sheets and bedspread had been thrown off.

"Should we call the police?" Liam asked.

Timothy's brow shot up. "And say what? That we suspect a ghost vandalized a guest's room?"

"Good point," said Liam.

"Your mother has been under a lot of stress," Mr. Fletcher said. "I really don't want her to know about this. But I felt I had to tell someone."

Liam looked thoughtful for a moment. "Between the frigid water and the vandalism, seems Inez really has it out for you too." He smiled weakly. "Guess I'm not alone. But why you?"

Autumn scooped up the papers that had fallen to the floor. Immediately, Autumn noticed photocopies of Canton Corp's holdings, newspaper clippings about Mick Canton, and maps of his properties. She rose slowly. "You're researching Mick Canton?"

Mr. Fletcher puffed out his cheeks like he was holding his breath. "My editor in Tampa wants me to write a profile on him."

Liam bent down and picked up notes. He read the man's chicken scratch and furrowed his brow before handing Mr. Fletcher the papers.

"It's not a coincidence you're a guest here, is it Mr. Fletcher?" Autumn asked.

"To be fair, my editor suggested I stay here. But he must've known the connections your uncle had to Mick Canton."

Liam checked the time on his phone. "I have to go."

"Now?" asked Autumn.

Liam nodded. "I need to meet Randall."

Autumn slumped her shoulders. "Okay. I'll call you."

Liam's eyes hardened for a second before he kissed Autumn on the cheek. "We'll talk." He sidled past Mr. Fletcher and left the room.

Timothy glanced around. "I'd stay and help you tidy up, but my mama needs me in the kitchen. Let's just hope Inez was messing with you for fun." Timothy followed Liam outside.

Mr. Fletcher waited a beat and swallowed. "What do you think your ghost is trying to tell me?"

"You never saw her?" Autumn pointed to her cheek. "A brunette with a mole below her eye?"

He shook his head.

Autumn explained all that she had uncovered about Inez. "She likes to play games, and she doesn't seem to want anyone's help. So the question is, what was she doing?"

Their eyes moved to the antique rug. A headshot of Mick Canton stared back at them.

"Huh," Mr. Fletcher said.

"Huh is right," said Autumn.

Liam pounded on Randall's door. "Open up, dude. I know you're in there."

Liam waited a beat and then knocked again. Silence. He knew Randall was home. Whenever Randall had a setback, be it something small like when he and Liam lost the division playoffs in Little League, or big like when Randall's dad died back in junior high, Randall would hole himself up in his grandpa's trailer and play video games until his eyes blurred.

Liam peered into the grimy window. Sure enough, Randall, still in his boxer shorts, was chugging a beer and pressing furiously on the game controller.

"Just come in, dude," Randall called from the couch. "The door's not locked."

Liam stepped inside the trailer. The place smelled like an ashtray because Randall's grandfather smoked two packs a day. That was one of the reasons he and Randall were such good friends. They were the only boys in their kindergarten class whose grandfathers dropped them off at the classroom door. Randall's dad had been a good man, but he'd worked a lot of overtime at an auto body shop on Islamorada, leaving Randall in his grandfather's care. Pops always said Fred Bell was a worse drunk than him, and that said a lot.

Without taking his eyes off the screen, Randall swiped some empty candy wrappers from the couch. "Sit, dude."

"Okay." Liam wiped crumbs off the worn, beige cushions and sat down. "You going to tell me what's going on?"

Randall took a swig of beer. "Nothing to really say. Granddad up and sold my inheritance to Canton Corp without telling me."

Liam felt the air get sucked out of the room. "Dude, why?"

Randall shrugged before his thumbs tapped feverishly on the controller. "He sold the land that he promised me, and then he took off to Sarasota with the money to live with his girlfriend. I get to keep the trailer, so there's that."

Liam fell back into the cushions. "Jesus."

"Yeah. The old jerk said that property was my inheritance. His exact words were, 'I've never given you anything good, but at least I can give you that.' And then he freakin' sold it." Randall laughed, but it was a hollow, sorrowful sound. "You know what I don't get is, why now? Why wait until I was putting together this business with you and Keith to finally give in to Canton? All these years, he had said no, but why now? Did he not want me to have something?" Randall wiped his nose with the back of his hand.

"Wait, Canton had approached him to sell the property before?"

Randall nodded. "Yeah, but he always low-balled him. Said the property wasn't worth much because of its location. So, why now?" Randall stared at Liam as if the answer were written on his face.

"I, I don't know."

"Canton always seems to have it out for you," Randall said, his voice flat. "You don't think he doubled his offer on the property to get back at you, do you?"

Liam's head swam. Could Mick Canton hate him that much? "We're nobodies. Why would he waste his time with us?"

"Not us, dude. *You*. And I don't know why. All I know is we don't have a space for our business."

"I'll think of something," Liam said. "I'll come up with a plan."

Randall scoffed and sipped from the can. "Yeah. Let me know when that happens."

"What's that supposed to mean?"

"It means, ever since you hooked up with Autumn, you haven't been focused on what's important."

"That's unfair, dude. And who's been feeding you those lines? Every time you've texted me, I've shown up. You're the one making decisions without me."

"Whatever, man. I'm gonna rely on me this time. I'll find us a new spot. Don't you worry."

Liam rose from the couch and checked the time on his phone. He was supposed to meet Pops for lunch.

"Gotta date?" asked Randall.

Liam didn't respond. "You sure you want to live alone? You can crash with me and Pops."

Randall waved this idea away. "Nah. I'm sick of living with old men." Randall went back to his video game, leaving Liam to show himself out.

# CHAPTER TWENTY-FOUR

While most of the guests slept off their hangovers on Thursday, Autumn went upstairs to work on her college essays. The guidance counselor at school wanted to approve them before Autumn completed her applications. Besides Candlewick, Autumn had only a handful of other schools she was applying to— schools she had never visited and schools that probably wouldn't meet her mother's approval. Autumn was losing her drive.

She flopped on her bed and opened her laptop. Procrastinating, she checked her email. There was a message from her dad wanting to know if she'd like to visit for Thanksgiving. She had been in Key West more than six months, and this was the first time he had invited her to stay with him. He even suggested touring Candlewick during her visit.

Autumn knew she should feel elated, but inside, she was conflicted. Did she even want to go to Candlewick anymore? Did she want to move back? And how could one boy make her question everything she had considered? In truth, Liam was becoming increasingly important to her. She wanted to see him all the time now. But what if she stayed in Florida? Would she still be her mother's lackey, a chambermaid in this place? What if Liam got sick of her, and she missed out on her opportunity to go back north?

"Ugh," she cried before slamming her laptop closed. "Hey Katie? Are you around?" Autumn waited a beat for her ghostly friend to show up. "I have boy trouble." Still, nothing. Where was that ghost?

Just then, there was a knock on her door. Evelyn opened it up and popped her head in. Autumn opened her mouth to speak, but her mother cut her off. "Don't worry. I'm not here to ask you to do anything. I want to talk about your birthday."

Well, that was surprising. "My birthday?"

Evelyn entered the bedroom and sat on the edge of Autumn's bed. She heaved a great sigh. "I know I've been preoccupied with the business, but you're turning eighteen in two days. Don't think I forgot."

Autumn fiddled with a loose thread in the bedspread. "I know you haven't forgotten."

Her mother smiled. "I thought maybe we could bring in take-out and watch some of your favorite movies. Or watch the first season of *Veronica Mars*. And we can eat junk food." She playfully bumped her shoulder. "Cora said she'd bake a cake."

"Oh, she doesn't have to do that," Autumn said. "Liam wants to take me out."

Evelyn's face soured. "Oh. What are you guys planning on doing?"

KIMBERLY G. GIARRATANO

Autumn squirmed. In the past, Autumn's birthday was a celebration, not just of another year, but of the season. Like she had told Liam, her mom would bake an apple pie. There'd be cozy sweaters and a fire blazing. When she was a kid, her mom would take her trick-or-treating for hours. But now, Cora was going to bake her a cake?

It was different here. Liam suggested getting dressed up and checking out some Fantasy Fest events. But Autumn left that part out. She just shrugged. "You know, dinner. Maybe we'll go to Mallory Square."

Her mother got to her feet. "During Fantasy Fest? Do you really think that's appropriate?"

Autumn rolled her eyes. "Mom, seriously."

"There's a lot of public nudity. It could give the boy the wrong idea."

"Liam's not like that. He also grew up here. I doubt he's as shocked by what he sees as you are."

"Maybe that's the problem," Evelyn said. "If it isn't shocking, then what's to stop him from thinking it's okay to take advantage of you?"

"Mom!"

Evelyn waved her arm in the air, as if that could erase her words. "Fine, go, if that's what you'd prefer."

Autumn recognized this tactic. Guilt. Truthfully, she did prefer Liam's company on her birthday to her mother's. Since the divorce, her relationship with her mom had deteriorated, and she wasn't sure it would ever go back to the way it was. Didn't Liam say what she wanted was impossible now?

"But if I catch you drinking, I'll put you on the next flight to Jersey."

"Oh, is that all it takes?" Autumn muttered under her breath. When she caught her mother's glare, she softened her voice. "How about we have an early dinner together and I go out with Liam after?"

Evelyn went to the door. "Sure. We could do that." She put her hand on the doorknob, but stopped. "Be careful with this boy."

Autumn's cheeks heated. Was her mom going to give her a talk about sex and responsibility? "Don't give up the things you want for him. That's all I'm going to say." Evelyn nodded as if she'd made her point and then left the room, making sure to close the door behind her.

Autumn plopped back against the pillow. *Don't give up the things you want for a boy. Well, that's rich.* Autumn's mother had made her give up her life in New Jersey for what Evelyn wanted in Key West.

It became clear to Autumn that she no longer knew what she wanted. And it also became clear that what she wanted might have changed in spite of Liam or because of him. She couldn't be sure anymore.

On Halloween night, Liam stooped down and checked his reflection in the side mirror of a Smart Car parked alongside the curb near the Cayo. He tousled his hair. He didn't want to appear like he was trying too hard, even though he had been trying too hard. It took him an hour to get ready that evening.

Pops had knocked on the bathroom door twice and asked Liam if he had fallen in.

Liam straightened his back and adjusted the tie on Pops's old Navy uniform. Victoria once told him that blue brought out the color in his eyes. He hoped Autumn would think the same thing.

Liam clutched a bouquet of supermarket flowers to his chest, careful not to stain the white fabric, and opened the door to the lobby.

Timothy sat at the desk. He raised his brows the minute he saw Liam. "Well, don't you look dapper."

Liam smiled. "You're holding back. I can tell."

"Oh, lover boy. If I wanted to make fun of you I wouldn't do so when you're here to take Autumn out for her birthday." Then he lowered his voice. "But I will warn you, Miss Evelyn is in a mood. You better watch out."

Liam frowned. "Is she here now?"

Nodding, Timothy whispered, "She's in her office. Sulking. She wanted to celebrate her daughter's birthday. But Autumn, like all teenage girls, would much rather be taken out by a handsome young gentleman."

Just then, Autumn descended the stairs. Liam pressed the bouquet of flowers to his chest, his sweaty hands coating the plastic sleeve. Liam's stomach did that thing where it churned a bit like the drum of a washing machine. Autumn looked beautiful. And hot, even though she was wearing the same dark blue sailor uniform as Liam. The uniform, even though cut for a man, managed to hug Autumn's curves.

"Wow," said Liam.

"Thanks," said Autumn. "I found it in the attic. It was Uncle Duncan's."

Liam licked his lips and handed Autumn the bouquet. Her face lit up.

Timothy reached over for the flowers. "I'll put these in water and leave them in your room."

Evelyn emerged from her office and narrowed her eyes at Liam. "What do you have planned for this evening? Although, I'm afraid to ask."

"Mom!" Autumn exclaimed.

Liam cleared his throat. "First, we're going to check out the costume promenade on Duval. And then my buddy's cousin is taking us on an evening cruise."

Evelyn arched her brows. "Your friend's cousin?" She said the words slowly as if trying to process the connection.

"It's okay," said Liam. "His cousin is an experienced sailor. It's totally cool."

"That makes me feel so much better," Evelyn said dryly.

"Mom," Autumn hissed. "We'll be fine."

Evelyn crossed her arms over her chest. "What's the name of this boat?"

"Ladykiller," Liam said without hesitation. He clutched Autumn's hand. "Ready?"

She stifled a laugh. "Yes."

Liam and Autumn walked outside and headed to Liam's scooter.

Autumn said, "You're terrible. You totally freaked out my mom."

Liam smiled. "She deserved it a little."

"Yeah, she did."

Before putting on his helmet, Liam kissed Autumn on the cheek. "Happy birthday."

Autumn kissed Liam on the mouth. "Happy Halloween."

Autumn felt giddy and a little light-headed from the spiked fruit punch served on the boat. Liam warned her about drinking it, but the red liquid tasted so sweet. It also made her forget all about her problems with Inez, Katie, and even her mom. Autumn giggled as she stumbled through the gate and into the darkened patio.

Liam put his finger to his lips and whispered, "Shhh." Autumn waved him away. It didn't matter. All the guests, except for Mr. Fletcher, Autumn assumed, were outside enjoying the crazy festival.

Autumn threw off her sailor cap and flounced into a lounge chair. Her butt sank beyond the broken plastic slats. She laughed loudly.

"Autumn, your mother's going to wake up and kill us both," Liam said, not even trying to hide his nervousness.

Autumn grinned and shook her head. These last few days had been exhausting. There was no way Evelyn could stay awake.

She stared at Liam. The evening air cooled the heat radiating off her skin. She wanted desperately to put her hands on his hips and pull him down on top of her. Autumn wasn't sure if it was the rum punch making her think these things or the way her body tingled when she did, but she wanted to kiss him, and she wanted to kiss him now.

She sat up and tugged the thin white tie of Liam's uniform. He smiled and eased onto her. Liam pushed her hair off her face and stared at her lips. "We shouldn't be doing this," he said, his voice a soft whisper.

Autumn sucked on her bottom lip. "Absolutely, we should."

He smiled again and kissed her tenderly. Autumn couldn't take it anymore. She pulled Liam onto her, wanting him to crush her body with his own. She parted his lips with her tongue and Liam groaned. He stopped for a second and adjusted his body. "I don't know where to put my hands," he said, sheepishly. "I don't want to crush you."

Autumn guided his hands to her waist. "Start here."

He kissed her again, this time more urgently. Autumn adjusted herself so that she could wrap her legs around Liam's waist. Liam put his hands into Autumn's and slid them up so they were above her head. As they kissed, their bodies moved together in rhythm.

"We need to stop," Liam said, panting.

"Why?" she asked, her voice practically a whine.

Liam stood up. "Because I'm a gentleman. And you've had too much to drink. Also, making out near the pool gives me the willies. Aren't you worried about who's watching?"

Autumn doubted Liam meant guests. Perhaps, if she hadn't drank so much she'd care about ghostly voyeurs. But, even if she was sober, she'd still want to kiss Liam. A lot.

Autumn sat up a little and pouted.

Liam leaned down and kissed her again on her lips, but the kiss felt chaste compared to what they had just been doing.

Light flooded the patio and Evelyn's sharp voice rang out, "What's going on out here?"

Liam leaped off Autumn. He yanked down his shirt, but it was no use. Evelyn regarded him with those suspicious eyes of hers. Autumn could tell there was no escaping her mother's wrath.

"We were just—" Autumn began.

"I can see what you were doing," her mother said. Then she eyed the sailor uniforms. "What happened? Did you ruin Uncle Duncan's uniform?"

Autumn glanced down at the inky blood splattered on the front of her shirt. "There was a fake rubber octopus attached to me at one point during the festivities."

Evelyn tightened her robe. She steadied her voice and this unnerved Autumn more than her mother's screams. "Liam, I think you better go."

"Mrs. Abernathy," he began, but she held up a hand to stop him.

"I was never intending to keep you on past Fantasy Fest."

"Mom!" Autumn cried out.

"I'll pay you for this week."

Liam faced Autumn. "Did you know about that?"

"I'm sorry," she said. "My plan was to talk her out of it."

Liam squeezed Autumn's hand. "I'll call you." His voice was barely a whisper.

"Don't go," Autumn pleaded.

Liam smiled weakly. "It's okay." He kissed her lightly on the cheek and disappeared out the side gate.

Autumn whirled on her mother. "Mom, that was cruel."

"That was nothing. I knew this nonsense with Liam was going too far, but Aunt Glenda kept saying, 'You're young. Be free.'"

"So what's wrong with that?"

Evelyn's eyes flamed. "Don't throw away your future for some guy like I did. You'll have nothing to show for it."

Autumn stepped back as if her mother had slapped her. In a way, she had. "You mean Dad."

Evelyn softened her stance. Her eyes searched Autumn's face, looking for some trace of recognition. "Look, I'm forty-three years old. I'm divorced and broke. All I have is this ridiculous bed and breakfast, which I have sunk whatever money I had into."

Autumn blanched and felt the sting of tears about come. But she held up her head. "You have me, Mom. Am I not good enough? Was I not worth the sacrifice?"

Autumn brushed past her mother and hurried inside to the empty kitchen, where she hoped to cut a slice of Cora's Key Lime pie and devour her sorrows.

# CHAPTER TWENTY-FIVE

Liam straddled his scooter and patted his pocket for his set of keys. What a night. It started off so well until he got fired. He should've known Evelyn had no intention of keeping him on; he just wished Autumn had given him a heads up so he didn't feel like such a chump.

Liam dropped his chin to his chest. The keys must had fallen out of his pocket when he and Autumn had been making out.

"Crap," he muttered. He would have to go back to the patio and find them. He let his helmet dangle from the handlebars and dismounted the bike. He pushed through the white gate, which squeaked on its old, rusty hinges.

The pool water was still like the night air. The Cayo looked dark inside, aside from a light left on in the lobby for the nocturnal guests, still partying in town.

Liam skirted around the pool and sidled past an old patio chair. He scraped his leg on a rusty screw that jutted out from the chair. It ripped a hole in Pops's old uniform. Liam cursed under his breath. He walked over the old lounge chair and bent down, his hand searching for his keys. He patted the concrete, his palm scraping against it until his fingers touched metal. He clutched the keys tight in his fist.

He hated being alone in the pool area. Ever since his first day here. The dark dulled his sense of sight, but heightened his sense of fear. Goosebumps erupted along his arms, and the little hairs on his neck stood at attention. He swallowed hard and made a beeline for the gate. Then he heard a noise behind him.

He froze in place.

"There you are," a seductive voice called to him. He spun around and relaxed his shoulders.

"Autumn," he said, putting his hand to his chest to calm his breathing. "What are you still doing out here? I assumed your mom was reaming you out."

Autumn still wore Duncan's old Navy uniform, but her hair was all disheveled. And the way she approached him was different. When she walked, her hips swayed side to side in a hypnotic rhythm.

She came closer and touched his collar. Her fingers danced over his skin, but instead of feeling bolts of electricity, he felt chills.

"Should we continue where we left off?" she asked, breathless.

Liam arched his brow. "I don't think that's a good idea." He nodded toward the house where Evelyn was no doubt watching, infuriated. "I came back to get my keys." He dangled them.

Autumn giggled oddly. "Don't you want me?" Liam noted how her voice lilted a bit. She spoke with an accent.

He removed her hands from his uniform. "What's gotten into you? You sound funny."

Her eyes darkened. She backed away and yanked her hands through her dark hair. "*Dios*! You always do this to me."

Liam retreated. Something was wrong. Very wrong. "*Dios*? And what do I always do?"

"Tease me," she said, her voice sounding angrier. "You tell me it's Mariana you love, but I know that's not true. I see how you look at me."

Now, Liam started to panic. "Inez. I'm not Leo Breyer. I'm Liam." He emphasized the difference in the names. "William Michael Breyer and it's not 1966."

Inez growled. "You did this to me!" She lunged for him, brandishing a knife in her right hand. Liam screamed as the blade grazed his cheek. "Inez, no!" She charged him again, the knife nearly missing his arm. "Stop! I'm not Leo!" Liam ran to the pool shed.

Inez's eyes darted all around. Liam flung open the shed door and grabbed the shovel.

"Please Inez. Let Autumn back inside her body. I don't want to hurt you."

Inez cackled and spat, "You've already hurt me!"

Liam's stomach dropped. "I'm sorry."

"You should be." She charged him again.

Liam raised the shovel and brought it down.

Autumn felt trapped inside her body. She could see Liam's fear. The way his knuckles turned white as he gripped the shovel. But also the way he held it. Like a baseball bat.

Autumn screamed, but it was no use. Inez was too strong. Her dark energy kept Autumn caged inside her own head. Timothy was right. She opened the door for this, and now she was stuck. Autumn knew she had a knife in her hand. She felt Inez in control, thrusting the blade forward, hoping to cut Leo. *No! Liam! It's Liam you're trying to hurt.*

Just as Liam brought down the shovel, someone slammed into her body, flinging her into the pool. She heard the shovel clang against the pavement. Inez was gone and with her, Autumn's strength. She could barely swim to the ledge.

Autumn registered Timothy's grim face as he stood at the pool's edge. He waited a beat before saying, "Are you in there, Autumn?"

She spit out pool water and swung droplets from her hair. "Yeah, it's me."

Timothy pursed his lips. "Seriously?"

"Just help me out."

Timothy held the skimmer pole out to her like a lifeline. She grabbed it and both Liam and Timothy yanked her out of the water.

Chlorinated water ran from her sailor uniform in rivers. She wrung out some of the water from her shirt. "Thanks," she muttered, her eyes downcast, not wanting meet Timothy's I-told-you-so glare.

"Girl." He put his hands on his hips. "I told you not to let a spirit into your body, but noooooo! You know better, don't you? You refused to listen to old Timothy."

Liam rested his hand on Timothy's shoulder. "It's not Autumn we should be mad at."

Timothy shrugged off Liam's hand, crossed his arms, and huffed. "Maybe not, but the girl has got to learn. Now, you'll never know when miss evil thang wants to jump inside you for a little revenge. She could overtake you at any moment."

"We'll figure out how to stuff her back inside," Autumn said.

Timothy shook his head.

"What?" Autumn asked, her patience completely gone.

"You can't just go stuffing a ghost back into wherever you think ghosts live. You have to banish her. And to do that goes beyond séances. She must possess you before you can get rid of her."

"So let's do that," Autumn said.

"Uh-uh," Timothy said. "Her negative energy makes her strong. You nearly killed Liam with a knife because she was controlling you. To get inside her, could mean she'll overtake your body. The Autumn we know and love," he looked pointedly at her, "could disappear."

"That's what she wants," Autumn whispered.

"What?" asked Liam.

"She wants to live again. Inez lets me see the bits and pieces leading up to her death to tease me. She knows I want to solve her murder. She's playing me."

"Yeah," Timothy said. "Everytime she gets inside you, she takes over little by little. It's only a matter of time before she becomes you."

"So how do we get rid of her?" asked Autumn.

"She is fueled by both revenge and a desire to live. You need to take away her fuel."

"How do we do that?" asked Liam.

"Find justice for her," Timothy said, annoyed.

Autumn flopped into the patio chair. "Can you say with a hundred percent certainly that Inez doesn't know who killed her?"

"Honey, I wouldn't even say I'm Bahamian with a hundred percent certainty. I just know. Anyway, no more hanky-panky." Timothy pursed his lips. "You have detective work to do."

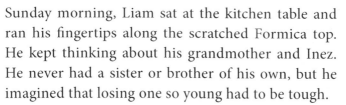

Sunday morning, Liam sat at the kitchen table and ran his fingertips along the scratched Formica top. He kept thinking about his grandmother and Inez. He never had a sister or brother of his own, but he imagined that losing one so young had to be tough.

Pops shuffled in. "Hey, sport, you're thinking hard." He chuckled, opened the fridge, and groped around until his fist encircled a can of beer.

Liam listened as the can hissed and his grandfather gulped down the amber liquid. Sometimes it took these quiet moments for Liam to realize just how much his grandfather drank.

Liam shifted in his chair. "How did you meet Abuela?"

Pops belched and flopped down in the chair across from Liam. Sweat trickled down his beer can, leaving a circle of water on the table. "I never told you that story?"

"Not really." He shrugged. "Maybe I never asked."

Pops smiled wistfully. "It was at her parents' bodega. I had just enlisted. I was only a little older than you are now." Pops winked. "I went in to buy gum every day until she agreed to go out with me. On our first date, I took her to dinner, and then we went dancing at the Green Parrot." He laughed. "She wore the most awful beige dress."

"Really?" Liam asked. "I thought you were going to say she was decked out head to toe in red or something like that."

Pops laughed, almost mournfully. "Nah. That wasn't her style. Not like Inez. She always wore bright colors. *She* liked to be the center of attention."

*This is good. He's talking.* "But not, Abuela?"

"No. She was more modest. That's probably why I liked her right away, because she wasn't flashy."

"Did other men ask her to dance?"

Pops lightly pounded the table. "You bet they did. But you think I'd let some other guy get to her first?" He shook his head. "Nope. We danced together the whole night. After that, we were inseparable." He was grinning now.

"So where was Inez when all this happened? I mean, I'd imagine she'd want to protect her sister from these devilish sailors."

Pops rolled his eyes. "It was us who needed protection from Inez. That girl . . ."

"Yeah?"

"Never mind."

"Come on, Pops. We're just talking."

"I'm no dummy. I know you think I am."

Liam was affronted. "I don't think that."

"You think I don't hear you tell your friend Randall about the Breyer curse?"

Liam shrank back. He never meant for Pops to hear those remarks. Pops was a decent person. Sometimes, it took seeing Randall's miserable grandfather to realize how lucky Liam had it growing up.

"Yeah, I know you, kid. I know you better than you know yourself."

"I don't think you're a dummy. I think you're a smart guy who is hiding something from me because you think I'm not old enough to handle it."

Leo sighed. "There isn't much to tell. Inez was volatile."

"Still is," Liam mumbled.

"Are we going to start with the ghost nonsense?" Pops took a long sip from his beer and shook the can. Empty. "Get me another one, will ya?"

Liam reluctantly went to the fridge and removed a beer from the top shelf. He plunked it down in front of Pops and sat.

Pops pulled back the tab on the can. "I know what you're trying to do. You're trying to get me to talk about Inez."

"I just want to know about my grandpa in his youth. Is that a crime?"

Pops got up from the table. "No. But that's not what you're asking here."

"I'm asking about a girl. A girl who was my great aunt, apparently, and who was killed."

"We never knew that." Pops wiped his mouth with the back of his hand. "She went missing one night after a dance at St. Veronica's. She picked fights with everyone that night. Me, your abuela. We assumed she took off. Mariana was worried, but I told her that Inez probably was necking with some guy on the beach to make Mick jealous."

"I thought they were engaged."

"They were." Pops belched, but his eyes grew soft, almost moony.

"When was this?"

Pops took a sip of beer and Liam could hear him swallow the liquid. "You think I remember? It was fifty years ago."

"Yeah, I'd think you remember when your sister-in-law disappeared and was never seen again."

Pops hesitated a moment before answering, "Early April." He cleared this throat. "Do you still wear my old dog tags?"

Liam lifted the chain from his shirt and dangled them in front of his grandfather. "I do."

Pops's words started to slur. "Maybe you should take them off when you're working. Just to be safe."

"I thought you didn't believe in ghosts."

"Just cover your bases, that's all."

Liam rose from the table and clapped his grandfather on the shoulder. "Well, I would, but I'm not going back there for work anymore. Evelyn fired me."

Pops patted Liam's hand. "You can blame that on the Breyer curse."

"No, Pops. This time, it was all me." Liam leaned down and kissed his grandpa on his head. "I'm going out."

"See ya, kid."

Liam made his way to the front door, but he thought he heard his grandpa curse Inez under his breath.

# CHAPTER TWENTY-SIX

That same morning, Autumn stormed into Evelyn's office. The sheer force of her entrance blew papers right off the desk.

Her mother frowned. "What's gotten into you?"

Autumn tapped her sneaker impatiently. "You know exactly what's gotten into me. You fired Liam!"

Evelyn softened her shoulders and shrugged. "I'm sorry, honey, but I really do think it was the best. He was a distraction to you, and . . ." her voice trailed.

"And what?" Autumn asked, her patience waning.

"I don't know. He didn't seem like a good influence. Plus, all those weird things happening as soon as he started working here. The chandelier. The pipes bursting. I mean, for God's sake, he fell into the pool and cut himself. He was a liability if nothing else." She sounded like she was practically laughing at the end. This only fueled Autumn's anger.

"You can't blame Liam for any of that," Autumn said. "It was Inez's fault, all of it. She has it out for him."

Now Evelyn truly was laughing, until she caught the serious look on Autumn's face. Evelyn cleared her throat and shuffled the papers on her desk. "I told you not to encourage your aunt about these ghost stories."

"They're not stories," Autumn said.

"They're not real!" Evelyn screeched. "Your father and I told you this in New Jersey. Ghosts aren't real."

Autumn balked. "Aunt Glenda is a believer. Timothy and Cora are believers. I'm a believer."

"If they're so real, why don't they show themselves to me?"

"Because you're not tuned into them. You don't even try to be open to the fact that the Cayo's haunted."

"That's ridiculous," Evelyn sputtered. "Anyway, I doubt the dead come back to wish us harm." She threw her pen on the desk and rubbed her eyes. "This place is messing with your head. You're blaming a ghost in order to stand up for that boy."

"That boy? He's the reason I'm happy here."

Evelyn's mouth tightened into a thin line. "There will be other boys."

"Mom, at some point, you have to let go of the bitterness."

Evelyn opened her mouth to protest.

"Forget it," said Autumn, turning to leave. "Forget everything."

Liam shuffled down the dock to the *Benny Blue Eyes*, which gently rocked on the waves. He stopped short of climbing on board and cried, "Randall!"

Randall stuck his curly head out of the porthole. "Dude! Be right out."

Randall didn't invite Liam on board. Not that it mattered much. Liam didn't care for Keith, and he figured the feeling was mutual. Of course, he wasn't there on friendly terms.

*Some merchandise was stolen from one of my warehouses. You wouldn't happen to know anything about that?*

Randall hopped off the boat and onto the dock.

"Walk with me," said Liam.

Randall cocked his brow. "What's up?"

The two set off down the dock and onto the wharf, which was quiet since most of the boats were out at sea.

"What's going on?" asked Randall, his voice hot. "You're freaking me out."

Liam faced his friend. "I want my investment back. All twenty-five hundred."

"What? You can't." Randall rubbed his eyes. "What the hell?"

Liam poked Randall in the chest. "I asked you if this was legit and you said totally. But guess what? Mick Canton is missing scooters from his warehouse. Tell me you didn't know. Tell me this was your cousin's doing and you didn't deliberately get me involved in a crime!"

Randall looked like he had swallowed a bowling ball. "Dude, at first, Keith just told me that they were cast-offs bought at auction."

"When did you find out?" Pressure built under Liam's skin. He walked away from the water, fearful that he'd push Randall into the ocean at the slightest provocation. "When?"

Randall flinched. "Before you gave me the money."

Liam grabbed Randall's collar. "You were supposed to be my friend. And now you've put us both in danger."

Randall peeled Liam's fingers off his shirt and stepped back. "What are you talking about? Mick doesn't know."

"Are you an idiot?"

"The bikes are hidden. They're going to be refinished and painted. Mick didn't even file a police report."

"You can't know that," said Liam through gritted teeth. "And Mick doesn't need the police. He has eyes all over this island. This friendship you have with Victoria is going to blow up in your face. She's using you."

"You're jealous!"

Liam hardened his eyes. "No, man. I wised up. I want out and I want my money back."

Randall shook his head. "That's not gonna happen. Keith used it to pay off the guys."

Liam pointed at his friend. "Mick's going to come after us."

Randall sputtered, "You're just trying to scare me."

Liam stared out at the vast water before him. "You should be scared."

Autumn stumbled on the rocky walkway that led to the fence in front of Mr. Blazevig's turquoise bungalow. Mr. Blazevig lived on a side street, at the south end of the island, in Mid Town. Locals called this area *the country* because the homes sat on larger lots and there were no sidewalks, just gravel that butted up against the property line.

Autumn had just finished reading Liam's text message about Inez going missing in April. She gently rapped on Mr. Blazevig's front door, careful not to crack one of the many panes of glass. The porch sconce was still lit, odd for the late afternoon. A broom leaned against a wobbly railing and the concrete had been swept. Apparently, the old man kept the outside as tidy as his family's graves.

Ralph Blazevig barely opened the front door, although Autumn could see he was dressed in loose-fitting brown pants and an old white undershirt. He hid behind the door and put out his hand as a way of stopping Autumn from entering the foyer. Odd. She had never been to his house, but usually people of his generation welcomed guests into their home.

"You got my text," Mr. Blazevig whispered.

"Are you okay?" Autumn tried to see around his head inside his house. What if he was the victim of a home invasion, the perpetrator holding a weapon to his back and forcing him to pretend everything was okay? Was Mr. Blazevig giving her some kind of coded signal?

Mr. Blazevig, sensing her unease, came outside and shut the door behind him. He stood hunched over, and when Autumn glanced down, she saw that holes riddled the man's socks. Autumn peered around him and through the glass door. She caught sight of faded yellow paint and floral couches with afghans draped over the cushions. A cat curled up on the loveseat.

Mr. Blazevig coughed into his fist. "Would you be willing to pass out tour brochures on Duval later today? I want to take advantage of the last day of Fantasy Fest before the island clears out. I usually do it myself, but I'm not feeling well."

Autumn met his eyes. Dark circles sat underneath. "Of course. Maybe, you should go to the doctor."

The old man hugged himself. "Psssh. It's only a cold. I'll be all right."

"Okay," she said, unsure. Maybe she'd ask Cora to mix up one of her herbal tea remedies. She could bring it by later.

"Wait here and I'll get the brochures." He shuffled inside his house and again closed the door on her.

Autumn waited until the old man retreated farther away, probably to his bedroom, and pressed her face against the glass panes.

*This is ridiculous. It's so muggy outside.* Autumn opened the front door and stepped inside. If the old man was embarrassed about his housekeeping, he shouldn't be. After all, she had to clean up after strangers at the Cayo.

She stood in the foyer, soaking up the colorful art on the walls, including a painting resembling a Chagall, the stacks of paperbacks in the corner of the room, the teacups and saucers that littered the coffee table, and the old black-and-white photographs lined up on the bookshelves. One appeared to be a wedding photo of Mr. Blazevig and his wife. Next to that, was a framed photograph of a little boy, and next to that was a photo of Ralph Blazevig in overalls smiling next to a little blonde girl.

Mr. Blazevig emerged from the far corner of the house carrying a stack of brochures. He stopped short at the sight of Autumn.

"It's too hot to stand outside," she explained.

"Of course. Where are my manners? Sorry. I just didn't clean today." He thrust the papers into her arms and pushed her toward the door. "Thanks for doing this. I'm sorry to leave you all alone tonight."

Autumn cemented her stance. She picked up the photograph of Mr. Blazevig and the blonde girl. "Is this your sister? You sort of look alike."

Mr. Blazevig smiled sadly. "Yes. That was taken several years before we arrived in the Keys."

"You came together?"

He took the frame from Autumn and traced his finger over the picture. "Our parents died when we were little and we grew up with my aunt, who was deaf, and she couldn't really look after us. So when I enlisted and was stationed here in Key West, I enrolled her at St. Veronica's so she could be nearby."

"Oh! Liam's grandmother went there too."

Mr. Blazevig smiled, and the skin around his eyes crinkled. "So she did. Except she was a few years ahead, I think."

"Speaking of the Cruces girls, how come you lied to me when I asked you about Inez?"

Mr. Blazevig's cheeks reddened, but Autumn wasn't sure if he was flushed with fever or embarrassment. "I'm sorry I wasn't more forthcoming. It's just she wasn't a nice girl, and I didn't want to speak ill."

"Why wasn't she nice?"

"Inez was a bully. Mariana was sweet, but Inez liked to, she liked to—"

"She liked to what?"

"She liked to hurt people," he said. "She made enemies quick."

"How do you mean?"

Mr. Blazevig took a cloth hankie from his pocket to wipe sweat off his face. "She'd say the most vile things to your aunt and uncle. Calling Duncan . . ." He stopped. "Insinuating he was—"

"Gay?" Autumn finished.

"It's not like nowadays," he said softly. "Being homosexual then was . . . well, he could've been dishonorably discharged from the navy had anyone found out."

Autumn couldn't believe she was about to ask this question. "Could Uncle Duncan have hurt Inez to hide his secret?"

"No! Duncan wouldn't kill a fly. He was too kind a person. Too good." Mr. Blazevig's eyes softened, and Autumn wondered if their friendship had meant more to each other than simply navy buddies. "That's the thing. No one knew she was killed until you said you saw her ghost. We all just thought she ran away from the dance. She got into a big fight with her sister that night, and Leo said some harsh things. She took off crying, and we never saw her again. We could never understand why Mick had proposed to that girl."

"You didn't know about the baby? Inez was pregnant. Mick was the father."

"N-n-no," Mr. Blazevig stuttered. "I didn't know." His face drained of color. With shaky hands, he shoved the handkerchief into his pocket.

Autumn opened her mouth to ask another question, but Mr. Blazevig grabbed a stack of paperbacks off the coffee table and pushed them into her open arms.

"You enjoy mysteries, Autumn? You seem to like playing detective. I can't read these anymore. My eyesight and such."

"Oh, okay." She accepted the books, taking the hint that Mr. Blazevig was purposefully changing the subject.

"I'm really tired. I should go lie down and sleep off this blasted cold." He ushered her outside and waved goodbye as he closed the door.

Autumn scuttled down the stairs and stopped dead with a realization. Mr. Blazevig's handkerchief was the same one Autumn and Liam had pulled out of the Cayo's bathtub. The cream one with blue trim.

The embroidered B stood for Blazevig.

"What do you mean it was the same handkerchief?" Liam asked.

Autumn and Liam stood shoulder-to-shoulder on Duval Street, handing out Mr. Blazevig's brochures and occasionally leaning back to allow a tourist to sidle past.

Today was the last day of Fantasy Fest, to Liam's relief. He'd had enough of naked tourists, crazy costumes, and impassable roads.

"Love ghost stories?" Autumn called to those strolling by. "Sign up for a haunted tour of the island. Midnight tours sell out quickly." Autumn extended the brochure, waiting for tourists to take it. Liam knew enough to shove the brochure in people's hands.

"It was the same piece of cloth. Same light blue embroidery," she said.

"You think that's a coincidence?"

Autumn gave him a pointed look. "Too many coincidences aren't a coincidence."

Liam considered this for a moment. "So Ralph Blazevig, the nicest man on the planet, killed Inez." He shook his head. "No way can I believe that."

Autumn smiled at a blonde family who graciously accepted her handout. "Me neither. But what else could Inez be trying to tell us?"

Liam threw the stack of brochures down at his feet. "Not only is Inez a bitchy ghost, but she's also a vengeful one. She's jerking us around. She wants to live again, and she'll say or do anything to get a host body."

Autumn squinted and nudged Liam's elbow. "Look across the street. At the corner. Is that—"

"Mr. Blazevig? What's he doing here? I thought he was sick, and that's why we're doling out brochures." Liam watched as the old man approached a black Escalade. "I know that truck." He glanced at the driver's flattop. "I recognize that driver. It's Mick's guy. His bodyguard or something." Liam snapped his fingers. "Finn."

Ralph Blazevig spoke to Finn through the driver-side window. Finn tilted his chin, and Mr. Blazevig climbed into the passenger seat.

"Why do you think Mr. Blazevig lied about being sick only to go off with Mick's driver?" asked Liam.

"I don't know," said Autumn. "But we're gonna have to find out."

# CHAPTER TWENTY-SEVEN

The following morning as Autumn got ready for school, Evelyn knocked on Autumn's door. Her mother stood in the doorway and picked at some loose paint flecks on the moulding.

Autumn sat on her bed and ran a brush through her dark hair. She glanced quickly at her mother. "What do you want?"

"Actually, I'm here to give you want you want," Evelyn replied. "I'm sending you to live with your father. You'll be back in New Jersey. Back with your old friends. In your old house. In your old life."

Autumn paused the hairbrush in mid swipe. Her muscles went rigid, and the brush suddenly felt as if it weighed a hundred pounds.

"Isn't that what you always wanted? To get away from here? To go back home?"

"That was before."

"Before what?" Coldness tinged her mother's voice. "Before Liam?"

Autumn wanted to say before she made a life here. Before she appreciated Key West, its stifling humidity, but also its festive life. People lived here. Maybe before, she just existed. But her mother wouldn't understand.

"I thought so," Evelyn said. "I was wrong to make you move here. I should've agreed to keep you in New Jersey."

"Agreed to keep me there? You said Dad didn't want me to stay with him. That you were moving me out of my high school in my junior year because Dad didn't want his old life intruding on his new family."

"God, Autumn. Is it so wrong for me to have wanted you to move with me? Did I really need to lose my house, husband, and daughter all at once?" Her voice sounded shrill.

Autumn bit her lip. Her mother was angry because she felt like no one loved her. But the truth was, Evelyn's anger made it hard for anyone to be close to her.

"I was never given a choice."

Evelyn crossed her arms. "Well, I'm sorry to say you're not being given a choice now. Go back home. Enroll at Candlewick. Get a degree and make something of yourself."

"You said I could do all that here," Autumn said.

"That was before you met a guy. A guy with no prospects. No future."

"Liam is nothing like Dad," Autumn said.

"No. He isn't. Your father had a good future ahead of him, and he still turned out to be a lying, cheating bastard." Evelyn turned to leave. "Your flight leaves next week."

And there was nothing more to be said.

Liam hung near the water's edge and scanned the ocean waves. A cool breeze blew off the water, and the sun was preparing to dip below the horizon. The past few days made Liam feel like his life was reeling out of control. Randall. Inez. Evelyn. Even Pops. They were all pushing against him, trying to ruin any semblance of normalcy and happiness he might be entitled to. Whether it was Evelyn bossing him around, Pops evading him, or Inez, whose only goal was to try and kill him—everyone wanted something from him without giving anything in return. And he was sick of it. Except for Autumn. She was the only person who made him feel valued. She wasn't trying to change him. And he loved her for it.

A rush of warmth flooded throughout his body. He loved her. He loved Autumn and today, he would tell her that.

Light fingers covered his eyes.

"Guess who?" a female voice said.

Liam whipped around and embraced Autumn. "My girlfriend."

Autumn beamed. "You cheated."

"I have your voice memorized. I don't need to guess."

Autumn sidled up to him and he put his arm around her shoulder. "It's beautiful tonight. The air is cool."

"It feels good," he said. "Sometimes, I get so sick of being hot."

Autumn nuzzled his neck. Then her eyes drifted toward the water. "Do you think you'd want to come to the northeast?"

"You mean to visit your dad? With you?"

Autumn cast her gaze downward, and Liam suddenly felt self-conscious about his ratty sneakers. He tilted her chin up so he could see her whole face.

"Are you still wanting to go back to New Jersey?" he asked. "I thought you had made a decision to stay here."

Autumn moved away from his touch. "My mom is sending me home to New Jersey."

"Your home is here. In the Keys. With me."

She rested her hands on the metal railing, but didn't make eye contact. "It's not that simple. On one hand, I love New Jersey. It's familiar and comfortable. On the other hand, I was just starting to enjoy Florida. I'm not ready to leave."

"Please tell me that I'm the reason you want to stay here," he said.

Autumn pushed off the railing and pressed her hands against Liam's chest. "Of course you're the reason."

Liam wrapped his arms around her. An iron pit settled in his stomach. He felt like he could sink to the bottom of the ocean if he was crazy enough to jump in. "Your home is with me. Tell your mom 'no.'"

"I can't," she whispered into his chest.

"Why not?" He rested his chin on the top of her head.

She didn't answer and Liam read her silence as doubt. He knew by insisting she stay in Florida, he was asking for a big commitment, not to mention defying her mother. They hadn't been dating long, but Liam couldn't imagine his life now without Autumn.

Autumn took Liam's hand. "Move to New Jersey with me. We'll go to college. We can get away from the Keys for a while. We can make a fresh start."

"I can't leave here," he said. "Sure, I lost my job and my scooter business is a criminal empire, but Pops is here. And I don't know if I want to start fresh somewhere new. I can't run from my problems. I'd be no better than my father or my mother."

"If you want to be with me, why won't you come home with me?" Her voice trembled.

"That's not fair. I could ask you the same thing. If you want to be with me, then why won't you stay?"

"Nothing is keeping you here," she said. "I have college prospects up North."

Liam splayed his fingers against his breastbone. "Ah, I see. Because I'm a high-school dropout, I have no reason to stay here."

"That's not what I meant."

"That's exactly what you meant. But you don't understand. My history is here. In the Keys. I don't belong anywhere else."

Autumn's eyes clouded with tears. "And I don't know where I belong. All I know is I can't defy my mother. I can't be one of those kids who doesn't have my parents' support. If you came with me, it would be easier."

They stared at each other for a moment, although to Liam, it felt like an hour. Finally, he said, "You know I can't leave. Not again."

Autumn glanced at the ocean waves and sighed. "I gotta go back to the Cayo."

"How much time do we have together?" He reached for her, and their fingers grazed.

"A week, maybe. I'll see you later." Autumn didn't kiss him goodbye.

Liam should've asked her to wait. He should've told her he would do anything for her or go anywhere to be with her. But Liam didn't have it in him. Autumn was the last person he thought would want him to change. But she was just like everyone else. She wanted something from him and wasn't willing to give something in return.

Liam woke the following morning and stumbled into the kitchen in nothing but a tattered pair of boxer shorts. Usually, Pops was awake by now, drinking coffee and reading the morning paper, but not today. His chair was empty. A note was tacked on the fridge. Liam pulled it off and read it.

*Went grocery shopping with neighbor. Then shuffleboard. See you later, kid.*

Liam crumpled up the note and threw it into the trashcan. The lid banged shut. Shuffleboard was Pops's joke about going to the Green Parrot for lunch. Just as well. Liam's only plan today was to throw himself a pity party and check on Craigslist for job openings.

The only good thing in his life was Autumn and now she was leaving.

It was probably better that Pops was gone for the day. Liam wasn't sure he could really look at the old man. Pops and his navy buddies all knew something about Inez's disappearance, and they were hiding information. Either that or they were covering for someone. But who?

Liam went into his room and threw on a dirty pair of cargo shorts and a stained gray T-shirt. No sense in showering—he ran his hand over his stubbly chin—or shaving. A pity party waits for no man.

Liam rummaged through the small fridge in the carport for a soda, but only found a six-pack of beer. Alcohol had ruined his father and was only slightly more kind to Pops. Liam exhaled, tired of resisting his fate. He pulled back the tab on the beer can. Pops would be annoyed, but Liam figured he could feign ignorance. Maybe his grandpa would think he drank it and forgot. Which had happened plenty of times in the past.

Liam plopped down into a beat-up patio chair. Its ribbed nylon weave dug into his back, but he didn't care. He took a sip of the cold liquid and let it cool his throat. A neighbor walked by with her snippy yorkie. She cocked her brow at him.

"Aren't you a little young to be drinking, Liam?" she called out.

Liam tipped his can to her. "Morning to you too, Mrs. Wiznewski." Then he took a gulp and belched. She clucked her tongue and kept on walking her dog.

Eventually, Liam got bored and dragged an old kiddie pool into the yard. He filled the pool with cold water from the hose and laid down in it, his arms and legs splayed like a starfish. After that, he made a salami sandwich and chugged another beer. He eventually fell asleep in Pops's beach chair and was woken up by a female voice. A tall, slender figure cast a shadow over him. He popped one eye open and then the other.

"You're drooling," Victoria said.

Liam wiped at the moisture on the edge of his lips with the collar of his dirty T-shirt.

"You look like crap." It wasn't her usual judgey way of speaking. She actually seemed concerned.

He sat up on his chair. "I've had a rough few days."

Victoria rolled her eyes. "You always had rough days."

Liam sighed. "Was I always this sad?"

She shrugged. "You're not what I would call a guy who radiates glitter and rainbows."

"I guess not. What are you doing here? I'm surprised you didn't send Randall to spy on me."

Vicky cocked her brow in confusion. "I'm not pathetic enough to send a spy."

"Right. You know he likes you, so you exploit him."

"I have no idea what you're talking about." Victoria opened up her coral, sequined clutch and withdrew an envelope. She snapped the clutch closed with a definitive smack that rattled Liam's nerves. "I have a proposition for you."

Liam stretched his arms above his head. "I need another beer. You want one?"

"Another beer? Since when do you drink?"

Liam got up from the chair and opened the fridge. "Since now."

"Ah." Victoria's face lit up with recognition. "Something happened with Autumn, didn't it?"

Liam stuck his head in the fridge so that Victoria couldn't read his expression.

"Whatever," she said, annoyed. "Listen, I'm loaning you money for your bike tour company."

Liam grabbed a can and closed the fridge door with his foot. "That's nice, but I'm not in business with Randall anymore."

"Good. You're better off." She thrust the envelope in Liam's direction. "Take it. I heard you got fired from the Cayo. Use the money for your own start-up. Just promise me you won't turn into—"

"My father? Pops?" Liam held the beer can in his hand, the cold stinging his skin. He put down the can but didn't accept the money.

"I was gonna say, a drunk."

"Same difference. Does your grandfather know you're doing this?"

"Yes," she said. "It's an investment, and there's nothing grandfather likes more than investing in the future." Victoria swallowed and stared at her flip-flops. "But, if you must know, there's a condition."

Liam fought back laughter. "Of course there is. Why would you do anything without strings attached?"

Her eyes hardened. "I will ignore that comment. With this money, you could be in business tomorrow."

"If . . . ?"

Her face reddened. Whatever this condition was, it sure embarrassed her to say it. "If you agree not to see Autumn anymore."

Liam blinked several times. Then he muttered, "pathetic" under his breath.

Victoria charged toward him and Liam backed into Pops's old workbench. A jar of nails rattled on the top shelf but held fast.

"If you must know," she said. "It was not my idea, but grandfather's. He's looking to purchase the Cayo Hueso, and he's concerned about your loyalties."

Liam pushed off the bench. "Tell him he doesn't have to worry."

Victoria relaxed. "I told grandfather you wouldn't do that."

"No, I mean, I'm not going to stop seeing Autumn." Even if Autumn returned to New Jersey tomorrow, there was no way he'd ever agree to such terms. Liam watched Victoria's tough exterior crumble. He felt bad for hurting her feelings, although it's not like she'd never hurt his.

"You won't take the money?"

He shook his head. "Not on those conditions."

Victoria paused for a moment. She softened her shoulders and stepped toward him, setting the envelope in his hand. "It's a check," she cooed. "A blank check. No more working for other people. You could be your own boss." Liam smelled her crisp perfume.

She sidled up to him and leaned in, practically pushing up against him. Liam's head buzzed from the alcohol. He flashed back to last year, before he went to North Dakota. Before his dad went to rehab. Before he met Autumn. Before a ghost tried to kill him. His life was no simpler now. Everything came full circle.

Victoria whispered, her warm breath on his skin. She turned her face toward his and looked into his eyes. He didn't pull away. Why wasn't he pulling away from her? She brushed her lips softly against his. It could barely have been considered a kiss.

Liam heard someone clearing her throat. Victoria slowly turned and a smile broke out on her face.

"Autumn," she said. "I didn't expect to see you today."

Liam squeezed his eyes shut. Now, he was truly done for.

# CHAPTER TWENTY-EIGHT

Autumn felt sick. She had borrowed her mother's car so she could apologize to Liam for arguing with him last night, but all she wanted to do now was get back into the car and run him over with it. Then she saw Victoria's smug smile. *Correction, I want to run Victoria over first.*

Victoria wiggled her fingers. "See you in school," she said to Autumn before climbing into her convertible and driving away.

Liam straightened up, but he stumbled, and Autumn noticed two beer cans rolling around by his feet.

"That's not what that looked like," he said.

Autumn's eyes weighed heavy on her face. Every time she blinked, she could feel how swollen her lids must have been. She'd been crying all night. She didn't have the energy to debate about seeing Victoria blatantly kiss him.

"It doesn't matter." Her voice shook. "I came here to apologize. I thought we could make a long distance relationship work."

"Thought? We still can." Liam reached for her.

Autumn snatched her hand away. She didn't mean to be so harsh, but what could Liam expect? She caught him kissing his former girlfriend. "No. I don't think we can."

"Because of Victoria?"

"Because of lots of things." Autumn scanned the carport, her eyes falling on a warped, wooden workbench; a tin trashcan attracting horseflies; and a dented white fridge that hadn't been scrubbed in ages. She wondered if the inside of the house was as equally depressing. "The Cayo isn't doing well. Aunt Glenda is going to sell, and my mom is likely to pack up and move to El Paso. Don't you see? Everyone I love is going to be hundreds of miles away from me."

"Including me," he said.

"Including you."

"Stay here with me," he pleaded. "Pops won't care."

Autumn scoffed. "I can't. You don't have a job. I won't have a job. Neither of us have money."

Liam crushed an empty beer can and threw it against the wall. "I love you, Autumn. Why isn't that enough? Are you just going to throw that away?"

The air rushed out of her chest. He loved her? She'd always imagined the moment a guy confessed his love, but Liam didn't appear sober. This wasn't that moment.

"You were kissing Victoria," she said.

"She kissed me before I could stop her. Don't you know me better than that?"

Impending tears burned the corners of her eyes. She was amazed she had any tears left inside her. "This is for the best."

"You don't want to throw your life away on me," he said, flatly.

Autumn narrowed her eyes and gave Liam a hard look. "I don't love you." Something pressed on her heart, as if an invisible fist had grabbed hold and was squeezing tightly. "Liam, I didn't—I don't." She couldn't finish her thought. She didn't mean to say she didn't love him. Where did those words even come from? "Inez."

"Don't blame her for how you feel. If you don't love me, it's okay." Liam turned away from her. "Go home to Jersey where no one can get to you. Not Inez. And not me." Liam fled the carport and went inside, slamming the door so hard, it practically fell off the hinges.

The pressure lessened its grip and Autumn exhaled slowly. She climbed into her mother's car and drove away. It wasn't until she was nearing the Cayo that she realized she had meant to tell Liam she loved him. Instead, Inez had spoken for her.

Pops crouched down and smacked Liam's face. First they were light taps on the cheek, but as Liam became increasingly hard to wake, the taps became slaps.

"Wha? Wha?" Liam asked, rousing.

"Come on, kid," Pops said, shaking his head. "What's the matter with you?"

Liam draped his arm over his face. "Ugh, go away."

Pops lifted Liam's legs and sat down on the couch. He kicked aside empty beers cans that littered the carpet below. "You can't be drinking beer like this. You're only eighteen."

Liam curled up and turned away. "Oh, like you and your navy buddies didn't drink when you were my age."

"That's different. The times were different. Get off the couch and go to your room. Tomorrow, I'm throwing out all the alcohol."

Liam rolled off the couch. He could barely get to his feet. "Then how will you survive?"

"What's that supposed to mean?"

"What do you think it means? Why is Dad in rehab? It all starts with you. You drink more than anyone, you're just good at concealing it. Did Inez's death drive you to drink? Out of guilt?"

"We're not talking about this," Pops said through gritted teeth. "You don't know everything."

"Why? If you killed her, tell me. If you didn't kill Inez, then you're protecting the person who did." Pops left the room. Liam shouted, "Autumn dumped me! Another Breyer loser whose woman left him!"

But Pops was out of earshot. Liam went to his room and slammed the door. Truth was, Autumn didn't dump Liam because of Pops. She dumped Liam because of Liam. Just like Victoria. Just like the few other girls before them. Liam was not the guy everyone wanted him to be, even when he tried.

By the time Autumn returned home, she had no more tears left to cry. So, she flopped into one of the dusty chairs in the parlor and stared at the floral wallpaper.

Her cell phone buzzed in her pocket. She slid the phone out to see her father's name on the screen.

"Hey, Dad," she said, forcing her voice to sound perky. She wanted her father to think she was excited about coming home. The last thing she wanted was to hurt her dad's feelings. Besides, Autumn had burned her bridges. It was time to start fresh in Jersey.

"Hey pumpkin. Are you excited to move back?"

Autumn forced a smile, even though she knew her father couldn't see her. "You bet." She reminded herself that she'd been wishing for this moment, and at last it had arrived. If only it wasn't at the expense of her and Liam. But seeing him with Victoria just made her understand that Liam wasn't serious about her, even though he said he loved her. And why should he be? They were only eighteen.

Now, Autumn genuinely smiled. "I'm super excited to see you."

"That's great," her father said. She noted he seemed more relaxed now. "I've almost got all the boxes moved out of the guest room. I hope you don't mind sharing the space with old tax records."

Autumn's smile disappeared. The guest room? It was a tiny closet at the end of the hall that looked out onto the neighbor's overgrown yard. "What about my old room?"

Her father cleared his throat. "Remember, honey, we turned that into Jennifer's craft room. For her business."

Autumn cringed at his use of the word, "we," as if she too had agreed to let Jennifer take over her old bedroom.

"I never expected you to move back so soon," he said. "We can't really ask Jennifer to fit her new business into the little guest room. Besides, you'll be in college next year. It's only for the short-term."

Autumn had never felt so transient. Just when she was moving back home, her father was anticipating her moving back out. "Well," she said, her voice ripe with sarcasm. "I appreciate the welcome home."

"Autumn," he warned. "You can't be upset. Your mother just sprung this on us."

"I can't be upset? First, I was told to leave. Now, I'm being told to move back. I thought, of all things, I would get to return to my bedroom. Because last time I checked, it was my room before it was Jennifer's craft space." Somewhere in the background, Autumn heard Jennifer's high-pitched voice say, "If she doesn't like it, she doesn't have to come here."

"I was there first!" Autumn cried out.

"We'll have to talk about this later," her dad said.

"There is no later." Autumn's voice was losing its steam. "I come home next week."

Jennifer's grumblings grew louder. "She's being ungrateful."

"I gotta go," her father said quickly. "I'll text you flight details later." And then he hung up.

Autumn stared at her cell phone in disbelief. She felt like a ping-pong ball being batted between her parents. She had no control over her life anymore. A rise of heat crawled up her spine. Autumn threw the cell phone at the wall and screamed. "Inez! This is all your fault."

Just then, a swirl of darkness surrounded Autumn and Inez materialized in front of her. Before Autumn could step back, the ghost lunged for her, and Autumn screamed.

Liam shuffled into the bathroom and rummaged around for painkillers. His head pulsed and throbbed as if someone had taken a drill to his skull.

He twisted the cap off the bottle of aspirin and threw two back in his mouth, washing them down with tepid tap water.

Pops stood in the doorframe with his arms crossed. "You might be surprised, but I wasn't always a drunk."

Liam spoke to Pops's reflection in the medicine cabinet mirror. "No?"

"No, smart-ass. Sure, I used to drink in the service. We all did. It got bad after your mother left your father, and it got worse after your grandmother died. Let's just say I don't handle my issues well."

Liam ran his hands over his face. "Well, that makes two of us."

"I don't want you to be like me kid," said Pops. "You can have a good life if—"

"If, what?"

"If you quit trying to be like me. You're better than I ever was."

Liam stared into the sink and examined a glob of dried toothpaste he never washed down the drain. "Pops—"

"You know I never liked Inez." Pops leaned against the doorframe, facing away from Liam, as if he couldn't look his grandson in the eye. "She tried several times to break up me and your grandmother. On the night she disappeared, she made a pass at me, and Mariana caught her."

"Where was this?" asked Liam.

"At the school dance outside the St. Veronica's gymnasium. Inez shoved me against the lockers and kissed me right in front of your grandmother. You could hear the record scratch. Your abuela was furious at her sister. She slapped Inez and threatened her."

"Did Inez leave after that?"

"She laughed it off, trying to save face. Eventually, she split. And we never saw her again." Pops rubbed his arms as if trying to warm his body. "Your great aunt was a cruel woman. Alive, she was manipulative and nearly split me and Mariana apart. And dead—she was no better. Her disappearance marred my marriage. Your grandmother blamed herself all those years. But it wasn't her fault. It was never Mariana's fault."

"I'm sorry, Pops."

"Me too, kid. If I could do everything over again, I'd do it all different."

"What do you mean?"

"Maybe, I could've stopped—." He shook his head. "Never mind. I don't think I could've done anything." Pops shuffled off to his bedroom.

Autumn's body jerked as she was transported to Inez's memory. She opened her eyes and found herself in the old gymnasium at St. Veronica's. But something was different about this memory. Autumn was no longer a close observer, seeing Inez's world directly from inside her. Now, Autumn felt like someone had shoved her into the closet in Inez's mind and she was peeking out through the window.

Purple and white crepe paper decorated the gym, and cardboard stars coated in glitter hung from the rafters. A nun swayed near the record player, examining each record before sorting them into piles, even as she tapped her black shoe to the music. Inez assumed each pile represented good vs. evil. Just like her and Mariana. Except Inez wasn't evil. She just took what she wanted when she wanted it—like any man would.

The freshmen girls huddled together under the basketball hoop while the upperclassmen danced in the center, making sure to maintain a respectable distance from the chaperones.

Inside, Inez moved in rhythm to the music, bunching up her red dress as if she was a flamenco dancer performing for the king of Spain. She was feeling better finally, like her old self, and Inez figured tonight, after the dance, she would have to conduct the dirty business of breaking Mick's heart.

Outside, distant thunder rolled. Inez could feel it in her bones—a storm was forming off the coast.

One of the senior girls changed the record and a crowd rushed the floor, eager to dance to The Rolling Stones until the record player scratched and a Perry Como song played instead.

"¿Dónde está tu anillo?"

"¿Qué?" asked Inez.

Mariana pointed to Inez's naked ring finger. "Tu anillo? You're not wearing it."

Inez glanced at her empty finger and shrugged. "I can't find it."

"It's still in my jewelry box. I picked it up the last time you threw it in your fiancé's face. I'm surprised you haven't retrieved it since then."

Mariana was too astute, too keenly aware of Inez's behavior. Inez had been careful with Leo, making sure only to corner him when he was alone. She knew Leo would never say anything to Mariana for fear her sister would not believe Inez made the advances. Mariana was astute, but she was fiercely loyal as well.

"Won't Mick be upset to see you're not wearing it?" said Mariana.

Inez tapped her foot in her black pumps and swished the crinoline. "I don't care."

"Inez—"

"I don't know why I let you put me on this dance committee," Inez interrupted. "Now, we're stuck here. Where are the boys?"

Mariana hovered near the refreshment table and adjusted the napkins, but her shoulders tensed. She smiled at Ralphie's sister, an S-shaped stick with blonde hair, who was doling out the punch. A chestnut cane leaned against the table.

"They'll be here any minute," said Mariana. "They're at Duncan's setting up for later."

Thunder boomed. "We should go before it rains."

"Nonsense," said Mariana. "The dance isn't over for hours. We all agreed to come here first and then we'll go to Duncan's. The night is young."

"Doesn't feel like it," Inez murmured. Anxiety surged through her skin. She wanted to get Leo alone so she could show him that she was the better Cruces sister. Sure, Leo claimed to only have eyes for Mariana, but Inez knew that once he kissed her, he'd see that Mariana was like tepid water.

Mariana shrieked and Inez whirled on her heels. Leo had appeared and planted a kiss on Mariana's cheek. She swatted him away. "Stop it before Sister Therese sees."

"Those old nuns don't scare me," said Leo.

Inez's heart swelled when she saw Leo in a sports jacket with a red tie. Civilian clothes. He even matched her dress. A good sign! Inez caught Leo's eye. She blew him a kiss, but Leo averted his gaze. Leo held out his hand to escort Mariana to the dance floor.

Inez's stomach twisted into a chignon. She sidled up to the refreshment table. Ralphie's sister, whose name Inez never bothered to remember, ambled up and grabbed the ladle to dole out punch into a paper cup. She handed it to Inez with a big smile. Inez accepted the punch and eyed the girl's cane. A cruelty came over her and she said to the girl, "I love dancing, don't you?"

Ralphie's sister grimaced and sat down.

Inez removed a silver flask from her dress pocket and tipped the contents into her cup. She thought she was being discreet until she caught Ralphie's sister's raised eyebrow. "Oh, you're not gonna say anything, are you?"

The girl shook her head.

"I didn't think so." Inez downed her punch and went back for seconds, this time doling out a portion herself.

Inez watched Mariana laugh and twirl with Leo. Then she ducked out of the gym and into a small alcove near the boys' locker room. She skipped the punch and took a swig from her flask. Inez liked how the gin burned her throat and lit a fire inside her belly. From here, she had a perfect view of her sister and Leo. Unfortunately, the booze did little to calm her jealousy, it just fueled her bravado.

She watched Leo escort Mariana over to the bleachers where the rest of the gang had gathered. The gang. Leo, Ralphie, Mick, Duncan, and Glenda. Inez and Mariana had been last-minute additions, but despite being Mick's girl, Inez was the outsider. Mariana fit right into their card games and fishing trips on Ralph's little boat, but Inez was too big for the group. As if she was a volcano, and they were the little town down the mountain. An eruption from her would destroy them under a blanket of fire.

Leo disengaged from the gang and headed her way. Inez hid her flask in her skirt and smoothed down her hair. She waited for him in the shadows.

Leo strode past her, but Inez reached out and grabbed Leo's sleeve. He skidded to a halt.

"Where ya going?" Inez crooned.

"To the boy's lavatory," Leo said, impatiently.

Inez pushed herself off the wall and slinked over to him. The gin made her head fuzzy, and her body move like liquid. "Why don't I join you?"

"In the bathroom?" Leo's cheeks colored. "Now, listen, Inez."

"No, you listen," she purred. "Why don't we skip this kiddie party and head back to Duncan's house where we can be alone?" Her fingers danced along his arm to his collarbone.

Leo squirmed out of her grasp. "Dammit, Inez. Take a hint."

Inez felt the magma inside her churn and bubble, rolling up her legs and thighs, through her torso and exploding from her hands. She shoved Leo against the lockers and kissed him hard on the mouth. Leo pushed her off him and wiped his mouth with the back of his hand, as if Inez's lips tasted like poison. "I can't take you anymore!"

Inez felt a harsh tug on her elbow. Mariana was hauling her down the hallway and toward the janitorial closet. Inez didn't have time to brace for the slap.

Inez gasped and cupped her cheek. "Puta."

Leo trotted down the hallway to separate Mariana and her sister.

"If you touch him again, I will kill you," Mariana hissed.

Inez smoothed her cheek and laughed.

Leo tugged lightly on Mariana's sleeve and led her back into the gymnasium. The last thing Inez heard was Leo telling Mariana, "We have to stop her."

# CHAPTER TWENTY-NINE

Seawater soaked Liam's shirt, but he didn't care. He just laid there on the floor of the yacht and observed the stars. The rocking of the boat didn't help the buzzing in his head. He took a swig from the bottle of Jack Daniels. Somewhere below deck, he could hear the laughter of the other people on board.

Even though he tried to clear her from his head, he couldn't help but wonder what Autumn was doing right this minute. Probably packing her suitcase. Or sleeping.

Liam closed his eyes, which didn't ease the nausea, then sat up. He felt his brain swirl around his head, sort of like the liquor in the bottle whenever the boat rocked.

He hadn't spoken to Autumn since she broke up with him several days ago. He really hadn't spoken to anyone, choosing to mope around Pops's house like he was in mourning. Then his phone rang, and he agreed to an invitation by the one person he should've been avoiding.

"There you are. Have you been hiding?" Victoria knelt down next to him. "We're going to dock soon. You okay?"

"I shouldn't be here." He brought the bottle to his lips.

Victoria put her hand on his hand and lowered the bottle. "Don't be so melodramatic. Enjoy yourself. You're with good company." She smiled.

Liam really did love Autumn, although she was willing to just up and leave, and she had made it perfectly clear she didn't love him. Those words stung.

Liam reached out for the Jack Daniels bottle and took a sip. "You know what? I think I *am* enjoying myself."

Victoria leaned in for a kiss. Liam turned away. The boat lurched and Liam slammed his head on the hard deck and then everything went black..

When his vision cleared, Mick Canton stood over Liam and held out a bag of frozen peas for the back of his skull. Liam groaned, but waved Mick off.

"Come on son, we'll chat in the saloon." Mick helped Liam to his feet and led him inside to a spacious room with shiny wood floors and built in cabinets. There were cream draperies on the windows and recessed lighting that made everything sparkle like diamonds in a jewelry store. Mick pointed to an oversized leather chair and held out the frozen peas.

Liam dropped into to the club chair, feeling more embarrassed than in pain. He waved him off. "I'm okay."

"Take the peas, boy," he said, gruffly. "I don't want you suing me for getting a concussion on my boat."

Liam accepted the frozen bag. "I'm not the litigious type."

Mick scoffed. "Everyone's the litigious type." He sat down in the opposite chair and lit a cigar. Mick offered one to Liam, but he said no. Smoking had never been one of Liam's vices.

"Did you hear I'm buying the Cayo Hueso?" Mick asked point blank.

Liam pressed the frozen peas to the back of his head and winced.

"The property is becoming too much for the ladies to handle. I always tried to get Duncan to sell, but his batty wife loved the house too much."

Liam wanted to say that, in Duncan's defense, it had been his childhood home, but he decided against it. He just nodded along, like a puppet, to whatever Mick said.

Mick leaned in close. Liam smelled tobacco and alcohol on the man's breath. "To be honest, I got the place for a song." He reclined. "I mean, it's run-down. It'll need a million dollar in renovations just to be presentable."

Liam thought about the worn parlor chairs. The mahogany bar top in reception. The teal shutters that framed the ornate windows. It certainly had charm. "I don't know about a million dollars."

Mick grinned. "It was a steal."

Liam shifted uneasily. First, it seemed to him pretty ridiculous, not to mention underhanded, for a nearly billionaire to be bragging about getting a property for a lot less than it was worth. Second, it sounded like Mick took advantage of Aunt Glenda's financial situation. Liam couldn't share in Mick's celebration, so he just sat there like a dope.

"Heard my Victoria is going to bankroll your endeavor." Mick examined his cigar.

Liam choked on the smoke. "I didn't take her money. I don't know what I'm going to do."

Mick flicked the ashes into a crystal dish and shrugged. "You could always come work for me. I value loyalty, and I need someone to supervise my current scooter rental space off Petronia." He put his cigar down and turned to Liam. "What do you say?"

"Um, can I think about it?"

"What's there to think about? You're a Breyer, Liam. Besides, a deal's a deal."

Liam didn't know what Mick was hinting at. He sank into his chair and tried to make himself look smaller. He sure felt small.

"And you better warn your buddy, Randall. What he did amounts to grand larceny."

"You have to know I had no idea where he got those bikes," said Liam.

"I'll keep that in mind. Provided you're a good Canton soldier now."

Liam set the bag of peas on the small side table. He wasn't sure if it was the booze talking or his possible concussion, but his curiosity would not subside. Liam looked Mick Canton straight in the eye. "Where were you the night Inez disappeared?"

Mick blanched, but then steeled his eyes. "I was at the school dance at St. Veronica's. Everyone was there."

"Did you and Inez fight?"

"Detective Breyer," Mick joked. "Should I get my lawyer?"

"Only if you have something to hide. Did you fight about the pregnancy? Leo? What?"

Mick raised his brow. "You presume to know an awful lot." He poured himself a drink from a crystal decanter. He swirled the butterscotch-colored liquid before throwing it down his throat. "We did fight about the baby."

"What about the baby?" Liam had always suspected that Mick killed Inez because she was pregnant, and he didn't want to be tied down to her, but Autumn claimed that Mick really loved Inez.

Mick took another swig and set down the glass. "There was no baby. Inez had miscarried and then lied about it."

Mick tapped the ashes from his cigar, but missed his crystal ashtray. Instead, the ash fell to the man's pressed gray pants and burned a small hole. Mick Canton didn't even flinch.

Inez stumbled into the gymnasium, but held her head up. They were all standing on the other side, Mariana whispering into Glenda's ear as if they were confidants.

Inez ignored the stares of the nuns, who were too cowardly to confront her directly.

Inez smiled and wiggled her fingers at them. She bumped into the refreshment table. The punch sloshed over the bowl and stained the white tablecloth pink.

Ralph's sister sopped up the mess with cocktail napkins.

Mick charged toward Inez and snatched her hand, leading her out of the gym and into an empty chemistry classroom. His eyes flashed. "What's this I hear about you kissing Leo?"

Inez pressed her hands against his broad chest, trying to both cajole him and shove him away. "I was just playing a joke."

"Are you drunk?"

Inez slipped her hand in her pocket and withdrew the flask. "It's gin. You want some?" She giggled.

Mick pushed the flask away. "Mariana told me something else."

Gin sloshed in her belly, seeking payment.

He lowered his voice to a whisper. "She said you miscarried weeks ago."

"She could never keep her mouth shut!" Inez tried to brush past Mick in an attempt to leave the classroom. She wanted to strangle her sister.

Mick grabbed Inez's wrists. "How could you lie to me like that? I gave you my grandmother's ring." He ran his thumb over Inez's finger. "Which you're not even wearing. Do you even love me?"

Inez stepped back, but she didn't dare look up at him.

Mick's eyes appeared moist and an odd satisfaction coursed through her.

"I want my ring back," Mick said.

Sobriety crept back in. "I don't have it."

Mick's eyes widened. "Where is it?"

"I sold it." Well, she was going to sell it. Along with some treasures she planned to steal from Duncan's house. Inez had hoped the money would be for her and Leo to run off together, but now, it seemed, Inez would need the money to leave Key West alone. There would be no going back to the gang after this.

Mick balled his fists at his side. "This is unforgivable. You've made a chump out of me for the last time." He loomed over Inez and then stepped around her, heading back toward to his group of friends.

Liam awoke groggy and filled with guilt. After his fight with Pops, and slinking off the Canton boat, Liam had been avoiding the old man. It wasn't Pops's fault he made a mess of things with Autumn. Autumn only did what she was likely to do later—dump his sorry ass for better things. Liam sighed. He had hoped things would've worked out.

Liam yawned and stretched as he made his way into the living room. "Pops," he called out. Liam tripped over a beer can. "Pops." Liam was met with silence. His heart raced. Pops slumped in his battered armchair, his head dipped to the side. Liam noticed a line of drool slinking down his grandfather's stubbled chin.

Liam crouched and gently slapped the old man's face. "Wake up, Pops." His grandfather groaned. Liam relaxed only slightly until he saw an empty handle of Jack Daniels on the side table. There wasn't even a glass. "Jeez, Pops. What did you do?"

Pops's eyes rolled around in his head before fluttering open. His voice came out raspy and barely audible. "I'm sorry, kiddo. I had to do it. She'd never leave us in peace." Pops closed his eyes.

Liam frantically tapped his grandfather's face. "Pops. Wake up." He noticed the cordless phone. "Who did you call?"

Pops began to weep. "You'll thank me, one day. You will."

"Pops, who did you call?"

Liam heard the sound of sirens.

Inez watched Mick go, her heart thumping wildly in her chest. For a moment, she was grateful there was no one to see her humiliation. Mama always said she shined like a jewel. Jewels didn't lose their luster no matter how often they were mishandled. She would overcome this. A few classmates glanced her way, but none were so stupid as to dare approach her to fuel their gossip mill.

No one except Ralph's sister, who watched Mick Canton with wide, appreciative eyes.

Inez flicked her dark hair off her shoulder. "You like Mick, don't you?"

The girl raised her brows in surprise at being caught. "I-I don't—"

"Oh, you think I don't see how you look at him with those big eyes, following him around like a puppy dog. It's pathetic." Inez wasn't sure why she was teasing the poor girl. But she was hurt, and she wanted to hurt someone else. Inez tilted her chin toward the girl's body. "But you do know why Mick could never find someone like you attractive?"

"I'm not as pathetic as you," the girl dared to answer.

"As long as there are beauties like me, the Mick Cantons of the world won't have time for the likes of you." Inez grabbed the punch bowl ladle, but the girl snatched it away first. Inez dug her red nails into the girl's flesh, drawing pops of blood, and then let go.

The girl winced and cried out. "You're a monster." She pressed a linen handkerchief to the wound.

Inez ladled punch into a cup, drank it all down, and crumbled the cup in her hands. The volcano inside her rumbled. She needed a release.

The dance would not be over for a couple more hours. It was time to go to Duncan's house and say her goodbyes.

# CHAPTER THIRTY

Liam squirmed in a hard plastic chair while he waited for an officer to escort him to the interview room to see his grandfather.

"It might be a while," the officer said not unkindly. He was an older man with salt and pepper hair and a Santa Claus body shape. His nametag read Sgt. Flips. "Is there someone you can call?"

Liam swallowed down his tears. He wanted to call Autumn, but he doubted she'd want to hear from him, especially now that Pops had been arrested for killing a woman. Liam slid his cell phone out of his back pocket and waved it at the officer. "I'll call my dad."

"That's a good idea. This is a lot for a teenager to handle."

*No shit.* Liam dialed the phone number to the rehab center in North Dakota. After being patched to the operator and then to his father's floor, he finally got a nurse on the phone. "I'm calling for Raymond Breyer. This is his son, Liam. Tell my father it's an emergency."

The nurse sputtered a bit before saying, "Are you okay?"

Liam stood up and paced the floor. "Yes, I'm fine. It's his dad. My grandpa. Just tell him Pops is in trouble."

He could hear the nurse sigh on the other end of the line. "Oh, honey," she said softly. "I wish I could, but your dad checked out of here days ago."

Liam closed his eyes and let out a big breath. Of course, his father couldn't hack a few weeks in rehab. "Did he say where he was going?"

The nurse hesitated. Liam wondered if she was planning to lie to him on the phone. "He said he was going to find a woman."

Liam fell back against the wall. The tile felt cool against his skin but did little to alleviate the rage inside. His father ditched his rehab stint to go on some wild goose chase to find his mother. Liam's mother. She was the only woman he'd ever loved. It was probably the reason he became a truck driver so he could search the country for her. *Well, screw them both.*

Liam mumbled a quick thanks before hanging up on the nurse. Sgt. Flips returned with a cup of coffee and handed it to Liam. "Did you get a hold of your dad?"

"Yup," Liam lied.

Sgt. Flips smiled. "Good. Because your grandpa is going to need a lawyer." Then he whispered, "And the new public defender they hired is a putz. You don't want him." Flips gently patted Liam on the shoulder. "You can see your grandpa for a few minutes."

Acid churned in Liam's stomach as Sgt. Flips led him into the interview room. There wasn't that two-way mirror Liam expected, just a large window with crisscross lines over it.

Pops hunched in the chair. Liam remembered that the poor man had been interrogated for hours and was still hung over. He dropped into the chair across from his grandpa and slid over his cup of hot coffee. "Here, you need this more than I do."

Pops cupped his hands around the Styrofoam. "Thanks, sport." He took a sip of the dark liquid and stared at the wall, his eyes glazing over. "Your grandma never got over her sister's death. Inez was like a dark cloud over our entire marriage. It didn't seem to matter what I did, she was never happy."

"Pops." Liam reached for his grandfather's hand. If the cops were recording this conversation, he didn't want his grandfather to say anything incriminating. "Let's not talk about this now. I need to get you a lawyer. Are any of your shuffleboard cronies lawyers?"

"Just Leonard, but he only worked with patents or copyright."

Liam leaned back in his chair. "I could call Mick Canton."

"No!" Pops's outburst startled him.

"Come on, Pops. Once upon a time you were friends. He has the money to help you out."

Pops vehemently shook his head. "I'd rather go to prison."

"You don't mean that."

"I do."

Anger bubbled beneath Liam's skin. He wanted to leap across the table and shake Pops's pride from him. This wasn't just about whether Pops went to prison. It was about Liam keeping the only member of his family with him. "Mr. Fletcher," Liam said.

"Who?"

"Mr. Fletcher," Liam repeated. "He's a guest at the Cayo. A friend, almost. He used to be a lawyer."

"Don't be bothering strangers. I'll use the public defender."

"He's a putz. You don't get a choice. I'm not letting them take you to prison."

Pops sighed and wiped at his wet eyes. Liam had never seen his grandpa cry before. Liam choked back his own sob.

Just then, Sgt. Flips came in. "The detectives would like to resume. Will your lawyer be coming soon?"

Liam stood and nodded. "Yes, I'm calling him right now." Liam slipped out of the room and quickly dialed the Cayo. The phone rang and Timothy answered, "Cayo Hueso Bed and Breakfast."

"Timothy," Liam choked out. "I need to get a hold of Mr. Fletcher."

"You all right, lover boy?"

"No." It took all his resolve not to burst into tears.

Autumn emerged from Inez's vision disoriented. It took her a few seconds to realize she was in the Cayo's parlor, her legs brought up tightly to her chest. She rose from the chair to retrieve her cell phone. The screen was cracked, but otherwise appeared all right. Autumn inhaled deeply and went outside to the patio to get fresh air. The vision had exhausted her and scrambled her brain. Autumn felt uncertain as to who killed Inez. As it turned out, Inez had pissed off enough friends that any one of the gang was a likely suspect.

Autumn laid down in the rusted lawn chair and stared out at the pool. By some miracle, Liam had managed to get the water to a normal pool color, rather than the green haze it had been not that long ago.

Liam. She wanted so badly for things to have worked out. For her mother to have been wrong. But the minute she saw him with Victoria, she knew. Liam's life was cemented here in Key West. And her life was, well, she wasn't sure. She didn't feel like she belonged in New Jersey anymore. Her own father was counting down the days until she moved into the college dorms. Still, maybe it was all for the best. She'd be back home. She could try for a slot on the school newspaper and get some real journalism experience. Then she'd be eligible for the scholarship the following year.

Mr. Fletcher crossed her path, carrying his brown leather briefcase. He loosened his tie. He must've been roasting in that charcoal suit.

Were you interviewing someone?" asked Autumn.

The man raised his brows in surprise, and then scanned his clothing. A look of understand dawned on his face. "Ah, no. I was coming back from the jail. I put on my lawyer suit today."

Now it was Autumn's turn to be surprised. "The jail?"

Mr. Fletcher plunked down at the end of the lawn chair, his weight pushing the weathered plastic strips to their breaking point. "Liam's grandfather has been arrested."

Autumn swallowed a big lump in her throat. "For Inez's murder? "

Mr. Fletcher sighed. "Are you still going back to New Jersey?"

"I leave the eleventh."

"I haven't known you long, Autumn, but you seem like a real good kid. The type of person who cares about people." He studied her. "I know Liam could use your support."

"He has you. He has Victoria and his Conch friends. He doesn't need me. Besides, I'm going home."

"Don't you think you are home?" Mr. Fletcher asked.

"My family is in New Jersey. Or at least my dad is and my soon-to-be half brother."

"True, but you and I both know that family isn't always blood."

Autumn thought about that for a moment. Timothy felt like a brother to her, and he and Autumn weren't relatives. She shook her head. "It doesn't matter. What's done is done."

Mr. Fletcher rose from the chair. "If you think so."

"Aunt Glenda is selling this place," she said.

"To who?"

"To me," came a deep male voice. Both Autumn and Mr. Fletcher turned around to find Mick Canton standing underneath the trellis wearing a blue-collared shirt. His large frame took up the whole space.

Mr. Fletcher didn't seem fazed. "You bought the Cayo?"

"It's not a done deal, but it will be." Mick smiled, showing a row of white teeth. They reminded Autumn of a shark.

"And what are your plans for the Cayo?" Mr. Fletcher asked.

"Why, to level it to the ground," Mick said casually.

Autumn leaped out of the chair. "You can't do that. This place is historic. It was in Uncle Duncan's family for years. There are . . ." She caught herself before saying ghosts.

"Perhaps, young lady, there are parts of one's past that are best left in the past," said Mick.

"You mean Inez?" A chill crawled up her spine.

Mick flinched. "You have no idea what you're talking about." His voice was ice.

"I know that you were a couple." Autumn jutted out her chin. "I also know that she broke your heart." She swallowed a lump. "And I know about the baby. Is that why you killed her? You didn't want to be a dad?"

"Autumn," Mr. Fletcher warned.

Mick's eyes flashed. "I was willing to accept my responsibility. And she didn't just break my heart, she crushed it. She could've had me, she could've had this life. Instead, she died wanting a man who would never return her love. The Breyer men destroy everything they touch."

Autumn approached Mick and stood her ground. "That's not true. Not Liam."

Mick glared at her. "Liam is just like his grandfather. The only way to save that boy is to bring him into the Canton fold."

"What did you say to Leo Breyer to get him to confess?" Autumn said.

Mr. Fletcher raised his brow.

Mick growled. "What makes you so sure Leo Breyer is innocent? Inez loved him. She couldn't stay away from him."

"Were you jealous? Jealous enough to kill her?"

Mick pointed a finger at Mr. Fletcher. "I don't like what this girl is implying."

"Is she telling the truth?" asked Mr. Fletcher.

"No. I don't know who killed Inez." Mick sniffed. "Leo was the last to see her alive. He must've killed her."

Autumn recalled Inez's memory of the night of the party. "No, Mr. Canton. Leo was not the last person to see her alive." She stared hard at the broad man. "You were."

"There's no way for you to know that," he said. Except his voice didn't sound angry, just confused. "When I left her, she was alive. Everyone was at the dance."

"Not everyone," said Autumn. "Somebody killed her."

Mick stared past Autumn. "I came to have a chat with your mom, but she seems to be out. Anyway, Bernadette will be stopping by with my contractor to talk renovations. I'm going to suggest we level this place to the ground." He sneered at Autumn before pushing past her and out the side gate.

Liam sat in a chair on Pops's cracked patio. He stared into the distance, his eyes glazing over the white pebbles in the backyard. The potted Mandeville flopped to one side. Liam got up and unraveled the hose, drenching the pink flower in water. The least he could do for his grandfather was to keep the plant alive.

Liam longed to talk to someone, but he was fresh out of friends. Pops was in jail. His father was missing. Autumn hated him. Randall was a criminal.

His eyes blurred, and his brain felt as if a goldfish was swimming circles in a murky bowl. He had no idea how he was going to get Pops out of this mess. There was no way his grandfather was a killer.

Liam's cell phone buzzed and he grunted as he struggled to grab it. He swiped the screen and grumbled, "What do you want?"

"Dude," came Randall's voice. "You sound terrible."

"Seriously? My grandfather's in jail."

"Okay," Randall said slowly. "I'm calling with good news."

Liam scoffed. *Yeah, right.*

"Mick Canton agreed not to press charges."

Liam didn't say anything. "Dude, you still there?"

Liam tried to sit up, but his limbs felt as strong as paper streamers. "I'm here. Why? How?"

Randall coughed. "Doesn't matter. He said he wouldn't report us. In fact, Canton agreed to lease us a property for free. For the first few years."

"Mick agreed to do that?" Liam's head buzzed. "Why would he agree to that?"

"I don't know why. It doesn't matter anyway. We're back in business, and we want you to come along, provided you focus on the scooter shop."

"Focus? If I remember, you were drunk off your ass just a few days ago," Liam said.

Liam couldn't see, but he imagined Randall shrugging, not seeing the similarities.

"Whatever, dude," said Randall. "You in?"

Liam held the phone away from his ear and stared at the screen. This was what he always wanted. He wanted to create something and be in charge of his own life. He wanted to work for himself. Randall was giving him another opportunity. But why now? Why the change?

Liam pressed the phone back to his ear. "Screw you, Randall." He pressed the end button, hanging up on his best friend of twelve years.

Liam knew exactly why Mick had changed his mind. This was what Pops had agreed to. His grandfather gave up his life for Liam to have one of his own.

# CHAPTER THIRTY-ONE

Liam stood over the Cayo's swimming pool and debated on whether he wanted to fall into the water and let Inez put him out of his misery.

Glenda approached him cautiously and rested her wrinkled hand on his shoulder. "It's going to be all right, William. My Duncan will see to it. Come, sit." She led Liam over to a bench with a weather-beaten floral cushion and ushered him into the seat. He felt like a zombie. His brain was mush, his body numb, and he was being led around by a seventy-year-old woman with a few loose marbles.

Glenda sat next to him and opened up her arms. Liam nestled into the crook, just like he used to do with Abuela. Glenda even smelled like his grandmother, a mixture of rose water and Aquanet hairspray. Glenda pressed her hand against Liam's head, and he sobbed. He couldn't even be embarrassed at this point. Everything was a mess. Pops was in prison for murder, his drunk father was gallivanting across the country trying to find a woman who didn't want to be found, and Autumn hated him.

Liam cried for a few minutes before straightening up. He wiped his runny nose with the back of his hand and sniffled. "If Duncan were here, he'd figure out a way to tell Autumn the truth."

Glenda stared at her hands in her lap. "Perhaps he can't tell her." Her voice was barely above a whisper. "Because perhaps he isn't here at all." Glenda sighed heavily. "Ghosts are rare and enigmatic beings. But I was never scared of them. Even as a child, I was never frightened. My mother used to call me crazy for communicating with them. Although, eventually, I stopped seeing them. Sometimes, I think my mother frightened them away, or maybe I did. I don't know. You, Timothy, and Autumn all have a gift. My gift disappeared long ago." Glenda's voice took on a childlike quality. She sounded both sad and terrified, as if those memories were as real now as they were when she was small. Maybe to her, they were.

"The truth is, I loved Duncan with all my heart, but I don't know if he felt the same way. I don't think he's here watching over us. I kept holding on to the Cayo, even when I was running it into the ground, because I couldn't imagine walking away from Duncan's spirit. But, I think he left long ago—maybe long before he died. Whatever happened here with Inez affected him. Before he died, he wanted to sell the Cayo. He said the building didn't hold the happy memories it used to. I should've listened."

"Mick Canton is going to destroy this place," Liam said.

"He will." Glenda absently patted Liam's hand and stared out at the pool as if in a trance. "But in doing so, he might take Inez down."

"And Katie," said Liam.

"Death is sad business. And the afterlife is no life at all. You'll be okay, Liam."

Liam rubbed his eyes. "Not without Pops."

Glenda played with her long beaded necklace. "Leo Breyer has made many bad choices in his life. But murder isn't one of them. I don't, for a second, believe he did such a thing, no matter what he confessed to."

"I know he didn't do it," said Liam.

"Then why'd he confess?"

"To protect me. I got into trouble with Mick, and I think Pops is covering for me."

Glenda focused on Liam. "If that's the case, then Mick must've asked him to. Which means—"

"Mick's guilty of murdering Inez."

"Or he's involved in the crime at least."

Glenda gently tilted Liam's chin up toward her. "You and Autumn have to figure this out. Together."

"How?"

Glenda let go and rose from the bench. "First, you both must start with an apology."

After Autumn heard rummaging in the attic and went to check it out, she found Liam stacking boxes and sweeping dust from the corners.

Her heart ached at the sight of him. His biceps flexed as he worked, and she wanted to go to him and put his arms around her. She wasn't going to see him ever again. Once Evelyn relocated to El Paso and Autumn moved in with her father, there was no reason for her to return to the Keys. The thought unnerved her. Weeks ago, all she wanted was to leave the oppressive humidity of Florida, and now the idea of moving back to the northeast gave her chills—and not the good kind.

Autumn coughed loudly as Liam kept on sweeping. "I've known you were standing there for the last minute. I can feel your presence in a room."

His words were like an arrow through her chest. "I wasn't trying to startle you."

"I'm not fragile, you know?"

"I know. What are you doing here?" She winced at the roughness of her words. "I don't want you to get in trouble with my mom."

"She texted me and told me she needed help cleaning out the attic. For the sale. I need the money to help pay Mr. Fletcher. He's giving me a huge discount, but I won't take a handout."

"Oh." The sale. Autumn had lived at the Cayo for less than a year, but she couldn't imagine this place belonging to anyone but her Aunt Glenda. She blurted out, "I'm so sorry about everything."

"Don't be. If anything, I should be apologizing to you." He cleared this throat. "About Victoria." Liam leaned the broom against the unfinished wall and glanced out the window. A warm breeze flowed into the attic and ruffled Liam's hair. "I didn't mean for us to kiss." He shook his head. "I do know. I was drinking and—"

Autumn navigated her way to Liam. She wiped some dust from on an old box and sat down, the cardboard bucking under her weight. She hoped Aunt Glenda's fine china wasn't packed inside.

He turned to her. "I'm a mess, Autumn. I was feeling sorry for myself, and I let my guard down. I don't deserve a nice girl like you." Liam wiped dirt off his face with the back of his hand. "The worst part is I made Pops think I was ashamed of him. And now he's copped to a crime he didn't commit to protect me."

"How do you mean?"

"Randall called to say Mick has given him a reprieve and his blessing to start our scooter business. He isn't going to report us to the police. I could've been charged with grand larceny. I'm telling you. Pops confessed to help my sorry ass build a business."

"Which means Mick asked him to," Autumn said.

"Because he killed her."

Autumn bit her lip. "Maybe."

"What do you mean, maybe? He's involved in Inez's murder. I can feel it in my bones. Based on everything we know, Mick is the most likely suspect. He was jealous. Not to mention Inez lied to him about miscarrying."

"And she claimed to have sold his ring."

"Based on that evidence—"

"Mick is her killer."

An object hit the floor, startling them. Autumn jumped. She padded over to a corner of the attic and saw the brown leather book. Uncle Duncan's high school yearbook.

"I thought Timothy had packed it away. It's just my uncle's yearbook. His mother sent him to boarding school in Connecticut."

Liam bent down to pick it up and put it back in the box just as Timothy rushed into the attic. He wiped a line of perspiration from his lip.

"You're sweating!" cried Autumn, not hiding her surprise.

"Yes, it happens during times of stress," Timothy said.

Liam nodded at Timothy. "What's going on?"

Timothy put his hands on his hips and exhaled. "I came up to tell you Mr. Blazevig collapsed. The neighbor found him, and he's in the hospital."

Autumn and Liam shared a look before hustling down the stairs.

Autumn hated hospitals. During Career Week at her high school, Evelyn tried to convince Autumn that nursing would make for an excellent profession. A job that could sustain her through all phases of her life. But Autumn could never get past the septic smell of a hospital. The beeping of machines. The cold tile. The looming death. The ghosts.

Now, Autumn paced around the nurses' station on the ICU floor, waiting for someone to acknowledge her. She shouldn't have even been allowed up here, but Timothy distracted the security guard with some serious flirting while Liam parked the car.

Autumn adjusted the strap on her backpack and addressed the dark-haired nurse in her most adult voice. "Can you please tell me what room Mr. Ralph Blazevig is in?"

The nurse narrowed her eyes at Autumn. "Are you family?"

"Granddaughter," Autumn said without missing a beat.

The nurse, whose nametag read Debbie, softened her expression. "Your mom visited earlier. He's in room three-twelve."

"Thank you."

"Just be aware, your grandpa is hooked up to a lot of machines. He's also heavily sedated."

Autumn nodded. She swallowed hard and made her way down the hall. She passed an open door where she glimpsed a gray-haired woman sitting on the bed covers, gently patting the man's hand in the hospital bed. Autumn shivered.

When Autumn arrived at room 312, she rapped on the heavy door, not even knowing if it mattered. Could Mr. Blazevig hear her? No, the nurse said he was heavily sedated.

Autumn entered the room. Mr. Blazevig lay in his hospital bed with a thin blue blanket pulled up to his chest. He wore old-fashioned pajamas, the kind she recognized from black-and-white films. His eyes were closed and his lips were cracked and dry. As he slept, a machine pumped up and down. Autumn pulled up a chair and sat next to the bed. She watched his chest rise and fall with the cadence of the machines. If she hadn't seen him breathe, Autumn would've thought he was dead. This was why she didn't like hospitals. Aside from the maternity ward, no one ever looked healthy in a hospital.

"Your grandfather had a stroke."

Autumn whipped around. Debbie entered and began changing a plastic bag that hung from a tall metal pole. "Will he be okay?"

"He was very dehydrated when he came in," said Debbie. "He needs a lot of care. But I'm sure your family will be able to get him the best home care around."

Autumn wasn't sure about that. She swelled with sadness. Who was going to look after poor Mr. Blazevig?

She glanced up at the nurse. "Can he hear me?"

"Probably not. But hearing your voice might help his brain heal. I believe that much."

Autumn turned around and took out some yellowed paperback books out of her bag. She held them up to show the nurse. "They're mysteries. He loves them. He's probably read them a hundred times."

Debbie patted Autumn's knee. "You're a real sweet girl."

Autumn settled into the cushion of the chair and poured herself a cup of water from the plastic pitcher. Then she selected one of the mysteries Mr. Blazevig had given her days ago. It was a collection of short stories about a detective's secretary who solved all the cases. The pages were yellowed from age, and there was a price on the cover. Fifty cents. Autumn opened the book to the first page, saw that the copyright date said 1962, and inhaled its musty odor. She began to read. The first story had an interesting premise. A store owner goes missing and the police assume his body was dumped in the lake. Except a storm blew in, and the murderer couldn't get on the boat, so she buried him near the fence in a vacant lot. Autumn scoffed. The secretary figured that out in three pages.

Autumn didn't understand the appeal. These were dime-store mysteries. She thought for sure Mr. Blazevig would like newer releases. Even her mom liked a good Grisham novel every once in a while. In Mr. Blazevig's books, the characters still used rotary phones.

Autumn was halfway done with a story about a librarian who murdered a patron when Timothy and Liam entered.

Autumn set the book down and glanced up. "That took you a while."

Timothy adjusted the strap on his heavy messenger bag before smoothing the back of his hair. "Girl, I got his phone number and his family history. That boy loves to talk."

Liam pulled up a chair and nodded at Mr. Blazevig. "How's he doing?"

Autumn sighed. A bubble of hurt crawled up her throat, causing her to choke on the words. "Not too good. He needs someone to care for him."

Timothy softened his eyes. "Don't you worry. Mama and I will check in on him."

Autumn didn't have the heart to tell Timothy that his reassurances didn't make her feel better.

"Come on, Autumn," Timothy said. "The man's asleep. Not much more you can do for him today."

Autumn started to stand when Mr. Blazevig grabbed her wrist. His bony fingers dug into her skin. Autumn tried to shake him off, but she couldn't.

His brown eyes flashed open for a second. "I'm sorry," he croaked in a hoarse whisper.

Autumn struggled against the old man's unusual strength. "Are you okay? Do you need me to get the nurse?"

"I lied," he repeated.

"I know." Autumn's voice trembled. "You told me already. About Inez Cruces? You did know her. It's okay. You didn't do anything wrong." She leaned in and whispered, "I think I'm close to finding out who killed her anyway."

Mr. Blazevig's eyes widened in fear.

Machines beeped and alarms sounded. Debbie rushed into the room and ordered Autumn, Liam, and Timothy out.

# CHAPTER THIRTY-TWO

The trio huddled outside Mr. Blazevig's room. A doctor flew past them.

"This can't be good." Autumn bit her thumbnail.

A blonde nurse snapped her fingers at them and pointed to a room down the hall. "You'll have to wait there for a while."

They all nodded while Liam led the way. The waiting room was a cramped space with a stained carpet, but there was a television with a broken remote, a vending machine, and a coffee pot.

Timothy dropped his messenger bag to the linoleum floor. It landed with a thump.

Liam eyed Timothy's bag. "What's in there? Sounds heavy."

"Well, Mr. Nosey," Timothy said, sitting down in a chair with worn blue cushions. "My sketch pad, colored pencils, and my tablet."

Liam opened the bag's flap with his toe. "And Duncan's yearbook?"

Timothy arched his brow. "Why would I have Duncan's yearbook?"

Liam bent down and removed the leather-bound tome from the bag. "You tell me."

"That's weird. I didn't put it in there."

Autumn paced around the small room. "The nurse said something weird to me." She paused to get their attention. "She said, 'Your mom visited earlier.' At first, I thought she meant Evelyn. But, I told the nurse I was his granddaughter."

"So who visited Mr. Blazevig?" asked Liam.

"Mr. Blazevig said he had a sister. Maybe she's still around," said Autumn. "If so, I could talk to her about Inez. Ralph's sister was actually the last person to see Inez alive. Maybe she knows something I'm not seeing."

"He's sick," Liam said. "Maybe she flew in from out of state."

"Yeah, but the nurse said his family would be able to get him the best care in the state. That implies money. Mr. Blazevig wasn't a wealthy man. So, who's his sister?"

The boys shrugged.

"The girl you saw in Inez's memories. Did she have a name?" Liam asked.

"No, Inez didn't know or she never made an effort to learn it."

"Would you recognize the woman if you saw her?" asked Liam.

"If I saw her now? I don't know. The girl from the vision was a teenager. Today, she'd be an old lady. She could look so different." Autumn's toe bumped up against Timothy's bag and she snapped her fingers. "The yearbook! The answer is in a yearbook."

Liam held the yearbook and flipped through the pages. "Your uncle's yearbook is from some boarding school in Connecticut."

"Not *his* yearbook. *A* yearbook. Mr. Blazevig said his sister went to St. Veronica's. We need a St. Veronica's yearbook. I'll flip through the book, find her name, and we'll identify her. Then we can find her."

"Where are we going to get a local yearbook?"

Autumn beamed. "The library has them in their historical reference collection. At least, the local library in Jersey did."

"Nice plan," said Timothy. "But the library doesn't open until tomorrow."

"Well then, we go tomorrow," Autumn said. "What's one more night?"

That night, Autumn crawled into bed, slipped under the covers, and turned off the light. She didn't even bother checking to see if her mom was awake. She didn't care. Her mind buzzed. Maybe there was a way to solve this mystery after all. They were so close.

Her eyelids fluttered like butterfly wings before closing. Autumn turned to her side and felt a cool draft. She opened her eyes and bolted upright. Katie floated over her bedside.

Autumn clicked on the light and pulled her covers to her chest in a protective hold. "Dammit, Katie, you scared the crap out of me."

But Katie didn't look sorry. In fact, she hardly looked like Katie at all.

"Katie, are you okay?"

The ghost hovered and stared straight ahead, her mouth opened into a black void. Autumn felt panic rise.

"Inez," she whispered. "Stop whatever it is you're doing to Katie."

"You want to see my last moments?" Inez hissed.

"Yes!" Autumn said. "Show me your last moments on earth."

A black mass left Katie's body and slammed in Autumn's. She fell back on her pillow as if she was falling asleep. Except when she woke, she wasn't Autumn Abernathy anymore.

Inez left St. Veronica's and made her way toward Duncan's house.

Thunder rumbled, and a strong breeze lifted up the hem of her dress, catching her off guard. She stared up at the darkening sky as clouds rolled in. Maybe the storm would cover her tracks.

Duncan's parents were wealthy and often out of town. Tonight was no exception. Inez knew where Duncan's parents kept the silver and she overheard Duncan tell Ralph there was cash in a cookie jar in the kitchen for such emergencies. Tonight was one such emergency.

Inez peered around, checking for nosey neighbors, before unlatching the back gate and entering the patio. Duncan, and presumably Ralph, had set up a card table near the pool with the record player on top. A stack of records lay piled up next to it. Inez kicked the records. A few landed in the pool and sunk to the bottom.

Inez started toward the French doors, until a blow to the back of her head sent her to the concrete patio floor.

She tried to push herself up but was struck again. A trickle of red, sticky liquid streamed down her forehead and dipped into her ear before she was rolled into the pool.

Autumn bolted upright, panting and out of breath. She'd never seen her killer's face. Timothy had been right. All this time, and Inez never saw who hit her.

It could've been anyone.

Liam hurried up the curved concrete stairs of the Key West branch of the Monroe County Public Library and held open the glass door for Autumn. Even as a kid, especially as a kid, Liam loved coming to the library with Pops for story hour. Pops would drop off Liam with the librarian before heading into the mystery section, where he'd read the latest Jack Reacher novel and return as story time ended. Liam would show off his craft and Pops would ruffle Liam's hair and compliment Liam on how well he cut out the storybook characters. Just thinking about those days made Liam's chest ache.

Autumn followed Liam inside the library, and he welcomed her nearness. Everything awful that had happened occurred from the moment he took the Cayo Hueso job, and yet, he wouldn't have changed these past few weeks for anything. He knew Autumn was going back to New Jersey. She didn't have a choice. But he'd rather have whatever time they had left than no time at all.

Liam made a beeline for the reference desk. A middle-aged man with thinning brown hair and wire-framed glasses oversaw the desk. His nametag read "Jon," and his brown eyes crinkled when Liam and Autumn approached.

"Can I help you?" the librarian asked.

"We need to see local yearbooks," said Liam. "Specifically from St. Veronica's."

"Huh," said the librarian. "What an interesting request. How far back do you need to go?"

Autumn glanced at Liam. "Nineteen sixty-six?"

Jon stood up and ushered them to the stacks in the back of the library. "We keep them on a shelf in the back." He wheeled over a small step stool, climbed up, and took down a dusty tome. Handing it to Autumn, he said, "Unfortunately, you can't check it out."

"That's okay," Autumn said.

Jon nodded and smiled. "Just leave the yearbook on my desk when you're done." He adjusted his glasses before retreating to the reference area.

Liam led Autumn to a rectangular table on the other side of the stacks. He didn't sit down, just immediately started flipping through the pages until he got to the senior class photos. All the women wore white blouses with black ties, the school pin affixed near their collars. The same pin Liam found buried in the dirt near the tree in the Cayo's backyard.

"We only need to find a name," Autumn said. "Maybe Timothy has some connections with other island hotels and we can find out where she's staying."

It didn't take long to find Inez's yearbook photo. Autumn stared at the photo and shuddered.

"Are you okay?" Liam asked.

Autumn pressed her hand to her temple. "It's like she's trying to claw her way out of my head."

Liam quickly flipped through the pages.

"There's no girl here by the name of Blazevig."

"Try the other classes," Autumn said.

Liam scanned the sophomore class photos and then juniors.

Autumn pointed to a photo. "There. That's the girl in Inez's last memory. Bernadette Blazevig."

He fell back into the chair. "Only now it's Bernadette Canton."

Autumn tucked a strand behind her ear and narrowed her eyes. She tilted the yearbook toward her. "It makes sense, that Bernadette would cover for Mick. She loved him, even then." Autumn examined the photo once more and closed the book. "Let's take a trip to Louie's and see who signed for Inez's ring. I want my suspicions confirmed."

"Louie isn't going to tell us that," Liam said. "Privacy is the only moral he has."

"That's okay." Autumn's tone darkened. "He doesn't have to. We'll get it out of him."

Liam hesitated, gently grabbed Autumn's face, and angled her chin until he could look into her eyes. "Autumn, are you in there?"

She put her hand on his. "I am. Don't worry. I'm not gonna hurt him. I can be clever, not cruel."

Liam smiled with relief. "Okay, let's go to Louie's."

Autumn's heart pounded in her chest as she tugged open the door to Louie's pawnshop. She'd been here a few times with her mother, trying to get cash for antiques they found in the Cayo's attic. She never liked how Louie would talk down to Evelyn, like she was a dumb female. Today, Autumn would try to get one over on Louie.

The bell chimed, signaling Autumn's entrance. Louie popped his baldhead out of his office and peered into the shop. He smiled, although to Autumn, it looked like a smirk. "What can I help you with, sweetheart? Got more junk to pawn?"

Autumn swallowed down a retort. Instead, she made her chin wobble and her voice teeter on hysteria. "Louie, I'm in big trouble. Remember those records you bought a few months back? Well, one of them was Aunt Glenda's favorite Doo-wop group, and I need to replace it, but I can't remember which album it is."

"Listen, kid, you think I can remember everything you bring in?" Louie rolled his eyes. "I don't have time for this. Why don't you get your aunt a nice CD instead? She's so kooky, she won't know the difference."

Autumn dug her finger into her palm hard, hoping to muster tears. Liam was outside waiting for her cue. "Please, Louie. You write everything down. Can't you just look in your book?"

Louie put out his hands like he was trying to stop a freight train. "Don't cry. I hate crying. Hold on a sec." He lumbered into his back office. Autumn put her hand behind her back and crossed her fingers. That was Liam's signal.

As instructed, Liam pushed open the door with his foot and hefted a large, moldy box from the Cayo's attic. It was filled with Duncan's old magic tricks.

Louie came back with his ledger and opened it up in front of Autumn. It was organized by customer name, price paid, price sold, and to whom. Jackpot.

"Hey, kid," Louie greeted Liam. He took a second glance at the box and grimaced. "Watcha got in there? It stinks."

Liam dumped the moldy box on the glass counter. "Some of Pops's stuff. Figured he doesn't need it anymore."

"Cold. Some grandson you are." Louie shifted his attention to Autumn as he flipped through the book. He tapped his finger on the entry.

Autumn squinted. "May I?"

Louie sighed and flipped the book around for Autumn to see better, but he never took his hands off the ledger. Just then, he jumped at the sound of metal hitting glass. Liam had dumped the box's contents onto the counter.

"What are you doing?" Louie cried out. "You're gonna crack my glass." He left Autumn alone with the ledger while he went to inspect the countertop.

"The box ripped. But look what I got. Come see." Liam held up one of Uncle Duncan's old Chinese finger traps.

Autumn didn't waste time. She flipped a few pages until she found Liam's name. She glanced at the entry. Disappointment flooded her. Priscilla Newman. The name was completely unfamiliar to her. The Cantons didn't buy back the ring? Another entry, right next to Liam's, caught her attention. *Well, that's weird. I wonder if Liam knows about this.*

*Huh.* She memorized the name and address.

She gave Liam a sad shake of her head, a cue for him to wrap things up. This mission had been a bust.

Autumn closed Louie's ledger. "All yours, Louie."

"Great, sweetheart. Get what you need?" Louie tugged at the Chinese finger trap. "How do I get this thing off?"

Autumn pressed a small button to free Louie's fingers. "No, *sweetheart*. Unfortunately, I didn't."

# CHAPTER THIRTY-THREE

Liam trudged up the Cayo's front porch and yanked open the door. He ushered Autumn into the lobby. The Cayo was suspiciously empty, save for Timothy, who lazily drew circles on a pad of paper.

"Where is everyone?" Autumn asked, deflated.

"Your mom and Aunt Glenda are meeting with a lawyer, Mama's scouring the want ads, and Mr. Fletcher is at the jail. The last guest checked out an hour ago. And the contractor is here. Which reminds me, Evelyn wants you to tidy up the January and February rooms."

"What does it matter if they're selling the place?" Liam asked.

Timothy yawned. "I don't know." He dropped his pen and stared at them. "What's gotten you two all mopey besides everything?"

"The Cantons don't have Inez's ring," Autumn said before explaining that Ralph's sister was Bernadette Canton. "Liam and I went to Pawn Louie's to sneak a glance at the ledger to confirm that Mick Canton bought Inez's ring. After all, Mick had seen Liam minutes before he sold the ring."

"If you suspect Mick Canton killed Inez, then he might not want a reminder," Timothy pointed out. "Maybe he didn't want the ring."

"I don't buy that," said Autumn. "In Inez's vision, he claimed the ring was an heirloom. He was pissed she wasn't wearing it, and he wanted it back."

Timothy's eyes bugged. "I told you not to—"

"I'm fine," said Autumn, her hand raised. "I'm here. It's still me."

Timothy exhaled. "So who did sign for the ring?"

"Some woman named Priscilla Newman."

Timothy pursed his lips. "I've never heard of her."

"Us neither," said Liam. "We have no proof of anything except Inez was hated by everyone."

"And I'm days away from leaving," Autumn said.

Timothy handed Autumn furniture polish and a rag. "Please clean the winter rooms." He handed Liam a cardboard box. "And Evelyn asked you to take down all the art and photos from the walls."

Liam cocked his eyebrow. "Seriously? Now?"

"The Cayo waits for no man."

Liam grabbed the cardboard box and set it down on the wingback chair. Autumn reluctantly ascended the stairs.

Autumn stomped up the stairs toward the January room. She wanted to track down Mr. Fletcher and brainstorm leads. Liam's grandfather still sat in jail, meanwhile Autumn and Liam had to clean the Cayo as if nothing had happened. As if the Cayo wasn't sold and in danger of demolition.

Autumn opened the door to the January room. Katie was there, floating between the two twin beds. She turned her vacant eyes to Autumn and put her finger to her lips. The hairs on the back of Autumn's neck prickled.

Someone was humming a melody. Autumn set down the furniture polish and rag on the teak dresser, which had a wooden cane with a brass top leaning against it. Uncle Duncan's yearbook rested on top of the bureau.

"Hello?" said Autumn hesitantly.

A head of gray hair popped out of the bathroom. "Oh, hello dear." Bernadette Canton, dressed in a bright red blouse and pleated slacks, unfurled measuring tape. "I'm thinking of combining the January and February rooms to make one large suite."

Autumn swallowed a lump. Mrs. Canton appeared a lot different now than Autumn knew who she really was. "Oh." Autumn held up the dust rag. "I just came to tidy up."

Bernadette shooed the idea away. "Don't bother. We'll be gutting the interior. No need to clean. You could put that yearbook away, though. I'm sure it's sentimental to someone."

Katie slowly shook her head at Autumn.

She slid the yearbook off the dresser just as the dizziness overcame her. Autumn's vision clouded and turned black. When she opened her eyes, she was in the same bedroom, except Bernadette Canton was gone. The room had blue walls with baseball pennants tacked up above the bed. This was Uncle Duncan's room. Was Inez in Duncan's room?

Autumn caught her reflection in the mirror. She wasn't in Inez's memories. She had channeled Uncle Duncan. His curly brown hair was slicked back and his hazel eyes shone bright. His cheeks were flushed. Duncan gathered a stack of records from the trunk at the foot of the bed, giddy still from having kissed Ralph behind the St. Veronica's gym. The two of them left the dance early. Glenda stayed behind to help Leo and Mariana clean up. Mick stormed off in a huff. Duncan had hurried upstairs to retrieve his music collection while Ralph set up by the pool.

Thunder boomed, and Duncan wondered if he should tell Ralph to move the record player inside. They could move the parlor furniture to make room for dancing.

Duncan moved the curtain aside to steal a glance at Ralph on the patio. Ralph was crouched on the ground next to Bernadette. A body floated in the pool.

Bernadette rocked back and forth on her knees. "I didn't mean it."

Ralph ran his shaky hands through his hair. "They'll take you away."

Bernadette tugged at her brother's sleeve. "Help me, Ralphie. Take her on the boat. Take my cane. Dump them in the ocean."

Bernadette sobbed and Ralph hugged her, smoothing down her hair. "Go home. I'll deal with this." She nodded and took off just as the clouds split open with drenching rain.

Duncan hurried down the stairs and onto the patio.

Ralph's eyes widened. "I didn't—"

"I know," Duncan finished. "But I'll lose you if someone finds out."

Ralph gagged, like he was going to vomit, and pressed his fist to his mouth. He shooed Duncan away. "Go back to the dance. I don't want anyone to know you were here." He waded into the pool, as rain pelted the surface, to drag out Inez's body.

Duncan stepped forward, prepared to help his friend, but then Ralph cried, "Go!" The intensity of his outburst frightened Duncan so much that Duncan fled down the street, slipping on the wet asphalt.

Autumn woke to find Bernadette hovering above her, shaking her.

"Are you okay, Autumn, dear?"

Inez wasted no time in coming for Autumn's body.

"I never did tell you how sorry I was about your grandfather," Timothy told Liam. Timothy had a cardboard box on top of reception. After dusting one of Glenda's trinkets, he'd wrap it up in tissue paper and place it carefully inside the box.

"Thanks, but he didn't do anything to be sorry about." Liam removed a photograph from the wall. It was one of the photos Autumn had found in the attic. Liam guessed Evelyn had them framed after all.

"I know." Timothy inspected the cracks on a porcelain figurine. "But he confessed."

"Doesn't matter. I'm going to the jail to turn myself in for the scooter theft. Pops will recant his confession, and he'll be released. I'm waiting on Mr. Fletcher to return first. I want to ensure I do this right." Liam examined the picture of Duncan and Ralph, their arms around each other. They stood in front of a little boat. Liam nearly dropped the framed photo. "Uh, Timothy?"

"What?"

Liam ran up to him and thrust the photo in his face. "Look!" He pointed to the boat's name that was written in sloppy, red capital letters along its side.

Timothy peered at the picture and gasped. "Ralph Blazevig's boat was called Priscilla Newman."

"Which means Bernadette Canton did buy that ring. She used Ralph's boat as the fake name."

"Pretty clever of the Blazevigs." Timothy glanced at Liam's expression and explained, "Priscilla Newman was the main character in these old whodunits from the sixties. She was the gumshoe's secretary, who always solved the cases, but her boss got credit because it was the sixties and sexism and all that. Mr. Blazevig was always reading them."

"Okay," Liam said. "But, why would she want a ring her husband had given a former fiancé?

"It was a Canton heirloom," Timothy said. "She must've wanted it returned to the family."

"I suppose you're right. Except, why use a fake name?"

"Because she didn't want anyone know she purchased it."

"Why?" asked Liam.

Timothy exhaled. "I don't know. Because she didn't want—she didn't want anyone asking questions."

"Why?"

Timothy rubbed his eyes. "Because—because she was involved." Then like a thermometer showing a plunge in temperature, Timothy's cheeks drained of color. "Liam, she's here. Mrs. Canton is here. She's upstairs taking measurements."

Liam's eyes darted at the staircase. "With Autumn."

Autumn felt paralyzed even though Bernadette didn't seem to realize anything had changed. Mrs. Canton pushed the yellow tape measure out until the metal tip touched the edge of the wall. She went about her business, unassuming, and quiet. She ducked into the large closet squawking something about extra square footage.

Autumn retreated back into the desk as the dark cloud of Inez's spirit came toward her. Inez growled before she turned around and fell back into Autumn as if Autumn was the Cayo's swimming pool and Inez its daring swimmer. Autumn clutched her chest and gasped for breath as she glanced in the mirror.

Mrs. Canton withdrew her cell phone and typed into it, completely unaware that Autumn's eyes darkened with amber and the edge of her mouth had curved up into a sneer.

"I see you still walk with a limp," Autumn said in Inez's soft, lilting accent.

Bernadette's eyes darkened. "Is that supposed to be funny, young lady?"

"So Mick married you anyway? Must've been so easy without me in the way." Inez jutted out her hip and tilted her chin at Bernadette's slight frame. "I see you lost the cane. Of course you would. I imagine the blood stains where you bashed my brains in would be unsightly to look at all these years."

Bernadette stepped backward into the dresser, rattling a ceramic pillbox and a statuette. Her eyes darted around the room, seeking an exit, an escape. Her voice trembled. "Autumn, dear?"

Inez pressed up against Bernadette. She lifted Bernadette's white silky scarf and pulled. Mrs. Canton yelped.

"Autumn is not here anymore," the ghost crooned. "Only I am. Inez Cruces. You remember me, don't you?"

Autumn felt like she was trapped in a coffin, alive and imprisoned. She screamed like a maniac, but no one could hear her, except for Inez who hissed, "Cállate."

Liam appeared in the doorframe and studied Autumn as she loomed over the older woman.

"What's going on?" he asked slowly.

Bernadette's face twisted into fear. "Get her away from me."

Liam approached Autumn cautiously. He put his hand on Autumn's and tried to loosen her grip on the scarf. "Autumn? You're choking Mrs. Canton."

"I'm not Autumn!" Inez snapped.

Liam jumped back. He raised his hands defensively. "Okay, Inez. I'm your great nephew, William."

*Inez! Don't you touch him!* Autumn cried.

"I don't care who you are," Inez said through gritted teeth. She turned her attention back to Bernadette.

Liam cried out for Timothy to get upstairs.

"You followed me to the Cayo Hueso that night," Inez whispered into Bernadette's ear. "You snuck up behind me, and you hit me over the head with your cane."

*How do you know this?* Autumn asked.

"I hitched a ride when you channeled Duncan," Inez told Autumn. "I saw everything you saw."

Bernadette tried to squirm free of Inez's grasp. "No, no."

Timothy entered the room and skidded to a halt. "What's going on?"

"Inez has totally taken over Autumn's body," said Liam.

"I'll go get help!" Timothy cried as he fled down the hall.

"All these years, I should've known it was you," Inez practically spit. "You loved Mick and the only person standing in your way was me. But you made a big mistake when you took that swing. Mick and I had ended our engagement that same night."

Bernadette's eyes widened. "No."

"Oh, yes. He was done with me. I had plans to leave the island that night. You would've been free of me no matter what. Instead, your whole life has been a lie. Your marriage to Mick was founded on my death." Inez wrapped her hands around Bernadette's throat.

Liam stepped toward Inez.

"Take one more step and Autumn disappears for good," Inez said, her hands still wrapped tightly around Mrs. Canton's neck. "I want to hear her say it." She squeezed harder. "Say it!"

Bernadette coughed, sputtered, but she couldn't get out the words.

"You have to loosen your grip or you'll kill her," Liam said. "She can't tell you anything if you're choking her."

"Say it!" yelled Inez.

Bernadette sputtered out the words. "I killed you."

Inez's mouth twisted into a sick grin, but her knuckles were still white. "And now, I kill you."

Liam slammed into Autumn's body, and Autumn tumbled to the floor. "Autumn, I know you're in there, you have to fight this!" Liam wrapped his arms around Autumn, holding her down. Her body thrashed as Inez struggled to maintain control. Liam's grip tightened.

*I'm trying!* Autumn attempted to recall her own memories—her eighth birthday party when her father dressed as a magician, her mother's apple pie, the family's trip to Disney World where Autumn broke her arm—the bits and pieces of her past that made up who she was. Autumn was not going to lose herself to a vengeful ghost.

Inez pushed through Liam's hold and leaped to her feet. Mrs. Canton grabbed a porcelain figurine and hurled it at Autumn's body. Liam ducked as the figurine hit the floor and shattered.

Liam rushed to Autumn's side and shielded her body. "No! You'll hurt her."

"She tried to kill me," Bernadette said through gasping breaths.

"Inez tried to kill you," Liam said. "Autumn is innocent." He grabbed Autumn's shoulders. "I know you're in there. You need to fight this."

*Let me out!* Autumn pounded on the door of Inez's mind with her fists. *My first kiss behind the school gymnasium. That time Natasha and I rescued a kitten on the side of the road. My first-place win at the spelling bee. Crying inconsolably the day my parents announced their plans to divorce.*

Inez cupped Liam's cheek. "Lion? Is that you? You've come back for me."

Liam opened his mouth to protest, but then he stopped. He kissed the inside of Inez's palm. "I missed you. I'm sorry for everything that had happened."

"I thought you had done this to me," Inez said, her voice whimpering. A tear gathered in the corner of her eye and slowly made its way down her cheek.

"I would never hurt you," Liam said carefully. "You're family. We've missed you all these years."

Autumn felt the prison bars of Inez's control tighten. Inez wasn't ready to let go.

"I want to come back," Inez said.

*My move to Key West with Mom. The first night at the Cayo. Aunt Glenda's old movies. Cora's cookies. Meeting Timothy, Katie, and Liam.*

"We're the not the same anymore," Liam continued. "I'm an old man now. And Mariana is gone."

"My sister is dead?" Inez asked.

Autumn could feel Inez's anger lift, leaving a residue of sadness. "I want to tell her I'm sorry."

"You can," Liam said. "Drop your hold on this world so you can move on to the other. Release Autumn, and be with your family."

"No!" Inez bolted upright. "You just want me to go away. Like before." Inez pushed on Liam's chest. "I don't have to go. I can stay in Autumn's body and be young again."

Liam drew Autumn toward him. "I'm not letting go. Autumn, get out of there!"

*My mom. Meeting my new brother. Studying journalism. Swimming in the warm Florida water. I will not let you take me, Inez!*

Inez cackled. "You can't stop me!"

*Kissing Liam. Loving Liam. Being with Liam.*

Autumn banged on her coffin lid. It felt like steel. She tried again.

*Liam. Liam. Liam.*

"Get used to me." Inez's mouth turned up at the corners. "Because I'm not going anywhere."

Liam leaned down and kissed Autumn on the mouth.

*Liam. Liam. Liam.*

Autumn punched the lid and the lock rattled. She hit it again and the lid popped. Autumn climbed out of the coffin into a cell.

*Love.*

Autumn wrapped her arms around Liam's neck and kissed him back. The prison bars of Inez's hold transformed into loose strands of silk. Autumn pushed through them and emerged.

# CHAPTER THIRTY-FOUR

Autumn embraced Liam. He nuzzled her neck and mumbled, "You came back to me."

"I wasn't going to leave you," she said.

"Ever?" he asked.

But before Autumn could respond, Mrs. Canton broke in, her voice hoarse. "Is she gone?"

Autumn and Liam broke apart. Autumn pressed her hand against her temple, hoping to subdue the lightheadedness. She relished the coolness of her own touch and exhaled with relief. "She's gone."

Bernadette stood tall and limped toward the door. "Good. I'm done with this performance. Your little show is over. Forget the renovations. I'm siding with Mick. I want this place leveled."

Timothy blocked her exit. "Where do you think you're going? I called the police."

Mrs. Canton pushed him aside. "No, dear, I don't think so. You see, you have no proof. What are you going to tell the police? That a ghost identified me as her killer?"

"We'll tell the police we heard you confess," said Liam.

"And I'll say you're lying to get back at my family. Your grandfather confessed to the crime. They won't charge me. You have no evidence. No body. No murder weapon."

Uncle Duncan revealed he was complicit in the cover up of Inez's murder. But he didn't see what Ralph did with Inez's body. As far as Bernadette and Duncan believed, Ralph dumped Inez in the ocean. But Autumn knew differently.

"Priscilla Newman," Autumn whispered. Her thoughts churned.

"What are you talking about?" Mrs. Canton asked impatiently.

"Priscilla Newman was the secretary in your brother's detective novels. She was the smart one. That's why you used her name. She was the unassuming star of the books. The clever girl. The one who figured out the murders before her boss did. She always knew where the bodies were hidden."

"So what?" Bernadette sneered.

"So," Autumn replied. "There is a body. And I know just where she is."

Bernadette laughed nervously. "That's impossible."

Autumn shook her head. "There's a good reason why Inez haunts the Cayo. Not just because she died here, but because she's buried here. Liam, where did you find the St. Veronica's pin?"

"Next to the Marlberry bush by the fence," he replied.

"That's where she's buried," Autumn said triumphantly.

"There's no way for you to know that," said Bernadette. "Ralphie dumped her at sea."

"Except he didn't. A storm rolled in and your brother wouldn't risk taking the boat out on such choppy waters. So he buried her in the only place he could—the hole dug for the Marlberry bush in the Cayo's backyard. He just never told you."

"How you know that?" Timothy asked.

"Easy. It was the same thing the killer did in one of Mr. Blazevig's paperback mysteries. Priscilla figured it out. When they dig up Inez, they'll find the murder weapon—Bernadette's cane. I'm sure I don't need to be Priscilla Newman to know that a body and the murder weapon are pretty damning evidence."

Timothy, Liam, and Autumn all watched as the color drained from Bernadette's face. She spun on her heels and fled the room, only to smack into Mr. Fletcher.

"Well, this should make a nice conclusion to my profile on the Cantons," Mr. Fletcher said. "Officers, you can come in now."

Two police officers came around, one holding handcuffs that he slapped on Bernadette's wrists.

Then they read Mrs. Canton her rights.

Liam rolled his scooter up Pops's driveway before cutting the engine. He didn't even take off his helmet before charging toward the house, bolting inside, and calling for Pops.

"In the kitchen, kiddo," cried Pops, his voice sounding scratchy and older.

Liam's heart swelled as he entered the kitchen to see Pops sitting at the kitchen table, wearing a set of freshly laundered shorts and a T-shirt, sipping a cup of coffee. Liam dumped his helmet on the table and wrapped his arms around his grandfather. Coffee sloshed over the edge of the mug.

"Take it easy, sport. I'm an old man." Pops's light voice betrayed his fake annoyance.

Liam rested his chin on his grandpa's shoulder. "I missed you."

Pops reached his arm up to tap Liam's cheek. "Missed you too."

"Liam," someone said, and he turned to see his father. Liam stood frozen, his feet cemented to the tile floor.

Ray Breyer opened his arms wide, but Liam made no moves.

"What are you doing here?" Liam's eyes ran up and down his father's frame. He was wearing one of Liam's old T-shirts, a pair of Pops's shorts, and a belt, cinching the waist tight. His father looked gaunt and at least fifteen pounds lighter than when Liam had last seen him.

Ray dropped his arms and leaned against the sink. "I've come home."

"For how long?" Liam's voice rose. "A week? A month? How long until you take off again?" Liam knew he sounded antagonistic, but he didn't care.

"I don't plan on leaving again." Ray didn't meet Liam's gaze, and so Liam took that for what it was —a lie.

"Right," said Liam.

Ray didn't respond and a tense moment hung in the air until it was cut by the sound of the telephone ringing.

At first, no one made a move to answer until Pops slowly rose from the table. "Who could be calling now?" He ambled to the wall and picked up the phone in the middle of a ring. "Hello? Who's this?"

Liam and Ray stopped glaring at each other to watch Pops's face twist into an unreadable expression.

"Everything all right, Dad?" Ray asked.

Pops closed his eyes and ran his hand over his scruff. "Okay, okay. How'd you get my number?" Leo's eyes shot up. "Oh, I didn't know that. Thank you." Pops hung up the phone, looking stunned.

Liam and Ray faced Pops with their hands cupping their elbows, that same stance passed down from Breyer man to Breyer man.

"What's going on, Pops?"

Leo took a moment to register Liam's face. "That was the hospital calling. Apparently, I was Ralph's in-case-of-emergency person on his insurance forms."

"Is Mr. Blazevig being released from the hospital? Does he need a ride home?"

"Liam," Ray said softly. "I don't—"

"He's dead," Pops cut him off. "Ralphie passed away in his sleep."

Liam and Ray stood there helpless until Pops began to weep. Ray and Liam stepped toward the old man and wrapped their arms around him.

Autumn took the long way to school for fear that cutting through City Cemetery, and not seeing Mr. Blazevig at his usual post by his family's graves, would turn her into a weeping, blubbery mess minutes before homeroom.

After everything that had happened, Autumn was in no rush to return to New Jersey, although that didn't mean she and her mother were secure in their home either.

For reasons that seemed obvious to Autumn, Mick Canton ended his contract on the Cayo. Instead, he had larger issues to deal with—including the arrest and murder trial of his wife, Bernadette. Considered a flight risk, Bernadette was not granted bail, despite the arguments made by an expensive team of lawyers. Thus, the Cayo Hueso Dead and Breakfast was still on the real estate market.

"We're still going to have to sell," Evelyn had told Autumn that morning at breakfast.

She and her mother hadn't really spoken much about their fight. After Bernadette had been arrested, Autumn told her mother she didn't want to move in with her father and Jennifer.

"I know you don't want to leave Liam," her mother had said.

"It's not that," Autumn said. "I don't want to leave

you. And if it means moving to Texas to live with Grandma, then that's what we'll do."

Evelyn brought Autumn into a hug and mumbled into her hair. "I don't want to move to El Paso either. Hopefully, a miracle will happen before then."

Now, as Autumn stood on the steps to her charter school and met the cold gaze of Victoria Canton, perched only a few feet from her, Autumn needed that miracle.

"Listen Victoria, I'm—"

Victoria held up her hand. "Shut it."

Autumn balked. That seemed harsh. After all, it was Victoria's grandmother who murdered a girl fifty years ago.

"I don't need any crap," Victoria said. "I've heard enough from everyone else."

It took Autumn a moment to realize Victoria wasn't flanked by her usual posse of Amazonian followers. "I wasn't going to give you crap," Autumn said. "I was going to say that I'm sorry you're going through this."

Victoria narrowed her eyes as if trying to decipher Autumn's angle. "Sure you are."

Autumn climbed the stairs until she could meet Victoria's red-rimmed and puffy eyes. "I *am* sorry. This isn't your fault."

Victoria's shoulders drooped. "No one should feel sorry for me. Walk me to class, will ya?"

Autumn adjusted the strap on her messenger bag. "Sure." They stepped toward the school building. "Do you want me to quiz you on the new material for American lit?"

Victoria nodded and bit her lip.

Later that afternoon, after the last bell, Autumn watched Victoria climb into the backseat of a black Escalade. The car's driver left, kicking up gravel and revealing Liam, who leaned against his scooter.

Autumn's heart sped. "What are you doing here?"

Liam kissed Autumn on the cheek, a sweet gesture that also felt chaste and disappointing. Autumn wasn't sure what she had expected. It wasn't like Liam was going to gather her in his arms for a dramatic make-out.

*Get a grip, Abernathy.*

"Your mom asked me to come and get you." Liam pressed his mouth into a line. "There's a woman at the Cayo Hueso."

"A new guest?" asked Autumn, disappointed. "I don't feel like cleaning any rooms today."

"No," Liam said. "She's not that. She's a lawyer for Mr. Blazevig. She's there to read his will."

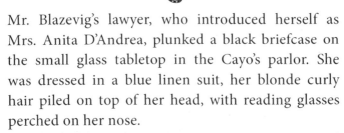

Mr. Blazevig's lawyer, who introduced herself as Mrs. Anita D'Andrea, plunked a black briefcase on the small glass tabletop in the Cayo's parlor. She was dressed in a blue linen suit, her blonde curly hair piled on top of her head, with reading glasses perched on her nose.

Everyone scrambled to find a seat. The parlor had never catered to this size a crowd before. Aunt Glenda squirmed in a floral armchair. Cora stood beside her, her hand resting on Glenda's shoulder. Evelyn fussed over Mrs. D'Andrea like a waitress, asking if she wanted a bottle of water or Cora's homemade cookies. Pops and Ray were there too, clearly feeling out of place. Meanwhile, Autumn, Timothy, and Liam hung in the back of the room, leaning against the wall, trying to stay out of the adults' way. Mr. Fletcher shook the lawyer's hand, and they exchanged pleasantries about a mutual colleague.

Liam had never been to the reading of someone's will. That was something only rich people did on television. And up until recently, no one knew that Mr. Blazevig even had money. Of course, Mr. Blazevig had been a man of many secrets.

Mrs. D'Andrea withdrew papers from her briefcase and snapped it closed. She sat down and addressed the group, looking less like a lawyer and more like a presiding judge. She rambled off some legal jargon that Liam barely paid attention to.

"I hereby leave my tour company to Mr. Liam Breyer," Anita had read.

His heart stopped beating for a second. "Huh?"

Anita smiled without teeth. "You're eighteen, I presume?"

He nodded, his mouth unable to form words.

"Great! You're now the proud owner of Blazevig Haunted City Tours."

Liam's mind raced. *A business. Mr. Blazevig left me a business. No more working for other people. No partnership with sketchy Randall. I can make a life with this. Mr. Blazevig would be proud.*

Mrs. D'Andrea cleared her throat and glanced around expectantly. "And for Autumn Abernathy, I leave you my house and savings."

Autumn's mouth dropped. "Are you serious?"

Everyone stared at her. The lawyer shifted nervously under their stunned gazes. "Um, I take it this is all very surprising."

Mr. Fletcher was the first to speak. "Thank you so much, Anita. Would you be able to draw up paperwork to transfer ownership?"

Anita nodded and collected her belongings. "I'll have my secretary take care of that." She shook both Liam and Autumn's hands before Evelyn escorted her to the lobby.

Autumn sank into a chair. "He left me his house."

"He left me his business," Liam said, equally surprised.

"Sounds to me like Old Mr. Blazevig was trying to make up for misdeeds by taking care of you two." Timothy examined his nails. "Would've been nice to have been included in that as well, but I guess I'm just not—"

Evelyn returned and thrust a large cardboard tube into Timothy's hands. "Mrs. D'Andrea forgot to give this to you. Apparently, Mr. Blazevig left it for you."

Timothy cocked his brow. "Do you know what it is?"

Evelyn shrugged. "Some piece of art he said you'd appreciate."

Timothy removed the plastic top of the tube and peeked inside. He gasped and pressed his hand to his chest. "Oh, my God."

Liam peered into the tube to see a tightly woken canvas. Timothy pulled it away. "You'll get your breathing on it. It's a Chagall. Mr. Blazevig left me a Chagall."

"Wait?" asked Autumn. "Like a real Chagall? Like in a museum, Chagall?"

"Yes," Timothy hissed. "What other kind is there? Oh, my word." He fanned his face.

"Are you sweating?" Liam and Autumn asked at the same time.

Timothy collapsed into a chair. "Well, of course I'm sweating!"

A month later . . .

Autumn sat on her bed with her laptop resting on a pillow and typed frantically on the keyboard. The spaghetti strap on her pale blue dress kept falling down as she reread the last paragraph twice, hoping to catch a missed spelling error before emailing it to Mr. Fletcher for his review.

Autumn glanced at the time on her phone. She only had a few minutes before Liam arrived to escort her to the winter dance.

"Whatcha doing?" Katie pretended to sound bored. It was laughable really. Katie glowed brighter than before, but not quite as strong as she had before Inez had appeared.

"I'm finishing up my piece about Inez's murder," Autumn said in her most businesslike voice, as if she really was an investigative reporter and this was the kind of work she did all the time.

Katie hovered near the side of Autumn's bed and leaned over, although Autumn doubted the ghost was actually reading her essay. "Ugh, after everything that's happened, you're still planning on ditching us to go back to New Jersey?"

Autumn closed the laptop and rose from her bed. She slipped on a pair of satin pumps, a vintage gem from her Aunt Glenda's closet. "I have to go to college somewhere. And it might be in New Jersey. But it might not. For the record, though, this article I'm writing isn't for my Candlewick College application. It's for Mr. Fletcher's newspaper in Tampa." Autumn slid a set of gold dangly earrings off her dresser and put them in her earlobes.

"To be published?" asked Katie, slightly incredulous.

Autumn dropped a pink lip balm into a silver clutch. "Yes. Hopefully, once people read how truly haunted the Cayo is, they'll want to come here. Business will pick up." Evelyn decided to take the Cayo off the market, even though she made it clear the old house was on borrowed time. "You're gonna have to do your share."

Katie pouted. "What does that mean?"

"It means you need to haunt. People are going to flock here in droves to see ghosts. You're gonna need to knock a few things off tables and write creepy messages in foggy bathroom mirrors."

"And if I don't?"

"If you don't, then we'll probably lose more business and someone else will buy the Cayo and turn it into a proper hotel. And then whose clothes and hair will you berate?"

"Ugh, fine." Katie pursed her lips. "I was going to say you look lovely, but I've changed my mind."

"Thanks anyway." Autumn spun in a circle. "Have you seen my cell phone?"

Katie pointed to the bookshelf in the corner of the room. "It's sitting on top of Duncan's yearbook."

There was still something that felt unfinished to Autumn. "Katie?" she asked tentatively. "How did Inez know Duncan had seen everything? How did she know to lead me to the yearbook?"

"Really?" Katie asked in that voice that made it seem like Autumn had asked the most stupid question on Earth. Had she? "The dead bird. The pin. Mr. Fletcher's April room being tossed. The handkerchief. The flood in the January room. And finally, the yearbook."

Autumn's eyes widened with a heavy realization.

Katie nodded, her mouth twisting up into a devilish grin. "Inez didn't leave you those clues."

Autumn inhaled deeply, not prepared for what Katie was about to say next.

"Your uncle did. And he's still here."

The sound of the doorbell startled them both. Liam had arrived to take Autumn to the winter formal.

Autumn dipped her toes in the Cayo's swimming pool while Liam hovered above her, hesitant. She grabbed a fistful of his cargo shorts and tugged him down. "Come on, sit with me."

Liam didn't budge.

Autumn glanced up and shielded her eyes from the sun. "Seriously? Inez is gone. There's nothing to be afraid of."

Liam exhaled and kicked off his sneakers. He sat close enough to Autumn that their hips touched, and sunk his feet into the crystal clear water. A surge of pride hit him—he might had been only been a pool boy, but he'd been a damn good pool boy. Of course now he was a business owner.

Autumn stared at the Marlberry bush, which still had crime scene tape, draped around its foliage. The medical examiner's office had exhumed Inez's body days ago. The police detective had just finished interviewing everyone yesterday. Liam hoped today things would go back to normal. He hoped he would go back to normal.

Autumn cleared her throat. "There's something I haven't told you."

*Okay, maybe not today.* Liam cocked his brow. "This sounds serious."

"It's not life or death serious. I don't think."

Liam sat up, attentive.

"You know how Louie's ledger is organized by last name?"

"Yeah."

"Well, you weren't the only Breyer in the book," she said softly.

"As far as I know, Pops has never pawned anything."

"It wasn't your grandfather," said Autumn. "It was your mother. Elena Breyer."

Liam's face paled. He rarely heard his mother's name mentioned. It sounded so formal. So definitive. She'd always been there in Liam's memories, but hearing his mother's name come out of Autumn's mouth like that made his mother seem undeniably real. "What did she sell?"

"Her wedding ring."

Liam scoffed. "Figures."

"That's not all." Autumn turned to Liam and paused, desperate to command his attention, for whatever she was about to say next. "Your mom left a forwarding address."

That was not what Liam expected to hear.

"It could be worth a try," said Autumn, pulling Liam out of his thoughts. "Talking to Louie, seeing what he knows."

Liam bit his lip before lying down on the rough concrete, his feet still dangling in the water. There was no way Louie was going to tell him anything. Maybe Louie and his mother once had some sort of relationship. Maybe that's why he was willing to hide her whereabouts. He didn't want to consider it.

Autumn laid down beside Liam. "Do you want to find her?"

"I don't know. My dad's been searching for her for years and look what it's gotten him. He's no closer to finding her, and he's lost himself in the process. Plus, my dad just came home. I don't want to open old wounds."

Autumn entwined her fingers with Liam's. "Fair enough."

Liam clutched Autumn's hand tightly, fearful of letting go. "Maybe I'll consider it, but first, I want to enjoy the moment. With you."

Autumn rolled over on her side. "I might go for a swim later."

"That's where I draw the line." Liam turned to her. "I'll take you to Bahia Honda this weekend. The beaches there are unreal. New Jersey—more like Old Jersey."

Autumn laughed. "I'd like that."

Liam ran his thumb along her bottom lip, desperate to kiss her, but fearful Evelyn was watching them. "Are you sad you're not returning home?"

Autumn grinned, her eyes crinkling, and kissed him. When she pulled away, Liam inhaled a sharp breath.

"Don't you know, Liam? I am home."

# ACKNOWLEDGEMENTS

There are many people I'd like to thank for helping *Dead and Breakfast* get published.

First, I'd like to thank my editor, Stacy Juba, for making the story far better than I could do on my own. I must also thank my friend and eagle-eye, Jill Ratzan, for proofreading the manuscript. Big hugs to Rachel Lawston, my talented cover designer, and Elizabeth Buhmann who dropped everything to critique *Dead and Breakfast* so I could make my deadline. I'm also indebted to everyone at Kindle Scout and Kindle Press. I'm so grateful for Amazon's backing and support.

I wish I could give Katie Moretti a winning lottery ticket. Her guidance, wisdom, and sense of humor mean the world to me. She's a talent and I'm lucky to know her.

Lastly, I'd like to thank my husband, Bob. Four years ago we took a trip to Key West where I discovered the perfect setting for a ghost story. Here's to many more inspiring vacations.

# ABOUT THE AUTHOR

Kimberly G. Giarratano lives in the Poconos with her husband and three kids. Her debut novel, *Grunge Gods and Graveyards*, won the 2015 Silver Falchion Award for Best YA at Killer Nashville. Connect with Kimberly on Twitter @KGGiarratano or visit her website, www. kimberlyggiarratano.com. To find out when the second and third books in the *Cayo Hueso Mystery* series will be released, sign up for Kimberly's reader club at http://kimberlyggiarratano.com/for-readers/

Also by Kimberly G. Giarratano

*Grunge Gods and Graveyards*

*The Lady in Blue: A Grunge Gods and Graveyards Mystery*

*One Night Is All You Need: A Short Story*

Made in the USA
Charleston, SC
10 December 2016